PRAISE FOR *THE MEASURE OF SILENCE*

"This poignant novel tells of trauma, abuse, young love, secrets, lies, and estranged family . . . A lovely story of family dynamics told with warmth and understanding."
—*Historical Novels Review*

"A riveting and emotional read! Langston takes us on a generational journey of discovery, uncovering secrets that threaten to tear a family apart. Fast paced and heartwarming, *The Measure of Silence* illustrates the struggles of motherhood and power of love and forgiveness with endearing characters."
—Eliza Knight, *USA Today* bestselling author of *Starring Adele Astaire*

"*The Measure of Silence* is a touching, compelling novel of the family secrets that bind generations and can also tear them apart. Elizabeth Langston deftly weaves the trauma of President Kennedy's assassination through the pain and difficulties of her characters' lives. The family dynamics are very relatable, and the characters' struggles with both their present experiences and the past kept me reading until the end."
—Georgie Blalock, author of *An Indiscreet Princess* and *The Last Debutantes*

"*The Measure of Silence* delves into the explosive results of a last wish that rips up deep family secrets. Elizabeth Langston powerfully illustrates the struggle of mental health issues in a world where they weren't understood and will leave you rooting for the heroine to succeed. This is a moving historical fiction with a past that will keep you riveted as all is revealed."
—Madeline Martin, *New York Times* and international bestselling author of *The Last Bookshop in London*

T0355788

Once You Were Mine

OTHER TITLES BY ELIZABETH LANGSTON

The Measure of Silence

Once You Were Mine

a novel

ELIZABETH LANGSTON

Text copyright © 2025 by Elizabeth Langston
All rights reserved.

Published by Lake Union Publishing, Seattle

www.apub.com

Amazon, the Amazon logo, and Lake Union Publishing are trademarks of Amazon.com, Inc., or its affiliates.

ISBN-13: 9781662521140 (paperback)
ISBN-13: 9781662521133 (digital)

Cover design by Jarrod Taylor
Cover image: ©Valentina Sani / ArcAngel; ©Peter Olexa / Unsplash

Printed in the United States of America

To Charles,
who raised his daughters to believe
we could achieve whatever we aspired to.
And we did.

CHAPTER ONE

December 1968

She had been relieved when her father told her she wouldn't have to leave home until January. She couldn't have imagined being anywhere else for Christmas.

Since she was already showing, she wasn't allowed out of the house. But she had been able to adapt most of her favorite traditions. Although her mother had done the shopping, she had made the list, wrapped the presents, and hidden them in her bedroom. Today, she and Mama had baked and decorated dozens of sugar cookies and gingerbread men. And later this evening, after her parents returned from babysitting the grandkids, they were staying up late to watch a holiday movie together on TV.

For the next hour, she would be alone, and that was fine. She liked having the house to herself. After loading a stack of Christmas albums on the stereo, she made a mug of hot chocolate, relaxed in a recliner by the tree, and tilted her head up, charmed by the blinking lights making patterns on the ceiling.

"What are you doing in the dark?" her mother called out.

She looked toward the kitchen. She hadn't heard her parents come in. "Enjoying the tree."

Her father switched on the overhead light. "Still interested in the movie?"

"Yes, sir." She pushed awkwardly to her feet.

When the phone rang, they all went still. Who would call after eight o'clock?

Daddy answered. "Hello? Yes, this is he." He tensed, glanced from his wife to her, then turned his back on them. "Just a moment." He walked into the living room, as far as the phone cord would stretch.

When he came back, he hung up the handset and frowned at her, his eyes bleak. "A space opened early for you at the maternity home. We'll take you in the morning."

She froze, hardly able to believe what her father was saying. Take her tomorrow? On Christmas Eve?

Her mother gasped. "Please, no."

He shook his head, his gaze never wavering from her. "Go on and pack."

Words of protest filled her mouth, but she held them in. There was no point. Daddy wouldn't back down from his decision. So she circled past him and went to her bedroom, closing the door behind her. It was dark and quiet in here. She paused, soaking up the peace.

From the den came the faint rise and fall of an argument. Her mother should stop. He wasn't going to change his mind.

Okay, there was too much to do to waste any more time. She flicked on a table lamp, surveyed the room, and took a moment to make a plan. Then she got to work.

Ten hours later, the room was clean and white, all color moved to three shelves in the closet. On top, she'd stored her record collection and a rolled-up Bee Gees poster. The middle shelf was devoted to nonfiction: her encyclopedias, dictionary, and reference books on biology and space. Lastly, and most precious, were her Christmas gifts from Galen. Hardcovers of *A Wrinkle in Time* and *The Prophet*, kept in place by a Murano glass paperweight. He'd gone to a lot of trouble to get them to her, convincing Aunt Trudy to smuggle them in.

If her father found out, would he throw them away?

She hated that she had to leave them behind, but the packing list from the Home said *No personal items.*

She was waiting on the edge of the bed, a small suitcase at her feet, when her father rapped on the open door.

"Ready, sweet girl?"

No, she would never be. "Yes, sir."

"Good. I want to leave by seven."

So the neighbors wouldn't see her. She understood. "Is Mama going?"

"Yes, she's already in the car." He held out one of his sweaters. "It's cold. You may need this."

"Thank you." She shrugged it on, looked around the room for the final time, and followed her father outside.

They backed out of the driveway before sunrise and headed east for the nearly four-hour drive to the Home. She sat quietly in the back, trembling with dread, doing her best to pretend she wasn't absolutely terrified by what lay ahead.

After a sleepless night, she must have dozed, because she awakened with a start. The sun was high and bright, and the rolling hills of the North Carolina Piedmont had flattened to the coastal plain. They exited the highway, wound through a charming town, and turned onto a long lane of stately mansions with big lawns. At its end, they bumped onto a circular driveway and parked before a wide set of steps.

She peered up at the house, a two-story redbrick box. It had black-shuttered windows, a porch outlined in Christmas lights, and a wreath on the door. To her parents, it must look reassuringly ordinary.

Daddy pulled her suitcase from the back and came around to open her car door.

Fighting to stay calm, she touched her mother's shoulder. "Goodbye, Mama."

Her mother merely nodded, ripped another Kleenex from the box, blew her nose, and tossed it on the mountain of used tissues at her feet.

"Come on," her father said and helped her from the back seat.

She clung to his arm as they climbed the front steps, her legs wobbling like Jell-O. On the porch, she stood numbly as he set the suitcase beside her.

"We'll be going now, sweet girl. You take care."

"Wait. Aren't you coming in with me?"

"No need for that. You'll be all right."

Frantic now, she grasped his arm with both hands and said, "Please, Daddy, don't leave me."

He tugged his arm free. "I'm sorry, but we've been over this. It's for the best." He kissed the top of her head, hurried down the steps, and hopped into the car. From the passenger side, her mother lifted her hand in farewell before pressing a fist to her mouth.

She stared in horror as the station wagon accelerated up the lane and braked sharply at an intersection before vanishing from view.

If she'd thought telling her parents she was in trouble had been the most terrible moment of her life, she had been wrong. Watching them leave her behind was far worse.

A minute passed. Then two. And still she waited, hoping they would realize their mistake. In the distance, a train whistled. The wind gusted, yanking a lock of hair from her ponytail. She shivered in her father's gray sweater, clutching it to her neck, breathing in the scent of Old Spice and pipe smoke.

They weren't coming back. She would be stuck here until May. Her parents had left her in this strange place and hadn't bothered to check inside.

It would be up to her to figure out how to survive.

"Miss Mitchell?"

She stirred painfully and looked over her shoulder. "Yes?"

A short, thin woman stood in the doorway in a pale-green suit with matching tights, a blond beehive, and an expertly made-up face. "I am Mrs. Lloyd, director of the Eastern Carolina Home for Mothers and Babies. Come along."

Lifting her suitcase, she followed the woman into a paneled foyer. Abstract art crowded the walls. A white Christmas tree perched in the corner, covered with orange glass balls, more forlorn than merry.

"In here." Mrs. Lloyd opened a door hidden by the paneling and led the way into an office. It had soft-pink walls, delicate furniture, and weak light filtering through sheer curtains. She sat behind a dainty desk, its surface bare except for a fancy phone and a folder.

Where were the other chairs?

The director noticed her confusion. "You will stand, Miss Mitchell. Girls do not sit in my presence without permission. Is that understood?"

She shivered with foreboding. "Yes, ma'am."

"Very well. First order of business. While you're here, you may not tell anyone your real name. We will call you Eve."

What? She had to give up her name too? "Why?"

Mrs. Lloyd's eyes narrowed. "I won't tolerate your kind of insolence here, *Eve.* Leave your attitude at the door, or we'll get rid of it for you." The director flipped open the folder. "I wish to confirm three details. Your eighteenth birthday is in April."

She nodded.

"Your due date is May third."

"Yes."

"And you plan to finish high school while you're here."

"Yes."

"Very well." Mrs. Lloyd pressed a hidden buzzer. A door opened at the rear of the room, and a woman in a mustard-yellow dress stepped in. "This is Mrs. Wilson, the assistant director. She'll explain the rules and get you settled in. Any questions, Eve?"

Oh, she had many, many questions, but the forbidding set of the director's jaw made it clear that only one response was acceptable. "No, ma'am."

The assistant director led her into a narrow hallway with blank walls and dark linoleum floors. The contrast with the public rooms was stark, like watching *The Wizard of Oz* in reverse, going from Technicolor to black and white.

"Come in, Eve." Mrs. Wilson was standing in an open doorway. Once they were both inside the room, she locked the door. "May I get you anything? A drink?"

"No, thank you."

"Okay, then. Strip to your panties and bra, please."

"*What?*"

The woman's voice was soft with apology. "I'm sorry, Eve, it's uncomfortable for me, too, but I have to ensure you didn't bring contraband."

Cool tears slid down cheeks burning with humiliation as she kicked off her shoes. With her back to the woman, she folded her sweater, removed her dress and hose, then stacked them on a chair.

"Stand here, Eve. Arms at your sides."

As the assistant director walked around her, she cast down her eyes, trying to ignore a stranger scrutinizing her body, the bulge of her waistline.

"Thank you, Eve." Mrs. Wilson indicated a screen in the corner of the room. "We provide uniforms. You can change over there."

A privacy screen? It was a kindness after the indignity she'd just suffered. She hurried behind it, her limbs stiff and cold. Once out of sight, she braced herself against the wall, afraid she might fall apart. How would she get through this?

"Eve, are you all right?"

"I'm fine." The words came out scratchy. She pushed away from the wall, only to discover another horror. A full-length mirror.

Did every kindness come with a mean-spirited kick?

She stared in shock at her reflection, hardly recognizing herself. Limp brown hair. Eyes a dull blue with dark smudges underneath. Lips ragged where she'd bit them.

Science was her favorite subject in school, and what she liked best was solving problems. *Make observations, find patterns, draw conclusions.*

Was she already seeing a pattern here? Kindness and cruelty coming in pairs?

After slipping on the brown tentlike top and elastic-waist pants awaiting her, she stepped from behind the screen to find Mrs. Wilson rifling through her suitcase, patting the extra change of clothes, feeling the insides of her sneakers. The woman unzipped the makeup case, sighed, and emptied its contents into a garbage can.

"What are you doing?"

Mrs. Wilson's smile was strained. "I'm so sorry, Eve. Makeup is a personal item. It isn't permitted. We supply all your needs."

"But . . ." She swallowed the protest. If the assistant director was as nice as she seemed, it would be smart to stay on her good side. "Okay."

The woman whispered, "Mrs. Lloyd is in the hall, listening to us. We have to be careful." Then she said at a more normal volume, "The Home has many rules. Follow them, and you'll be fine."

"What rules?"

"I'll tell you the main ones, but read the binder in your room. Every word. You don't want to be punished for breaking a rule. The first one is easy. Whatever tasks you're assigned, do them well."

No worries there. She would. "What am I assigned?"

"In the afternoons, schoolwork is your only responsibility. Mrs. Lloyd prides herself on the number of girls who finish high school here. You'll clean the bathrooms each morning or anytime they're soiled. Mrs. Lloyd will inspect them daily, so do *not* disappoint her." The assistant director held a finger to her lips and concentrated hard. After a moment, she relaxed. "Mrs. Lloyd has left." Mrs. Wilson looked at her clipboard. "Mealtimes are at eight, noon, and six. Don't be late, not even a minute. And no smoking inside the house."

"I don't smoke."

"Good. Finally—and this is *very* important—you're Eve here. Don't tell anyone your real name. Only Mrs. Lloyd and the doctors are allowed to know."

Assuming a different name might not be so bad. She could pretend to be a different person. When she left, she could shed who she'd been here along with the name. "I'm Eve."

"Excellent. Now, we will keep the clothes you traveled in, but you may take your sweater and your suitcase. Come on. I'll show you to your room."

They climbed a flight of stairs and stopped midway down a hall that ran the length of the house.

"Here you are."

The room was small, hardly big enough for the two twin beds. One was made with military precision. The other, a bare mattress. Beside each bed was a nightstand.

A tall, thin brunette with a Cleopatra haircut leaned against the opposite wall, blowing cigarette smoke through an open window. She stubbed out her cigarette and turned lazily.

Mrs. Wilson sighed, fighting to contain a smile. "Miriam."

"I promise, I won't ever do it again."

"Or at least, not until tomorrow. Anyway, this is Eve. Can I trust you to show her the ropes?"

"You shouldn't trust me ever."

Mrs. Wilson's laugh became a cough. "Take care." She left.

Eve set her suitcase on the end of the bare bed and looked at her new roommate warily. Who had they picked for her? Would they get along? Or would her bedroom be another place to fear?

The two girls eyed each other silently, assessing, although Miriam looked too mature to be called a girl. Early twenties, Eve would guess. It surprised her that someone so old would have to come to a place like this.

"Welcome to hell, Eve. Where do you want to start?"

She blinked at the raw greeting. Liked it. "The bathroom. I need to pee."

There was a brief silence, and they both laughed. The ice was broken.

Miriam gestured toward the hall. "Go and do your business. Second door on the left."

When Eve returned, her roommate was leaning against the wall again, the bare bed now neatly made, the suitcase stowed underneath. "I took care of yours. The lunch gong will sound soon, and we don't want to miss that." Miriam groaned and pressed a hand to her back.

"When are you due?"

"April Fools' Day. Appropriately." She smoothed a tender hand over the tiniest swell of a belly.

In that moment, Eve knew she would trust her roommate despite what Miriam claimed earlier. The next four months would be awful without someone to rely on. "What's it like here?"

Miriam's lips twisted. "You'll figure it out soon enough." She looked out the window. "Their sole focus is to get us to deliver a baby, sign the papers, and leave. It's tolerable if you go along with that."

"And if you don't?"

"It's a nightmare."

A loud bong reverberated through the house. Doors creaked open up and down the hall.

"The food will be the highlight of your day. Come on. We don't want to be late."

When they walked into the dining room, it was so quiet that Eve was surprised to find ten other girls there. All were dressed in the same ill-fitting outfits of solid-color tops with dark pants. All were unnaturally subdued for teenaged girls.

Two women entered from the kitchen, each carrying a large tray, their matching aprons starched. Silently, they set a plate before each girl and left. The pot roast and potatoes smelled wonderful, but nobody moved, still as statues. The women returned with rolls and a pitcher of water. This time, when they disappeared back into the kitchen, the girls ate.

Halfway through the meal, a girl clapped a hand over her mouth, forced her chair back, and ran from the room.

Miriam made a soft grunt. "You're on bathroom duty?"

Eve nodded. This was what Mrs. Wilson meant by *soiled*.

"I'll help but only this once."

They shared a smile, and Eve let her guard down. Just a little.

The Home enforced lights-out at nine. It had seemed ridiculously early when Eve first heard, but after her exhausting day, she was glad. She lay on her back, watching moonlight flicker on the ceiling.

There was a twitch on the side of her belly. When she rubbed it, it twitched again. No, it was more like a flutter. Was that the baby? The possibility filled her with wonder. No one had warned her about how this part would feel. That there was a person inside her, wanting to be known.

She waited for another flutter, disappointed when it didn't repeat.

On the other side of the room, bedsprings squeaked. Miriam must be awake.

Eve whispered, "The baby kicked me. I think."

"It's sweet, isn't it?"

"Yes." Was her roommate willing to talk? The darkness encouraged secrets. "How old are you?"

"Twenty-three." Miriam snorted. "Old enough to know better."

Eve had always been slow to build friendships. As the daughter of the high school principal, she'd felt isolated, never quite sure why people were nice to her. It had been easier to remain aloof.

She could tell a difference with Miriam. They might be six years apart in age, but circumstances had made them friends. At least, Eve hoped so. She would take a chance and ask an extremely personal question. "What happened?"

Miriam exhaled slowly. "It's humiliating how stupid I was. I was working as a teller at my stepfather's bank, and he hired a new branch manager. Handsome, smart, and *sooo* charming. He'd just moved to town and asked me to show him around. I was happy to." Her voice thickened. "I discovered I was expecting around the time his wife and kids arrived. My stepfather told everyone I was on vacation and sent me here. What about you?"

"A summer fling." Her parents' term. She couldn't believe how matter-of-factly she was using it. Galen was much more than a fling. "I was staying with my grandmother and met a boy."

"Handsome, smart, and *sooo* charming."

All true, but . . . "It wasn't like that." Eve still missed him. Hadn't received a letter in weeks. If it hadn't been for her Christmas gifts, she would've worried that he'd moved on. "He was my first everything. First boyfriend. First kiss. First—" She blushed in the dark.

"Aren't we a pair of clichés?" Miriam sounded amused.

No. Tears stung Eve's eyes. She and Galen were *not* a cliché. "Maybe he'll write me here."

"He can't, Eve. Mrs. Lloyd would throw his letter away."

"Why?"

"She censors our mail. Anything she deems inappropriate is cut out or destroyed."

"That's awful."

"It's part of the agreement your parents signed. You'll get used to it because you have to."

Was Miriam right? Would Eve ever get used to it here? Or would she get good at pretending?

"The worst part, though, is the social worker. Mrs. Kinsley lectures us on our sins with religious zeal. We are fallen, and it's her mission to ensure we don't forget."

Eve was so weary of the ugly words. Ruined. Shameful. *Slut.* Escaping the contempt of her brothers and sisters-in-law was the only good part of leaving home. "I'm not fallen."

"You'll think you are when Mrs. Kinsley's done with you. Stick close, Eve. I'll take care of you."

"You'll be gone before me."

"You'll be good at the game by then. Now, go to sleep." It wasn't long before Miriam's breathing grew even.

Eve stared wide eyed at the ceiling, plucking at her quilt, trapped in a prison without bars. She wasn't sure which part would be the hardest to deal with: Being homesick. Forgiving her parents for inflicting this on her. Or withstanding the sense of malice pervading the Home.

CHAPTER TWO

February 1969

In Eve's opinion, laundry was the very best duty. She had no decisions to make. Clothes were either clean or they weren't. Her mornings were blissfully boring, long periods of nothing interrupted by bursts of activity.

Today had been diaper day. A smelly process, although the odors improved with each step. Soak, bleach, wash in Dreft. Even though she'd finished thirty minutes ago, she sat on a stool in the corner, warm and peaceful and forgotten.

The basement door creaked open, and high heels tapped down the concrete steps. When Mrs. Lloyd reached the bottom, Eve was standing at a table, refolding a diaper.

"Hello, Eve. I have an extra task for you."

"Yes, ma'am."

"Perhaps you're aware that Delilah's daughter will greet her new parents today. Pick an outfit for her."

Eve went to the cupboard with infant traveling clothes. The request sounded simple, but it was as much a burden as an honor. Eve tried to think like the other girl. What would Delilah want to see her daughter in their last time together? Most of the outfits were frilly and pink, but Delilah didn't seem like a frilly, pink kind of girl. Eve selected a crocheted cap, diaper cover, and booties in plain white. And a yellow dress, embroidered with a kitten.

The director nodded approvingly. "Well chosen. Take them to Delilah on your way to lunch."

Eve dropped her gaze. She neither wanted to go to the nursery nor did she want the director to know. Mrs. Lloyd could transform splinters of information into weapons. "Yes, ma'am."

Upstairs, she slipped on her gray sweater, left the main house, and crossed to Transitions Cottage, where mothers and babies stayed after being discharged from the hospital.

Eve paused in the doorway to the greeting room, dreading what she was about to do. She'd never actually observed a handover, but she'd seen several of the surrendering moms afterward. Two had emerged with neutral expressions, as if they'd donned a mask, making it hard to tell if they were anxious or puzzled or relieved. The rest had been overcome with grief.

Delilah was in the distraught category, cradling her baby and crying brokenly. She was only fifteen, the youngest resident at the Home. Like Eve, Delilah had been dropped off by parents who hadn't bothered to tour the facility or visit. But where Eve had fallen for the father of her baby, Delilah hadn't understood what her tennis coach was doing to her until after it was over.

Despite that, she clearly adored her baby. Each morning, she would hover at the nursery door, eagerly waiting for the nurse to hand over her freshly swaddled daughter. Then she would stroll the halls for as long as she was allowed. Seeing Delilah's love for her child had been delightful and made the girl's current slide into despair even harder to witness. It was a frightening glimpse into what Eve's future might be.

"Delilah," Eve said, aching with sympathy. "I brought an outfit for your daughter."

The girl looked up with red, puffy eyes. "Oh, pretty. I like kittens."

"You've mentioned that before," Eve said with a smile.

Delilah lowered her head. "I've never dressed a baby."

As an aunt to nine nieces and nephews, Eve had plenty of experience. "Would you like me to help?"

"Yes, please."

Together, they laid the baby on a love seat. While Delilah put on each tiny piece, Eve encouraged, even as she struggled to hide her feelings. How incredibly sad and wrong it was that this would be the only time Delilah ever dressed her daughter, and she hadn't even been allowed to choose the clothes.

When they were done, Delilah lifted the baby to her chest and smoothed the tiny yellow dress. "My parents say that I'm too young to take care of her. That I'm a child myself. I know it's true." She kissed her baby's brow. "But I don't think my heart understands. How am I supposed to be okay with never seeing her again?"

Eve had no answer. Didn't want to think about it. So she stayed beside the younger girl, not speaking, just listening, until the lunch gong sounded. But with her appetite gone, she bypassed the main house and detoured to her favorite bench.

Mrs. Lloyd escorted a couple into the cottage. Ten minutes later, a piercing wail sounded. The side door opened, and the couple hurried out, the woman cradling a baby swathed in a yellow receiving blanket. They rushed through the gate and into a waiting car.

Blocking out the cries, Eve huddled deeper in her sweater. It had been washed so often that it no longer smelled of aftershave and smoke, but Eve could imagine the scent. She'd become so good at pretending, she sometimes fooled herself.

Miriam stepped onto the patio and scanned the yard until their gazes met. She lit a cigarette and puffed, the smoke snatched away by the breeze. She dropped the butt, stamped it out, and strolled over.

"Hard day?" she asked as she sat.

"Yeah."

"This'll cheer you up." She pulled two envelopes from the pocket of her jacket. "A card for you. A letter for me."

Eve smiled. She didn't get much mail. "How did you get these?"

"I'm working in the office this week. Go ahead. Open yours."

The pale-blue envelope had a rectangle in Sharpie-black blotting out her real name, with *Eve* scrawled over it. She swallowed her irritation and drew out a Hallmark card from her grandmother.

When you care enough to send the very best.

The card had a drawing of a girl in pajamas looking up at the night sky. Inside were a printed sentiment about two people watching the same moon and a handwritten message from her grandmother.

> My dearest Anne,
> I hope this finds you well.

Miriam frowned. "Is that your name? I can't believe it wasn't censored."

"It's my middle name. No one calls me Anne but my grandmother. It's our little joke."

> My camellias are blooming, big and pink. They fill me
> with joy. I'm planning my vegetable garden. Come
> and stay with me this summer. We'll pickle cucumbers
> and okra.

Eve wasn't sure she would accept the offer. Staying with her grandmother last summer had been what got her into trouble.

> Write back when you can. I miss you.
> Take care, my little love.
> Grammy

Eve slipped the card and envelope into her pocket. She would enjoy them again later. On her own. "What about yours?"

"It's from my mother." Miriam unfolded a creamy sheet of paper with lots of holes in it. "Looks like a snowflake, doesn't it?"

"It does. Doesn't she know it'll be cut up?"

"Of course. This is intentional. She deliberately adds words she wants cut out. What's left is a coded message." Miriam's eyes sparkled. "If anything is deleted in a sentence, the first word of the following sentence is important."

Eve read the first paragraph, picking out the "important" words. *Moving. To. New. Branch.* "What does that mean?"

"The baby's father will be transferred, so he won't be working at my branch anymore. Thank goodness."

"Would Mrs. Lloyd have censored that?"

"Maybe not, but my mother enjoys feeling like she's gotten away with something."

A door slammed at the back of the house. Mrs. Wilson appeared on the patio and spoke to the three girls there. They stubbed out their cigarettes and went inside. The assistant director stared next at the bench and pointed at the door.

Miriam and Eve rose too. Their break was over.

As Eve was finishing her physics lesson that afternoon, someone knocked on the classroom door. Mrs. Wilson stuck her head in and crooked a finger at Eve. The tutor rolled his eyes, then shooed her away.

In the hallway, she asked, "What is it?"

"You have an appointment with Mrs. Kinsley."

"Okay." Vaguely alarmed by the lack of warning, Eve walked slowly to the counseling room. This would be her fourth visit with the social worker. The previous three had been mild. Mostly conversations about her health and her grades. Nothing to account for the dread the other girls experienced.

When she entered the room, Mrs. Kinsley was seated with her back to the window and the blinds up. Sunlight streamed in, so bright it gave the woman a halo. Miriam claimed it was done intentionally to lull girls into believing Mrs. Kinsley cared about them.

"Welcome, Eve. Have a seat."

She lowered herself into a chair.

"How long have you been here?"

Mrs. Kinsley knew. Why ask? "Seven weeks."

"Mrs. Lloyd and I sense reluctance from you to talk about the surrender of the baby."

Eve didn't react. She knew their opinion and wasn't willing to discuss her own.

"Hmm. No comment?"

She shook her head.

"I understand you have a new niece. Born on New Year's Day."

She flinched, disoriented by the change in topic. Her personal news was none of their business. "My father wrote me about it." He'd also tried to explain away the silence from home. There had been the holidays. The new semester. Things in the family that kept him busy. All clumsy excuses. "Her name is Susan. Her three older brothers will spoil her rotten."

"It doesn't bother you?"

"Having another niece? No, it's fabulous."

"What I mean, dear, is the comparison between your situation and your sister-in-law's. She did things the right way and had her children within the bonds of marriage. Her accomplishment is celebrated. Unlike you, who must be hidden so your indecency won't taint your family."

Eve stiffened in surprise. The social worker had never spoken to her before with such brutal language. Clenching her fists against her thighs, Eve willed her outrage to stay in check.

"Your sister-in-law doesn't have to be ashamed. She can show off her baby."

Eve wanted to look anywhere but at the smirking face opposite her, except she couldn't seem to drag her gaze away. "Why are we discussing this?"

"Ooh, a bit of temper. But I'm happy to answer. We're discussing it as a reminder that every baby ought to be loved and nurtured like little Susan, to be welcomed into a home with happily married parents."

Her brother might dispute that last part.

"It's a good example of how adoption can save you."

Resist asking. You'll regret it. But she couldn't help herself. "Save me from what?"

"Your own depravity. And the baby from a lifetime of bastardy."

Eve swallowed a gasp. At the family gathering where her parents had announced she was in trouble, her sister-in-law—Susan's mother—had called Eve's baby *that bastard.* No one had said anything. Just let the ugly word go unchallenged. And now the woman who was supposed to be helping her had used it too. Eve clamped her lips to stop her own inappropriate words from spewing, but the gleam in Mrs. Kinsley's eyes said she knew her barb had hit home.

Rather than pursue the advantage, she switched topics again. "I understand your father is coming to visit this weekend."

Eve blanked her expression. Had they deliberately hidden this news from her? Waited until the right moment to spring it on her?

The social worker checked her watch. "Oh, look at the time, and such a nice chat we're having. What duty have you been assigned, dear?"

"Laundry."

"I'm going to recommend you work the overnight shift in the nursery next. Beginning in March."

She gaped, horrified. March was the worst possible month. "Please, not then. I have final exams in March."

"If you can't study and take care of a baby when you have a roof over your head, three meals a day, and nursing care round the clock, what do you think it's like in the real world for mothers without husbands to provide for them? Hmm?" The woman bared her Chiclet teeth in a smile. "You may go. I'll see you in a week."

Mrs. Kinsley had been right about Eve's father. He *had* been planning to come the Saturday after Valentine's Day, but he'd canceled at the last minute. Then rescheduled twice. She had her fingers crossed he would arrive this afternoon.

She could barely concentrate in the morning, her emotions oscillating between joy and dread. She hadn't seen her parents since Christmas. Would Daddy make it this time? How would she react to being around him? Pathetically eager? Politely mature?

Throughout lunch, she waited in the dining room, too nervous to eat much, eyes trained on the wall clock. How much longer?

After the dishes had been cleared, the kitchen door swished open, and Cook carried in the dessert tray. One by one, she distributed bowls of chocolate pudding, skipping Eve.

Cook met her gaze and grimaced apologetically.

Mrs. Lloyd came in. "No dessert for you, Eve. Dr. White says you're gaining too much weight, and I can't have any of my girls getting fat, now can I?"

Her cheeks burned with embarrassment. Miriam tensed beside her, about to erupt, but Eve laid a detaining hand on her friend's arm, sending her a silent message to *leave it be*.

"Now, come along. Your father's waiting for you in the parlor."

She'd never been so happy to flee the dining room.

He was staring out the window and turned at the sound of her footsteps. His suit was rumpled after hours in the car. "Hey, sweet girl." He opened his arms, and she ran into his embrace.

She had the answer to one of her questions. Her reaction was pathetically eager. As her belly pressed against him, she didn't miss the beginning of his withdrawal, but she held on for dear life.

He kissed the top of her head and eased away. "You look . . ."

"Big, I know," she said with a pained smile. Only seven months along and she looked like she'd swallowed a basketball.

"Yes, well." He jammed his fists in his pockets. "Would you like to go out for a drive?"

Escape this place with her father? Absolutely. "That would be great."

A throat cleared behind them. "I'm sorry, Mr. Mitchell," the director said. "We discourage leaving the property during visits."

A muscle twitched in his jaw. "My daughter, my decision." Thrilling words from him.

Mrs. Lloyd's nostrils flared, but she said mildly, "Of course." She spun on her heel and left.

"Come on," he said.

They stepped out into sunshine under a vivid blue sky. She hadn't left the Home through the front door since December. Hadn't seen the cheerful yellows of forsythia and daffodils. The world seemed brighter out here.

The station wagon surrounded her with familiar smells. Tobacco. Mama's cinnamon rolls. The scent of clothes washed in Tide. It made her tear up.

Daddy's hands gripped the steering wheel. "Where to?"

Her brain felt like mush. The girls didn't go out in the town often. Too much gawking. But she hadn't eaten much lunch. "How about dessert? There's a drive-in nearby with ice cream."

Ten minutes later, he was drinking a Pepsi, and she was eating an ice-cream cone. Chocolate dipped.

"How is school going?" he asked.

"Almost done. I take my exams week after next. Once I pass, I'll have my diploma."

"Your mother will be happy to hear it. What classes are you taking?"

Her smile faltered. If he'd read her letters, he would already know. "English. Trigonometry. American government. Physics."

He perked up. "Physics?" He'd been a science teacher before becoming a principal. "How are you taking that?"

"I told the main tutor how much I loved science, and she talked the physics teacher from the private academy into taking me as a student." Eve wouldn't get credit for it. She'd started too late, and the labs were impossible to schedule. But she loved the lessons. The calculations. The practicality.

He sipped his Pepsi. "How are they treating you here?"

Miriam had warned her about addressing this topic. It was impossible to make clear what it was like in a way her father would understand. Most of the staff handled them like prize sows, their primary purpose to produce offspring. They were kept clean, housed, and fed. Expected to be grateful for their care, with kindness as a reward for good behavior. Eve was afraid that her father would think that sounded about right. "It's fine."

"You're certainly fed well." He coughed.

Her pleasure in the treat vanished. She glanced sideways at her father. He was staring straight ahead, his eyes watering as if overcome with grief. Which was all her fault.

Desolation was contagious. She wrapped the remainder of her melting cone in a wad of napkins and tossed it in a garbage can.

On the trip back to the Home, he talked in bursts. Family news. Plans for the senior prom. After that, they lapsed into silence.

He parked the station wagon and shut off the engine. Overhead, thunder rumbled. The wind sent the tree branches thrashing.

"It's time for me to go, sweet girl."

"So soon?" Her protest was half-hearted. Their conversation had been stilted. She couldn't have taken much more.

"I want to get home before dark."

"Daddy, do you ever talk with Aunt Trudy?" Eve had so many things she wanted to tell an adult but not her parents. They would think she was exaggerating. Trudy lived in a city. Nothing surprised her.

"I'm stopping in Raleigh on the way home. I'll see her then."

"Please ask her to visit me."

"I will." He adjusted the knot of his tie. "I don't think I'll be able to return. It's such a busy time of the year. Family things. And graduation is only—" He sighed.

"Two months away. Yes, I know." She didn't appreciate the reminders of what she'd lost. "But you'll be here when my baby is born, won't you?"

He shook his head.

"What?" Dread tickled down her spine. "Will Mama come?"

"No, she can't. Your mother is too upset. She doesn't think her nerves can take seeing you like this." He gestured vaguely toward her middle.

"Daddy, please. I'll need you." But she could see he wasn't convinced. "The baby is your grandchild."

"No, it isn't. My grandchildren were born to my sons and their wives." His jaw flexed stubbornly. "Your situation is different, and I trust the people here to manage it correctly. Once the matter is settled, you can come home."

"Manage *it*?" she repeated in despair. "I'm having a baby. Not an *it*."

"I have nothing further to say on the subject." He pulled out his wallet and handed her a five-dollar bill. "Here's some spending money."

She crumpled it in her fist and looked out the windshield, too distressed to speak.

The mood inside the car grew tense. His hands gripped the steering wheel. Released. He was building himself up to say something she wouldn't like.

It didn't take long. "You have to come home by yourself," he said. "You understand that, right?"

The world around her faded into sepia tones. Sounds muffled. She felt gut punched. From the moment she'd told her parents, they'd made it clear the "situation" would be handled through adoption. She hadn't been consulted, so she'd locked away her opinions, unexamined.

That had been tolerable when her pregnancy had seemed like a problem to solve. A shame she had to hide. But she *knew* her baby now. She didn't feel like the matter was settled. "Or else what?"

His face hardened. "Or don't come home at all."

Choking back a sob, she pushed the door open, stumbled to the stairs, and climbed as fat raindrops pelted her with increasing speed. At the top, she stepped under the roof and peered back into the veil of rain, but Daddy's car was already gone. Clamping a hand over her mouth to contain her cries, she leaned against a pillar, hoping no one would come out to check on her, desperate to be left alone.

Why was everyone so certain what the right thing was for her baby—except her?

CHAPTER THREE

June 2024

It had been the perfect kind of Friday Allison Garrett often dreamed of but rarely got. No customers had called to complain about their software. Meetings had ended when they should have. And all ten babies in her Water Tots class had been adorably fearless. She left the aquatic center in a great mood, hoping her perfect day would include an uneventful evening.

She drove out of Marlowe and merged onto a quiet highway. The route home took her through a rural area of wooded hills, shallow creeks, and houses with lots measured in acres. On the gravel road into her own small community, she made a stop at a cluster of mailboxes before taking the quarter-mile driveway up to her log cabin.

She parked her Camry in the carport and went inside, thumbing through the mail. Nothing of interest, so she tossed it onto the kitchen table, glanced at her phone, and sighed. Airplane mode. She reconnected, and the texts flooded in. Two from her mother. Three from her best friend. Several from her boss. But it was the alert from Ancestry.com that grabbed her attention and sent her pulse into overdrive.

Her DNA results were in. The message she'd been waiting on for the past month. Actually, her whole life.

Her purse and gym bag slipped to the floor. She crossed to the couch, where her cat lay sprawled, warming his belly in the sunlight streaming through the sliding glass doors to the deck. Otis obligingly rolled over so Allison could sit, waited for his *Hello!* rub, and contorted his body against her thigh.

She opened her laptop, brought up a browser for the Ancestry website, and then stopped. With answers only a click away, she was afraid to look. Was she ready for whatever was coming? Did she really want to know? It wasn't as if she was unfamiliar with the process. She'd been doing genealogical research for years—first with her father, and more recently as a search angel assisting strangers.

Her findings sometimes led to happy reunions with long-lost family members who were welcomed with open arms. But she'd witnessed awful stories too. Vile people lurking in the shadows of the family tree. Furious birth parents who'd planned to take their secrets to the grave. Saddest of all, dads who had to be told they didn't share DNA with a beloved child they'd raised.

Allison wasn't concerned about her father's side of the family. Dad and his brother had had their DNA results for years and cajoled many others into testing as well. The Garretts had accumulated a massive amount of data.

No, if there were any surprises, they would come from her mother's side.

Mom had been adopted as a newborn. Her birth parents were a mystery, and as far as Mom was concerned, they could stay that way. She'd never searched for them or had her DNA tested. Originally, she'd claim it was loyalty to her adoptive parents. But after they had both died, Allison had approached her mother about initiating a search, only to be taken aback at the ferocity of Mom's refusal. She wasn't able to get past a lifetime of hurt, of wondering why her birth mother had given her up. Heather Garrett feared her story was of the awful type and decided she was better off never finding out.

Then last month, completely out of the blue, Mom reversed her decision with no explanation. She'd simply given the okay for Allison to test her DNA—with one condition. It was *not* okay to tell Mom the results.

Okay, enough procrastination. Allison navigated to her DNA matches on Ancestry and scanned the list. The top two matches were totally expected: Dad and his brother. But the next one was not. Her third-closest match was an unknown female, identified only as *MP*.

Allison felt a quiver of, what? Nerves? Elation? She had dozens of other aunts, uncles, and cousins on the match list, and MP was closer. She clicked the entry.

The unknown female wasn't related to Dad. MP had to be from Mom's birth family.

The knowledge shuddered through Allison. Made her eyes sting. She'd been so focused on how this would impact her mother that she'd overlooked its effect on herself. The unknown female could be the key to locating their missing family.

Allison dropped her head to the couch back and stared at the wooden beams of the ceiling, taking a moment to let this sink in. Fear and joy warred within her, and so far, joy was winning.

The keypad on the carport door beeped four times. She rotated her head to the side and watched her best friend enter.

"Hi." Bree held up a cloth bag. "I'm here."

Allison frowned, still tangled in her discovery. "Why?"

"We're having dinner together."

"I don't think I knew that."

"You would have if you ever replied to your messages."

Allison checked her phone and skimmed the three previously ignored messages. Sure enough, Bree had invited herself over.

"Is it okay?" She looked contrite. "Would you rather I leave?"

"No, I'm glad you're here." Allison had always been so logical about DNA results, remaining clearheaded as she mined the information for bits of gold. But these results were *her* gold, and it was overwhelming. It would be wonderful to share them with her friend.

She started to stand when Bree said, "I'll fix everything. Stay there."

"Fine with me. What are we having?" She slouched back into the cushions.

"Your leftovers."

Alllson grinned. "Do you know what I have?"

"No, but whatever they are, they'll be good. My contributions are ice cream and wine." Bree put the carton in the freezer and a wine bottle on the counter, then opened the refrigerator. "Chicken salad. Pimento cheese. Marinated green beans." She smiled happily. "Do you have crackers?"

So much for *stay there*. "Coming." Allison went into the kitchen to help. While her friend filled a platter with salads, fruit, and pita chips, she poured two glasses of wine. They set everything on the coffee table and flopped onto the couch, the cat between them.

She and Bree had been best friends since they'd held hands in line at kindergarten. Their friendship had endured a lot. Middle school. *High* school. Colleges that were hundreds of miles apart. Broken engagements for each. After they'd both moved back home to Marlowe, it hadn't taken long to realize how much she'd missed having someone who always seemed to show up precisely when Allison needed her most.

As she ate a grape, she studied her friend. Bree wore her own personal style of business comfortable: blue capris and a sleeveless yellow shirt. But something was different. Her red-gold curls were . . . golder? "Did you do something to your hair?"

"You can tell?" She wagged her head, sending the short curls bouncing. "I rinsed it with apple cider vinegar. If you noticed, it must be working." Bree fed Otis a piece of chicken, fed herself a green bean, and moaned. "It's hard to believe that anything green can be this good."

"Thanks. I think. So how's life?"

"Awesome." Instant animation. Bree loved talking about Write Style, the shop she'd opened last autumn near the center of town. Initially, she'd only sold stationery and pens, but a wider variety of products was finding its way onto the shelves. Bree had an unlirhited supply of ideas. "Lots of online orders this week. Another month of not being in the red."

"A worthy goal." Allison finished a pita chip slathered with pimento cheese and tried not to gaze with longing at her laptop. How rude would it be to log back on?

"Are you wondering if you'd be a poor host to resume whatever you were doing before I arrived?"

Caught. She laughed. "Yes, I am."

"And what have you decided?"

"That it would be very rude, but I'd like to anyway."

"Be my guest." Bree scooped more chicken salad with a chip.

Allison reached for the laptop and returned to MP's entry. Unfortunately, there wasn't much to glean. The woman's information was private, which meant she was probably alive. That was good news. But Allison wouldn't be allowed to contact her directly, which would slow down progress.

Bree peered at the screen. "What has you so captivated?"

"Genealogy. I'm on the hunt."

"Whose family?"

"Mine." It gave her chills to say it.

"Oh, wow. Your results came in!" Bree moved Otis off the couch to shift closer. "Learn anything?"

"I've got a match with someone from my mom's birth family." Allison pointed at the entry.

"It can't be that easy. Can it?"

"Theoretically, yes. But not likely. I'm sure this one will get harder." Plenty of effort remained, and some of it could get painful. Especially if Mom's cooperation was required.

"MP, huh? Are initials all you get?"

"It depends. Each Ancestry user can decide what they're called on the site. I always use my full name. But MP has someone else managing her account, so initials are all we'll get. For now."

Bree reclined into the couch and sipped her wine. "Can you tell how MP is related to you?"

Allison stared through the wall of glass opposite her as the sun sank in a blaze of red behind a hill. Her connection to MP was *very* close. The possibilities were limited, but any of them would have a huge impact. "She could be an aunt." Allison swallowed hard. "Or my grandmother."

"Oh, Allison. That's amazing."

It was. Scary too. She might have located Mom's birth mother. Life was about to get complicated.

Allison had uncovered this kind of information many times for other people and had seen a spectrum of reactions. She should have anticipated how unsettled she would feel. And what about her brother? She hadn't asked Perry whether he would want to know, and now wasn't the time to broach the topic, not while he was embroiled in a custody battle with his ex-wife.

It was a big responsibility, figuring out how to handle whatever the search revealed next. "Here's where I have to proceed carefully. If MP is my aunt, she might not know she has a sister. Telling her could be a shock."

"And if she's your grandmother?"

"I won't have to worry as much about contacting her. If she has her DNA results public, it's likely she wants to be found."

"Whoa. After all this time. What will you tell your mom?"

"Nothing yet. At her request."

Her friend nodded slowly. "I get that. What happened to your mom is sad."

And hard to understand. The birth mother had left her baby on a porch late at night. Fortunately, the porch had belonged to the town doctor. Yet there had to have been other, less risky options available to the girl, no matter how desperate she was.

Allison had been a search angel long enough to know that oral histories could be unreliable. Maybe MP could shed light on the story. Or maybe not, and they'd never know.

"What do you do next?" Bree asked.

"Send an email to MP's contact person."

"And then what?"

"Wait." In a typical search, there would be three major phases. Collect the data. Analyze the findings objectively. Reveal the conclusions. This search wouldn't be typical, since there was no way for her to be objective. But she could remain hopeful. She'd found a door into her family's past, and she was excited to follow where it led.

CHAPTER FOUR

March 1969

After nearly a month on the nursery shift, Eve was exhausted. Two babies with stuffy noses had kept her up all night. Whatever message Mrs. Kinsley was sending had been received.

When Eve left the nursery at seven, she skipped breakfast and went to bed. It hardly seemed like any time had passed before someone was shaking her shoulder.

"Get up, Eve."

"No." She didn't bother to open her eyes.

"You have a visitor." It was Miriam's voice. So annoying.

"Go away."

"She says she's your aunt."

Eve's eyes popped open. "Aunt Trudy?" She swung her legs over the edge of the bed. Pushed to her feet. Swayed and dropped back down again. "Where are my shoes?"

"Slow down, or you'll hurt yourself," Miriam said and nudged the missing shoes closer. "Who is she?"

What could Eve say about her aunt? Trudy was a career woman who wore gorgeous clothes and drove a glamorous car. She'd never had a husband or kids nor planned to, yet her life seemed full of joy. "My dad's sister. She's fabulous."

"She's waiting in the foyer. Mrs. Lloyd has her cornered."

Eve laughed. "Whatever happens, my aunt will emerge the winner." She stood carefully and stepped into her shoes.

"Your clothes are wrinkled, but I don't think you should take the time to change." Miriam handed her the gray sweater. "You'll need this. Okay, come on. I'll make sure you get down the stairs in one piece."

Her aunt was standing in the foyer, keys in hand, a lemon-yellow scarf wrapped around her head, her white coat open and sunglasses on. Mrs. Lloyd hovered nearby. "Here she is."

Trudy pulled Eve into an exuberant hug. "I am so happy to see you. How are you doing?"

She sent her aunt a wary glance. They had an audience. "Fine."

Trudy pushed her sunglasses to the top of her head, eyes narrowing. "Yes, I can see that." Her gaze flicked to the director and back again. "The weather is nice. Why don't we get some fresh air? I saw a cute little park on my way in."

"I'd like that." Leaving the house would be wonderful.

"Miss Mitchell," Mrs. Lloyd began, "you're not on the approved list."

"I'm sure that's an oversight. Call my brother and ask, if you must, but my niece and I are leaving." Trudy linked arms with Eve and sailed out the door, leaving a whiff of Chanel perfume in her wake.

Eve controlled a smile. Minutes later, they were racing away in her aunt's purple Mustang.

Trudy turned out of the neighborhood and wound through the streets of the town. "I stayed with friends in Wilmington this weekend, but of course I stopped on the way home to see how you were faring."

"Thank you. I'm glad you're here."

"Sorry I couldn't come sooner." Trudy breathed deeply through her mouth. At a stop sign, she glanced sideways, her eyes unreadable behind her huge round sunglasses. "When your father was here, did he tell you . . . the news?"

Eve looked away. "Yes, and I'd rather not talk about it." On her rare chance to escape the Home, she didn't want to think about what the future held.

"I understand. Completely." Trudy cleared her throat. "It's been hard."

Hard for her? Why? Had Daddy and Trudy argued over his edict? Eve waited for more, but her aunt didn't supply any details.

"Okay, honey. Tell me what's going on with you."

Eve hadn't had time to plan how much to reveal. "I've graduated from a private academy in town. We didn't go through the ceremony, but I got a diploma." On the line for the location of the school, they'd typed in *Eastern Carolina Home for Mothers and Babies*. Another little dig to make sure her future employers knew where she'd been for her last semester.

"That's wonderful. Ooh, here's the park." Her aunt screeched into the deserted lot and braked. "Want to take a walk?"

"Sure."

They were strolling along a paved path when her aunt spoke again. "How are you? Really?"

The question brought such relief. "Miserable."

"I'm sorry. Do they treat you badly?" Trudy's voice tightened.

"Not physically. It's just . . . Ugh." Here was her chance to explain the daily humiliations, the constant nastiness. "They serve delicious food, but if you're getting too fat, you have to sit and watch the others eat. The doctor is awful. He only speaks to the nurses. His hands are hard and cold." Like his heart. "And instead of answering our questions, he simply glares like we're more disgusting than dog doo. Our mail is censored. Our showers are timed. And the vicious names they call us, you would never say in polite company."

Trudy gave her a hug. "I'm sorry."

They finished a loop around a fountain and headed back toward the parking lot. Two more cars had pulled in. Church must be letting out.

"Do you know what you'll do about your baby?"

Someone had asked her opinion. Why did no one else act like she should have one? "I try not to think about it."

"You have to, honey. You don't have much longer."

From the moment she'd told her parents she was expecting, it had been assumed she would relinquish the baby. Everybody believed that the only way to redeem herself and save her family's reputation was adoption. She wasn't positive she agreed. But what did she want? And what was right for the baby?

"Your parents are adamantly opposed to bringing your child home."

Irritation flared with surprising strength. "Are you on their side?"

"I'm on the side of you and the baby. I want what's best for you both. I won't comment on your parents' choices, but I've told them I'll come for the birth. If you want me to."

"Yes, please." If she couldn't have her mother, Aunt Trudy would be next best.

"I'll make sure Mrs. Lloyd has my number to call when you go into labor. Now, listen to me. This is important. Wait until I get here to sign the papers. You ought to have someone from the family with you when you do. And if the people here bully you into it before I arrive, you have a week to change your mind."

"Okay." Eve was *so* relieved. She wouldn't be alone after all.

"Don't forget. It's your right to revoke." Trudy flicked her hand, as if dismissing the topic. "Now, I can stay another hour. What shall we do?"

"A drive in the country?"

"Let's do it. Is it too cold to put the top down?"

"Never."

"That's my girl. There's a blanket on the back seat if you need it."

Once the top was down, her aunt reversed from her parking space in a chorus of popping pebbles and raced out to the highway at a thrilling speed. It was too noisy to talk, but Eve didn't care. Lifting her face to the sun, she laughed with pure joy. She had only been away from the Home two times in the last three months and never outside the town limits. The land in this part of North Carolina was so flat that, if there weren't so many trees, they could have seen for miles.

At last, they circled back to the town and drove through an old neighborhood with its big, beautiful homes and massive azaleas in pink and red and purple.

"I bet Grammy's azaleas are fab." Eve looked at her aunt, about to ask a question she shouldn't but couldn't resist. "Do you ever see Galen?"

"No. I haven't been to Marlowe in weeks."

"Why not? Don't you visit Grammy on the weekends?"

Trudy went pale. "I thought Warren told you the news."

"He did. I can't bring the baby home."

"Oh, honey," Trudy said hoarsely. "That's not what I meant." She pulled into an empty parking spot below a huge pecan tree, twisted in her seat, and took off her sunglasses. "This isn't the way I wanted you to find out."

Eve's pulse quickened with foreboding. "Find out what?"

"I am so sorry to tell you this, but Grammy died."

Eve pressed back until the car door blocked her from going any farther and shook her head in disbelief, certain she hadn't heard that right. "Grammy died? Your mother?"

"Yes." Her aunt's eyes shimmered with tears. "On Valentine's Day."

She let her head drop to the seat back and looked up at the tree branches overhead, her mind almost numb from shock. "Why didn't anyone let me know?" She was proud of how calm she sounded.

"Mrs. Lloyd asked your father not to say anything so close to your exams. She didn't want you distracted."

The director had long ago won the title of the vilest person Eve had ever met. So her collusion in this terrible decision came as no surprise. But her family? Maybe their haste to imprison her here had been understandable. But withholding the news of her beloved grandmother's passing? Not allowing her to mourn with them? It was unforgivable. "You went along with them."

"No. I mean . . . Warren said he would tell you in person. I assumed he had when he visited you."

"Clearly, he did not." Closing her eyes, Eve fought off a wave of nausea. How dare they? "Did you tell him I deserved to know? That he shouldn't wait?"

"I tried. But he's your father, and I'm just your aunt. I—"

"Didn't think it was your place to interfere." Her eyes blinked open. "Daddy was here four weeks ago, and you haven't checked on me since."

"No."

Her aunt had always been so special to her. Someone she relied on completely. But Trudy had let her down, and that hurt in ways Eve could barely take in. "Take me back. Now."

Her aunt looked like she would object but, instead, cranked the engine. The drive to the Home was completed in silence.

Before the car had fully stopped, Eve was opening the door and squirming out. Her aunt came around to help, but Eve waved her off. "Was the real reason Daddy didn't have me attend the funeral so people wouldn't know?"

"Yes."

Eve looked up at her aunt. "How has he explained my absence?"

"You went away to take care of your sick grandmother."

"People will figure it out now, and I still wasn't allowed to grieve with my family." Eve stared ahead at the house. A curtain twitched in the parlor window. She was being watched. "I know I did something wrong, but my family has too. Only there's a difference. I made the mistake of loving someone too much. My family is guilty of not loving me enough, and that's a far worse crime."

Tears pooled in Trudy's eyes. "I'm so sorry. I don't know what to say."

Eve's whole body ached. "You should go."

She held herself together until the rumble of the Mustang had faded, then she hung on to the railing and yielded to her grief.

Mrs. Wilson pulled Eve aside later that afternoon. "Mrs. Kinsley would like to see you."

"When?" Eve didn't want to speak with the social worker but knew she couldn't refuse.

"Now. She's waiting on you."

When she arrived in Mrs. Kinsley's office, the older woman was sitting in her chair, hands pressed together as if in prayer, lips curled in a feral smile.

"Welcome, Eve. Have a seat."

She sat clumsily and shifted around until she was less uncomfortable.

"I understand your aunt was here this morning. Mrs. Lloyd thinks it might be wise to discuss how you're feeling."

Eve didn't want to discuss how she felt. Not with the social worker. Not even with herself. She would have to be careful. Mrs. Kinsley could be relentless when she wanted to know something.

"So tell me. How was your visit?"

"Fine."

"I don't think that's true. Did your aunt say anything troubling?"

Eve glared in disgust, although she wasn't sure at whom. "Did you keep my grandmother's death from me?"

"No, dear, of course not." The smile went wider. "But I concur with the decision. We couldn't have you do poorly on your exams. Getting your diploma is important."

If Mrs. Kinsley really believed that, why had she tried to ruin Eve's chances by putting her in the night nursery? She looked at her hands, clenched in her lap. Among her family, Aunt Trudy, and the staff at the Home, she had no one to trust.

"So is making the right decision about adoption. You're only five weeks from your due date, and you're running out of time. After girls carry their children for months, you want the best for the baby. It's a natural longing. I understand. I have four. But you aren't the best, are you, Eve?"

Her defenses might be damaged, but she wasn't giving up. "I love my baby."

"I know you do, which is why you'll sign the papers, because you'll realize your love isn't enough." Mrs. Kinsley sighed mournfully. "Think about the situation from the baby's perspective. Would any child want a mother like you? Of course not. You have no job. No prospects. No money. Your father's made it clear that you'll have no family, either, if you insist on keeping the child. I'm sure you don't wish to doom the baby to a life of poverty. Adoption gives him a chance to be raised by a married couple living in a nice house, with a mother devoted to caring for him."

Eve knew she ought to just tell them she would sign the papers and be done with it. But she wanted to hold her baby first. Look into its sweet eyes and touch its soft skin. Only then would she be able to give him or her what they really needed. Even if that wasn't her.

The nursery was unusually quiet that night, just what Eve did not need. Without anything to do, she sat in a rocking chair, unable to relax, thoughts churning.

The night nurse had nodded off, confident Eve could manage on her own. They had only five babies. Two were scheduled to be handed over this week.

Eve made the rounds, stopping at each bassinet. All were sleeping peacefully, their cheeks plump and rosy. No wet diapers. Blankets snugly in place.

What would her baby look like? Golden like Galen? Brunette and blue eyed like her? A little of each?

She could honestly say she hated this assignment, but not for predictable reasons. Mrs. Kinsley had forced it on her so she could see how hopeless it was to manage life with a baby. But Eve was smart enough to know that the care of five babies couldn't compare to the care of one. Just like the care of one would be different when the child was completely dependent on her, and only her, for everything.

No, the argument that had chipped away at her confidence had been planted weeks ago. It was the thought of her mother doting on little Susan and all her other grandchildren except Eve's child. Her baby deserved to have a loving family who reached for him eagerly. Without reluctance or distaste. If she denied that to her child, what kind of mother was she?

She paced restlessly, too agitated by her dilemma to sit while her head and her heart battled it out.

Her family had been wrong to keep Grammy's passing from her, especially her parents. It was as if they'd abandoned her again. Exposed how they cared more about appearances than her. If they'd been wrong about that, what else had they been wrong about?

They'd certainly been mistaken about the Home. It wasn't a good place. She realized now that her banishment to the middle of nowhere had been in *their* best interests. Not hers. Not the baby's.

Into the stillness of the room, the sobs came. Harsh sobs that shook her shoulders and twisted in her gut. She'd never felt so alone in her life.

The baby gave a mighty kick. Then another. And suddenly, Eve was giggling. *Making a liar of me, huh? Reminding me I'm not alone, not while I have you.* Such a lovely thought.

She lowered herself into a rocking chair, closed her eyes, and enjoyed the party going on in her belly.

A sickening pain in her back brought her out of a doze. She wobbled to a stand, needing to pee, only to continue gripping the chair, worried by how odd her legs felt. When the pain finally subsided, she made it to the bathroom, mostly in time.

By 5:00 a.m., the backache had spread around her sides, the whole of her abdomen tightening rhythmically. She watched the clock. Timed the contractions.

Her sisters-in-law had nine children between them. Eve had watched them go into labor for five. She knew she had most of the signs yet didn't want to believe. She wasn't due for another five weeks. *No, no. Please, no.* It was too soon.

But there was no doubt. She was in labor.

"Wake up." She shook the night nurse's shoulder. "The baby is coming."

CHAPTER FIVE

Bree Harper arrived at her shop Saturday morning to discover that online orders had poured in overnight. Most would require gift wrapping.

It wasn't a bad problem to have: her business doing better than its first-year projections. She would never complain. That would be ungrateful. She was happy with how things were going. If success meant she had to work harder than she'd expected, so be it.

She was sealing a carton when there was a banging on the alley door. An Allison kind of banging. Bree pushed it open. "Come in."

"I brought breakfast." Her friend carried two large to-go cups and a white bakery bag to the office desk and set them down. "Coffee and cinnamon scones."

"Just what I needed. Thanks." Bree took a seat and went for the coffee first. All treats were welcome, but caffeine was a priority.

Allison went over to a table stacked with empty cardboard cartons. "Still packing up?"

"Yeah. It's wedding season, and pens appear to be a trending groomsmen gift." All shipped separately with customized note cards. Not. Complaining.

"Want some help?"

When Bree had dreamed up the idea of a stationery shop—a place to rekindle the lost art of writing letters—banks hadn't been willing to fund her. Presumably, they'd considered her too much of a risk after she'd wiped out her savings to pay off her student loans from graduate school. So the bank-of-Allison-and-Dad had "invested" what Bree needed to open Write Style. She'd vowed then that she would never *ask* her friend for any other help. But when it was offered? She was happy to accept. "Sure. I'll wrap the gifts and write the note cards."

"And I'll box them for shipping." Allison got to work with no further prompting, sifting through the labels and packing lists, pursing her lips as she analyzed what to do and how.

Bree envied her friend's innate practicality and drive. Allison's movements were seamlessly efficient. Her focus, total. Bree would bet her morning routine lasted no more than ten minutes. Allison would throw on whatever was clean. Shorts and a T-shirt in solid-color neutrals. She kept her brown hair clipped sleek and short, so even it obeyed. Yet she always looked put together. Striking.

The two of them finished less than an hour later. Forty packages wrapped, sealed, labeled, and ready to ship.

The staff-only door swished open, and her salesclerk stepped in. "I'm here." Lola looked gorgeous today in a purple sheath, her silver hair up in a french twist. "Need anything?"

"Thanks, but we're done."

She gestured at a cart brimming with new items. "Want me to put out the stock?"

"That would be great." Bree felt weepy. Maybe it wouldn't be such a hard day after all.

Lola wheeled out the cart. She'd barely left before the delivery guy arrived. He handed over a couple of boxes and hauled off the rest.

Once it was just the two friends again, Bree sagged against the wall with relief. She was caught up.

"Hey, are you okay?" Allison asked.

"Yes." Bree straightened. At her friend's raised eyebrow, she said, "No. Owning a business is never-ending work."

"You have me."

True, and she was grateful. But Bree was already in danger of abusing her friend's willingness to pitch in. She had to pace herself. Dropping onto her desk chair, she reached for the last bite of her scone and glanced at her phone. "Oh, I have an alert from Ancestry. My DNA results are in."

"You sent in a test?"

"Yeah. In solidarity." She opened the Ancestry web page on her laptop and selected Origins. "I'm mostly from England and Ireland. What about you?"

"I haven't checked my ethnicities." Resting a hip against the desk, Allison pulled out her phone. "Do you see where it says DNA Matches? Select it next. Those are all your matches. They're sorted in descending order of how close they are to you."

"Wow. This is amazing." Bree's half brother Tristan was at the top. Their mom would be fuming about his taking the test. If she knew. "My brother is listed first. After Tristan . . . that's strange. I have someone called MP too."

"Really?" Allison's fingers tapped on her phone screen. She swiped. "Amazing," she echoed oddly and sat down hard. "Who do you have listed after MP?"

Bree checked—and gasped. "Allison Garrett?"

"Yeah. We're related." Allison had a tremulous smile. "And we're *really* close."

Bree was related to her best friend? That was a wonderful surprise. "How close?"

"Interpreting DNA results isn't an exact science. I can't say for sure, but—"

"Can you guess?" Bree interrupted, before her friend went into more details. Allison tended to overexplain.

"There are several relationships that qualify," she said, "but based on our ages, we're almost certainly full first cousins."

"*First* cousins?" That was *really* close. As in, *that can't be right.* "What exactly does *full* mean?"

"We share the same grandfather *and* grandmother." Allison set her phone down and stared at the desk, lost in thought. When she spoke again, her tone was soft and awed. "You're a member of Mom's birth family, Bree. *Your* father and *my* mother must be full siblings."

Wait. Siblings? Bree felt breathless with panic, like she was driving along hairpin curves through the mountains, hoping a Mack truck wouldn't appear around the next bend. "What makes you think that?"

Allison looked up, her gaze clearing, the wisps of pleasure fading to something more pensive. "Check your match list again. If my dad is your uncle, he'll be listed higher than me."

"He's not there."

"Then you must be related to me through my mother. And I don't have your brother on my list. If Tristan and I aren't a match, you and I can't be connected through your mother. So I must be related to your dad." She dropped her head back. "Everett is my uncle. Mom is his *sister.* This is unreal."

Bree usually found her friend's confidence reassuring, but right now, it was tiresome. She considered her top three matches again. Tristan. MP. Allison. "Remind me how MP fits into all this."

"What?"

"Allison. Focus. Who is MP?"

She shook her head. Blinked. "MP is our full aunt," Allison said carefully, "or our grandmother."

"So you're saying that either MP is a sister to Dad and Heather, or Dad's birth mother is not my Granna."

"Correct."

Bree felt the color leach from her face. "That can*not* be true."

"DNA doesn't lie."

In this case, it had to. "There has to have been a mistake. Maybe the sample was contaminated."

"It wasn't. The results are either all right or all wrong. If yours had been contaminated, you wouldn't have matched with your brother."

This was unbelievable. Except she'd listened to Allison's search-angel stories for years. It was common for people to deny the facts. Bree had always wondered how they could doubt when presented with the evidence. In every case, if they kept digging, the facts were always confirmed. Also common? Families were ripped apart by the revelations.

Bree had to think this through calmly. If she assumed that the DNA results were accurate, what else could have happened? "If Dad really is the son of my grandparents, it would mean they gave away your mother and our aunt MP."

"That's one possible explanation."

"Which I don't believe." Bree closed the lid of her laptop, shutting away the results. "If Granna isn't Dad's biological mother, then Grampa had an affair." With the same woman? Producing three children, where they kept the boy and gave away the two girls? No, that was ridiculous.

"We don't have enough data to draw that conclusion."

Data? These were people, not data. And they were people she loved, unsuspecting of the damage ahead. "I can't accept this," Bree said and popped out of her chair. She paced back and forth, her thoughts in disarray. Everything she believed about her family was about to change. What monster had she unleashed?

If only she could rewind this conversation. Even better, forget she'd ever taken a DNA test. But she had, and, deep down, she didn't doubt what her friend was saying. Allison hadn't gotten this wrong.

Her salesclerk poked her head in the door. "Got a moment?"

Bree looked up. "Sure, Lola. What is it?"

"A customer has come in to make a special order for a fountain pen."

"I'll be right out," she said, glad for the reprieve. Her world had changed in the past ten minutes, and she needed to get away. She looked at her friend. "I have to see to my customer."

Allison's eyes narrowed in concern. "Bree, you've just heard some major news about your family. Don't you think—?"

"No. I'll be fine."

"But we should talk about—"

"Not now. We'll talk later, okay?" As Bree pushed through the door, she glanced back over her shoulder, surprised to find a look of sympathy on her friend's face.

For twenty-five years, they'd been closer than sisters. "Family" by choice. Would being cousins by blood change them?

CHAPTER SIX

After leaving her friend's store, Allison drove home through the rain, the soaking kind that kept her concentrating on the climb up her driveway and into the carport. Once inside the cabin, she tossed her keys onto the island, then collapsed on the couch. Otis permitted a quick belly rub before assuming his nap position.

The adrenaline rush she'd had earlier had faded, leaving her shaken. Today's news ought to have been some of the happiest she'd ever received. She'd long been curious about her mother's birth family. Learning that her best friend was actually related to her should have been pure delight. Instead, the reality had brought complexities Allison didn't know how to deal with.

What was she going to do about her mother?

As if on cue, her phone rang with Mom's ringtone. Allison took a steadying breath and answered. "Hi. What's up?"

"Are we still on for dinner?"

She searched her mental calendar and . . . nothing. "Sure?"

Mom laughed. "Did you forget?"

"Completely." She had a good excuse. She'd had an eventful day.

"Can you come? Although, I warn you, it's just spaghetti."

Just spaghetti? Mom's was epic. "I can. I made brownies. Should I bring them?"

"Yes," her father shouted in the background.

Mom laughed again. "Well, there's your answer. Around six?"

"See you then."

Allison set down her phone and groaned. Should she say anything about the Harpers? Her mother couldn't spend the rest of her life bumping into them, unaware that they were her brothers and niece. Allison would have to tell. But when? It would be wrong for Mom to be the last to know.

She wished she'd had the forethought to introduce her own condition on the DNA testing—that if she found something explosive, Mom would listen. Or maybe Dad would and choose the appropriate course.

Should she tell him what she'd discovered anyway? No, that wasn't fair. Once he knew, he would be forced to tell his wife, and that would make him the bad guy.

Allison would have to be the one to initiate the conversation. When she'd uncovered more facts. When she could be more definitive than *we're related to the Harpers*. In other words, not tonight.

Allison packed brownies with homemade fudge sauce for Dad, added angel food cake with berries for her mother, and started the trek back to town.

She admired their house as she strolled up the sidewalk. It wasn't the home she was raised in. Her parents had moved here as empty nesters, downsizing to a contemporary ranch, all cedar and glass and stone. It suited them. "Mom? Dad?" she called out as she entered the cool interior.

"Back here," her mother yelled.

But the smell of garlic and oregano was already drawing her to the kitchen. Mom stirred sauce in a pan and kept an eye on pasta bubbling in a pot. Dad sat at the table, engrossed by something on his tablet. When Allison walked in, he slipped off his headphones.

"Hey, Alli."

"Hi, Dad." She kissed his cheek, then set her container on the counter and began to unpack. "How's work?"

"Fun. Easing my way to retirement." Her father had owned a plumbing business for nearly thirty years. He was ceding control to a manager much more slowly than necessary.

"Easing?" Mom laughed. She gave Allison a hug on the way to the sink.

Dad gave his wife a look over the top of his glasses. "Can't be too careful," he said mildly.

After they were all seated with steaming plates of spaghetti, Allison asked about one of her parents' favorite subjects. Their son and grandson. "Any news from Perry and Liam?"

When Mom nodded a *go-ahead* at Dad, he said, "It's getting ugly again."

Perry's divorce had been finalized two years ago. It had been nasty, but, for their son's sake, they'd eventually settled into an armed truce. And it had held until Perry's ex-wife moved to Oregon with her new partner. When he'd refused to grant permission for Liam to leave North Carolina, a new battle ensued. "I'm sorry to hear that."

"Yeah. We are too. At least Liam seems to be oblivious. He's loving his soccer camp." Dad switched to a story about a recent game he'd attended, convinced his five-year-old grandson was a prodigy. Not really accurate, but Dad's loyalty was charming.

"Allison?" her mother asked. "Are you okay?" The question was pointed, as if Mom could tell something was up.

"Yeah. I'm good." And that was true, in every aspect of her life except one.

"You seem preoccupied."

"A little." Allison had been lucky when it came to parents. In high school, she'd been the envy of her friends, having a mom and dad who'd given her the right blend of interest and independence. But the right blend had come with a disconcerting sixth sense for detecting when she was upset and trying to mask it. "I'm making plans for a trip to Scotland."

"On business?"

"Mostly, but I'm also taking a week of vacation." She hadn't booked much yet. A train pass. A few out-of-the-way bed-and-breakfasts in popular tourist areas. But she'd left most days unplanned.

Dad narrowed his eyes in paternal concern. "Are you traveling by yourself?"

Mom patted his hand. "She'll be safe, Rod."

"I reserve the right to worry," he said as he pushed up from his chair. "Since you two cooked, I'll wash the dishes."

"I won't argue with that." Mom turned to Allison. "Up for a walk?"

"Sure," she said and followed her mother outside.

Her mother took off on her usual mile-and-a-half scenic route through the neighborhood, past houses with carefully tended flower beds and lawns. Once they'd reached the first corner, Mom launched into a monologue, shifting smoothly from one topic to the next. Liam. Dad's too-tentative foray into retirement. Her job.

Mom had been a registered nurse before having children, but she'd put her nursing career on hold until Allison and Perry had made it into middle school. Then Mom had pursued becoming a nurse anesthetist full steam, gaining the necessary credentials, studying for her doctoral degree. Yet she'd still been available most afternoons when Allison got home from swim team practice. Her mother's career had modeled the expectation that "it's never too late to find what makes you happy."

"Your turn," Mom said. "Are you teaching much at the pool?"

"Just one Water Tots class, and I substitute when they need me."

"How's Bree?"

Dangerous ground. Allison would have to be cautious. "Staying busy with the store."

"Still helping her out?"

Allison grinned. "As much as she'll let me." She maintained her friend's website. Neither of them was sure how successful that experiment had been.

"I'm concerned about Perry," Mom said, circling back to her son's custody battle.

Allison really ought to call him to see how he was doing and offer to babysit her nephew.

Her mother halted. "Have you been paying attention?"

"Not entirely."

"Okay. You've been cagey all evening. What's happened?" Mom hesitated; then her eyes widened. "Did you get your DNA results back?"

Allison nodded. "Last night."

Mom bit her lip. Looked around the street and back again. "Did you learn anything that surprised you? Is that why you're distracted?"

"Yes."

Mom took off again.

Allison hurried to catch up. They continued to walk, waved at neighbors, petted several excited dogs. But as they came into view of her parents' house, her mother asked, "Is the surprise about the Garretts?"

"No."

Mom stopped on the driveway. Took a couple of slow breaths. "Why do you want to know about my birth family so badly?"

"They're my family, too, Mom. I wonder about them. What kind of people are they? Good? Bad? Ordinary? Extraordinary? Do I look like them?"

"You look like a Garrett."

Mostly true, although not her eyes. "I'm curious about my family history."

"I'm not."

"I get that. Which is why I've had the results for twenty-four hours and hadn't mentioned it to you." Mom was sending mixed signals. Why was she asking questions if she didn't want to be told?

Her mother stormed into the house through the front door and went straight to the kitchen. Dad stood at the sink, drying his hands on a dish towel.

"Her DNA results are in," Mom blurted.

"Ah." Dad's gaze went back and forth between them, trying to gauge the mood. Then he frowned, possibly recognizing something on Allison's face that troubled him.

Maybe she should feel them out. Clarify the boundaries. "If I discover something that's really important, Mom, what should I do?"

"Alli," Dad warned softly.

Mom stared, interest and denial warring in her expression. "Like what?"

Allison wished they would just trust her to determine if ignorance was acceptable or not. "They live in Marlowe."

Mom paled. "Okay, nothing else." She rushed out into the backyard and kept on going until she reached the gazebo.

"Does your mom know them?" Dad asked.

"More than knows them. They're friendly."

"Whoa. She didn't anticipate this. None of us did. I'll talk to her." The back door banged shut behind him. Once he reached the gazebo, he sat beside his wife, pulled her into his arms, and held her close.

Allison watched her parents through the window, sorry that the evening had ended this way. Why hadn't they predicted such an outcome? In retrospect, she couldn't imagine how they'd believed it would be fine for Allison to have knowledge that Mom did not. Because today's discovery guaranteed that there was more to come, and no matter how hard Allison tried, her mother was going to be hurt.

CHAPTER SEVEN

After Bree had placed a special order for a fountain pen, she'd helped with a rush of customers, signed someone up for a calligraphy class she was teaching soon, and returned to the workroom. But instead of handling other tasks that ought to be done, she'd sat like a lump in her desk chair, staring into space, her brain on overload. Anything important could wait while she adjusted to her new reality.

The door to the showroom opened. "Bree?"

She spun the chair slowly. How long had she been out of it? "Yes, Lola?"

"I've locked up. Is there anything else I can do?"

"No. Thanks." Bree smiled at the older woman. Lola had become a godsend in the six months she'd worked in the shop. After thirty-five years of marriage, her husband asked for a divorce and moved in with his girlfriend. Lola had moved to Marlowe to be closer to her daughter, a student at Duke's medical school, and her son, a paralegal at a Durham law firm. Armed with an MBA and no recent experience, Lola had applied for an open salesclerk position at Write Style. Bree had known instantly she was ideal for the job. "You can go on. Enjoy the rest of your weekend."

"Great. See you Tuesday." Her clerk slipped out the alley door.

She should get out of there too.

But what should she do? Go home? Forget what she'd learned in hopes it would go away?

No, it would be impossible to have a normal Saturday evening, not while she had this huge secret consuming her thoughts. Awful or not, she had to tell her father. Tonight. She reached for her phone and called.

"Hi, Bree," he said, a smile in his voice.

She trembled. He wouldn't be smiling much longer. "Are you home?"

"Yes." He sobered. "What's up?"

"I need to come over and talk with you."

"Are you okay?"

"I'm fine." Well, not really. Everything was wrong and would never be right again. "I just have some questions to ask."

"Sure," he said. "When?"

"I can drive over now."

"Okay. See you soon." The call ended.

She hesitated. Her father would be devastated and might not want witnesses. Yet, if Dad had questions, Allison could respond with confidence about family trees and DNA, where Bree might flounder. She needed her friend. Her text to Allison was almost instinctive.

Are you there?

Yes

I'm going to tell Dad. Could you meet me at his house?

Leaving now

Bree pulled into the driveway of the home she moved to when she was ten. A Low Country, it was called. One and a half stories. White with black shutters, a wide veranda, and a yard filled with dogwoods, pine trees, and crape myrtles. Her old room had a dormer with a window seat where she could sit and watch the world and dream. So many happy memories.

When Allison's Camry pulled smoothly to a stop at the curb, Bree got out of her car and waited for her friend to join her. "Thanks for coming," she said, trying to stay composed. "You've helped people share this kind of news before. How did you handle it?"

"Usually, the family member starts the conversation. I only jump in if necessary."

"That'll work. If I stumble, you take over."

"I'll do my best. It's just that . . ." Allison exhaled shakily. "This time, I'm a family member too."

The statement shuddered through Bree. Having her friend as a cousin hadn't quite sunk in.

Dad was standing at the front door. "Hi, Allison," he said and pulled Bree into a hug, holding on slightly longer than normal, no doubt sensing the depth of her distress. "Come in."

Bree led her friend over to adjacent club chairs while Dad dropped onto the center of the couch.

"Okay, Bree. What's going on?"

"Dad." She hated what she had to do. When her parents split up twenty years ago, there had never been any question about who would get primary custody. Her mother had remarried, moved two hours away, and started another family. Bree had stayed with her dad. He'd been her anchor in the midst of all the pain and confusion, and she was about to wound him badly. "Allison and I had our DNA tested."

"Interesting. I didn't know you'd done that. So the results must be in?"

"I got mine yesterday. Something unexpected popped up." She frowned at her hands, twisting in her lap. "The same unknown female appeared on both of our lists."

"That *is* unexpected, but kind of cool." He smiled at Allison before looking back at Bree. "Does that mean you're related? Like cousins?"

"Yes," Bree said gruffly. "First cousins."

"First?" Emotions flickered across his face. Surprise. Confusion. Concern. "I don't understand. How can that be?"

Could she do this? Could she find the words?

No, she couldn't. She shot her friend a pleading glance.

Allison took over. "Ancestry.com gives us enough information to narrow down the relationship between two people who have a DNA match. I think that Bree and I are first cousins. And that my mom is your sister."

"What?" His head jerked back as if slapped. "Heather is my sister? *No. That can't be right.*" He hitched forward to the edge of the couch and rested his forearms on his knees. He shook his head over and over. "No."

"It's true, Dad. I can show you." Bree tried to open the app on her phone, but her hands shook so badly she dropped it.

He flicked the offer away with his hand, launched off the couch, and scanned the room restlessly. The fireplace drew him like a magnet, his attention zeroing in on the collection of framed photos, especially the one of him as a baby with his brother and parents. "I can*not* believe this."

He spun around, his gaze falling on Bree for a long, tense moment before directing rapid-fire questions at Allison. "How sure are you?"

"Very sure."

"Wasn't Heather adopted?"

"Yes."

"Am I?"

"It's possible." Allison looked pained. "I don't know."

"I don't either. Obviously." He dug out his phone. "But I know someone who will." He tapped a contact and waited a beat. "Are you busy?" Dad's voice had a sharp edge. He glanced at his watch. "As soon as you can. Okay, thanks." He slipped his phone into his shorts pocket and met Bree's gaze. "My brother will head over in a few minutes."

Would her uncle have any answers?

Yes, he had to. He'd been in high school when her father was born. He would have noticed if Granna had been pregnant.

The wait was excruciating. Dad paced into the foyer and back. Bree didn't know where to look, so she stared at her feet. From the chair beside her, Allison shifted closer. In comfort? Support?

Bree couldn't acknowledge her friend, too overwhelmed by the catastrophe exploding around them. They shouldn't have come. Shouldn't have told Dad. She wished she could take it back.

After two raps on the front door, her uncle walked in, but his steps faltered when he saw them gathered. "What's going on?"

Dad glared at his brother with burning intensity but didn't respond.

Bree found her voice again. "Uncle Galen, Allison and I had our DNA tested."

He blanched. If there had been a faint hope that this had all been a terrible mistake, the hope died with her uncle's reaction. He wasn't surprised; he was alarmed.

"Everett," he asked roughly, "did you have your DNA tested too?"

"No. Why?"

Ignoring the question, Galen looked back at Bree. "What did you find out?"

His harsh tone gave her pause. Her uncle was usually so easygoing. "Allison and I are first cousins."

He frowned. "What?" Clearly, that wasn't what he'd expected to hear.

Dad lifted his chin in challenge. "It appears that Heather Garrett is our sister."

Galen steadied himself against an armchair. Gripped it for support. "Sister?" he whispered, horrified.

"You know something." Dad's voice was raw with anger. "Tell me."

"Everett, I . . ." Galen bowed his head, as if it was too heavy to hold up. Bree had never seen him look so defeated.

A long, silent moment passed. Then he nodded to himself, straightened to his full height, and met Dad's gaze. "Everett, I'm not really your brother. I'm your father."

CHAPTER EIGHT

Allison had wondered from an early age what it would be like to meet her birth grandparents, to learn their story and have it become a part of hers. As she'd grown older, she'd come to believe that what had happened all those years ago had to have been bad. Why else would they have given up their child the way they did? But she'd clung to optimism and hoped for the best.

Finding out Bree was a member of her family? That was amazing. But as happy as it would one day make her, Allison couldn't celebrate yet, because something bad *had* happened. And uncovering the rest was going to hurt.

She looked at each of the three Harpers, all devastated by the news. But their reactions were quite different.

Everett leaned against a wall with his fists jammed in his pockets, head thrown back, breathing slowly through his mouth while he made a visible effort to bring his emotions under control.

Galen had fumbled his way into an armchair and was hunched over, arms resting on his knees, hands loosely clasped, not meeting anyone's gaze. She thought she saw shame, but that was eclipsed by something stronger. Perhaps grief.

Bree worried her most. She was motionless. Frozen. Her face a blank mask.

Allison shifted to look out the window into the fading light, trying to reconcile what she'd just heard with her mother's abandonment story.

A desperate young woman had been passing through Marlowe, spotted the town doctor's sign outside his home, and left her baby on his porch, the safest place she could find. Then she'd disappeared into the night. A tale that implied the town had been a random choice.

Galen's announcement meant that Marlowe hadn't been random at all. It also raised a lot of questions. Which parts of Mom's story were real and which were fabricated? Who had hidden the truth? The doctor? Mom's parents? Everett's?

Stop. Allison shouldn't speculate until she'd uncovered and verified more facts.

Everett pushed away from the wall and crossed the room to study the collection of family pictures again. "Galen, why does my birth certificate say that my parents are Bernice and Marvin Harper?"

"Because, legally, they were. They adopted you."

"Adopted me." The words were hard and flat. "The three of you didn't think to mention that sometime in the past fifty years?"

Galen shook his head helplessly.

"Wow. My parents are my grandparents, and my brother is my father. That is . . . obscene."

The two men locked gazes for a long moment, the air crackling between them. Everett faced away from them, his body held rigidly.

Stricken, Galen turned to Allison. "Did you learn anything else from the DNA results?"

"We did. We've found a woman who's a close match to us both." She watched him intently, hoping he would confirm the woman's identity. "I think it's likely she's our grandmother."

He made a strangled sound in his throat. "How can you be sure?"

"It's there in the data we're given. The closeness between family members is measured in something called centimorgans. The higher the number, the more DNA you share. For instance, parents share over three thousand centimorgans with their children. Full siblings share over two thousand with each other." She swallowed against the thickness in her throat. "Bree and I each share more than seventeen hundred centimorgans with the unknown female. That's very close. Nearly as close as siblings."

He lowered his gaze. "Molly," he said reverently.

Molly. The M in MP.

Bree jerked at the name. "Galen, was she your girlfriend?"

His smile flashed and died. "Yes."

Bree drooped. She must regret that she sent in a DNA sample. Her impulse in "solidarity," an amazing gesture of support, had cracked wide open the one thing Bree thought was rock solid: her family.

Allison's world had been disrupted, too, but it wasn't the same. She'd been aware her whole life that her mother had family they didn't know. The revelations were filling in gaps, not creating them.

"Allison," Galen said. "Can you tell whether Everett and your mother are full or half siblings?"

"Yes, sir. They're full."

He shook his head. Blew out a shaky breath. "No one ever told me we had a daughter."

CHAPTER NINE

April 1969

Slowly, reluctantly, Molly grew aware of her surroundings. First came the smell of antiseptic cleaner, fresh flowers, and her own soiled sheets. Then came sounds. Cooing babies. Soft conversations. Squeaky shoes.

Her eyelids fluttered open. She was lying beside a wall lined with steel cabinets. Tan curtains hung from the ceiling, separating her from the rest of the room. A nurse slipped through an opening, carrying a baby, and continued into the corridor.

The memories of the past twenty-four hours flooded in. She'd been forced to lie on this bed naked as she was given an enema. Held down as her privates were shaved. Restrained when she fought against their hands groping her in unmentionable places.

There had been pain. So much pain. There still was. When she'd asked for relief, she'd been told, "We don't waste medicine on sluts."

She hadn't spoken after that, but she had cried, and the waking nightmare had grown worse. They'd yelled at her to shut up. Slapped her for resisting. Finally, someone had clamped a mask over her face. She'd slipped into merciful oblivion.

She was conscious now. Cold, naked, aching, and alone.

Another nurse passed by the end of her bed.

"Help," she said. The word came out as more of a croak.

"Yes?"

"Can you bring me my baby?" She didn't even know if she had a boy or a girl.

"No one is bringing a baby to *you*." The nurse disappeared through the door.

Had she awakened to a different nightmare? She closed her eyes and hoped for oblivion to return.

◆ ◆ ◆

"Good afternoon, Miss Mitchell. I'm Dr. Lambe."

Molly roused enough to look in the direction of the voice. A short, slender woman in a white coat stood at the side of her bed. She had kind eyes.

"I'm the pediatrician for your babies. How are you feeling?"

She dropped her gaze, too exhausted to speak.

"You're not okay, are you?" The doctor came closer. Leaned over the bed. Stiffened. "I do *not* believe what I'm seeing here." Her clipboard clattered onto a side table. "I'd like to examine you, Miss Mitchell. Is that all right?"

"Yes." She was gripped with a sudden need to hear her real name from a kind voice. "Please call me Molly."

"Okay, Molly. I'll be quick."

A cool hand touched her forehead. Her neck. When the sheet was lifted, she shivered as cold air flowed over her hot, naked body.

Dr. Lambe hissed. "Excuse me a moment, Molly. I'll be right back." She marched into the hallway, barking out orders.

Thirty minutes later, Molly had a clean bed, a sponge bath, and a hospital gown. She was sitting up and sipping water when Dr. Lambe returned. A nurse trailed anxiously behind her.

"You'll be getting antibiotics soon for an infection. Would you like something for pain?"

"Yes, please."

"Why don't we let you hold your babies first?"

"Thank you. What did I have?"

The doctor shot a fierce frown at the nurse and gestured toward the door. "Get them." She turned back and smiled. "You have twins. A boy and a girl."

She had twins!

A nurse came in carrying the two prettiest creatures Molly had ever seen. Soon she was propped up with pillows, cradling her children.

"Your son is ten minutes older than his sister," Dr. Lambe said.

Molly heard the words but didn't acknowledge them. As awful as the past twenty-four hours had been, the bad memories were crowded out the moment she gazed down into her babies' faces, watched them yawn and squirm in her arms, and felt a love so consuming she could think of nothing else.

Molly reclined against the hospital bed, suffering from one of the worst headaches of her life. She hadn't eaten breakfast today, too nauseated and worn out after being kept up half the night by noise from the hallway and the excited laughter of other people on the maternity ward.

The nice pediatrician hadn't been by yet today. Neither had her babies. But she had other visitors. People she did *not* want to see.

"Eve," Mrs. Lloyd said, "we're here about the papers." She set a document on the hospital tray and held out a pen.

"My name is Molly. Molly Anne Mitchell." She pushed the pen away irritably. Why were they bothering her now, of all times? She felt dopey, her brain all fuzzy from drugs and pain. She shifted on the bed, moaning when agony sliced through her. "I'm not making any decisions without my family here."

"No one is coming, Eve."

"What about Aunt Trudy?" She *promised.*

"*Nobody* will be here." Mrs. Lloyd smacked the pen on the tray again.

"Eve," a familiar voice said in her calm, sensible way. "You've run out of choices."

It was Mrs. Kinsley. Why was she here? *Lord, help me.*

"Why delay the decision, Eve? No one is going to save you."

Molly closed her eyes as another wave of nausea rolled over her. "Are you sure everyone knows the babies are here?"

"Of course they know, dear. It doesn't matter. Your family won't let you bring the babies home."

"What about Galen?"

"You'll get no help from the father. He's moved on and doesn't want any part of you. I'm sorry to say it, but you're completely alone. You can't take care of yourself. How can you take care of the babies?"

She gulped a sob. "Please go."

"Look around you, dear," Mrs. Kinsley droned on. "The maternity ward is full of happy couples preparing to take their precious gifts home. But no one is happy for you. Why would you want your children to grow up burdened by your shame? Your little darlings will learn words like *bastard* and *slut* on the playground. They'll be raised poor and lonely. Is that what you want for your children?"

"My aunt—"

"Wants you to give them up too. Why are you being so selfish? Let your babies have a chance at a good life."

She lifted her hand. Batted away the words. Everything seemed so muddled in her head.

"We choose the parents carefully. A married couple, with a father who makes a good income and a mother who stays home to lavish love on her child. Think of these couples, desperately wanting babies but unable to have them. Would you deny them and your little ones such a bright future?"

She hated how much sense Mrs. Kinsley made.

"Eve, if you love your children, you must do right by them." The social worker placed the pen in Molly's hand and closed her fingers around it.

She choked on a moan. And signed the papers.

With her infection under control, Molly was discharged Saturday. But the twins were not. Although they were fine and healthy, she was told they needed more time in the hospital.

She was moved into Transitions Cottage, where she would remain until she was ready to leave. The recovery rooms were much nicer than in the main house, but it was only to impress visitors. Since families were allowed to come into the cottage to pick up their girls, they could recommend the great facilities to any friends with wayward daughters.

She slept most of that first day but awakened around 8:00 p.m. It was dark and quiet. She switched on the nightstand lamp and found two letters. One from each of her parents.

She read her father's first. It was inexpertly typed.

April 2, 1969

Dear Molly,
Have you received a high school diploma? You'll need one when you look for a job.

I'm sorry to learn you've been ill and pray for a speedy recovery.

I have missed you, sweet girl. We're looking forward to having you at home again.

Love,
Daddy

Trudy knew she'd received a diploma. Were her father and his sister not speaking?

It was true that Molly would be living at home but not for very long. She was going to college. Had been saving for years. Had it slipped his mind? Or was it too late to apply this year? Probably that was it.

Mama's letter had been postmarked a day later.

Dear Molly,
I hope you are feeling well and strong after your hospital visit.

Hospital visit? She'd given birth to premature twins!

I have your bedroom ready for your return. You are allowed to stay where you are through the end of April, but we'd like to pick you up a week from Sunday. Your father and I will be there around noon. We'll stop somewhere for a nice lunch before bringing you home.
Love,
Mama

Neither letter had mentioned the babies nor any of the events of the past four months. She'd lost her grandmother. Suffered through a torturous labor and delivery. Surrendered their two youngest grandchildren for adoption. Did they not realize she wasn't their little girl anymore? She could never be the same.

Next week was her eighteenth birthday. She might not be able to vote yet, but she was an adult in every other way.

She pushed off the bed onto aching legs and crept down the hall. All rooms for new mothers were full. If any more girls gave birth, they would have to double up.

Miriam was in the room next to hers. They had delivered on the same day, although Miriam's son was six hours younger than the twins. The door was closed. Lights out.

Two girls in robes were sitting in the TV room, laughing at a show. They didn't look over when she walked in. She grabbed an apple from a bowl and walked out again. Back to her room and blissful sleep.

Sunday morning, after a shower and dressing in her own clothes, she went to the nursery. A pregnant girl sat in a rocking chair feeding a baby its bottle. Mrs. Clancy, the night nurse, was changing a diaper.

"Morning, Eve. I hear you have beautiful babies."

The comment sobered her. They wouldn't be hers much longer. She didn't want to think about that. "I do. When will they be discharged?"

"Maybe tomorrow. Maybe Tuesday. They've talked about keeping the girl an extra day since she's smaller than her brother. We'll have a full nursery when they're both here." The nurse swaddled the baby in blue, then lifted him to her shoulder. "This is Miriam's son. Would you like to feed him while I check the others?"

"Sure." She held out her arms.

"You did the right thing, giving them up."

Giving them up? The words shivered through her.

"Mrs. Lloyd does a good job finding new parents, Eve. So many people want babies that we can pick the best."

She shook her head. "I'm not glad."

"I understand. It's hard." Mrs. Clancy reached into another bassinet. "But if you come to this place, you don't have a choice."

After Molly fed and burped the baby, she left the nursery, stopped outside Miriam's door, and rapped lightly.

"Come in."

When she walked in, Miriam lay on her side, pale and listless, staring at the wall.

"Hi."

She gave a tiny nod.

"I gave your son a bottle tonight."

"Thank you. He's quite handsome." She smiled faintly. "Like his father." She struggled into a sitting position, legs dangling over the side of the bed, head bowed. "They've selected his parents, although the handover won't be until May. I'll already be home in Richmond. Frank, my stepfather, is sending his driver on Friday to pick me up. How about you?"

"My parents say they're coming for me next Sunday." It was too soon. She wasn't ready to say goodbye to her twins. "I'll miss you. We won't stop being friends, will we?"

"Nobody stays friends after this, Eve. Too many bad memories."

"Not all of my memories are bad."

"No, mine aren't either." Miriam grasped her elbows with her hands and looked up. "You were the best part of this place for me."

As Molly reclined in bed that night, sipping her evening cup of hot chocolate, feeling sleepy, she worried about the moment she would say goodbye to her babies. To Miriam. And dreaded how it would feel to be home again.

When Molly awakened Tuesday morning, she felt dopey, her head aching fiercely. The room was filled with bright light. What time was it?

She grabbed the alarm clock. It was nearly noon! How could she have overslept on the day the twins would be discharged? Throwing on a robe, she raced to the nursery. "Did they release my babies from the hospital?"

"Yes," the nurse mumbled around the diaper pin in her mouth. "They arrived early this morning. Here is your daughter," she said and placed her in Molly's arms.

Her daughter was tiny compared to the other babies. Molly touched a fingertip to a soft cheek. So lovely and peaceful. "Hi, little one," she said and was rewarded with a pucker of the lips.

She looked around for her little boy, but the only blue-swaddled baby was Miriam's. "Where is my son?"

The nurse lifted another baby to her shoulder and patted. "Gone."

"Gone?" She frowned at the nurse. "Where?"

"His new parents have taken him home. The handover was this morning."

"What?" Molly must have misunderstood. He got here and was immediately handed over? "That doesn't make sense. I'm supposed to be part of the handover."

"You were sleeping, so Mrs. Lloyd made an exception for this couple."

"Why didn't someone wake me up?" It wasn't as if she was far away.

"I'm not sure." The nurse sat in a rocker and offered a bottle to the baby, who eagerly ate. "It's not as if you have to be there. You signed the papers."

Yes, but she'd looked forward to holding him again. Felt cheated that she hadn't. Molly kissed her daughter, returned her to a bassinet, and watched her settle. Did she miss her big brother? Did he miss her? "When will they return for his sister?"

"Aw, sugar. They aren't."

She gasped. "What do you mean *they aren't*? Won't they be adopting both twins?"

"No."

"Why not?"

"His parents didn't want the girl."

CHAPTER TEN

Allison could hardly believe what she was hearing. "Galen, are they twins?"

"We only . . ." His face flamed. "They would have to be."

She reeled from a flood of emotions. Disgust for whoever had made the decision to split up twins. Anger that her mother had been deprived of her brother for her entire life. Grief for all of them at what they'd lost. It was that last emotion that had her needing to disengage. The information had come in too fast to absorb. She would have to put her feelings on hold until she didn't have an audience.

"Explain to me," Everett bit out, "how our parents could have adopted me and not her."

Galen stared at his clasped hands. "I can't explain it." He sounded hollow. "They adopted you directly from the maternity home where Molly was sent. I can only hope they weren't aware."

"Ya think?" Everett turned to Allison. "What have you told your mother?"

"Nothing, really. Mom doesn't want to know."

"I can sympathize." He stalked to the foyer. "I need some air." The door slammed behind him.

Bree remained statue still.

Galen—Allison didn't know what to call him anymore—sat in a chair, breathing hard.

Allison stood. She had to get out of here. "I'll go."

No one objected.

She cranked up the AC in the car as she drove away. But a block ahead, she had to brake suddenly when Everett stepped out in front of her. He continued across the street, oblivious to what had nearly happened, and blended into the shadows of a greenway.

She listened to '70s hits on the drive, not wishing to think until she was home. But the instant she entered the cabin, the questions rushed in. What kind of private adoption agency would have allowed twins to be separated? Why had they facilitated a family adoption for Everett but hadn't handled an adoption for Mom?

Allison dropped on the couch, gathered Otis in her arms, and checked her phone. There was an alert from Ancestry. A response from MP's contact person.

As soon as Bree had left the cabin last night, Allison had sent the woman a message.

> Dear Gwendolyn,
> I am Allison Garrett, a close match with MP. You're listed as her account manager. Can you help me get in touch with her?
> My connection with MP is through my mother, Heather, who was adopted as a baby in 1969. I hope that MP will be able to share information about my mother's birth family.
> Sincerely,
> Allison

It was common to wait months or years for a response on Ancestry. This one had come back in a day.

Allison uncoiled from the couch and crossed to the sliding glass doors overlooking the backyard. There wasn't much to it. A short expanse of lawn, bordered on two sides by overgrown perennials and a thick stand of trees along the back.

She'd bought the A-frame log cabin two years ago, against the advice of her parents. Too isolated, they'd said. But that was one of the things Allison loved about it. The area might feel rural, but it was the ideal distance from everything that mattered to her. Twenty miles from the office in Durham. A three-minute walk to her closest neighbors. An easy drive to her parents' home in Marlowe.

Okay, enough indecision. She eased back onto the couch, rearranged Otis on her lap, and opened the message.

> Dear Allison,
> We prefer the first contact to be with Heather. Please have her email me directly.
> Regards,
> Gwen Reeves

The response disappointed her. Mom wouldn't get involved. Connecting would be delayed.

But it was a positive sign too. If Molly was willing to be found, she had a story she wanted her children to know.

CHAPTER ELEVEN

April 1969

Molly peered at the nurse in disbelief. Surely she'd misheard. "They're splitting up my children?"

"Yes. I think it's terrible too." Mrs. Clancy tutted.

"She's his sister. They go together." Molly groped for a chair and sat. She would never have signed those papers if she'd been told what Mrs. Lloyd had planned. This was horrible. It had to be fixed. "That other couple has to bring my son back."

The nurse gave her a curious look. "Why?"

"So that another family can be found to take them both." As she said the words, she knew she was right. It calmed her.

"There's nothing you can do, sugar."

Oh, yes, there was. *You can change your mind.*

If Mrs. Lloyd didn't have the decency to keep the babies together, Molly would reclaim her children.

She stormed over to the main house. When she reached the director's door, she rapped and walked in, not waiting for an invitation.

"Well, Eve." Mrs. Lloyd's penciled-on brow rose sharply. "Why are you here?"

"I'm revoking my decision. I'm keeping my babies."

Mrs. Lloyd cleared her throat. Smoothed the cuffs on her silk blouse. "Unfortunately, it's too late."

"Aunt Trudy said I had a week."

"I doubt that your aunt has as good an understanding of adoption laws as I do. As our attorney does."

"She wouldn't be wrong about this. The week isn't up, and I want both of my babies."

Mrs. Lloyd pushed up from the desk. Even though she was shorter than Molly, her personality loomed tall. "You've signed the papers. The boy has been placed with a fine couple from Boston. A doctor whose wife is a homemaker. The girl's parents will be here next Monday. You're too late."

"I want to speak to the attorney."

The director straightened a stack of papers on her desk. "That won't be possible. He's busy."

There was a knock at the door, and Mrs. Wilson stepped in. "Eve, are you all right?"

"I changed my mind, but Mrs. Lloyd says I'm too late. I have a week."

"That's true. When did you sign the papers? Last Wednesday?"

"Yes."

Mrs. Wilson turned to the director. "She's made the deadline."

Mrs. Lloyd gave them a cold stare. "Very well. I will see if the attorney can come tomorrow. Now leave. Both of you."

Mrs. Wilson followed Molly out the door. "Is this about there being two adoptions?"

She nodded, too upset to speak.

"I understand, Eve. But if you revoke, you need a plan for what comes next. Your circumstances haven't changed. On Sunday, your parents will pick you up, and they're not taking the babies home."

Molly was up early the next morning to feed her little girl a bottle. It felt so different this time, knowing that instead of leaving with strangers, her daughter would be reunited with her brother.

She made such adorable smacking noises. Molly could understand why the staff discouraged giving them names. Since Molly wasn't relinquishing after all, it made no sense to call her daughter *the baby*, and she'd picked the prettiest name. Diana. Goddess of the moon. She'd first thought of it in December while watching *Apollo 8* on TV.

"Diana," she said and kissed her daughter's brow.

The nurse walked over. "Don't get attached, sugar. It'll only make it harder to hand her over."

"I won't have to. I changed my mind. I'm taking my babies with me."

"Uh-uh. Mrs. Lloyd told me not an hour ago that this little doll has a couple coming for her Monday."

"There's been a mistake. Here, take her please."

She returned to the main house. This time, when she entered the office without invitation, Mrs. Wilson was there too.

"Mrs. Clancy says my daughter has a couple coming for her."

"That's right."

"You can't. I revoked. I get to keep them."

"No, you don't," Mrs. Lloyd said in a singsong voice. "A signed revocation letter is required. You didn't turn one in, and the deadline has passed."

Molly was unsure how to respond. The woman had deceived her with no apparent remorse. "But I told you."

"Verbal isn't enough."

"Pearl," Mrs. Wilson said in disbelief. "You knew her intent."

"Sorry. That's the law." Mrs. Lloyd gave a tiny shrug. "The girl's new parents have been selected. They're thrilled."

The director was utterly contemptible. Didn't the government oversee places like this? Require the babies to be treated like the precious human beings they were? The woman shouldn't even be allowed around children, much less control their destinies.

"You tricked me," Molly said incredulously. "You let me think I'd done what I needed to."

"It's your responsibility to know the rules."

"Pearl—"

"Hush, *Mrs.* Wilson." She flapped her hand at Molly. "Go, Eve."

Molly had dissected a frog once in freshman biology, something that had both fascinated and repulsed her. She studied Mrs. Lloyd the same way now, a specimen to be dealt with. While the director might think she'd won a victory, she would soon find out otherwise. Right or wrong, legal or not, Mrs. Lloyd had forfeited the right to make decisions for Diana.

Molly would get through whatever came next. It wouldn't be pleasant. She didn't have a plan yet, but when she did, it would succeed.

"Fine. I'll go."

The director's eyes narrowed suspiciously.

Molly went out to her favorite bench. It was a nice, warm day, with a strong breeze lifting tendrils around her face. Behind her, the morning train whistled past. She took slow breaths. Not ready to make decisions. Needing to let herself mourn. In the brief time she'd thought her babies were coming home with her, she'd fallen in love with them. With the idea of being their mother. It had been silly.

Her little boy was lost to her, but Diana was not. It was Molly's responsibility to make things right for her. Pushing to her feet, she strode calmly to the cottage and knocked on Miriam's door.

"Come in."

Molly shut the door behind her with a soft click. Her friend was sitting against the headboard of her bed, wrapped in a silk robe, knees up, hair falling about her shoulders in a tangled cloud. She looked at Molly through bloodshot eyes. "What is it, Eve?"

She hesitated. For months, Miriam had seemed indifferent to having a baby, but the birth of her son had affected her too. "I'm sorry. Are you okay?"

Miriam gave her a tight smile and lowered her head to her knees.

Molly perched on the end of the bed. "I went to Mrs. Lloyd's office," she said and gave an account of what happened. She ended with, "I don't get my babies back after all."

"Because that witch deceived you." Miriam slid off the bed, tightened the belt on her robe, and paced. "She's evil."

If her son's new parents weren't decent enough people to keep him with his sister, why should Molly expect the next couple to be any better? "I can't let her choose parents for my daughter."

"What can you do?"

Molly had only one option. "Steal her." The idea was frightening. Where would they go? Could Molly be arrested if they found her? But the thought of leaving Diana at the Home was more terrifying than breaking the law. "I have to do it before Monday. That's when the handover is scheduled."

"How will you sneak her out of here?"

"I don't know, but I have to try."

"Then we need a plan."

We? Hope shivered through her. Molly wasn't in this alone. "Okay. Let's make one."

Miriam opened a side table and pulled out a pad of paper and a pen. "Train, bus, or car?" She frowned. "Not bus or train. They'll be watching at the stations for a girl with a baby. You won't get far."

"By car, then." Could she call Aunt Trudy to pick them up? No, that option had its problems. She might try to talk Molly out of it. Or worse, tell Mrs. Lloyd.

"Eve, it'll be fine. Don't panic."

"I won't. And my name is Molly."

"I'm Gwendolyn. *Gwen.*" She jotted a note on her pad. "My driver will be here Friday. Clive will take you anywhere you want to go."

Optimism flared, then quickly died. It was the perfect solution, and Molly couldn't accept. "It would be impossible for me to get into your car unnoticed. There are always staff watching when a girl leaves, and we can't count on the baby not crying."

"True. So we'll just have to pick you up somewhere away from the Home."

She would have to slip the baby out of the nursery without the nurse noticing, escape through a brick wall, and wander who knew how far through the woods. Which all sounded crazy, but she would figure it out. "I steal the baby and leave unseen. Then what?"

"We'll find a safe place to rendezvous." Her friend's smug confidence was contagious. "It'll work. We just need to refine the details."

Molly would put up one last warning. "No matter what we try, if the baby and I disappear on the same morning as you, no one will believe it's a coincidence."

"Doesn't matter. If they don't see us together, they can't prove a thing."

"You'll have to lie."

"A fact which gives me great satisfaction." Gwen's laugh had a wicked edge. "Let's make a checklist. What do we need to steal a baby?"

Molly held her gaze. Afraid. Excited. Ready. "Diapers and formula."

Gwen wrote it down. "A suitcase for you would be too risky, I'm afraid, but we can stuff some of your things in mine. We'll also retrieve your important papers. Driver's license. Social security card. They have them locked up, but I know where they are."

"Diploma too?"

"If it's there. What else?"

They spent the rest of the day working out the details and sorting through the options. By lights-out, they had an unbeatable plan.

CHAPTER TWELVE

Molly's plan wasn't quite as flawless as she'd hoped.

Gwen's diversion had gone well enough. On her way to the car, she'd dropped a folder full of "important" papers, which sent them flying about in the wind. All available staff had joined the chase, except the night nurse. She hadn't been tempted by the commotion, not when she had a crying baby to soothe. Precious minutes were wasted waiting for Mrs. Clancy to change a diaper before Molly could tiptoe in and steal her daughter.

A rarely used gate in the brick wall squeaked loudly as Molly pushed through it. Luckily, no one followed.

And the path through the woods was a quagmire, sucking at her shoes. It took much longer to reach the rendezvous location than she expected. But at last, Molly stood near an empty highway, swaying in a desperate attempt to shush a wailing newborn. By her mud-soaked shoes lay a torn paper bag with diapers and cans of formula spilling out.

She shivered in her father's sweater, securing its edges more closely around Diana. The plan hadn't accounted for how cold it would be under the trees.

The minutes ticked by. Two trucks passed. Then silence. She didn't know what the time was, but the getaway car should have been here already.

In the distance, a dark car crested a hill and slowed. Molly blew out a sigh of relief. It was a black Continental. She emerged from the tree line, hoping she wasn't wrong.

The Continental stopped. The rear window rolled down, and her friend stuck her head out. "Get in here. Now."

When Molly bent over to collect the baby's things, her friend hissed, "Stop. Leave it. Come on."

She hurried over and ducked in. The car was accelerating before the door had completely shut.

"Hand me the baby, and lie down on the floorboard until I tell you to get up."

She was barely out of sight before a vehicle screeched past, heading in the direction of the Home, sirens blaring. A second shrieking vehicle followed.

Clive drove sedately for another mile or two, then made a left turn. Another minute passed before he gunned the engine and they were off.

Gwen released a breath. "Okay, you can get up."

Molly sank onto a seat. "What happened?"

"Mrs. Clancy noticed you and the baby were gone far sooner than we expected. A policeman got there fast. Clive and I were interrogated, and the car was searched." Her friend shuddered. "You were right about going through the woods in the opposite direction from town. They're probably crawling all over every possible path to the train station."

"But we're safe?"

"Yes," the driver said. "We'll stay off the main roads until we get to Raleigh."

She sank into the back seat, cold and fear shivering from her body. While Gwen held the baby, Molly closed her eyes and drowsed.

"Molly?" Clive asked. "We're in Raleigh. Can you give me directions?"

Once she'd directed them to Trudy's apartment complex, Molly groaned at her own stupidity. The Mustang wasn't there. "It's a weekday. She's at work."

"An obvious oversight," Gwen said as she cuddled Diana. "But it's the only mistake we made."

"I know how to call my aunt."

Clive caught Molly's gaze in the rearview mirror. "We passed a pay phone on the main road."

Molly walked back from making the call and took her baby. "You go on. My aunt's on her way, and it's best if you don't see each other."

"So she can plausibly deny me? Understood. Okay, take care." Gwen hugged her, baby and all, and stuffed a scrap of paper into Molly's pocket. "My address and phone number. Find me if you ever need me. Being coconspirators in the same crime qualifies us as friends for life."

Molly tried to smile. "Thank you."

The Continental had barely exited the parking lot when her aunt's Mustang raced into it and screeched to a stop. Trudy slammed the car door and stomped up the walkway. "What have you done?"

Molly felt the urge to cry. The past week and a half had been hard. She could have used her aunt's help. "Why didn't you come to the hospital?"

Trudy's shoulders slumped. "I'm sorry, honey. They never called. I didn't know until three days ago that you'd given birth."

"Mrs. Lloyd is a despicable person."

"You're more gracious than I am." Trudy glanced around, but the neighborhood was quiet. After unlocking the door, she dragged Molly inside. "Well, it's done. We'll fix it."

Molly wasn't sure what that meant, but she didn't want to think about fixing anything. She just wanted to enjoy her baby. "Look at her, Aunt Trudy. How could anyone not love Diana on sight?"

"Oh, she is beautiful." Trudy lifted a tentative hand. Hesitated.

"Go on. You can touch her."

Trudy brushed her fingertips over the fuzz on the baby's head. "What's in the grocery bag?" she asked and led the way to the kitchen.

Clive had stopped by a store, or Molly would have nothing. "Formula. Pampers."

"Any baby clothes?"

"Only what she has on."

"Is she hungry?"

"We fed her in the car." Molly patted Diana's diaper. "And she's wet."

"Are *you* hungry?"

"Yes."

Trudy set her purse and keys on a table. "Take care of your daughter. I'll make you a sandwich."

Molly changed Diana into a fresh diaper and rejoined her aunt. A cheese sandwich and glass of milk awaited her.

"Here, I'll hold her," Trudy said, reaching for the baby. "I know I sounded upset when I got home, but I'm glad you're here. I'll take care of you. Both of my nieces."

Molly felt almost faint with relief. Her aunt's help had been the biggest question mark in the whole operation, and now she could relax. A little. "Will you tell Daddy?"

"No, I won't. He's abused my trust."

While she ate, her aunt wandered about the living room, Diana in her arms.

"Your father called just before you did," Trudy said. "He asked if I'd heard from you. I told him I hadn't, and he hung up. But they're looking for you, and they'll come here eventually." Humming a lullaby, she disappeared into the back of the apartment.

By the time Molly had finished her meal, Trudy had reappeared carrying a basket with Diana tucked inside.

"If you're finished, let's go. I have to move you and the baby."

"Where?"

"To Mama's house. You can stay there. I'll come when I can."

Molly waited until they were out of the city limits to tell her story. Trudy listened without comment until the end.

"You told the director in front of a witness that you'd changed your mind?"

"Yes. Mrs. Wilson said I'd made the deadline."

"And the director didn't tell you the letter of the law?"

"No. Just waited a day and said it was too late."

"What she did was unethical. Probably illegal too." Trudy made a clicking sound with her tongue, then thinned her lips. "I know someone over in the state's department of social services. I'll ask some questions. Not just about the revocation, but also what I'm hearing about Mrs. Lloyd and her lawyer."

"What will happen to them?"

"I hope they get the consequences they deserve." She sniffed. "I'm so proud of you, Molly. You did the right thing for your daughter."

She'd forgotten what it was like to receive praise. As tears slid down her cheeks, she brushed them away with the back of her hand.

"What's wrong?" Trudy reached over and squeezed Molly's arm. "We'll get this sorted out, although it'll be tricky. I'm not sure the police will have any sympathy for you, so you'll have to stay hidden at Mama's house. I'll tell the neighbors not to worry if they see someone walking around inside. We'll have to hope they don't get nosy."

Molly loved her days alone with Diana. It was like they were existing in a kind of dreamworld in this lovely, big house. The weather was mild. Spring was blooming everywhere in a riot of color, the azaleas in the backyard a wall of pink taller than she was. When she slipped outside after dark, the scents were glorious.

Diana was sleeping well. Her tiny sounds—burps and toots and sneezes—made Molly laugh. They had plenty of food and a clean house, so her only chore was washing diapers. Pampers were too expensive to use every day.

The doorbell rang on Wednesday. The sound startled the baby in the middle of her morning nap. Then she settled down again. Close call. The last thing Molly needed was the neighbors knowing who was here.

It rang again. Then a knock. But she didn't dare go down the staircase.

The veranda boards creaked, and whoever it was walked away.

She hurried to the front window and peeked through the curtains. Their across-the-street neighbor was walking up her driveway, disappearing into the backyard.

Had Molly been seen? Had the baby been heard? Trudy had warned the neighbors of the possibility of someone working inside, but a baby's cry would be hard to explain.

They wouldn't be able to go out. Not to the store or the park or anywhere, which made Molly weepy. As much as she loved being with her angel child, she was pathetically eager for an adult to talk to, and Trudy wouldn't be here for another two days.

Why couldn't Molly have her mother do for Diana what she did for her other grandbabies? It would be so lovely to ask Mama for advice or simply to hold the baby.

If Molly could barely manage to be a mother on her own for one week, how could she hope to manage for years?

Diana stopped being an angel on Saturday. Thank goodness Trudy was there.

The baby would not stop crying. Nothing made her happy. Feed, burp, change, cuddle. All useless. Molly had to endlessly repeat the cycle until Diana cried herself to sleep. When she was up again before dawn, Trudy suggested a drive. Out they went in the Mustang with the top down. After the baby fell asleep against Molly's chest, she was able to doze along country roads through tobacco fields and silent towns. The sun was rising as her aunt swerved onto a rutted lane bordering a meadow and stopped near the Eno River. Trudy and Diana went walking through the trees while Molly napped.

A soft rain began to fall. The top went back up, and they drove home. Feed, burp, change, cuddle.

By midafternoon, Diana was squalling again.

"You have to get that baby quiet," Trudy hissed from the doorway.

"I'm trying." Molly was crying too.

Her aunt came in and sat on the end of the bed. "My brother called. He's suspicious that I'm not more worried than I am. He says the police are still looking for you." She gently patted the baby's back. "We can't keep doing this. You have to decide what you're going to do next."

"I will." *Soon.*

It didn't take long. By the following weekend, Molly knew she'd failed.

She couldn't live like this. Staying away from windows. Never going outside unless it was night. Dreading every time Diana cried for fear the neighbors would hear. It wouldn't be fair to keep her daughter, but making the decision would be so final. So *forever.*

When her aunt showed up Saturday morning, Molly was sitting at the table, feeding her daughter a bottle, trying not to cry.

Trudy scanned the disaster of a kitchen and shook her head. "How are you?"

Molly shrugged. Pressed kisses to her baby's face.

"You're worn out, honey. I hope you've been thinking hard about what to do." Her aunt dropped her purse on the counter and waited.

Molly had no answers, but she had plenty of things to think about. Taking care of a baby was a full-time job. How could she hang on to a paying job when she was exhausted from staying up all night with a baby?

It would be impossible to raise her daughter alone.

The staff at the Home had been right. She *was* unfit. She couldn't be the kind of mother she wanted her daughter to have. And no one would help her. She couldn't even count on Trudy. "Mrs. Lloyd told me while I was in the hospital that you said I should give up the babies."

"She lied. I would never have shared an opinion with any of those people." Pulling out a chair, Trudy sat and rested her forearms on the table. "But it *is* my opinion, Molly. You are wonderfully capable. Smart. Appealing. There's a grand future awaiting you. But raising your baby will mean a lesser life for you both. You have to make the best choice for you *and* your daughter."

You aren't the best, are you?

Tears seeped from her eyes. Dripped onto Diana's bib. Molly was so weary of fighting. "I won't take her back to the Home." *And I can't keep her.* Hadn't she known that all along?

"I agree, but you can't stay here either. You must know what you're up against."

"I do."

"You'd have to get a job and a place to live, probably in the city."

"I know."

"And someone to watch Diana while you work."

"I *know.*"

"Watch the tone." Trudy leaned back and brushed a short curl behind her ear. "I would suggest signing up for food stamps or whatever aid we could find, but I'm not sure you should be contacting the government anytime soon."

Pinching her eyes shut, Molly whispered, "What else can I do?"

"Let me give it some thought," Trudy said, not even trying to hide the relief in her voice. "There will be plenty of couples who'll want to adopt your daughter, but I won't risk you going to jail. We have to find a solution where we don't expose who you are."

CHAPTER THIRTEEN

Bree had to get away from her father's house and find something mindless to distract herself. *Now.*

She drove through the town center and then five blocks farther, to a neighborhood of 1950s-era homes. Her studio apartment was in the daylight basement of a brick ranch. The apartment was tiny and Spartan, but it saved her on rent. She was rarely there anyway.

After changing into shorts, she poured a glass of chardonnay and carried it to the brick patio outside her door. It was pleasant for a June night but noisy. She sipped wine, listened to a symphony of insects, and reflected on her day.

Her great-grandparents—that would be hard to adjust to—and her grandfather Galen had hidden an important part of their family history. She didn't understand why, and she wanted to. *Needed* to. These people she loved and admired had deceived her and Dad in a way she was struggling to accept.

Slow down. That was anger talking. She ought to wait for more facts.

She'd always been so proud of her family. Well, with the exception of her parents' divorce. When Mom relocated to Charlotte with her boyfriend, Bree had been allowed to choose where to live, and she'd chosen to stay with Dad and his family. They had been the one true thing she could count on. Now, she couldn't.

Her phone chimed. Allison had texted.

Are you okay?

No

Want to talk?

No. I just need to be quiet

All right

The exchange depleted her. Bree honestly didn't know what to say, a circumstance she'd never experienced before. She would snap out of it eventually. Not tonight, though. She had to process a bit more of her grief.

When life got tough, Allison had always been her pillar to lean on and vice versa. They had built their relationship to withstand something like this. Bree had never expected that the "something like this" would have her friend at its center.

Bree was overthinking this, right?

No, she couldn't face Allison yet. Not when her world had been knocked askew and their actions had been responsible. Maybe her thinking wasn't fair or reasonable or mature, but her feelings were real, and she wanted to deal with them. Alone.

Bree had been awake since five but stayed in bed. Watching the sky lighten. Listening to birds, sporadic traffic, the slapping feet of the occasional runner.

It was Sunday. Supposedly her day of rest. But that wasn't really true. She was a business owner. It wasn't possible to ever be completely off.

Rolling to her side, she looked around her home. Four hundred square feet. Bedroom, living room, kitchen—each occupying a section of the same space. Normally, she loved her little apartment. Felt smug with how compact, pretty, and sufficient it was. Today, it was closing in. She slid from under the sheet and secured the Murphy bed out of the way. Took a shower in the tiny bathroom. Dressed, grabbed her bag, and headed out. She chose to walk the long route to downtown. The one with oak trees shading the sidewalks and gardenias scenting the air.

She entered her store through the front door, simply because it made her happy. The showroom was charming and cheerful. Exuding creativity and possibilities. She liked to be in Write Style when it was quiet like this, with the lights off and faint sunlight filtering in from the front windows. She made a cup of coffee in the back and took it out to the small conversation area at the rear of the showroom. It had been Lola's idea. A love seat, two armchairs, and a side table. An inviting place to relax.

They held writing classes here, with room for eight attendees if they squeezed in extra chairs. Holding the classes where shoppers could hear the laughter had served as its own advertisement. All of her June classes were filled, with wait lists.

The journey to owning this shop had been bumpy and full of detours.

Even with a master's degree in library and information science, Bree hadn't been able to find a full-time job as a librarian. She'd been offered a position with the State of North Carolina, only to have it put on an indefinite hold by a hiring freeze. While waiting, she'd taken other temp jobs, anything remotely related to books or writing. Teacher's aide. Proofreader. Bookstore clerk. It was at that last job where she'd begun to dream about starting a business. She'd spent a year thinking and planning, taking business law and finance courses at a community college, and immersing herself in the specifics of running a stationery store. The results had been nothing short of gratifying. Everything about Write Style was going well.

Except her.

Since Dad and Allison had believed enough in her to invest, Bree had been determined to prove them right. They'd told her to chill about paying them back, but she'd worried anyway and cut corners in her life. Saved every spare penny. Hired only Lola and two college-age clerks to mind the retail space while Bree worked in the back. But the exhilaration of the shop's early success had given her false energy, and she was worn out. It was unnatural for her to be all work and no play.

She took a sip of coffee and gazed out at the shopping district. Cars passed by. There was more foot traffic than she would've expected. Families headed to an early service at church.

Families.

Why had she sent in that DNA test?

No, it was ridiculous to have regrets. She and Allison had distant cousins who matched on their shared lists. It would've only been a matter of time before Allison dug through those trees and worked her way to the Harpers. But the end result would've been a process, giving them a warning of the connection before it smacked them down.

What was she going to do about Allison? How did they weave *cousin* into their friendship?

She pushed the thought away. Not solvable yet.

Tasks she'd ignored last night were waiting. She went to the back and opened the laptop. A flood of orders had arrived overnight, and half were marked RUSH. Nope. Not today. Tomorrow would be *rush* enough.

When she turned on the printers, they started spewing out packing lists, note cards, and shipping labels. As they piled up, she sagged into her ergonomic chair, also known as her second home, and cried.

The ache in her head finally roused her. Whether it was the aftermath of tears or lingering emotion from yesterday, the cure was caffeine and calories.

She locked up the shop and left. Done for the day. She walked into the diner across the street and waved at her favorite waiter, her former

AP history teacher, now retired. He had to be nearing seventy. After his spouse had died two years ago, he'd started working the breakfast rush. Bree assumed he was lonely and came here for the company, not the tips.

"Breanna, the usual?"

"Yes, sir."

She was halfway through her waffle when the door chime sounded and her father came in. He spoke briefly with the waiter and then walked her way. It was no coincidence that he was here. He knew her Sunday routine.

She had his cup of coffee poured before he slid onto the bench across from her.

"Morning, Dad."

"Morning." His smile was strained.

"How are you?"

"Not great. You?"

"Same." At least they were being honest with each other. "I'm really sorry, Dad."

"Don't be." He added cream and sugar to his coffee, rare for him. "Galen made a conscious decision to keep the information from me. There was no way we could've imagined a secret like that in our family." He took a sip of coffee. "I went over to his place last night."

"To confront him?"

"Not exactly. To satisfy my curiosity. I asked for more of the story, but he couldn't manage much. Knowing that Heather Garrett is his daughter has torn him up. Plenty of lies to go around." He set the mug down. "Nell knew that I'm his son."

Wow? Or *of course she did?* Aunt Nell had died just before Thanksgiving. Galen had been lost without his wife, and this shock wouldn't have helped. "So what's next?"

"I don't know. I can hardly think. I need time to let it soak in."

Their waiter set down Dad's order, asked if they needed anything, and left.

Dad crunched a slice of bacon. Drizzled molasses over his biscuit. "Have you told your mom?"

"Not yet. Do you want me to keep it to myself?"

"No, you should tell her. It's been hidden long enough."

"Okay. Soon." Mom would be interested in that weirdly detached way she got over anything related to Dad.

"Have you talked with Allison since yesterday?" he asked not so casually.

Bree stiffened. "No."

"What happened wasn't her fault."

Dad had noticed her withdrawal. Had Allison? "I know, but I'm not ready to discuss it the way she'll want to." Their relationship had changed in ways Bree couldn't adapt to easily. She wasn't prepared to pick it apart, analyze the pieces, and rebuild it into something new.

"Don't shut her out. The two of you could be supporting each other through this."

Bree shrugged. Her friend wasn't affected by the revelation in the same way. What she needed was someone who could be more objective.

Dad had the right idea about talking to her mother, and Bree would do it in person. She desperately needed to get away.

Tomorrow, she would head south. To Charlotte.

CHAPTER FOURTEEN

April 1969

Molly stared out the window, heading north through the Virginia countryside, bleary eyed after a night spent on a bench in the Raleigh train station. She hadn't consciously thought through her need to leave North Carolina, but, with no one there she trusted anymore, she'd simply had to escape.

Her grandmother's suitcase rested on the floor, protectively behind Molly's legs, stuffed with a hodgepodge of items chosen for their ease of grabbing. There were the things that Gwen had sneaked out of the Home. Cash that Grammy had left lying around. And some of Grammy's clothes, although they were likely too big.

"Richmond, next stop."

The train lurched, banged, then slowed.

She'd barely had time to glimpse a river full of boulders and frothing water before they plunged into the city. Grim city blocks yielded to wide, charming streets. The train squealed to a stop at a building almost too pretty for a train station. She joined the line of people getting off, then another line at the pay phone.

When it was her turn, she dropped in a dime and dialed. It rang and rang. Would her friend pick up? It was Sunday. She might be at church.

"Hello?" Gwen answered, sounding breathless.

"Hi. It's Molly."

"Molly! Where are you?"

"The train station. In Richmond."

"What?" There was a pause. "Never mind. We'll be there shortly."

Molly waited outside under the colonnade. It was a lovely day. Warm. A slight breeze. People wandered in and out of the station, wearing their Sunday finest.

A black Continental pulled to the curb, and Gwen was out of the car, rushing toward her. They held each other tightly, as if it had been years rather than weeks since they'd last seen each other.

"I've missed you. So much. You just don't know," Gwen whispered and stepped back. She was dressed in pink from head to toe. Quite a contrast to huge brown smocks.

"I think I do."

Clive joined them and gestured toward her suitcase. "Is that all you have?"

"Yes."

He put it in the trunk, then helped them into the car.

Shifting sideways on the back seat, Molly considered her friend's outfit. The headscarf in psychedelic pink and orange. Pink swing dress and stockings. Pink platform shoes. "Do you go to church that mod?"

"Obviously." Gwen grinned. "You don't?"

"No, never." Molly wasn't brave enough. She would be branded as disrespectful for life. Not that Molly wasn't already branded for life.

"Are you Baptist?"

"Methodist."

"Well, there you go," Gwen said. "Presbyterians are more relaxed. Although, even with them, I'm teetering on the edge."

From the front seat, Clive laughed.

"Okay, a little over the edge. My stepdad doesn't approve, but Mama thinks it's a fantastic idea. Gives people something to talk about besides where I was for five months."

Molly's smile vanished.

"I'm sorry," Gwen said. "Want to talk about what happened?"

"No."

"That's cool. I can guess most of it."

Molly looked out at the open window. They were whipping down a boulevard. People strolled along the sidewalks. Azaleas were in full bloom. Buildings rose many stories on either side of the street.

Clive parked the car in an alley behind a narrow three-story building. When they entered a small lobby with a tile floor, he charged up the curving staircase with her bag.

Molly and Gwen climbed more slowly. At the top, the only door on the landing stood open, with Clive waiting beside it.

"I left your suitcase in the living room, Molly."

"Thank you."

"Of course," he said and turned to Gwen. "Should I wait?"

"Please. I'll be down soon."

He gave a brief nod and descended the stairs noiselessly.

Gwen led the way inside. "Here we are. My little apartment."

Even though Molly could see only the living room with a large picture window, the "little" apartment felt like it wasn't much smaller than her childhood home.

"It's charming." A bank teller couldn't afford this. Was Gwen rich? Maybe the "driver" should have been a bigger hint.

"So," Gwen started, slipping off her scarf, "is this a visit? Or have you moved?"

Molly had fled with no specific thoughts about what she would do once she got to Richmond, but one thing she knew for sure. It wasn't a visit. She crossed her fingers. "I've moved."

"Good. You're staying with me."

"For now."

"An argument for later, because I have to meet my parents for lunch soon, and I want to get you settled before I go." She went to a pink phone tucked into a small alcove in the wall, picked up the handset, and dialed. "Hi, it's me. I'll be delayed a few minutes. Something's come up." She listened. "No, it's a happy delay. Bye." She crooked her finger at Molly. "Follow me."

Gwen went down a dim hallway and opened the first door with a flourish. "This used to be my junk room. It's your bedroom. *For now.* Move whatever you like out of the way. You'll find sheets for the sleeper sofa in the linen closet." She crossed to the closet and pushed aside the louvered doors. "This will be yours, too, in about five minutes." Reaching in, she scooped up two armfuls of clothes on hangers and walked out.

Molly hauled her suitcase onto the sleeper sofa and snapped it open. The sounds of clothing transfer continued behind her.

"Okay, Molly. What else?"

She looked up from the jumble in the suitcase. "Are you sure about this?"

"Yes. Very sure. I cannot begin to tell you how happy . . ." Gwen stopped. Pressed a hand to her chest. "We'll talk more when I get back." She glanced at her wristwatch. "Sorry, but I really have to go. Does your family know where you are?"

Molly shook her head.

"Use my phone and call them direct. It's fine."

Her friend pulled her into a perfumed embrace, the scent soft, subtle, and sweet. Like Gwen. Well, maybe not the subtle part.

"Make yourself at home." She hurried into the foyer. Seconds later, the front door slammed.

Before doing anything else, Molly explored her new home. She peered in an open doorway into the other bedroom. It was much larger and furnished by someone with good taste. This room also had a picture window and a bathroom in the corner.

The door across from the spare bedroom was a second bathroom with a small shower. She flicked on the light, splashed her face with water, dried her hands, and continued to the kitchen. It was stuffy in the apartment, so she cranked open a window.

Her gaze fell on the phone alcove. Yes, she should let her family know she was fine. It would have to be her aunt. *Collect.*

"I'll accept the charges," Trudy said crisply and waited until the operator had dropped off the line. "Where are you?"

"Staying with a friend."

"I see." Trudy might suspect which one, but she didn't know Gwen's real name or where she was from. "For how long?"

"I don't know. A while."

A disapproving sniff. "Will you call your parents?"

"Someday. Not yet." Molly had to ask what she really wanted to know. "How is Diana?"

"She's fine. Safe." Trudy's voice gentled. "With her parents."

A tear slipped from the corner of Molly's eye.

"May I tell your father that you called?"

"Sure." She might not want her parents to find her, but they deserved to know she was safe.

"Okay. Please keep in touch, honey."

"I will. Bye, Aunt Trudy."

Molly took a shower, changed into a loose dress, and hung up the rest of her clothes. When her stomach growled, she went to the kitchen and found an apple and an Oreo. Then she stood, completely alone for the first time in months, no one telling her what to do, no one finding her a disappointment.

Gripped by a weariness that was soul deep, she slumped on the couch and looked out the window at the rooftops of other buildings, trees undulating in the breeze, a flock of birds winging past. And allowed herself to absorb the peace.

◆　◆　◆

The lock clicked in the front door.

"Molly? What are you doing?"

She opened her eyes to fading daylight. She must have napped. "Nothing. Absolutely nothing."

"It's nice having nothing to do." Gwen sat on the couch, her body tensing. "That's about to end for me. I officially return to work tomorrow."

"Are you worried?"

"Some. Frank told them I've been in Europe. A delayed gift for my college graduation. Like anyone believes that." She snorted. "I wasn't showing when I left, so they may be suspicious but won't dare say anything."

"What about the father?"

"He's already been transferred to another branch. Since he and everyone else know it's an insulting move, I'm sure he'll find a different bank." She shrugged. "It isn't much of a consequence. He'll recover soon."

"But at least your stepfather did something to him. Most guys barely feel a ripple in their lives."

They lapsed into silence, shoulder to shoulder on the love seat, the faint sounds of traffic, people talking on the sidewalk three stories below.

"How are you, Gwen? Really?"

"I miss my son."

The grief in those four words touched a chord. Gwen hadn't spent a couple of weeks with her child like Molly had. Did that make it harder or easier? "We're mothers."

"We are."

"And we can never talk about it."

"Except to each other." Gwen cocked her head, as if thinking. She popped to her feet and wandered over to the picture window, staring down at the street below. "Do you have a plan for what's next?"

"No." Molly ought to make one rather than sit here like a lump, but it had been so nice not to think.

"Well, then, no worries. Mama and I made a plan for you."

100

That surprised a laugh from Molly. "You would take over my life if I let you."

"Yes, I would. And do a good job of it too."

She rose and joined her friend at the window. It was a pretty view, if she ignored the TV antennas crowding rooftops. "I have to find work."

"Mama has ideas about that. She wants to help."

"Why would she do that?" Molly had only met Peggy Abernathy twice, when she visited Gwen at the Home. "She barely knows me."

"She knows you better than you think. I wrote about you constantly. Coded letters, remember?" Gwen turned serious. "She says you'll have a hard time finding a job if they see you graduated from a maternity home. You need something besides your diploma, and a recommendation from Mama will carry weight. Do you have any experience?"

"Babysitting, but I won't do that." Not now and possibly never. "I took care of my grandmother when she was ill. That's about it. Unless you count the chores we did at the Home."

"I don't." Gwen linked her arm through Molly's. "Speaking of chores, I have laundry to do. The machines are in the basement. After I'm done, it's dinner, TV, and bed. I don't want to be late for my first day back."

Molly made the right choice to come here. "Thank you. For everything."

"Trust me, Molly. I'm the one who's grateful."

A cabinet door slamming somewhere awakened Molly. Sunlight filtered through blinds into the room. Stretching, she yawned and looked around, realization of where she was flooding in. She slid from the bed and went into the living room.

Gwen stood at the kitchen counter, eating a piece of toast. She was dressed more soberly today in a knee-length blue dress. Slim fitting.

Short sleeves. Peter Pan collar. She looked prim and sexy. Molly wished she could pull that off. Maybe one day.

"Good morning, sleepyhead. Coffee?" Gwen pointed at the percolator.

Molly shook her head. She'd never acquired the taste.

"My mother might drop by this morning to chat with you about jobs. Do you have any cash on you?"

"A little."

"Come to the bank during my lunch hour, and we can set up an account for you."

She picked up a leftover toast triangle. Mmm, cinnamon sugar. "Won't I need a man to cosign?"

"I don't think so. Frank's bank lets women have their own accounts. They might worry that you don't have a husband, but if it's a problem, Frank will take care of it."

Molly was glad she'd come to Richmond, but it had been more impulsive than anything she'd ever done. Would she become a burden to her friend? "How can I ever thank you?"

Gwen chewed her toast thoughtfully, then set the crust down. "Let's make a deal. No more thanking each other for everything. We're just two friends."

"Okay." But Molly would find a way to pull her own weight. "When will you be home? I could cook dinner."

"Not refusing that. There's money in the cookie jar and a grocery store three blocks south of here. I'll be back by six."

"South?"

"Downhill. Toward the James River." Gwen picked up her purse and gave Molly a hug. "You'll be glad you've moved here. Promise."

CHAPTER FIFTEEN

Bree had done nothing productive for the rest of Sunday, focusing on her favorite mood-altering activities. She'd painted her toenails. Streamed a cute documentary about puppies training to be guide dogs. Reorganized her bookshelves, this time by the color of the covers.

Maybe she should take up a real hobby. Something as different from running a business as possible. Not cooking. Failure could make people sick. Nor exercise. Bleh. Besides, she had that covered by walking to work occasionally. When it wasn't raining. The distance was short enough not to get sweaty and long enough to feel virtuous.

Officially, the store was also closed on Mondays. For Bree, they were days off in name only. But not today. She was going to Charlotte. It had been over a month since she'd been there for Tristan's high school graduation party.

She pulled up the family calendar. Tris was going to freshman orientation at the college he was attending in Charlotte. Her younger brother Carter was lifeguarding at one of the public pools. Mom only had a clear two-hour block from eleven to one. Bree would try to fit herself in it. She texted.

Want to have lunch with me?

Yes. Is this spontaneous, or is there
a reason?

Both. Something to do with Dad. Nothing bad

11:30 at Claude's

I'll be there

She chose the kind of outfit that would be comfortable enough to drive in and wouldn't embarrass her mother at her favorite bistro. A flirty little dress with lavender peonies against a cream background. Neutral flats.

Before she left town, she would get the weekend rush jobs out. She drove to the store and hurried inside. The delivery guy usually stopped by around nine thirty. She had to get the packages ready.

Everything was wrapped and ready to go by nine. If the delivery guy was late, she'd have to go on. Nobody kept Mom waiting.

The knock came at nine twenty, just when she was on the edge of panicking. She pushed the full cart to the door and flung it open. "Hi, Kai. I have packages."

"So I see." He smiled.

"Can I help you?"

"No, I've got it."

As soon as his truck was out of the way, she would leave. She crossed to her desk for her purse, phone, and a gift for her college-bound brother.

When Kai had loaded the last package, she followed him out the door and locked up. "Thanks."

"Sure. In a hurry?"

"Yeah. Going to see my mother. In Charlotte." She flushed. Why had she told him so much? He didn't care.

"Have fun." Another smile and he was swinging himself up into the driver's seat of the truck.

"Kai? So this may be outside the rules, 'cause I know you're only supposed to check for pickups when your route brings you past the shop. But would it be okay to text me if you can't make it by nine thirty? Just on Mondays."

"That is outside the rules."

She shouldn't have said anything. "Okay."

"And I'll do it." He grinned. "Just on Mondays."

She handed her phone up to him. He texted himself and gave it back, then waited until she'd stepped safely out of the way before driving off.

When she arrived at the restaurant two hours later, the host led her across the dining room to where her mother sat at a table for two. Mom was a beautiful woman, mostly natural assets with a few carefully selected enhancements. She called Bree her mini-me. Same strawberry-blond hair and clear skin. Both had blue eyes, although Bree's were a shade darker. She'd inherited all of her mother's best features. From her father, she got the "Harper Build."

Translated: Bree wasn't slender.

Mom rose and gave her a touch-and-go hug. "I already ordered a Cobb salad for you."

Bree had been craving grilled cheese. "Thank you."

She let her mother fill her in on her brothers until the waiter had served their salads. Then Mom asked, "So what's this all about?"

Bree had what she thought of as a "guarded" relationship with her mother. She'd never forgiven Mom for the divorce, and Mom had never forgiven Bree for choosing Dad. It made for hazardous conversations.

Her mother favored blunt honesty, another trait Bree hadn't inherited. But she'd voluntarily put herself in the line of fire today. Another indication of the depth of her agitation. "Allison had her DNA tested. It sounded like fun, so I did too."

"And were there skeletons in the Harper closet?"

She narrowed her eyes. "Not nice, Mom. It's my closet too."

Her mother had the grace to look chagrined. "Sorry."

Bree ate a bite of her salad. Gazed out at the other diners and back to her mother. "The DNA results had some unexpected discoveries. Galen is Dad's birth father."

"Ooh. I ought to be surprised, but I'm not."

Really? The rest of them had been stunned. "Why?"

"I've always wondered about their age difference. Bernice made no secret that she'd wanted more children and that she'd had two miscarriages between her boys. So the story she and Marvin told about an oops baby made sense. Even then, Galen seemed more taken with Everett than the average much-older brother."

The next part would shock Mom. "Dad also has a twin sister."

"Damn." She pushed back in her chair. "You've found her, haven't you?"

"Heather Garrett."

Mom's eyes widened. "As in, Allison's mother?"

"Yeah. It's been distressing." What a mild word. Bree's whole world had been knocked out of orbit. She had no idea where she was anymore. "For Galen too. He never knew he had a daughter."

Mom took a long swallow of her tea. Swirled the glass, clinking the ice. "How does this affect you?"

"I don't know yet. I'm trying to hold off on obsessing over it, so I can return to some kind of normal cadence in my life."

"To recap, your best friend is your cousin. Your father was adopted. And Uncle Galen is Granddad." Mom shook her head. "I think we've wrung all we can out of that topic. Why don't you tell me about your business?"

"It's doing well." Bree would leave out the part about her no-frills existence. It was a sore subject, since her mother had refused to fund college after Bree declared a major in information science. That her mother had been correct about the meager job prospects hadn't helped.

"I've been referring friends to your website for wedding gifts."

Ah. That accounted for the surge in online sales beginning in May. She couldn't decide whether to be irritated at the intervention or grateful. At least Mom's gesture could be viewed as a backhanded compliment. She wouldn't have referred friends if she had the slightest concern her recommendation was unwarranted. "Thank you."

"A good-quality pen is never wrong."

Bree shouldn't ask, but she would. "Do you tell them it's your daughter's shop?"

Mom shook her head. "Not because I'm not proud. I am. It's just hard to know whether it would help or harm if they know who you are." Her lips twisted.

Bree totally understood. Her mother had a strong, edgy personality. The whole *you love her or you hate her* applied.

Mom had been involved with her husband, Fort, before she'd split from Dad. Her second marriage seemed happy, as far as Bree could tell. Fort was able to provide the kind of lifestyle Mom preferred. Bree's brothers were great guys. She didn't begrudge what they had, but her mother's betrayal had devastated Dad. He hadn't bothered much with a social life since. Was he afraid of rejection? Avoiding another mistake? Whatever the reason, she wished he would try.

Bree shook the thoughts away. "I have a gift for Tristan. Can I leave it with you?"

"You brought a gift to his graduation party."

"This one is more of a *welcome to college* present. A grab bag of things he might find useful as a freshman."

"That's prescient. He's planning to live on campus."

"Yeah, he told me." At Mom's raised eyebrows, Bree felt her own tickle of surprise. Of course she was close with her brothers, or as close as she could be living over a hundred miles apart. "We text a lot."

"Really? Define *a lot*."

"Not every day, but a few times a month."

"Since when?"

Her persistence was strange. "I don't know, but it isn't recent. Why? Does that bother you?"

"No, it delights me. Neither of you ever mentioned it." She glanced at her phone. "I should get moving. I have an appointment uptown."

They walked out together. Bree set the gift bag in Mom's trunk, waved as she pulled away, then started the two hours back to Marlowe.

Bree was streaming *Bridgerton* on Netflix that night and pondering the idea of a class on Regency letter writing when her phone pinged. It was Tris.

I checked my DNA results. You really are my sister

Was there any doubt?

You're Mom's mini-me, so not unexpected

Thanks for the care package. Surprisingly good choices

I did go to college. Twice

Long ago. This might be a rude question, but how expensive is the pen wholesale?

Expensive

Could you be more precise?

No. Why do you care?

Just curious how upset I should be if I lose it

If you do, I'll tell you the price, and you'll be upset

Gotcha

You could sell care packages like mine. Pens, notebooks, and journals are excellent. But other stuff too. Duct tape. Burner phone. Protein bars. Postage stamps

The idea was worth considering. She could experiment with how many items she could fit into a standard box. Research more online to see how much she could reasonably mark up. Or make the packages customizable so that buyers could adjust what they were willing to spend.

Great idea. I'll think about it. Any other suggestions?

Condoms

Uh, no. Parents are my buyers

Solid point. I'll give it more thought

Thanks

Later

The conversation had her feeling a spark again. Something she'd lost with all the necessary but tedious tasks. She traded her phone for her laptop, brought up a spreadsheet, plugged in some numbers, and got to work brainstorming care packages.

CHAPTER SIXTEEN

Allison had met her brother and nephew at the ballpark Sunday evening to watch a Durham Bulls game. The outing had devolved into Liam sleeping on her lap and Perry sharing his fears over possibly losing custody of his son. Once she reached home, she took a call from a guy in Alaska who was hunting for his birth father.

She'd gone to bed late and had a restless night, saturated from the emotional pain of her family and others'. She ended up oversleeping, something she never did.

Now here she was, trapped in traffic on the interstate. When it became clear she wouldn't be able to reach the office in time for the development team's staff meeting, she joined by phone. Five minutes late.

It took her a minute to catch up, but she finally figured out that the team was talking about the website of a local chain of hardware stores. The customer had made a request to add 3D animation to the site. The topic immediately engaged her, and not in a positive way. As the software architect for this project, it was her job to design the website to make sure all parts worked together well. Adding animation would create nothing but headaches.

It was a terrible idea.

The account manager, however, seemed to be taking it seriously. "What can we show users while they're waiting for their invoice to load?"

Team members started throwing out suggestions. Spinning hammers. LEGO towers imploding. Dancing traffic cones.

The lead developer said, "Allison, you're quiet. Do you have any thoughts?"

Yes, she did. "I'm trying to wrap my brain around why we're discussing this. Done well, animation might be cute. But that's the only plus. Besides being hard to implement and even harder to maintain, it'll create performance problems. And after all that work, users will beg us to turn it off. Instead of trying to distract users from how slow we are, why don't we focus our efforts on being faster?"

Her comments were met with a heavy silence, and then someone cleared his throat. "Hi, Allison. This is Burt."

The *customer*? Why was he on the call?

"So I'm guessing you're opposed to my idea."

She stifled a groan. How could she salvage this? "It has issues."

Burt huffed a laugh. "Well, okay."

A text came in from the account manager.

Drop off now

Gladly. She ended the call and sucked in a breath. That had been so bad. Ahead, traffic was moving again. As her car lurched forward, she mentally flayed herself for not checking the agenda before leaving home.

After parking near the office building, she stopped at the coffee shop in the lobby, bought a large Americano, and took the stairs up to her office. When she unlocked her computer, a meeting request popped up from her boss, marked "Private." It gave her a chill. Allison didn't have to wonder what Fawn wanted. After responding to a few emails and answering one phone call, Allison gave up trying to concentrate and watched the clock. With a minute to spare, she walked to the corner office.

Her boss looked up from her screen, stood, and smiled neutrally. "Come in. Shut the door." Fawn wore a light-gray skirt suit, a mint-green top peeking out from the collar, and taupe shoes with four-inch heels. The silver hair curling about her shoulders didn't quite mask the hoop earrings. She looked sophisticated. More like a marketing director than the head of Research and Development who could still write code.

Allison could never pull off that look, and she didn't want to. T-shirts and jeans or shorts were her uniform. She would upgrade to business professional if she had to, but that didn't happen often.

Her boss gestured toward the small table in the corner of the room. They both took seats at it.

Her sense of foreboding strengthened. "Is this about the meeting this morning?"

"Yes, it is. I just fielded a long, irate phone call from Burt. Did you really tell him he had a bad idea?"

"I didn't use the word *bad*." Allison was known for her honesty, and she appreciated it in others, but she would've been more diplomatic if she'd known Burt was there.

"Why weren't you aware we had a customer on the call?"

She hated to admit it. But no excuses. "I didn't check my messages yesterday."

"Or today." When Allison started to speak, Fawn raised her hand, halting any response. "We've had conversations about your people skills."

They had, in her last "quarterly" review. Six months ago. Her boss had warned Allison about coming across as impatient. She couldn't argue with that adjective. Most of their meetings lacked efficiency. Without an agenda, they often discussed details that could be handled over email. They spent too much time talking about sports or craft ales or potty training. Yes, she knew the other team members found those topics fascinating, but why was it necessary to cover them in *business* meetings?

"Should I call him to apologize?"

"He's not interested in hearing from you at the moment. Which is a problem for *me*."

Allison felt like her chest was in a vise. What kind of problem? "Okay. I'm sorry. I don't intend—"

"Your intentions aren't important," Fawn interrupted. "What matters is how others perceive you. Your team knows that you don't mean to be abrasive."

Allison stiffened. "That's a strong word."

"It is. Also apt."

Had Fawn been this clear in their last review and Allison hadn't paid attention? "Can you give me an example?"

"You're condescending with technical explanations. You make people listen to twenty words when ten will do."

That stung. "Ten words are rarely enough to explain adequately."

"It's better to give people the minimum and let them ask questions."

"Not everyone will. They don't want to look stupid."

"Then that's on them. Look, Allison. You do brilliant work, but if our customers are uneasy around you, you're less effective."

Abrasive? Condescending? She stared at her boss, wounded.

Fawn's voice grew brisk. "I've promised the customer I'll take action to fix this. You've focused on your technical skills to the detriment of your people skills. It's past time for you to be great at both."

"Okay." Allison had accepted a position here right out of college, and she liked it. Was her job in danger?

"I've asked HR to create a training program for you. You'll be hearing from them soon. Whatever they assign, it's your top priority." Her phone vibrated against the tabletop. She picked it up, frowned, and stood. "Anything else?"

Other than *I have no idea what just happened here*? Allison shook her head.

Fawn made it back to her desk and stared with a show of concentration at the screen. "One last thing. I'll be sending Jax to Scotland in your place."

"You're giving him my trip?" It was a blow. She could hardly breathe. "Why?"

"The timing conflicts with your training program."

"But Jax isn't technical enough."

"That's why you'll be on call to back him up while he's there."

"Please, Fawn." Allison had been working on the Glasgow project for months, and Jax didn't have a clue. "Can we adjust the schedule?"

"Sorry." Fawn sat and flapped her hand dismissively. Done.

Allison returned to her office, too on edge to interact with anyone. She packed her things and left.

HR called while she was driving home. They had a long, painful conversation over Bluetooth, followed by a short, painful email awaiting her when she got to the cabin. Her training plan consisted of a virtual class entitled *Soft Skills for Software Professionals* as well as an in-person intensive workshop, beginning later this month. During the week she should have been in Scotland.

The training was serious business. It bothered her that, if she'd needed this so badly, why hadn't it been serious all along? Why so sudden?

She had no meetings on her calendar this afternoon and, with Jax taking over the Glasgow trip, nothing urgent with her other projects. So she signed into the e-learning site and opened the virtual class. It had twelve lessons, each video lasting about an hour. Might as well get started.

She watched a short introduction, which could be boiled down to *Embrace what resonates; set aside what doesn't.* Were they really inviting her to ignore what she didn't like?

She clicked on lesson one. *Words wield power.*

Sigh. A cliché.

Stop. If management deemed this training essential, she should too. It was time for an attitude adjustment. Clichéd or not, her continued employment might depend on this class. She returned her attention to the video and hoped it would become more interesting.

Two hours later, she took an assessment covering the first two lessons and passed with 92 percent. But it hadn't really been an assessment. More of a review to emphasize the points they were trying to make.

Words wield power.

Honesty shouldn't shred people.

Was that how she came across? Someone who shredded people? She hoped not.

This class targeted software professionals who were unaware of how they affected others until someone pointed it out. In other words, the class was speaking directly to her. Since the training site had a whole course developed on the topic, she wasn't the only technical person who needed help.

It was only midafternoon, and she was already wrung out.

A message came in from the company's travel concierge. Allison's arrangements for Scotland had been canceled. She'd have to decide whether to cancel or postpone her vacation too.

Jax sent a meeting request for the following morning with a link to his PowerPoint slides. She reviewed them and had lots of feedback, but her new reality had left her uncertain about how honest to be.

Jax was confident. Assertive. It would be hard to shred him, so this would be a great opportunity to practice tact. He was no doubt delighted to get the trip to Scotland and expecting her to be upset about it. So she wouldn't be. Well, she wouldn't let him detect it.

This wasn't a punishment. It was a challenge.

Bree was an expert at people. She loved talking with them. Sharing advice. Finding common ground. Soft skills were natural for her. Had she ever noticed Allison being rude? She texted her friend.

Let me know when you're free

The response hadn't come in until after Allison finished a load of laundry.

Driving back from Charlotte

A visit to her mother? Interesting. Bree must be in complete disarray if she turned to her mom. She rarely wanted Tracy to see anything other than perfect Bree. Actually, it was strange. She'd always waited to share things with her mother until she'd polished the rough edges with Allison first.

A prime example had been Bree's breakup with her former fiancé. Caden had often gone on weekend "fishing trips." Bree had been shocked to learn those trips included more than fish. When she'd confronted the jerk with damning photos on his social media accounts (Caden wasn't particularly smart either), his answer had been "it's not cheating until we're married."

Bree hadn't told her mother about the broken engagement for weeks afterward, avoiding all wedding talk, unable to say his name without crying. Instead, she'd been a nightly visitor at the cabin, eating her favorite comfort foods and bingeing *Fast and Furious* so she could watch things explode as she worked through the grief.

That month had given Allison an unexpected bonus—insight into how insubstantial her own relationship was with her then-fiancé. After he'd moved to California without warning, she'd barely noticed his absence.

Okay, done. Allison was restless from all the time spent on introspection. She ought to get away from her computer and move. A hard swim was what she needed. She grabbed her gym bag and headed for the aquatics center.

She'd been on the swim team in high school but not in college. While she'd lost interest in competing, she hadn't lost her love for swimming. The water restored her. Became her own private, peaceful world.

Today, she swam laps without counting. Just pushed her body to the point of failure. She rinsed off in the shower, feeling worn out in a better way, her sense of competence restored.

Out in the lobby, she checked her messages. Two texts from the office and one missed call from her brother. She'd try Perry again when she got home. As she continued toward the external doors, Everett came out of the men's locker room, his hair wet, focused on his phone. She waited for him to notice her.

Everett was a man she'd admired for twenty-five years. The father of her best friend, who had built forts out of sheets in the living room when Allison stayed over. The English teacher who had valiantly tried and failed to make a writer out of her in seventh grade. The news this weekend hadn't magically turned him into a different person. She didn't expect any real change in their interactions, but their relationship could never be the same. He was no longer only "my best friend's father." He was *her* uncle. "Hi, Everett."

He looked up and smiled. "Allison." He caught up to her. "Enjoy your swim?"

"Yes."

"Me too. Well, water aerobics." He gestured toward the snack bar. "I'm heading over there to get a drink. Want to join me?"

"Sure." She was hit with an odd twinge of guilt. As if they were going behind Bree's back.

"What can I get you? Water?"

"That works."

After he bought their drinks, they drifted over to an empty bench.

He drank half the bottle. Picked at the label. "What have you told Heather?"

They had dispensed with the small talk. Allison was good with that. "Only that she has family members who are local. No other details yet. She'll have to adjust between each new piece of data."

"So I shouldn't call her?"

"No, please don't." Allison could tell he was struggling to rein in his curiosity. "I'll tell you when she's ready."

"Okay. I'll wait."

"Thanks. Have you talked with Callum?" Galen's son with Nell. Everett's half brother. Formerly his nephew.

Everett frowned at his water bottle. "No, Galen wants to call him first."

Wow. What would it be like to suddenly adjust how she felt about Liam? She adored her nephew, but it wasn't the same feeling she had for Perry. Everywhere she turned, this whole situation spawned complications.

"What I learned this weekend blows my mind. I have a sister. A *twin* sister. It doesn't seem real." He drained the last of his water. Crushed the bottle. "Have you found her?" he asked casually.

Allison knew which *her* he meant. "I've exchanged messages with her contact person. But not directly with Molly."

She couldn't say the news hadn't sunk in, because it had. What still was out there, beyond her grasp, was what she would do about it. Could they ever be normal again? Could she form the kind of family connection with the Harpers that she had with the Garretts?

Would this alter her friendship with Bree?

She and Everett rose together, tossed their empty bottles into the recycling bin, and stood staring at each other hesitantly. If she was with Dad's brother, he would have pulled her into a hug so tight she would laugh and fake-beg him to let go. But she and this uncle had yet to create their own conventions.

Everett must have read her thoughts. "Allison, let's not push this. Until Heather is comfortable with the news, it doesn't feel right to act as if everything's fine."

"Sure," she said, more disappointed than she'd expected. She wished they would all agree to stop tiptoeing around. The new reality was here to stay.

As she watched Everett walk to his car, she thought about whether she should call out to him and mention Molly's interest in contact from her child.

No, it could wait. Even though he was the child more likely to respond, Mom ought to have the first shot. But the delay was frustrating. There were mysteries to be solved. If the answers were painful, Allison would need time to present the story in the least hurtful way.

She had sufficient information to locate the Molly Mitchell who was raised in North Carolina and likely born around 1951. But Allison felt honor bound not to poke into her grandmother's life yet.

She had, however, looked up the contact person, before she knew not to. Gwendolyn Abernathy Reeves was from a prominent family in Richmond, Virginia, and, from all appearances, had lived there her entire life. How had her path crossed Molly's?

CHAPTER SEVENTEEN

May 1969

Peggy Abernathy's name worked like a miracle with potential employers. Molly had landed two jobs by week's end. Busing tables at a tearoom and mopping floors on a local college campus. Both jobs were part time and minimum wage. Molly was glad to have them.

The tearoom waitresses had a tradition of sharing tips with the person busing by leaving nickels and pennies in a mason jar. There was a five-and-dime store on her walk home, so each Saturday, Molly would collect her coins and stop by Woolworth's to treat herself. She spent, at most, one precious dollar, but she would go batty if she didn't have something to look forward to.

The first Saturday, she bought undies. Desperately needed. The second, Breck Shampoo, because she loved the smell. Today, she got a nice pen and a postcard, and took them to the lunch counter, which had already closed for the day. She dashed off a note to her parents. Nothing momentous. *Hello. I'm fine. Miss you.*

They would see the postmark and know she was in Richmond, but she wouldn't include her address. She wasn't ready to hear from them yet.

When she returned to the apartment, it didn't feel empty but was way quieter than Gwen was capable of. Molly crept down the hall and paused outside the master bedroom. She heard a hiccup. A snuffle. A sob.

She knocked. "Gwen, are you okay?"

"No."

She nudged the door ajar. Gwen was curled on her side, fist pressed to her mouth, a knitted blanket draped over her. Molly walked in and sat on the rug by the bed. The snuffling sobs continued for a moment, then slowly faded.

"What happened?" she asked.

It took a while for Gwen to respond. "I saw a friend from high school in the park. Pushing a baby carriage."

"I'm sorry." Molly dropped her head back on the mattress, eyes watering. "Will we ever be able to see babies and not cry?"

"Maybe someday." Gwen grabbed a tissue, blew her nose, and wiggled under the blanket, but she seemed calmer. "I've talked with someone. One of the ministers at my church."

"You talked with a minister?" Molly tried to picture herself confessing to Pastor Norton at her childhood church. His response would be a long, painful monologue on fornication and sin and the rocky road to redemption. Nope. It boggled the imagination.

"I know. It sounds crazy, and maybe I have been. It's just been so hard since I returned, and I can't seem to get going again. But he was helpful. I talked. He listened. No lectures or judgment. Just sympathy."

Molly envied her that. Not only finding help, but being brave enough to ask. "Did you tell him about me?"

"I told him about *Eve*. How fabulous you were. How miserable I would've been without you. But not your real name." She pushed into a sitting position and wrinkled her nose. "You smell like Pine-Sol."

A not-so-subtle way of letting Molly know the weep session was over. "I'll go shower."

It was mid-June before Molly decided she was ready for her family to know where she was. On her next Saturday splurge, she bought stationery, sat at the lunch counter with a Coke, and wrote her parents. She added her return address and dropped it in the mailbox. The whole walk home, she fought back nerves. Would they respond?

No, she wasn't worried *if* they would. It was *how* they would. Would they be angry or reproachful? Would she read disappointment between the lines?

Too late. The deed was done.

On the following Saturday, Molly had her first real mistake at the tearoom. For seven weeks, she'd bused tables without incident. That changed today. She dropped a tub of china plates, and they broke, which was awful enough. But it startled one guest so badly, she spilled tea on her blouse. The manager on duty gave Molly a thorough scolding after her shift.

Dispirited, she skipped Woolworth's and dragged straight home. From the landing outside the apartment, she could hear a muffled conversation inside. Gwen wasn't alone. Molly pressed her ear to the door and gasped. She recognized the voices.

Her parents were here.

Choking back a sob of joy, she burst through the door. The three people in the living room turned. Then her mama was running to her, and they were in each other's arms. Hugging, laughing, crying.

Her father joined them at a more dignified pace and dropped a kiss to her head.

She took a step back. She hadn't seen Mama since December. "You should have told me you were coming."

Her parents exchanged glances before looking back at her with strained smiles.

Ah. She got it. They had worried she wouldn't welcome them. A reasonable concern. "I am *so* happy to see you."

Daddy exhaled with relief. "You look well."

"I am."

Mama pulled her in for another hug that lasted and lasted. When she finally let go, she said, "Are you free tonight?"

Molly was free every night. "Yes, ma'am."

"Wonderful. We'd like to take you out. The steak house near our motel looks nice."

"And there's a movie theater nearby," her father said. "We haven't seen *The Love Bug* yet."

Molly had, and it was cute enough to see again. "Okay. Let me change."

At the steak house, they were shown to a table by the windows. After the waiter took their orders, they looked at each other. Smiled. Toyed with their silverware. It was awkward, and Molly didn't have a clue how to make it better. She'd been out of their lives for six months, and they'd been out of hers. She was a stranger to them now. What was there to say?

"You've changed your hair," her father said with a sniff. He didn't care for it.

"It's a bob." She loved it. So easy to take care of. She smoothed it over the tips of her ears, not wanting him to notice they were pierced. He would hate that even more.

"Heavens," Mama exclaimed. "I nearly forgot. I brought pictures." She drew a photo album from her purse.

Molly's interest changed to stunned silence as her parents flipped through the pages, oohing and aahing over their "youngest grandchild," Baby Susan—who was three months *older* than her twins. Molly was grateful when the waiter showed up with their food.

As Daddy plopped liberal amounts of butter on his baked potato, he shot her a glance. "How can you afford that apartment?"

"It's subsidized." She chuckled. At their narrowed eyes, she lost the smile and added, "Gwen's uncle is into real estate, and he owns the building. She gets a good deal."

"Do you know her from . . . ?"

"Yes, sir."

His expression might be carefully blank, but disapproval radiated from every pore.

Mama jumped in. "Tell us about your job."

A safe topic. "I have two. I work in a tearoom mornings and afternoons, six days a week. Only minimum wage, but I get free meals during work hours. I'm also on a janitorial crew at VCU." She cleaned the third floor of the Business School, where the professors' offices were located. And only one bathroom! In Molly's opinion, it was the best assignment. She was glad the other cleaners hated climbing stairs.

"VCU?" her father asked.

"Virginia Commonwealth University." She leaned forward, enthusiastic over how the university fit into her future. "I plan to go to college there. They have a degree in education." For as long as Molly could remember, she'd wanted to be a science teacher. "I'll wait until I'm an in-state resident to start. I'm hoping for fall 1970."

Her mother gasped. "You're not coming home?"

Ugh, this topic had tumbled onto treacherous ground after all. "Mama, I was always going to leave Lowell after high school. Richmond is farther than expected, but I like it here."

Her father frowned. "How are you going to pay for college?"

With him, it was always about the money. "I'm saving everything I can. When I add my college fund account, there ought to be plenty to cover the first year's tuition."

Mama glowered at her husband. "You haven't *told* her?"

He ate a bite of meat and stared out into the dining area, not meeting Molly's gaze.

"Told me what?"

Mama lightly rapped her knuckles on the table to get his attention. "*Warren.*"

He sighed and put down his fork. "The account only has about a hundred dollars in it."

Molly didn't understand. Last time she checked, it held nearly five hundred. They must be mistaken. "How can that be? I've been saving for years, and I haven't withdrawn any. Not even a penny."

"We used it to pay the fees at the Home."

She stared at her father, dumbfounded. He couldn't be serious, could he? But he looked steadily back at her, as if he hadn't just admitted to an appalling violation of her trust. "What fees?"

"For your stay," he said. "And the baby girl's hospital costs."

She turned to her mother, who was flushed with guilt. "You must be joking."

Mama shook her head.

Icy rage cascaded down Molly's body. Closing her eyes, she gripped the edge of the table, imagining the embarrassing scene she was about to make. No, she wouldn't do that to herself, so she counted backward from twenty instead. When she reached *one*, she opened her eyes. "How *dare* you," she said coldly. "You had no right to touch my account."

Her father's jaw flexed. "I most certainly did. I signed for it. I can do with it as I please."

Did he really believe himself? "Legally, yes, but in no other way. It was immoral of you to spend my money."

"Immoral?" His eyebrows arched high, shocked to have such a word used against him.

"Yes. And for what? To pay that evil beast to torture me and give away your grandchildren?"

Mama said, "What do you mean by *torture?*"

Daddy talked over her. "*You* gave them away."

Molly shuddered at her father's words. He was right. She *had* signed the papers, a regret that would haunt her until her dying days. But she would not dignify his comment with a response. Instead, she rounded on her mother. "You would know what I meant by *torture* if you'd ever bothered to check on me."

"That's a harsh word," her father said.

"In my case, it fits. But you can't dispute what it was like there, can you? You never toured the facilities or asked questions or showed up at the hospital."

"We didn't go to the hospital," her father said sternly, "because there was no reason to ever see the babies."

His words were like a match to tinder. "*I* was a patient, too, and you left me at the mercy of people who despise girls like me. With no one there to protect me, my treatment was inhumane. The nurses chained me to a bed. Allowed me to lie in my own filth. Left me alone while I writhed in pain and burned with infection. If my parents didn't care enough to come, why should they?"

"It can't have been that bad." Mama sounded doubtful.

"It was worse. I was terrified and helpless. If the twins' pediatrician hadn't stepped in, I wouldn't have received the medicine I needed."

"What kind of infection?" Her mother paled. "Will you be able to have children?"

Molly had just bared her soul, and that was her mother's response? "I am a mother. I *have* children, and you wouldn't let me bring them home."

Mama's face fell. "I'm sorry, sweetie, but that wouldn't be right."

"Forcing me to surrender my babies wasn't right either." This topic had been treacherous ground, indeed. "Now you know why I'm not coming back. When I lost them, you lost me." She couldn't be with her parents anymore. Laying her napkin beside her plate, she rose. "Have a safe trip home."

She stormed from the restaurant, only to stop uncertainly on the sidewalk. It was breathlessly hot and muggy. Not that she would've tried to walk home anyway. The apartment was too far, and she couldn't take a taxi since she hadn't brought any money. She went back inside and borrowed a phone to call Gwen.

She answered on the first ring. "Hello?"

"It's Molly. Can you come and get me?"

"Just a sec." Gwen spoke to someone else, the words muffled. Then she was back. "Clive will. He can be there in ten minutes."

Precisely ten minutes later, Clive picked her up and drove her to the apartment in silence. When she entered, Gwen was waiting.

"Your visit didn't go well."

"No."

"Wanna talk about it?"

"Not now." Molly turned toward her room, then stopped short at the sight of two full laundry baskets under the picture window.

"Your parents brought your summer clothes."

With a curt nod, Molly continued to her room, crumpled on the bed, and stared, dry eyed, into the dark until well past midnight.

Molly was in the kitchen before dawn, plugging in the coffeepot and fetching a notebook and pencils. She had to throw out her budget and start over again. A whole year's worth of college tuition had been spent on a place she'd begged not to go to.

She had to put that thought behind her, or it might poison her future.

First, she listed the unavoidable costs. Her share of rent and groceries. Bus fare. Emergencies. And one optional cost. A tiny bit extra to have some fun occasionally. Otherwise, she would go bonkers.

Next, she added her college expenses for tuition and books.

She made estimates. Shaved them here and there. Calculated and recalculated. But no matter how hard she tried, she couldn't make the numbers come out right. She couldn't be a college freshman in 1970.

Well then, she would work until she could.

Gwen stumbled out to the kitchen around eight, still in pajamas. Molly looked up. "You're not ready for church."

"Not going today. You need me." Gwen poured coffee into two cups, added liberal amounts of cream and sugar, and brought them to the table.

Molly took a sip. Palatable.

Gwen frowned over the rim of her cup. "What are you doing?"

"Calculating my finances for the next year." Or three.

Her friend rested her forearms on the table, straining to see the notebook, studying the numbers grimly. "Why have you pushed college out until fall of '71?"

"My parents paid for the Home with my savings."

Gwen said a dirty word and slammed back into her seat. "That stinks."

"I agree." Moisture prickled her eyes, and she dabbed it away. *Not now.*

"I'm sorry to have to tell you this, Molly, but you left off dorm fees."

She froze. "Why? Will you kick me out?"

"No, I love having you here. It's just that female students under the age of twenty-one are required to live on campus. Unless you live with your parents."

She ran to the bookcase, pulled out the VCU student bulletin, and flipped to the page with fees. As she skimmed them, her mouth went dry. Living on campus meant paying for a dormitory room, laundry, insurance, and a meal plan. She'd counted on two hundred dollars per semester. Instead, she was looking at seven hundred.

It was too much.

She hadn't cried last night, but tears squeezed from the corners of her eyes, scorching a path down her cheeks.

"Hey, Molly. It'll be okay. Maybe we can get the age thing waived. Frank knows people."

Of course he did. She suppressed a hysterical urge to giggle. Was she destined to be rescued by the Abernathys for the rest of her life?

Time to save herself. She went back to the table and picked up an eraser. She had a budget to fix.

◆ ◆ ◆

Molly didn't hear from either of her parents until after Independence Day. Then a Hallmark card appeared in the post. The handwritten message was brief.

July 9

Dear Molly,
I am so sorry. Please forgive us.
       What can we do to make this right?
Love, Mama

Molly hadn't answered, but two weeks later, another letter arrived. The first paragraph made her laugh.

July 23

Dear Molly,
Did you watch the moon landing on Sunday? As much as your father loves the space program, you know we did. We must have the best TV in the neighborhood because we had a roomful show up. People sitting on the floor and leaning against the walls. The doorbell rang so much, I finally had to put a sign on the door that read: Come on in.

Mama's letters kept arriving, every other Friday like clockwork. Two pages, with a five-dollar bill tucked inside. The only grandchild she singled out was Walter, Molly's favorite. He was in the junior high band, playing the trombone.

She found herself eagerly checking the mailbox for her mother's letters. It was Mama's witty observations about life in a small town that Molly loved most. She was seeing a side to her mother she'd never known, and it was fabulous.

In place of a fourth letter, Molly received a heavy, shoebox-size package wrapped in brown grocery-bag paper. Inside were her Christmas gifts from Galen: one paperweight and two books. Her mother must've done that behind Daddy's back. He wouldn't be happy if he knew.

Molly responded this time.

> Dear Mama,
> Thank you for <u>all</u> the mail. I look forward to hearing from you.
> Tell Walt that I'll expect a concert when he gets good.
> Yes, Gwen and I watched the moon landing at her parents' house. They had a roomful too.
> Love, Molly

In October, her mother called long distance, late at night when the rates were down. She asked if she could pay a visit in November and spend the weekend after Thanksgiving together. Of course Molly said yes!

Mama brought Aunt Trudy, and the three of them had a wonderful time talking, eating, and shopping. While her mother was preoccupied with a Christmas-gift purchase, Trudy pulled Molly aside.

"I've talked with a friend at North Carolina's department of social services. They've grown curious about what happened to you at the Home, and they're investigating. They also assure me that the police won't look for you anymore."

Molly smiled her thanks, relieved that part of the ordeal was behind her. "What will happen to the Home?"

"I can't be sure, but it won't go well for them."

Throughout the remainder of their stay, neither her mother nor her aunt mentioned Daddy. Was he still mad at her? Or mad at himself? Whichever it was, maybe one day, he would come around too.

As winter gave way to spring, life brought Molly several fab changes that lifted her spirits.

She was promoted to waitress in the tearoom. Tips were creating a nice bump in her savings.

She received two letters on Good Friday. The first, from her mother, was fun and newsy as always, but the final two paragraphs really captured her attention.

> Your aunt was in Marlowe recently, something to do with probating your grandmother's estate. She saw Galen Harper coming out of the post office and stopped for a chat. He has enlisted in the army. He'll leave in May for boot camp. We'll keep him in our prayers.
>
> Are you up for visitors again? Trudy and I would like to drive up the third weekend in April.

To Mama's question? *Yes!* Molly would mail an answer tomorrow.

She reread the paragraph about Galen, folded the letter, slid it back in its envelope, and felt a quiver of fear. Should she write him?

No. Aunt Trudy had told her at Thanksgiving that Galen had no interest in her. Molly had more pride than to push herself on him. Even if she mailed something to his house, he wouldn't receive it.

The second letter was from her father. She hadn't heard from him since the argument last summer. Well, other than *Love, Daddy* written on a Christmas card. This note was marginally longer.

March 25, 1970

Dear Molly,
I hope you are well. It sounds as if you are. I enjoy the
letters you send your mother.
We miss you, sweet girl.
Love, Daddy

A simple message. Not asking for forgiveness. He would never do
that. But writing her at all was an olive branch. She would accept it.

On Easter Sunday, Molly attended the early service with the
Abernathys, her first time inside a church since . . . *before*. And what
a beautiful church it was. From up in the balcony, the sanctuary was
breathtaking. It had soaring rafters and gorgeous stained-glass windows.
There were lilies everywhere. The pipe organ and a brass ensemble
played as the ministers and choir processed up the aisle. It was unlike
anything she'd ever experienced. Majestic and inspiring.

The younger minister gave the children's sermon from the steps by
the altar, two little boys leaning against his legs, twenty more young-
sters at his feet. While she couldn't hear him clearly, she could see how
much he loved telling the story. And she *knew* he had to be Gwen's
"counselor."

Molly whispered to her friend, "Is he the minister who listened to
you?"

Nodding, Gwen whispered back, "He'll be listening to me again
Tuesday."

Molly didn't ask why. Tuesday was the first birthday of Gwen's son
and Molly's twins. They hadn't discussed it. Like a storm front on the
horizon, it waited for them. Potentially ferocious. Unavoidable.

They wouldn't let it slip by. Somehow, the day would be
remembered.

◆ ◆ ◆

Molly called in sick on March thirty-first. She'd never done that before, but she couldn't have worked today. With her red-rimmed eyes and raw pink nose, she looked ill.

She put on her favorite sweater and took a long walk after lunch. She window-shopped. Wandered around the library. Dropped by a grocery store for the ingredients of a German chocolate cake. When it was baked and frosted, she set it on the coffee table and pressed in three candles. Two blue and one pink.

Gwen walked in late, holding a single blue iris. "Hi," she said, setting her keys on the counter and reaching for a vase.

"The flower is beautiful." Another way to remember.

"Clive gave it to me."

Molly longed to ask about their relationship, but he was the one topic she was careful not to raise. Her friend was sensitive about Clive. She would discuss him when she was ready.

Gwen carried the vase and iris into the living room and stopped abruptly. "What's that?" She pointed at the cake.

"Dinner."

Gwen smiled sadly. "Perfect."

After Molly lit the candles, they sat on the rug and watched dripping wax form tiny puddles on the frosting. In unison, they blew out the candles, and Molly cut two big slices.

"Do you wonder where they are?" her friend asked quietly.

"Every day." Molly set her plate down and drooped against the couch. "Do you think we'll ever get over it?"

"I hope not."

CHAPTER EIGHTEEN

Bree spent the rest of her Monday evening ignoring the pressing tasks of her day off while she pursued Tristan's suggestion. A ping from her phone interrupted the fun. An incoming text from Carter.

Tris got a freshman care package from you

She couldn't help a laugh. Was someone feeling left out?

He did

Ever consider making one for high school seniors?

Not a bad idea either. Same items?

Mostly. Also candy, first aid kit, Uber gift cards

You've given this some thought

There's more where that comes from

What kind of candy? It can't melt

Breath mints, skittles, pop rocks

Got it

I volunteer to be your test market

Deal

Bree owed her brothers gratitude for yanking her from a business rut, because the care-package idea still had her buzzing with interest the next morning. She pulled the suggested items she already had in stock, organized them on the assembly table, then experimented with what she could fit in a standard-size box.

"Good morning," Lola said. "You look excited."

"I am." Bree pondered the permutations of items. It was a good mix, with a little space left over for snacks or candy or a few of the other ideas. Yeah, she could make this work with a nice profit for the effort. "My brothers brainstormed care packages for college or high school students with me. Customizable, if I can figure out how to do that on my website."

"Sounds fun. Let me know if I can help." Lola gave her a meaningful look. "Really."

"I will." And Bree meant it. Lola had been hinting that she would like to take a more active role in the shop. Bree was almost ready to consider it, once she could clear her mind enough to figure out which tasks she was comfortable turning over.

Okay, time to put the fun stuff aside. There were plenty of mundane things to do, and Lola left Tuesdays after lunch. Bree would be alone until the afternoon clerk showed up at four.

Midmorning, someone made a light rap on the staff-only door and came in. Must be friend or family. Lola wouldn't have let them pass otherwise. Bree finished stacking a new shipment of sustainable journals, turned toward the door, and forced a smile to her lips. Allison. Her best friend. Or was it best cousin? So far today, Bree had been having decent success at ignoring the weekend's revelation. Not anymore. "Why are you here?"

Allison flinched. "We haven't talked since Saturday. That's unusual for us."

"Not if you consider what happened."

"Are we okay?"

"Sure." A partial truth. They weren't entirely okay, but Bree owed her friend an explanation, and she didn't have one yet. She reached for another sealed carton and ripped it open. Colored pencils and coloring books from a new supplier.

"What are you doing?"

"Receiving new items. They were delivered this morning, and I'm just getting to it."

"Do you want help?"

Not really. "Sure."

Allison was as good at this as she was at everything she tried. Yet Bree was tense the whole time they worked, with *Don't say anything, please* sliding through her brain like a marquee.

"Fawn is sending me to customer etiquette training."

Bree eyed her friend. "What's that?"

"Soft skills for geeks."

"Sounds like a good idea."

Allison's hands stilled. "You think I need it?"

How could Bree agree without saying yes? "I think tech experts can become so exuberant about technology that they forget it's meant to serve people."

Her friend scowled. Not fooled. "Do you find me abrasive?"

Stall. "Did your boss use that word?"

"Yes."

"*Abrasive* is too strong."

"What word would you use?"

Why was Allison pushing like this? They'd made a promise as little girls to always tell the truth to each other, even when it hurt, before they understood how much worse the hurt could get as they grew older.

When it came to communication, Allison valued efficiency over nuance. Refreshing, usually. But she could be so focused on getting her message across that she bulldozed over the *how* and the *when* of what to say.

The worst example? Bree's breakup with her fiancé. Allison had never held back with her dislike of Caden. She'd thought he was bad for Bree all along and never minced words about it. While Allison proved to be right, Bree would have preferred sympathetic silence to *We both knew he was a jerk.*

Sympathy was what she'd given when Allison's engagement fell apart. The only thing she'd had in common with her ex-fiancé was their jobs at the same company. More workmates than soulmates. Bree had known it was doomed well before Allison had. She'd been the bright star in that relationship, he merely the wannabe. He'd ultimately moved to California to find a smaller solar system to shine in.

Bree had waited until he was long gone and her friend had been on the mend before giving the "I never really liked him" speech. Perhaps she'd been too extreme with subtlety, but Bree wasn't wired to inflict painful truths on those she loved. "I would say you're oblivious."

"Oblivious of what?"

"Oblivious of the way people react when you're on a roll about something."

"Well, that was honest."

Forget subtlety. "You shouldn't have asked the question if you didn't want honesty."

Allison gasped. Backed up until shelving stopped her. "What have I done to you?"

"Nothing. Everything." Bree combed her fingers through her hair. She hadn't intended to hurt her friend. To share how she felt so bluntly. Normally, she wouldn't have, but her filters had been knocked askew. She should just shut this down before it spiraled further. "The world is different than it was a week ago. We can't pretend that we're the same. Me. You. Any of us."

"But why has that made us so distant?"

"I need space to handle this."

"And I need my friend."

Bree dropped her hands. Shrugged helplessly. "I don't know what to say." Their needs were in conflict with no way to resolve. She was sorry about that, but she wouldn't yield.

Allison frowned and looked away, totally at a loss. "What's going on here?"

"I don't know. We're in the middle of an agonizing mess. The end isn't in sight. And it's our fault."

"Our fault?" Allison gaped. "It's not our fault. It's theirs. A fifty-five-year lie. We may never know the full story, but we don't have to tiptoe around the parts we do."

"My dad hasn't recovered. Or Galen. Or me."

"I haven't either."

"You haven't been hurt to the level we are, and you're a constant reminder of what I've done to my family."

Allison jerked. "I am your family. I was before."

All true, and the knowledge made Bree's heart hurt. Despite the turmoil they were currently experiencing, being Allison's cousin would bring something wonderful to their friendship, unless Bree ruined it with the way she was acting. "One day, that will fill me with joy."

"Wow. Okay. I get it." Allison rubbed a hand against the back of her neck. Tried to smile. Failed. "I'll leave you alone then." Her friend strode from the stockroom.

Words filled Bree's mouth, clamoring to get out. *Don't go. I'll figure this out.* But she also needed some peace to sort through her emotions. To forgive whoever needed forgiving.

The alley door banged shut, and her world was quiet again.

She closed her eyes. Why had she allowed that conversation to go so wrong? She'd hurt her friend and herself.

How could she make this better?

There was an obvious first step. She had to retake control. To stop floundering around and fill the holes in her understanding. The best way to do that would be to learn what happened all those years ago, to find the reasons her grandparents had stayed silent.

Legally, her father might have been their son, but he was born their grandson, something they hadn't forgotten. The deception had been deliberate.

Her friend had uncovered the *what*. Bree would seek the *why*.

CHAPTER NINETEEN

Allison worked remotely on Wednesday, attending a virtual meeting at 5:00 a.m. with their European office, feeling subdued and struggling to stay engaged. Afterward, she sent Jax feedback on the presentation he was giving to the Glasgow staff. Then she and Otis left her home office to take a break on the deck.

Eventually, the peace of the outdoors had the desired effect, and she headed back inside. But what to do next? She had no meetings. No urgent email. Just her top priority.

She signed back on to the e-learning site for soft skills training. Today's lesson: *Understand your audience.*

The instructor recommended thinking up a thorny issue facing the learner. Could be professional or personal. Allison settled on *What should I remember about Mom before sharing news that she's spent a lifetime avoiding?*

As Allison went through the lesson, she anchored that question in her mind.

One of the techniques for assessing her audience was to *enlist the aid of a trusted adviser,* something Allison had been doing since she learned the word *Dad.*

Not yet eight o'clock, but her parents would be up. It wasn't too early to pay them a visit. When she pulled up their driveway, she was glad to see her father outside, mowing the lawn. He would know the best way and the best time to ease Mom into the information.

Dad noticed Allison, shut off the mower, and stopped. "Good morning."

"Trying to get this done before the heat of the day?"

"Yeah." He mopped at his face with the hand towel hanging around his neck.

"The neighbors don't mind?"

"The neighbors mowed theirs an hour before me." He gestured with his head toward a wooden bench in the shade. "I'll take a break." He drank deeply from a bottle of Gatorade as they sat. "I can guess the reason you're here."

"I have an update on Mom's birth family that she has to hear."

"Alli." He sighed. "She won't discuss it."

Allison had noticed. "If she's so opposed to knowing, why did she agree to let me take the DNA test?"

"The medical history." He pursed his lips. "She's on board with gaining access to it, but not with hearing anything specific about the people."

"Well, as it turns out, I don't have to gain access to their medical history. I've known it for years." She willed him to trust her. "I get how strongly she feels about this, but I'm not exaggerating. Mom has to hear who our family is."

He rolled the bottle between his hands. Looked at her. "Who?" he asked resignedly.

"The Harpers."

"Bree's family?"

"Yes."

He whistled. Finished his drink and set it aside. "How closely is your mom related to them?"

Her father understood genealogy. She would let him sort through the implications. "Bree is my *full* first cousin."

He frowned. Considered. Groaned as he got it. "Okay. Let me hear the details."

"Everett is Mom's brother." Grief thickened her throat at the waste of it all. "*Twin* brother."

Her father swore. "Twins adopted separately. That is . . ." Dad dropped his head in his hands. "How did this happen?"

"We don't know. Everett was never told he was adopted."

Her father stared at the house, concern creasing his brow. Mom stood at the window in her nursing scrubs, grim determination in the set of her mouth. A moment later, she blended into the shadows.

"Dad, there's something else major. Galen Harper is their birth father."

"Can it get any more complicated?" he muttered. Facing her, he opened his mouth to say something and closed it again. His expression softened. "You've had to wrestle over what to do alone."

She dropped her gaze. Nodded. No matter what choice she made, Mom would be hurt. It had been confusing. And no one to share it with.

"I'm sorry, doll." He pulled her into a one-armed hug, sweaty T-shirt and all, but she didn't mind. It felt like the first kind touch she'd had in days.

"Tell me the rest, Alli."

"There isn't much more. Galen's girlfriend was sent to a maternity home. Everett's adoption was handled through them. Galen didn't know he had a daughter, so he has no idea why Mom's was handled differently."

"One baby had a private adoption, and the other was left on a porch?"

"It doesn't make sense." She turned sideways on the bench. "You and I both know this can't be the whole story. It's all tangled, and pulling the threads apart will take time. I've located the birth mother through her account manager on Ancestry, but she'll only accept contact from one of the twins."

"What does Everett say to that?"

"I haven't told him. I owe it to Mom . . ." Allison shrugged. Dad understood. If Mom still rejected participation after she heard the facts, at least it would be an informed decision.

"I'll go in and talk to her. I agree that ignorance is no longer an option."

"Isn't she working today?" For a nurse anesthetist, distracting news had to be handled carefully.

"She was on call and had to go in for an overnight emergency. Arrived home ten minutes ago." He stood, walked several steps, stopped. "I'll let you know when I'm done."

Allison got the message. Time for her to leave.

On her way home, she took a shortcut to the highway through the neighborhoods encircling downtown. Marlowe had been gaining popularity as a bedroom community for Durham. It had been affordable ten years ago, but that was changing.

She neared Galen's neighborhood and made a last-minute decision to swerve in. He lived in a home built in the sixties. It would've been solidly middle class then but worth much more now given its large lot and proximity to the center of town. They'd added a ramp for Nell's wheelchair during the final year of her life. It had been pulled down, but the porch still hinted at its presence.

She rang the doorbell.

He wore a delighted smile as he appeared at the storm door and pushed it open a crack. "Hello."

"Hi." She rocked back on her heels, not entirely sure what to do next. She was never this impulsive with someone she didn't know well. "Sorry for dropping by without a warning, but I don't have your number."

"We ought to remedy that." He held out his phone and waited for her to return it. "I suppose you've come for information."

His statement was tinged with disappointment. She was instantly contrite. She had to reassure him she wanted more than information. "I'm not sure why I came. I think it's mostly a desire to get to know you better."

His eyes lit up. "Thank you. I'd like that."

"I could return another time."

"No, no. Now is fine. Would you like to sit on the porch?" He gestured toward a pair of wicker rockers. "It's pleasant out."

It felt humid and hot to her, but whatever he wanted worked for her. "That would be great."

"Can I fix you a glass of iced tea?"

"Thanks."

He slipped back inside and shut the door firmly, but not before she got a glimpse of the living room. It was a complete mess. Did he have housekeeping help? Nell had kept the place spotless until her strokes made it impossible.

He brought out two full glasses, set them on a small wicker table, and sat across from her. "Now, how are you?"

It wasn't just a throwaway question. He sounded like he really wanted to know. "Trying to get used to the new reality."

"We all are." He sipped his tea, a faint tremble to his hand.

"Are *you* doing okay?"

"Well enough." He smiled and waved at a passing neighbor. "Allison, it's fine to ask. What would you like to know?"

His posture seemed relaxed. Did he actually *want* to talk? She would start easy. "Was Molly from Marlowe?"

"No, she was from Lowell, a small town near Winston-Salem. We met when she spent the summer of '68 here, caring for her grandmother."

"How did you meet?"

"I volunteered at the library. Brought books to shut-ins, like her grandmother." His gaze went unfocused. "Once I met Molly, I brought books to her too. And then I was a goner."

CHAPTER TWENTY

June 1968

It was the sad reality of Molly Mitchell's life that a fast ride through the countryside was the biggest adventure of her year. Yet here she was in her aunt's convertible, racing along a ribbon of highway, hair whipping wildly about her head, her hand surfing the wind.

When Aunt Trudy tapped her shoulder for attention, Molly turned. "Yes?"

"What did your father tell you about your job this summer?"

Job? That wasn't exactly what he'd called it. "Help Grammy around the house."

"It'll be more complicated than that." Trudy downshifted as they drove past the WELCOME TO MARLOWE sign. "Grammy doesn't feel well, and it makes her grumpy."

"Grammy's always grumpy."

"She means it now." Trudy braked at a four-way stop. "She has trouble walking, and she wets the bed. Sometimes."

Molly felt a twinge of worry. "How often is sometimes?"

"Once or twice a week. And she forgets things."

Daddy hadn't shared those details. Well, any details. Molly would've come anyway, but he should have told her.

They drove through the shopping district and turned onto Grammy's street. All the houses looked the same in her neighborhood.

White, two story, with verandas and shutters on the windows. What made the houses distinctive was their yards. The neighbors took gardening seriously.

Grammy's home had rested proudly on this corner lot since 1920. But as they parked in its driveway, Molly's heart sank. *Proud* was no longer the right description. She got out of the Mustang, surveying the yard in dismay, unable to remember ever seeing it so unkempt. Overgrown hedges. Straggly weeds. No flowers unless she counted the dandelions blanketing the lawn.

Her aunt shut off the engine and sighed. "We'll pay you fifty dollars a week."

That was good news, and if the yard was any indication, Molly would earn it. "Thank you."

Trudy shot her an unreadable look. "I'll be here on the weekends, but during the week, you'll have to be the adult in the house."

"All by myself?"

"You'll be fine, Molly. It sounds daunting, but you're up to it."

She went in the house and set down her suitcase. Her nose wrinkled. She'd expected the scent of cookies baking, but the house smelled sour and musty.

Grammy was sitting in a recliner. Gripping her cane, she wobbled to her feet, a yellow housedress billowing around her. "Come here, Molly girl, and give me a hug."

She hadn't seen her grandmother since Christmas, and the changes in her appearance were shocking. Grammy had lost weight. She had dark circles under her eyes and pasty skin. When she lurched forward, one arm outstretched, Molly had to prop her up, staggering under her grandmother's clumsy weight.

That was when the truth sank in. Molly would be in charge. *The adult in the house.* It wasn't something anyone had ever let her be before, and she'd been thrown into it without warning.

Aunt Trudy deftly maneuvered Grammy back into the recliner.

"Molly girl, I'm baking cookies. Go get yourself one."

Aunt Trudy gestured silently toward the back of the house.

"Sure, Grammy." When Molly reached the kitchen, she stumbled to a stop. Broken eggshells and dried yolk dotted the countertop. A canister had been knocked over, spilling flour onto the floor. The oven wasn't on, either, but when she peered inside, soupy cookie dough puddled on a tray.

"Molly," her grandmother hollered, "can you bring me a cookie too?"

"Yes, ma'am," she called back. "Give me a minute." Or fifteen. She found a clean bowl and got to work.

It was midnight, but Molly was too agitated to sleep.

Her oatmeal walnut cookies had been a success, almost as delicious as Grammy's. The nutmeg on the counter was the ingredient that Grammy had always kept secret.

Baking had been followed by an endless list of chores. Kitchen cleanup. Laundry. Cooking supper and washing up afterward. Helping Aunt Trudy bathe Grammy before bed.

Her grandmother slept in the den, no longer able to climb the stairs. Molly would be on call all night.

After Trudy disappeared into her bedroom, Molly had unpacked her suitcase in the guest room, lain on the bed, and tried to relax. But her legs trembled and her mind raced. She wanted to sleep, but tonight, she was consumed by a different kind of tired.

Teenagers weren't supposed to bathe their grandmothers. It was just wrong. She hadn't felt any better after Trudy told her not to worry because "Grammy only bathes once a week." That was wrong too.

The worst part? Tomorrow night, Trudy would return home to Raleigh. Molly would be alone with her grandmother for five whole days.

No. She should stop her thoughts right there. She could do this.

Tossing her pillow to the foot of the bed, she changed positions, bringing her body closer to the breeze flowing in the window, and drifted to sleep.

◆ ◆ ◆

By Wednesday, life had fallen into a pattern. Grammy's mornings went okay, but after lunch, she turned into a supergrump. Her feet were too cold. The tea too sweet. The TV too soft. Molly had to ignore reality and fix *something*. Only then would Grammy nap.

Once she heard Grammy snoring, Molly flopped onto the couch, head resting on the arm.

The doorbell jolted her awake. She checked her grandmother, whose eyelids were fluttering. Darn it all. Racing into the foyer, she peered through the screen door, irate.

The person waiting there made her angry words evaporate. He was a boy her age. Many inches taller. Dressed in a polo shirt and plaid shorts. His hair and eyes were a gleaming golden brown. She wouldn't call him handsome exactly. Pleasing? No, that wasn't quite right either. Mama had once told her there was a difference between handsome and attractive. Molly finally understood.

"Hi," he said. "I'm here to see Miss Ivy."

"Galen, honey," Grammy yelled, "come on in."

He opened the screen door. "Excuse me."

Molly was standing there like a lump, blocking him. "Oh, sorry." Flushing, she stepped aside.

"Afternoon, Miss Ivy. How are you?"

"Ready for my books. What have you got for me?"

While they talked, Molly checked her appearance in the hall mirror and suppressed a groan. Stained shirt. Gross shorts. Grubby feet. Sweaty ponytail. Clearly the boy had been expected. Why hadn't someone warned her?

"Molly?"

She stomped into the living room. "Yes, ma'am?" She forced the words through clenched teeth. If Daddy had been within hearing range, she would've had her mouth popped for insolence. But all she got from Grammy was a narrowing of the eyes.

"This here's Galen Harper. He brings me library books each Wednesday." Grammy patted the paper bag in her lap. "Galen, this's my granddaughter, Molly. She's visiting this summer."

He smiled. "Hello."

Molly nodded, long past ready for the spotlight on her to end.

He turned his smile on her grandmother and pointed at the paperback romances on the side table. "Are you done with those?"

"Uh-huh," she said as she shuffled through her new books.

He scooped up the stack, headed out, and stopped on the steps to look around. The veranda was swept. The flower bed weeded. He smiled at her through the screen door. "I think your grandmother's lucky to have you here."

"Thank you." Molly flushed again, this time with pleasure.

"So, hey. I'll be back next Wednesday. Would you like me to bring you a book?"

"Oh, you don't have to."

"It's no big deal. What kind of books do you like?"

It would be rude to blow off his question, right? Besides, he'd probably forget. She stepped out onto the veranda. "Anything to do with science. Especially space or biology."

"I meant . . . what kind of fiction do you like?"

"Oh. I don't read fiction." *Not unless a teacher requires it.*

"None?"

"Nope."

"I'm fixing that. Well, I'd better be going. I have other deliveries to make." He waved as he hopped into his car. She waited until his El Camino disappeared around the corner before going back inside.

Grammy had her reading glasses balanced on the tip of her nose with a paperback open. Molly ran upstairs to shower, shampoo, and change her clothes. Just in case more visitors showed up at the door.

After wrestling her grandmother into bed, Molly changed into her pj's and roamed around the house, looking for something to do. But the quiet chores were done. She ought to just turn off the lights and go to bed.

A car stopped in front of the house. She stood in the shadows of the foyer as someone crept stealthily up the steps, set something on the veranda, and hurried away. The car rumbled to life and continued down the street.

She crossed to the screen door and looked out. A paper bag? Inside she found a single paperback, well worn and thick. *Dune.* By Frank Herbert.

Science fiction? Ugh. She opened to the front page. Galen's name was written there in lovely cursive. He'd brought her a book from his own collection. She would have to read it. She didn't know whether to be pleased or irritated.

Tiptoeing up the stairs, she lay on the bed with the window open, lamp on, and floor fan grinding.

The first few pages were confusing. Too many names to keep track of. But soon the story sucked her in. Unlike anything she'd ever read. She lost track of time.

At midnight, she made herself put the book *down*. She would pay for her lack of sleep in the morning, but it had been worth it.

When Galen arrived the following Wednesday, Molly was waiting on the veranda for the book swap. As he climbed the steps, clutching a new bag, she whispered, "My grandmother's asleep."

He nodded his understanding. Silently, they traded bags.

"This is nice of you, Galen. She really enjoys her romances."

"No problem. See you next week." He turned to leave.

"Wait." She'd almost forgotten the book he'd loaned her. "Here. Thanks."

"You've already finished *Dune*." His smile was slow. "What did you think?"

"Better than I expected."

"Oh?" His eyebrow rose. "What were you expecting?"

"A tedious story with science so bad I wouldn't be able to stomach it."

He was two steps down from her, but their eyes were on a level. "And it was neither."

"Correct. I can't say I *liked* it, but I couldn't stop reading it either."

"Interesting reaction. Care to try something else?"

A happy glow spread through her. "Sure."

"Okay. Another sci-fi. Not tedious. Not bad science." With a wave, he left.

That same night, she was stretched out on a lawn chair in the backyard when she heard the El Camino approaching from the town center. She scrambled off the lawn chair and ran around to the front. Galen was climbing the veranda steps, a book in his hand.

"Hey, I'm here."

He reversed down the steps, meeting her at the bottom. "Your next book." He handed it over.

"*The Martian Chronicles*?"

"Don't judge," he said with a laugh. "Give this one a chance too."

She frowned skeptically. "Okaaay."

"Cool." He turned to leave, then hesitated. "Would you ever want to simply talk?"

"About what?" She held her breath.

"Books. Like a book club." He shrugged. "My friends don't read."

She hadn't either. Until him. "Yeah. Sure."

"How about Friday?"

"Yes."

As the rumble of his car faded into the night, Molly sat on the veranda swing, thinking about Galen. He'd interrupted his evening to bring her a book. Invited her to a book club for just the two of them. Made a date. Well, not a *date* date. More of a . . . well, she didn't know what it was exactly.

But what she *did* know? Their conversation had reminded her of how isolated she was, how tethered to this house. It had also made her feel special.

She flipped open *The Martian Chronicles* and immersed herself in its world.

CHAPTER
TWENTY-ONE

Grammy's string of good days ended Friday.

Molly was in the kitchen, fixing breakfast, when the sound of sobbing pierced her concentration. She shut off the stove and ran to the den-turned-bedroom. Her grandmother lay twisted in the sheets. The smell of pee was overpowering.

"It's okay." She crossed to the bed. "Let's get you cleaned up."

"Noooo," Grammy wailed. "Go away."

"Sorry, I can't." Molly yanked off the sheets and helped her grandmother sit. Everything, including the housedress, was soaked.

"Please." Grammy's neck was red with embarrassment. "You shouldn't have to do this."

It wasn't Molly's preference, either, but she'd chosen to come, and she'd do what was necessary. Kneeling before her grandmother, she said, "I'm not your granddaughter right now, okay? I'm the person who takes care of you. We'll be fine."

Grammy plucked at her sodden housedress, her face creased in despair.

Molly couldn't fix things if she had to fight her grandmother. What could she do to snap Grammy out of whatever funk she was in? To forget who her helper was? "Why don't you call me something besides Molly?"

Grammy's hands stilled. "Like what?"

"Anything that reminds you I'm your employee."

"I've always liked your middle name. Anne."

"Yes, Ms. Mitchell."

Grammy chuckled. "Miss Ivy to you, Anne."

"All right, Miss Ivy, let's clean you up." Molly went into the bathroom for a washcloth and towels.

At home in Lowell, Molly was only in charge of little things. Not the *what*s of a chore—those were prescribed. But she was allowed to decide the *how*. It created an invisible boundary between her and adulthood. Like a well-trained dog, she'd never stepped over the line. Why should she with her parents around?

But at her grandmother's house, she'd raced over the boundary without noticing. It felt good to be on the other side.

Molly was waiting on the veranda steps Friday night before nine, straining to hear Galen's car. So it was a surprise when he walked through a pool of light from a streetlamp before merging into the shadows again. He reappeared at the bottom of the driveway.

"Hi," he said. "Ready?"

"Sure. We'll have to sit in the back so I can listen for Grammy." She led him around to the backyard, dying to ask where his car was.

They sat in lawn chairs she'd left within hearing range of Grammy's room.

"So how does a book club work?" she asked.

"However we want. We could talk about characters, plot, themes—"

She held up a hand for him to stop.

He peered at her through the darkness. "What?"

"This sounds too much like English class. How about we say what we liked about the story?"

"But you didn't like *Dune*."

She sighed audibly. "Okay, then. What we found compelling."

"Ladies first."

She voiced her thoughts, starting with the way the story had exploited religion for both good and bad. It tugged at something inside her.

He was sprawled in his chair, long legs stretched before him. Something about his stillness stopped her in the middle of her sentence. "What?"

"Nothing. Just enjoying the discussion of themes."

"Like in English class." She giggled. *Giggled?* Her?

"Yeah. That's my hope."

"Your hope for what?"

"My life. If I could be whatever I wanted, I'd be an English teacher. Or anything to do with books." He sounded sad, as if it were a dream he had no chance of reaching.

"What's stopping you?"

"A furniture store." His bark of laughter was harsh. "It's been in the family four generations. I'm not allowed to break the chain."

"Why don't you just tell them you'd rather be . . . ?" Her voice trailed away. He was shaking his head firmly.

"I tried, but I'm 'too smart to be a teacher.'"

Oh, wow. What an awful thing to think. "Is there no one else to run the store?"

"I'm an only child." He looked at her. "What about you?"

"I want to be a teacher too. I guess you could say that it's my family business."

"Why?"

"My father's the principal at our high school. Has been since before I was born." She sighed into the darkness. "I have three older brothers, but I might as well be an only child. They were out of high school and working before I was in first grade."

"What subject will you teach?"

"Science. Like my dad." She shrugged. "My rebellion is about location. My parents want me to teach in my hometown. I'd prefer the city."

"Will you?"

She met his gaze. "Yes." But the word came out more hopeful than definite.

"Maybe we could rebel together."

"Maybe." Awareness shimmered between them. She didn't know what this was, but it felt dangerous. Enchanting. She looked away.

He rose reluctantly. "I'd better be going. Thanks, Molly."

She trailed him to the front. "When should we meet again?"

"I can't next Friday, but the Sunday after?"

He was serious about the club. Cool, because she was too. "Sure."

She watched him hurry down the block, waving as he turned the corner.

Nine days was a long time to wait.

Molly was in the kitchen Wednesday afternoon, washing up the lunch dishes, when she heard her grandmother call out, "Come on in."

"Hi, Miss Ivy," Galen said. "I'm early today."

"No problem. Let me see what you brought."

Molly put a pan in the drying rack, wiped her hands on her shorts, and walked to the living room. Grammy was rummaging through a bag with five new romances, beaming as she went. Galen had scooped up the finished pile.

"These look nice, honey. You know what I like."

"No, ma'am, not me. The librarian picks them." Looking over his shoulder, he caught Molly's eye and gestured with his head toward the door.

She nodded. "Grammy, I'll be right back."

"Hmm." She was already engrossed in her book.

Molly followed Galen onto the veranda. He held out a battered paperback and watched carefully as she took it.

Catcher in the Rye. She gasped. "Um, wow."

"Have you ever read it?"

"Absolutely not." Her father had banned *Catcher in the Rye* at the high school. Too vulgar, profane, and tempting.

"Okay." Galen held out his hand. "I'll find something else."

She clutched it to her chest. "No, I want to read this one."

"Good." His eyes glinted with admiration.

A gust of wind sent a lock of hair across her face. He reached up to tuck it behind her ear, his finger trailing across her cheek.

She leaned into his touch, surprised and thrilled. Wishing to memorize the sensation so she could replay it a million times.

He dropped his hand. "I'll see you Sunday."

"See you Sunday."

After the El Camino was out of view, she went back inside and started down the foyer toward the kitchen.

"Molly?"

She paused. "Yes, ma'am?"

"You spent longer than a goodbye out there with Galen."

"He brought me a book." She hid it behind her back.

"Be careful with that one." Her grandmother was somber.

The warning shocked her. "Why? He's cool."

"He's glorious. Better than this town or his parents deserve."

"I thought you liked him."

"Oh, I do. Very much."

"Then what's the problem?"

"His destiny is set, and he's sick about it. He hides it well, but I often wonder if he's about to explode." Grammy's tone softened. "It's a dangerous thing to cross paths with a glorious, tortured soul. Get too close, Molly girl, and he'll break your heart."

CHAPTER
TWENTY-TWO

October 1968

After Molly returned from her summer in Marlowe, she'd slipped easily back into the routine of her old life, consumed by getting ready for her senior year of high school—and keeping a nervous eye on the calendar as she prayed there would be no consequences from her final date with Galen.

August turned to September, and she'd missed a period. But stress could be the reason, couldn't it? Between the excitement of a new school year and missing Galen so badly, that could be it. She'd heard her sisters-in-law talk in whispers about the early signs of pregnancy, and Molly didn't have them. She wasn't tired or nauseous. Particular body parts were not swelling.

By October, though, she couldn't ignore the truth anymore. Molly hadn't had a period in ten weeks, and she was never late. She'd already suspected what it meant. This morning's nausea confirmed it. She was expecting.

After dinner, she went into the bathroom, leaned against the tile wall, and stared at her reflection in the mirror. Limp hair, red eyes, and tearstained cheeks. She didn't have to worry about Mama hearing her moan. The TV volume was too loud.

She couldn't decide what to do. Like a broken record, her brain had only one thought. *I'm having a baby. A baby. A baby . . .*

The thought of confessing to her parents made her ill. For seventeen years, they'd watched their youngest child with disbelief and a touch of awe. The "pleasant surprise" who'd arrived as they neared their forties. A girl who preferred numbers to words and the scientific method to people. She'd cruised through school and expected to cruise through college—the first of their children to do so.

But this choice she'd made would baffle them. Their most cautious child had gambled with nature and lost. Molly had brought shame on herself and her family, and nothing would ever be the same.

She wanted to let Galen know, to have him help her figure out what to do. So she'd sent him a letter, asking him to please call her, but a week had passed with no response. Was he ignoring her? Or was his mother keeping it from him?

She stumbled from the bathroom, tugged on a jacket, and headed for the backyard. She sat on a swing and looked up at the night sky. Was *Apollo 7* up there, flying over? The bravery of the crew—the first NASA mission since the fire in *Apollo 1*—cheered her. Gave her perspective. She had a serious problem to handle. The astronauts had worries of far more significance.

Okay, think. How long could she hide her condition?

The back door opened and shut. Mama came across the lawn and stopped a few feet away. She held up a Kotex box. "You haven't used any sanitary napkins since you've been home," she said, her voice rough.

Molly couldn't help it. She choked on a sob. And once the tears started, she couldn't control them.

"Molly." There was such pain and disappointment in her mother's voice. "Are you in the family way?"

She nodded, head bowed, shaking with fear.

"Warren," her mother screamed.

Life changed in that moment. Molly had walked out under the stars as a girl in terror of her parents finding out, refusing to acknowledge that this problem wouldn't go away by itself and she had decisions to make. Now she was ticking down the seconds until she would be forced to tell her secret to her father, knowing that she'd been absolutely right to be terrified.

The screen door thwacked, and Daddy drew even with Mama. "What's going on?"

"Tell him, Molly."

She started bawling. But her mother was relentless, repeating *tell him* until Molly finally got the words out.

Whatever she'd imagined she would see on his face, the reality was far worse. His eyes shimmered with grief, as if he'd just learned she was dying and he would be mourning her forever.

Daddy directed only one statement to her. "I need a name."

"Galen Harper," she whispered.

Her father growled in his throat. He'd been raised in Marlowe. He knew the Harper family. "Go inside, Molly. We'll be in shortly."

She was huddled on the couch in the den when her parents came in ten minutes later. Daddy went to the phone, called Aunt Trudy long distance, and told her to make arrangements for the two families to meet. Soon. There was no time to waste.

By the weekend, Molly had been quietly expelled, and she and her mother had taken a train to Marlowe. For the next week, they'd hidden at her grandmother's house while awaiting the Saturday meeting with Galen's parents.

If her family thought sending her to Grammy's was a punishment, they were wrong. It had been a relief to leave her hometown and the smirks of her brothers. They had been amused to see the golden child knocked off her college-bound pedestal. Their wives had been worse, spitefully calling her names. Disgusted that *the oops baby is having her own oops.* What had Molly ever done to them?

Daddy and Aunt Trudy had arrived last night. Molly had stayed out of their way, too tired and ashamed to speak with her aunt. Daddy blamed his sister for allowing Molly to run wild over the summer. But he was wrong. It hadn't been her aunt's fault. Molly was responsible for her own choices. And she hadn't been running wild. Her actions had been pure adult.

The Harpers were due to arrive anytime now. Molly was already waiting in the living room, sitting on a rocking chair in the corner. She was wearing the only dress she could fit in, but it was pretty, the same deep blue as her eyes.

"There you are," Aunt Trudy said, her smile strained. "Ready?"

"No, and I won't be."

"You'll survive." Trudy pulled up a stool. "Warren's found a place for you. A maternity home. You'll be able to finish your senior year there."

Molly nodded. Her father had told her last night, and the news had made her heart thump faster. She knew he wanted what was best for her. So why did she feel like this was all happening too fast to think? "He says I'll go in January."

"They come highly recommended. They'll take good care of you and find a loving home for the baby. You'll be able to slip right back into your old life as if you'd never stepped away." Trudy patted her arm. "Any ideas where you'll go to college?"

"Greensboro." To the teachers college.

Trudy tutted. "You can do better. Think about going to school in Chapel Hill. They have all kinds of science majors."

"I'd never get in."

"You might. I know some people."

Molly smiled, and it had been so long since she'd tried that her cheeks ached. "Of course you do, Aunt Trudy."

Her father entered the living room, wearing a suit and tie. He frowned at Molly's smile. "Is something funny?"

She blanked her expression. "No, sir."

"Good." He stood with legs apart, arms crossed over his chest. "The Harpers will be here shortly. I'd appreciate it if you would sit there and say nothing."

"Yes, sir."

"We'll leave as soon as this ordeal is over."

Mama rushed in wearing her best silk dress and wedding pearls, then perched on the edge of the couch, folded her hands neatly in her lap, and didn't speak.

Three pairs of shoes clomped across the veranda. The doorbell rang.

Molly stared steadily at the floor during the introductions, not wishing to acknowledge *his* parents. When she looked up again, sunlight blazing in from the picture window had turned the four parents into silhouettes. Her parents were side by side on the couch. Mr. and Mrs. Harper sat on two chairs opposite them.

Galen hovered in the foyer, leaving on his jacket as if he didn't plan to stay. A bolt of anger shot through her. There had been nothing but silence from him for weeks. Had their summer together meant so little to him?

But then his eyes swept the room and locked on her. His face could've been carved from stone except his lips, which pursed and twisted, trying to find a resting place. Her anger melted away. Across the space separating them, she felt a tug of attachment. He gave a curt nod, as if he felt it, too, while his eyes shone with longing. Misery. Grief. At least they shared that.

What would the adults do if she jumped up and ran to him? If they held each other or simply left the house to figure out between them what to do?

Uninterested in their children's opinions, the adults were already arguing. Well, her father and Galen's mother. Their voices were rat-a-tat-tatting like weapons. Two hostile factions, who, perversely, wanted the same outcome—for the problem to go away. With a real effort, she switched her focus from the yakking silhouettes to the rug beneath her feet. The adults' voices rose and fell as negotiations were finalized. She glanced up once and found Galen watching her. He'd changed since the summer, and it wasn't just the shaggier hair. He seemed taller, stronger, older. And more reserved. She couldn't bear what they'd become.

Her father's furious voice drew her attention.

"No, ma'am. No," he was saying to Mrs. Harper. "Molly didn't get into trouble by herself."

"She wouldn't have gotten into trouble at all if she was a good girl." The woman turned her head deliberately, glared at Molly, and snarled, "Nasty whore."

The word reverberated in her brain, stunning in its power. She'd never heard it spoken out loud before, and it had been used against *her*.

Daddy shot to his feet, hands fisted, eyes ferocious.

Mr. Harper gripped his wife's arm.

But it was Galen who shocked them most. "Mama," he said in a scarily soft voice. "Do *not* speak about Molly like that. Ever again."

She gaped at her son. Recovered quickly. "She went after you."

"No." Galen turned to Molly. "I went after her."

She drank in a breath. He'd defended her.

"Well," her father said. "I'm glad to hear you admit that, young man, but you're not planning to do the right thing, either, now are you?"

Galen's eyes widened in horror as he looked back at her father. "No, sir."

Molly had heard her mother mumble about marriage to her father last night, when they thought she was already in bed. She'd known Galen would never have asked her. Nor would she have said yes. They were too young to be married. Too young to be parents. But his reaction stung, just the same. She hunched over again, ignoring the buzzing voices, withdrawing into herself.

"Molly," her father said sharply.

She raised her head. Galen gazed steadily at her, regret and relief in his eyes. Why? She looked around and found the adults were all staring at her. What had she missed while she'd been tuning them out?

She concentrated on her father.

"We've agreed on reserving a place at the maternity home I mentioned." He licked his lips. "After the baby is adopted, you may come home."

These four adults had decided her future, dealt with her situation, as she'd sat here, so weighed down with shame that she'd avoided thinking about what she actually wanted. She pressed a hand to her thickening waist. It was easier to acquiesce. Go where they told her to go. Return when the problem was past.

They were gaping at her now. Rather, at her hand resting on her belly.

"Do you understand me?" her father asked.

Her temper sparked. He wasn't exactly giving her a choice. "I heard what you said."

His eyes narrowed at her insolent tone, but his lips stayed shut.

"After the adoption," Mrs. Harper said, "my son can forget you were ever born."

Gasps whistled like a cold breeze. How had such a wonderful boy like Galen been raised by this awful woman? What had happened in her life to make her so bitter?

Well, Molly didn't have to sit here and listen to another word. She stood and smiled. Pity wasn't an emotion she felt often, but here she was, feeling it for the other people in this room. The realization made her strong. "Your son can also forget that his child—your *grandchild*—was ever born."

She strode through the shocked silence, maneuvering past Galen, and out the front door. She didn't stop until she reached her parents' station wagon and leaned against its hood, breathing hard, willing her trembling legs to hold her up a little longer.

The screen door slammed. Familiar footsteps skipped down the veranda steps and approached.

"I'm sorry, Molly," Galen said from close behind her.

"About what?"

"About the way my mother acted." He rested his hands on her shoulders. "That you're having to go through all this. Because of me."

"Because of us."

"Yeah, but it will hurt you more."

She snorted. "It's not going to hurt you at all."

"That's not true."

Yes, it was, but she could understand that he didn't get it. That he didn't realize what a difficult course lay ahead of her. And when Monday came, his life would simply go on as usual. "I've been expelled." Her voice cracked on the last word.

"What? From high school?" He turned her and read the answer in her face. "I'm sorry."

The fight went out of her. She let him pull her into his arms and loved the feeling of being held. Over his shoulder, she saw that the four parents had stepped onto the veranda and were watching them grimly.

She hugged him back with desperation. It was time to say goodbye to Galen, to drive out of his life. Forever.

CHAPTER
TWENTY-THREE

Allison didn't move, afraid of distracting Galen from his story.

He was smiling at his memories. "The first time I laid eyes on her, I stood there, mouth hanging open, drinking in the sight of the prettiest, most vibrant girl I'd ever seen." He chuckled. "She was *so* pissed when I rang that doorbell. Miss Ivy had just fallen asleep after giving Molly trouble all morning."

"Who was Miss Ivy?"

"Molly's grandmother, Ivy Mitchell. She lived in that big house on the corner of Main and Oak."

Allison knew exactly where it was. "The Ivy Inn is named for a person?"

"Yes." He blinked, as if coming out of a trance. "She would be your great-great-grandmother."

Wow. "Is the inn still in the family?"

"I don't know." His forehead scrunched. "The woman who runs it isn't a Mitchell."

Allison made a mental note to see if she could discover who the owner was, then tried to nudge him back to his story. "So Molly was her grandmother's caregiver."

"Yeah." He grinned. "I'm sure Miss Ivy was a handful. She was stubborn—and a big woman, too, where Molly was not. She was short and curvy. I don't know what her family was thinking, leaving her to handle Miss Ivy on her own, but Molly did. She had it all under control." His next statement was barely a murmur. "How could I not fall for that?"

"When did you start dating?"

"We didn't at first. We formed a book club of sorts." He took off his glasses and wiped them on his shirttail as he talked. "She loved science, but she'd never read science fiction. I took it upon myself to educate her."

"Do you remember which books?"

"*Dune* was first."

"Wow. Zero to *Dune* is pretty fast."

He barked a laugh. "Well, sci-fi had slim pickings in the sixties."

"How did you progress from book club to dating?"

"It got serious pretty quickly." He sobered and put aside his tea. "We only had the summer."

He'd grown uncomfortable with remembering their romance. Allison would move on. "Did you ever try to find her?"

"Sure, but her aunt said she wanted nothing to do with me."

"And you believed that?" Okay, that came out more baldly than she'd intended.

Galen gave her a stern look. "Yes, I did. Molly knew where I lived. She could've found me if she wanted to."

"Maybe she'd been told you wanted nothing to do with her either."

"Hmm." Frowning, he gave that some thought.

"Did she know your parents adopted Everett?"

"I'm not sure. I assumed so."

"Did you ever ask them?"

He snorted. "I refused to discuss Molly with my parents."

"Why?"

"The way they talked about her was inexcusable. Called her filthy names, as if she seduced *me*. Or got pregnant by herself." His jaw tightened, as remembered fury gripped him. "Nell was the love of my life, but Molly was the only woman who ever came close. What they did to her—what *I* did to her—was wrong." He pushed abruptly to his feet.

Allison stood, too, and watched him shuffle toward the door, not making eye contact. Was he regretting how much he'd shared?

He turned to her with a half smile and stared at her intently. It felt like there should be something more to this moment, but she'd never had a private conversation with him. They had no precedent about what to do when they parted.

Her mother was in denial. Her best friend was agitated. Would either of them care how Allison proceeded?

No, wait. This man was her grandfather. She would set her own terms with him for their relationship.

He must've been thinking the same thing, because he held open his arms. "May I?" he asked wistfully.

She stepped closer, felt his arms wrap loosely around her. They embraced for longer than perfunctory, shorter than *all in*. And she loved it.

"Thank you," he said.

Nothing to say to that. This man had learned traumatic news. Some aspects he could be blamed for. But his world had changed, too, and he was going through it alone. She couldn't let that be true.

She was skipping down the steps when his question stopped her.

"Will you locate Molly?"

She nodded confidently. "I've contacted people who know her. I'll find her soon."

"So what's the holdup?"

She would leave Mom and Everett out of it. "I'm trying to work that out."

CHAPTER
TWENTY-FOUR

Bree put off her hunt for the truth a couple of days and caught up at the shop. Since Lola was closing Write Style Thursday evening, Bree allowed herself to head home early, ready to set procrastination aside and begin her research.

She retrieved a shoebox from the top shelf of her closet, its lid dusty after years of neglect, and carried it to her Murphy bed. Inside were bundles of letters Granna had saved, some tied with ribbons, others secured with rubber bands. The first bundle contained a collection of postcards from her grandfather. He'd traveled to furniture markets and estate sales all over North Carolina and the East Coast and faithfully sent his wife postcards. Since Bree had never reviewed them, she pulled off the rubber band, which promptly crumbled. After thirty minutes of deciphering Grampa's cramped scrawl, variations on *Having fun, miss you*, Bree set them aside. Nothing there.

She'd read the letters once before, but it might be worthwhile to reskim. Five bundles later, she was done, having again found nothing memorable.

Granna had been a pack rat. There had to be more somewhere.

Dad's attic was the likely location of any of the boxes and trunks that had been spared a trip to the landfill after Grampa's death. She remembered finding a cache of old newspaper clippings in a trunk, which she hadn't bothered with since bundled letters had been too enticing to deny. Now those clippings took on a different importance. They had been cut out and kept for a reason.

Tonight was Dad's darts night. She could check the trunks without bothering him. To be honest, she didn't want him asking questions until she understood what was going on.

She let herself in the side door of the house she'd been raised in. It was dim inside, with the lights out and blinds drawn. She dropped her purse and keys on the kitchen table, then strode down the foyer toward the staircase, pausing when she sensed she wasn't alone.

Her father was kicked back in his recliner, staring through the darkness at her, a beer bottle in his hand.

"What are you doing, Dad?"

"Thinking." He took a long drink of his beer. "Why are you here?"

The question gave her a pang of guilt. She had a key and knew she was welcome to come over anytime. He'd offered to let her live here, which would have allowed her to save money to repay her promissory notes earlier. But she'd ultimately refused. They both needed their space.

As much as she didn't want to reveal the true reason, she wouldn't tell a lie. They'd had enough of those. "There could be boxes of Granna's in the attic. I plan to go through them."

"To see if she left clues?"

Nothing got past ole Dad. "Yes."

"Be careful, Bree."

"I'm curious. I don't intend—"

"You didn't intend to hurt me by testing your DNA."

The accusation made her gasp.

"Sorry." He set the bottle down and rubbed his fingers against his temple. "What happened isn't your fault. If anyone, I hold Galen responsible. My *father*." Betrayal roughened his voice.

"He wasn't the only one who kept the secret from you."

"I know." His hand dropped to the armrest. "My parents did a terrible thing, but they're not here to accept blame."

"Have you talked to Galen since Saturday?"

"Briefly."

That was more recently than she'd seen him, a fact she would have to remedy. She refocused on her father's appearance. He wore wrinkled clothes and sported a scraggly growth of stubble. Had he been too distressed to take care of himself? "When did you last eat?"

He gave a nonchalant shrug.

She returned to the kitchen and poked around in the fridge. It held enough leftovers to create a decent plate of meat loaf and potatoes. After warming them up and adding a small salad, she handed it over. "Here, and don't argue."

She sat on the couch across from him and watched until she was certain he would clean his plate. Then she stood and headed for the stairs.

"Are you going to be in the attic?"

"That's the plan. Will you be okay?"

"I'm going out for a walk."

The front door slammed as she stepped into the attic. It was overly warm, hazy, and dark. When she flipped the light switch, two bare bulbs cast interlocking circles of light, leaving lots of shadows. But, happily, her grandmother's stash of stuff was well lit. Bree's gaze was drawn to the brass table lamp from Granna's bedroom. Nostalgia swamped her. Bree had been seventeen when her grandmother passed away. In Granna's final months, she'd been too ill to leave home, so she'd read to keep in touch with the world. When her eyes failed, Bree had done the reading for her. Books, magazines, catalogs, letters. That lamp had sat on the nightstand. Its short chain made the most satisfying click when pulled. The signal that had started and ended their time together.

Behind the lamp squatted a vintage Samsonite makeup case in aqua blue. As she unsnapped the locks and lifted the lid, a musty smell puffed out. The silky lining was loose in the lid, and the elasticated pockets held paper clips. Otherwise, the case was crammed with yellowed newspaper clippings, trimmed neatly with pinking shears, most from the *Marlowe Tattler*.

Bree took a cursory look. Advertisements. Gossip about weddings, cocktail parties, out-of-town guests, funeral notices, baby showers. Her grandmother hadn't always included the top line of the newspaper. Without dates, it was difficult to know if Granna had stacked them randomly or if the organization was intentional. What had been the motivation to keep them? Had she simply been nosy?

Bree was taking the makeup case home with her. She snapped the locks down.

Stuck behind the boxes, she found another old Samsonite, same aqua but much larger. This suitcase was heavy. She carried it down to the first floor.

Dad was coming in the front door, his mood visibly lighter. "Need help?"

"Sure. You can load this one in the car."

After she had both cases in the trunk, she reached for the driver's-side door. "Thanks."

"Will you let me know if you find anything that's intriguing?"

"If you really want to know."

"I do. So, um . . ." He kicked at a crack in the concrete with his shoe. "I saw Allison at the aquatic center Monday. We had a nice talk."

Bree wasn't thrilled by the idea, which should've been beneath her. But dissatisfaction wormed its way in regardless. "Why?"

"We were both headed out at the same time. I've always liked Allison. It's odd to think of her as my niece. A happy surprise, I guess. Something to get used to."

Allison had always had a connection with Dad but *through* Bree. Now that connection was direct. It *would* take getting used to. "Did she say how her mother is doing?"

"Heather didn't know the details as of Monday." He pulled Bree into a hug. "Hey, it might take a while, but we'll be okay."

And there it came, the quick tightening of his arms he normally made before dropping them. A relief. Dad was centered again.

After hauling her discoveries into her basement apartment, Bree began a careful review, placing items into different piles on the living room rug. She sneezed over vintage dust and dabbed at her nose with a Kleenex. It was strangely enthralling to unearth what had been important to people in the past.

In the large suitcase, wrapped in tissue, was the entire front section of a Charlotte newspaper, dated March 31, 1969. The day Dad was born. President Eisenhower had been lying in state at the US Capitol. John Lennon and Yoko Ono were on their honeymoon.

Next came a postcard from Grampa, postmarked from Providence in April 1969, promising to *hurry home soon*.

Two letters were addressed to Galen, typed so hard she could feel the text through the paper. One was from the Selective Service about registering for the draft. The second, about his student deferment.

Bree rewrapped the items in tissue and placed them to the side.

Granna had saved several clippings from a newspaper column with the uninspired title of Gossip About Town. One clipping had a small set of paragraphs highlighted by a red-ink box, drawn with an unsteady hand.

If you've been wondering for the past few weeks why Bernice Harper has been wearing loose dresses, wonder no more. Bernice had her own little bundle of joy on the way. He's here now, and, boy, is he a cutie patootie.

I won't ask why the pretense, but I have it from excellent authority that she would rather not answer questions. I speak for us all when I say, "We understand."

Granna had worn loose dresses to trick people into believing she was pregnant.

Bree looked at the items arranged on the floor and tried to fit the bits and pieces of information she'd gleaned into her uncle's story. His girlfriend had given birth, then disappeared. His son's adoption had been planned months in advance and apparently never mentioned again.

Galen had told her once that he'd dreamed of being a teacher, although it hadn't worked out for him. He'd ended up running the family business, which he sold after both parents passed away. In his sixties, he reclaimed a piece of his dreams by self-publishing a series of historical cozy mysteries.

She would've sworn that she had a solid grasp of his history, as much as a niece ought to. But now the holes seemed ragged and large.

Galen hadn't dated much in high school or college and hadn't married until he was thirty, to an older divorcée with two sons. He and Nell had waited several years to have a son together. Dad was seventeen years older than Callum, a person he'd always thought of as his nephew and now knew was his half brother.

Had the turmoil of his relationship with Molly driven Galen to change his goals in life, to set aside his dreams? Had he been trying to atone?

Bree burned to know more. Even though it was late, she texted him.

Are you there?

Yes

Want some company?

His response took longer this time. Much longer. Was he worried she would grill him?

It struck her how scared he must be. With Aunt Nell gone, he had no one to lean on except her and Dad, and after this past weekend, they were leaning away.

I can bring cake. I promise I didn't bake it

Okay

He had a carafe on the coffee table with cream, sweetener, dishes, and silverware. He'd gone to a lot of trouble in the short time since she texted. It made her feel guilty. For the past several months, Bree had been too busy with the shop to give this lonely, grieving man the attention he deserved.

If she'd known he was her grandfather, would she have acted differently?

Absolutely.

She poured two cups of coffee and sliced the carrot cake. She moaned over a forkful of frosting, in all its cream-cheesy goodness, while Galen watched.

"You're here to ask questions."

"If you're okay with that."

"Ask away." He sounded resigned.

No, this was wrong. "The questions will wait. We can talk about something else."

He held her gaze a moment before saying, "Okay. Did you have another topic in mind?"

She stared at him wide eyed, thought hard, and couldn't think of a thing. "No?"

They both laughed, and the mood lightened.

"Go ahead, Bree," he said quietly.

She had so many things she wanted to know, but she would pace herself. In the weeks and months to come, she would have plenty of time to learn all the details. She would start with the present. "Does Callum know?"

"Yes, and he's angry at me too. Being a brother is different than being a nephew. I hadn't thought of that."

Galen would find it hard to make things right with his son. Face-to-face would be best, and Callum was living in Singapore until the end of the year.

Maybe it would be better to stick with the past. "Did you know your parents planned to adopt Dad?"

"I had no inkling till I came home from high school one day, and there he was. Since Molly wasn't due until May, I didn't realize at first he was my son. He was so small." Galen smiled with fierce pride. "And completely awesome."

"What was it like being around Dad when he was little?"

"He was a lively one. Curious." Galen's smile widened. "Everett was a good kid. Handsome. He definitely inherited the Harper gold eyes and hair. But I could see her in him too. Her mouth and chin and long fingers."

Bree's next questions might be harder for him. She would tread cautiously. "Did you love Molly?"

"With everything I was capable of at the time." His smile dimmed. "Which, sadly, wasn't enough."

"Did you try to stay together?"

"Never considered it, and if her parents had pressed me, I would've refused. Too selfish and afraid to give up college." He hung his head.

"What about her? Did she want to go to college too?"

"Oh, yes. She was determined. I'm sure she found a way."

Bree grew more intrigued about Molly with each answer. "You didn't contact her?"

He shook his head. "I couldn't at the maternity home. It was forbidden. By the time I finally rebelled, she was gone. I asked her aunt a couple of times where she was. At first, I'm sure Miss Trudy didn't know either. Eventually, though, she knew but declined to tell me. Said it wouldn't do either of us good to reconnect. So, no, I didn't know where she went. I don't to this day." He blew on his coffee, slurped, and set the cup down. It rattled against the saucer.

"Didn't Molly's family live in Marlowe?"

"Just her grandmother, and she died before Everett was born. I only saw Miss Trudy 'cause she inherited the house."

"Did you ever question whether everything you were told was true?"

"We didn't in those days." His lips curved up at the corners. "We just assumed people were being honest. Not like now. Your generation is bombarded with information. Conflicting versions of the same story. You have to wade through too much noise to find the facts. I don't think people revere the truth anymore. They don't have the time or energy." He huffed a laugh. "My generation expected only one version of the truth to exist. There was no point in seeking others."

Bree could understand why Allison pursued genealogy with such passion. His stories from the past were fascinating, the perspectives shaped differently by the world he'd lived in.

Millennials never had to wonder about anything. They had access to all the information, all the time. It was nearly impossible to hide secrets. Her generation had to assume that, someday, their private data would be exposed. Persistence would ultimately win.

For baby boomers, *not* knowing things had been a given. Galen had no choice but to leave Molly and their shared past a mystery. "Allison thinks it's likely that Molly made her DNA public on Ancestry because she wants her twins to find her." That felt weird to say. *Her twins.* An unknown woman had played a key role in their family, whether they wanted it to be true or not. "Does that bother you?"

"No, I hope Everett does meet her and they become part of each other's lives. She was a wonderful girl. I suspect she's wonderful still." Galen's chin lifted with resolve. "But I'm staying out of it. What Everett builds with Molly should be his decision. Believe me, I understand how sharp regrets can be if you've been persuaded onto a different path than what your gut knows is right."

There was so much she hadn't known about this man. When the churn settled down, she would like to know him better. "Have you ever tried to look her up?"

"Never saw the point. Bad or good, there's nothing to be done."

"Did you ever see her again?"

"Once. Back about twenty years ago, at her aunt's funeral. It was graveside only. Small and private. Trudy Mitchell was buried beside her mother. I went to the cemetery to pay my respects but didn't go close enough to speak."

This story felt unbearably sad. Bree couldn't imagine passing up the opportunity to check in with someone she'd loved. Unless the love had turned to hate. It didn't sound that way for Galen and Molly. Was that also a generational thing? To lock regrets in the past and leave them unexplored?

"Did she see you?"

"I'm fairly sure she did." His face reflected sweet memories. "Molly wasn't alone. There was a young woman on one side, holding a baby. And a man on the other. Molly was leaning into him. She seemed secure with him. Content. If you've ever truly been in love, you recognize the look. They were together."

CHAPTER
TWENTY-FIVE

March 1972

Molly chose her college major—or, really, it chose her—for its practicality and earning potential. When she'd learned that VCU offered associate degrees, she'd been intrigued. Although law enforcement and secretarial science hadn't interested her, information systems caught her eye.

Earning potential? Check. Computers were only going to become more useful.

Practical? Double check. She would be done in two years, and the department chair, Dr. Little—her favorite professor from the floor she cleaned—liked her!

The decision had turned out better than she could've dreamed. After a semester and a half, Molly had discovered a real affinity for computer programming. She *loved* it. Code was either clean or it wasn't. Unfortunately, she'd found a bug in her next programming assignment, and it was due tomorrow. She glanced at the clock. It was well past ten. She didn't like the idea of walking the ten blocks to campus in the dark, and the thought of passing by Monroe Park so late gave her the creeps. But she had no choice. She wouldn't hand in a buggy program.

The computer center was unexpectedly deserted. Had everyone left a day early for spring break? The basement corridor was dim, no sounds other than a slow tap-tap coming from the card-punch room. She recognized a classmate typing on a keypunch machine with his index finger.

Jerry wasn't a typical student. He was older by several years. Formerly a soldier in Vietnam who'd been medically discharged because "the army doesn't need a sniper with a shattered hand." She'd never thought much about how time consuming it must be to punch a program onto a deck of cards one handed.

"Hi, Jerry," she said, sitting at the machine beside him. She loaded some cards into the hopper and punched her corrections. She'd finished ten cards before he punched two.

As she was packing up, he said, "It's kind of late for you to be here."

"I just found a bug. It's kind of last minute for you too."

"I have no choice." Wearily, he indicated a sign on the wall.

BETWEEN 8 A.M. AND 8 P.M., THERE IS A 15-MINUTE TIME LIMIT FOR KEYPUNCH MACHINES.

She felt a spike of outrage on his behalf. That wasn't fair. Why did the world make life easiest on the people who did *not* need help? Well, she couldn't solve the problem for everyone, but she could solve it for him. She pointed at his coding sheets. "Move over. I'll punch in the rest of your program for you."

He looked up at her with narrowed eyes, considering. "How can I repay the favor?"

"Do you have a car?" At his nod, she said, "You can give me a ride home."

"Sold." He slid out of his seat.

Fifteen minutes later, they had both run their programs, picked up their printouts from the computer operator, and walked out to the parking lot.

Gwen was just getting home from her night out when Molly was dropped off. They went in together and started up the stairs.

"Who was the guy?" Gwen asked. "He's a hunk."

"A classmate, and we've established there is no interest in either direction." A fact that Molly appreciated very much.

"Why?"

"Me, because no man will be allowed to distract me from my studies. Jerry didn't say why I'm not his type, nor do I care." She entered the apartment ahead of her roommate and headed to the kitchen. "I'd like hot chocolate. Want some?"

"Sure." Gwen flung herself onto a chair and watched as Molly collected ingredients from the fridge and pantry. Once the cocoa was heating in a saucepan, Gwen asked, "Are you interested in making easy money over the next two weekends?"

Molly didn't look up from stirring. Her friend knew how to get her attention. "Sure, if it fits into my schedule."

"It will. Five hours on Palm Sunday and on Easter. Babysitting in the nursery at the church."

She stiffened. "You know I can't."

"Toddlers, Molly. Just one-year-olds."

"You have a nursery for just one-year-olds?"

"We have a separate nursery for every year up to kindergarten. Big, wealthy church. Having lots of kids."

It had been a while since she'd been around toddlers. That age didn't seem quite so daunting. "How much?"

"Ten dollars for five hours."

Wow. "That's more than minimum wage."

"Big, wealthy church."

"Will I need to interview?"

Gwen grinned. "Mama is the head of the nursery committee. If you want the job, it's yours."

On Palm Sunday, Molly was shivering in her coat outside the church's education building by eight o'clock. An elderly man with a ring of keys jangling in his hand walked up the sidewalk.

"Hello," he said, unlocking the door. He held it for her, flicked on the lights, and disappeared into a stairwell.

She stood there uncertainly until a woman wearing pearls and a modest green dress poked her head out of a room at the opposite end of the hall.

"You must be Molly. You'll be in here."

Once she reached the room, the woman said briskly, "For the early service, you'll likely have one child. That'll grow to four or five by the late service. I've put a stack of books beside the rocking chair." She gestured toward a closed door. "Parents should bring everything their child needs, but we have Pampers, graham crackers, and juice, just in case. Any questions?"

"None."

"Let me know if you need anything." The woman rushed out.

Barely a minute had passed before a tall man wearing a clerical collar came in, a tiny girl cradled in his arms. It was the junior minister. Gwen's former "counselor."

It had been over a year and a half since Molly had seen him. She'd attended church here with Gwen in 1970. Then that fall, Reverend Palmer's wife died from complications of childbirth. When he returned from bereavement leave, he'd merely gone through the motions, rarely speaking, sitting behind the pulpit with his face blank and hands clenched.

He'd told Gwen once that it must be hard for her to mourn in the shadows. Molly thought what he went through—mourning on a stage—must be even harder. He had nowhere to hide while hundreds of people watched and judged. Witnessing his grief had dredged up her own. She'd taken a break from the church and hadn't come back. Until now.

His gaze locked on her. "You must be the new sitter."

"Yes, sir." She approached them slowly. The little girl eyed her with suspicion.

"This is my daughter, Naomi."

"Hi, Naomi. I'm Molly." She smiled, then looked up at him. This close, he looked thin and haunted.

"Ward Palmer." His smile looked forced. "I'm sure the church checked your references, but may I ask a few questions?"

"Sure."

"What experience do you have with children?"

She ignored the sting. "I've worked in a nursery before and had many babysitting jobs as a teen. Lots of nieces and nephews."

"How old are you?"

"Twenty-one." In two weeks but close enough. "I'm a student at VCU."

"You used to come with Gwen Abernathy and sit in the balcony."

She nodded, surprised that he'd remembered.

"Welcome back," he said, his tone warming. He hung a diaper bag covered in Raggedy Anns on a wall peg. When he tried to put his daughter down, she whimpered and wound her arms more tightly around his neck.

Molly held out her hands. The little girl shook her head.

"Okay, Naomi. I'll be reading over there." Molly went to the rocking chair and reached for *The Little Engine That Could*.

Stories proved too tempting. Naomi wiggled to be put down and toddled over. After settling the little girl on her lap, Molly opened the book and began to read.

When Reverend Palmer reached for the sign-in clipboard, Naomi twisted, watching her father intently. After he left, she patted the book, and Molly continued.

Three more toddlers were dropped off throughout the morning. By eleven fifteen, she had four little ones napping.

Parents collected their children after the late service until only Naomi remained. They sat on the floor and went through another round of books.

Twenty minutes passed before an older woman came in, two little boys in tow. "Reverend Palmer is late, *again*, and I have to leave. Can you watch them?"

"That's fine."

The woman released their hands and indicated each boy in turn. "David is four. Nathan is six." She walked away.

Molly waved them over. "Join us. We're reading."

David sat beside her and leaned in. Nathan stood at the door, vigilant in watching both the hallway and the nursery. But with each story, he crept closer until he was kneeling in front of them.

They had nearly finished singing their way through a picture book of children's hymns when their father appeared in the doorway. The boys were at his side in a flash, both receiving a smile and a shoulder pat. Naomi squealed, pushed to her feet, and hurried to him, laughing when he swung her high and pressed a noisy kiss to her cheek.

"How'd it go?" he asked Molly.

"We had fun."

The boys nodded rapidly.

"Thank you, Molly. I apologize for being late."

"It's no problem."

The Palmers walked away, their footsteps echoing down the hall.

Molly was sitting at the kitchen table, textbooks and notes spread around her, when her roommate came in from Sunday brunch. She looked up as Gwen put three blue irises in a vase.

"I love that Clive gives you flowers each year for your son's birthday." Despite the twelve-year difference in their ages, Gwen maintained an intense friendship with him. Molly thought she'd detected it deepening recently. "Do you—?"

"Please don't ask." Gwen wandered over to the record player. "What are you listening to?" She shuffled through the album covers. "The Carpenters. Carole King. Feeling mellow, are we?"

"I need mellow when I'm studying. Especially marriage and family." Molly was taking the class as an elective because she'd heard such cool things about it. It had opened her mind to so many myths she'd completely believed. The "traditional" family she'd grown up in hadn't been traditional after all.

Gwen picked up another album. "Helen Reddy?"

"I am woman."

Gwen laughed as she pulled out a chair. "So what is all this?"

"I have two projects due after the break. Sociology and programming. I'm trying to think of a way to combine them." She pointed at the textbook. "The more I learn about marriage laws, the more I want to run analysis against the data."

"Like what?"

"Like, does the increasing proportion of married females in the labor force really affect family structure?" Molly stacked her books and pushed them aside. Her friend seemed chatty. "How was brunch?"

"Same as always. How were things at the nursery today? Any problems?"

"Not really. I had the three Palmer children at the end."

Gwen got squinty eyed. "Did Mrs. Lake dump the boys on you?"

"I didn't mind. They're sweet."

"Yes, they are. Still inappropriate of her. How did Ward seem to you?"

"Like he's dazed."

"Christmas and Easter are especially hard for him. Brenda *loved* holidays." Gwen sighed. "The congregation is being patient with how tuned out he's been, but some have begun to grumble. They expected him to be over it by now."

"He doesn't have to get better on their schedule."

"You and I understand that, but not everyone does." She pushed out of her chair. "So, will you stay on?"

"Stay on? I thought the job was only for two Sundays."

"It's not. I said that to get you hooked." She grinned with no remorse.

"Gwen." Molly rolled her eyes. She should've guessed. But was she willing to continue? It wasn't easy to find jobs that fit around her class schedule. She'd quit the cleaning job when she started college last fall and could only help out at the tearoom occasionally. With her savings account dwindling, it didn't make sense to refuse. "Count me in."

CHAPTER
TWENTY-SIX

June 1972

Molly was mesmerized by the storm pounding Richmond, transforming the streets into small rivers. A hurricane was raging out in the Atlantic and making itself noticed all along the East Coast.

Two days ago, she'd found the patter of rain soothing, not worried that Agnes's fury could reach this far inland. But the rain had been relentless. Richmond received a flood warning yesterday. Some neighborhoods were without power. Bridges over the James were closed. The downtown had been evacuated when the river overflowed its banks. National Guard troops, armed with rifles and raincoats, had been mobilized.

With no college classes this summer, Molly had recently started a job at a local movie theater, but her new boss had called to say it flooded and would be closed indefinitely. Bad news for her in a more personal way. She had enough savings to pay next year's tuition. *Or* living expenses. But not both. Five hours each week at the church nursery or the occasional Saturday at the tearoom wouldn't be enough.

Gwen had left Monday for a girls' week with her mother in New York. She'd phoned three times in the past twenty-four hours to check in, but it seemed like she knew more about Hurricane Agnes than Molly did.

When the phone rang yet again, she almost didn't answer. "Hello?"

"Molly, this is Ward Palmer," he said, sounding tense. "Would you be able to babysit my children this afternoon? The church is helping with flood relief, and I should be there."

She was surprised. In the three months since she'd taken the church nursery position, many of the parents had hired her to babysit, but this was the first time for the Palmers. "I can. When?"

"As soon as you can get here safely."

Thankfully, Gwen's car keys were hanging on a hook by the door. "I'll leave now. Just give me directions."

It was eerie driving through the empty streets. Trees had fallen over from their own weight, the sodden ground unable to hold them up. Houses were dark. Emergency vehicles raced past.

The Palmers lived in one of those neighborhoods where the houses had no driveways, just alleys edging the backyards. After she located their bungalow, she parked at the curb and climbed the steep concrete steps leading to their porch. Before she could ring the bell, Reverend Palmer wrenched the front door open. Dressed in denim and work boots, he looked deeply stressed as he jiggled his red-faced, sobbing daughter against his shoulder.

"Thank you for coming," he said.

Molly stepped directly into a company-ready living room. "Sure—"

Before she could finish the thought, Naomi flung herself into Molly's arms and hiccupped.

"Hello, little one," she said and kissed a sweaty brow.

"The boys are in the library." Reverend Palmer pointed through an open entryway into a room lined with bookshelves. His two sons lay belly down on a rag rug, watching TV. "Boys, Molly is here."

David waggled his fingers but otherwise remained statue still.

Nathan jumped to his feet. "Hi."

"Okay, what next?" The man ran his fingers through his dark hair. "I should give you a tour."

"No need. Nathan will."

"Yeah, Dad, I can."

"Okay." He sent her a vague frown. "I don't know how long I'll be gone. Just call the church if you need anything."

"We'll be fine."

He disappeared into the kitchen, then a door slammed. Moments later, a car roared to life behind the house and whined down the alley.

Molly looked expectantly at Nathan. "Tour time?"

Staying put, he gestured to his left. "On this side of the house is the library, kitchen, and Naomi's room." He nodded toward the right. "On that side is the living room, bathroom, and Dad's room."

"Where do you and David sleep?"

"In the attic."

"Where are the stairs?"

"In the kitchen. You have to go to the kitchen to do everything."

"Cool. Thank you." An efficient tour. No walking required. "Any suggestions for what I should do next?"

"Naomi needs a nap."

His sister shook her head vigorously, then rubbed her eyes.

"Thanks, Nathan."

When he went back to the library, Molly walked down a short hallway into the kitchen. It was the heart of their home, with a kitchen table in the corner and doors leading in every direction. Naomi's bedroom was straight back. Inside were a crib, changing table, toy basket, and rocking chair. Molly focused on getting the little girl comfortable again. A fresh diaper replaced the soaked one. Desitin ointment soothed a tiny bottom the same angry red as Naomi's cheeks. After pulling a clean top and shorts on her squirmy body, Molly said firmly, "Nap."

There was no protest. She laid the little girl in the crib and rubbed her back. Naomi hugged a stuffed lamb and closed her eyes, her thumb near her mouth.

Molly returned to the kitchen. Lunch dishes waited in the sink, ready to be washed. She peeked into the library. Other than a forgotten pile of laundry on the couch, it was fine. The boys were still engrossed in the TV show.

Okay then. With the three children occupied, Molly would do chores.

Once the children's show ended, Molly turned off the TV. She handed the boys a box of crayons and let them color until Naomi woke up. Then they played games. But as the clock ticked closer to five, interest waned. And still no word from their father.

Molly checked the fridge and pantry while the Palmer children watched, standing in a stair-step row.

"Are you making us dinner?" David asked.

"Yes." She settled on sandwiches and fruit. Boring, but she had ideas for kicking up the fun. "Let's have a picnic."

"A picnic?" Nathan scoffed. "It's wet outside."

"We'll have one in the library. Any tablecloths we could use for a picnic blanket?"

"I can get that." He took off.

David tugged on her shirt. "Can I help?"

"Yes, you may. Pick out three apples and leave them on the counter. Then help Nathan spread the tablecloth over the rug."

Ten minutes later, they were seated on their makeshift picnic blanket, feasting on peanut butter and jelly sandwiches and apple slices, with the promise of Jell-O chocolate pudding as soon as it set in the fridge. They were nearly finished when the children froze, concentrated hard, then scrambled to their feet. The boys raced into the kitchen, with Naomi toddling behind them.

"Dad!"

Molly followed them more slowly and found Reverend Palmer standing in the mudroom, David clinging like a limpet to one leg, Nathan beaming while his dad tousled his hair. Naomi stood a careful distance away, nose wrinkled and head shaking in determined denial. She was not going any closer to her muck-covered father.

He laughed. "I know, missy. I need to clean up." He met Molly's gaze. "How'd it go?"

"Great. Are you hungry? We've just eaten PB&Js."

"A PB&J sounds good. Thanks."

When his sons seemed reluctant to let him go, she clapped her hands lightly. "How about pudding while your dad cleans up?"

That did the trick. The kids crowded around the family table, Naomi in her high chair. The bathroom door shut quietly.

When footsteps creaked in the hallway, the boys were out of their seats. Naomi howled to get "down." Molly cleaned the little girl's face and hands and released her from the high chair.

She made another two PB&Js, added an apple, and carried them into the library. Her heart squeezed as she took in the scene. Nathan sat on the rug at his father's feet, "reading" a picture book to his siblings. Reverend Palmer, in a fresh T-shirt and jeans, snoozed on the couch behind them.

If she ever created a list of the traits she found attractive in a man, *good father* would be high among them.

After setting the plate within his reach, she returned to the kitchen. Time to clean up. Again.

When the wall phone rang thirty minutes later, she snatched up the handset. "Hello. Palmer residence."

The person at the other end hesitated. "Is Ward there? This is Bob." He said his name as if he expected her to recognize it.

"Yes, he's here." She heard a groan from the library. The floorboards creaked. "Just a moment." She pressed the receiver to her chest.

Reverend Palmer was leaning against the doorframe to the hallway, rubbing his face. "Who is it?"

"Bob?"

He held out his hand. *Thank you,* he mouthed. "Yes, Bob, this is Ward." He listened, brow furrowed.

She rejoined the kids.

The phone made a faint ping, and he was dialing again. He had another brief conversation. She couldn't understand the words, but his tone was clear. He wasn't happy.

He stuck his head in the library and gestured her into the kitchen. "It's bad out there, Molly. I have to go back," he said softly. "I called my mother-in-law, but she can't come over tonight. Can you stay?"

"Sure. As late as you need."

"Thanks. Oh, and the water plant is compromised. So let's skip baths tonight. Naomi goes to bed around seven. The boys an hour later." He grabbed a can of Coke from the refrigerator. "I shouldn't be too late."

"Don't worry. We'll be fine."

He went out through the mudroom without telling the kids goodbye.

After the children were in bed, Molly tried to watch TV, but not much was on besides flood reports. So she wandered into the living room, browsed the sheet music on the piano, and studied the family photos on the mantel. Two were professional portraits. One of him with his wife and boys. The second of their wedding. There was also a Polaroid shot of his wife in a hospital bed holding newborn Naomi. The children had taken after their father. Thick, dark hair. Beautiful brown eyes. An attractive family.

Molly dozed in the library until the back door creaked open. When she walked into the kitchen, Reverend Palmer stood by the sink, pulling bills from his wallet.

"Sorry I'm so late," he said tiredly.

"No problem. Your kids are wonderful."

He smiled with pride as he handed over the money. "Can you come again tomorrow? I've been asked to be at the church in the morning by eight."

She didn't have to think about it, liking the idea of helping in some small way. "I'll be here by seven thirty."

"Thanks. Be careful out there."

193

Gwen returned to Richmond Monday. "Hi." She set her suitcase down with a thump. "That trip home was fun."

Molly looked up from the couch, a magazine open in her lap. "Glad you're back safely."

Fanning her face, Gwen went into the kitchen. "Were you lonely?" she called out.

"Busy, actually," Molly answered. "We don't have running water yet."

"That's too bad." She came out of the kitchen with two cans of Coke and handed one over. "I guess I haven't heard the worst of it yet. So what kept you busy?"

"The Palmer kids. I babysat them while their father volunteered."

"Oh, yeah?" Gwen perched on the edge of an armchair. "How did that go?"

"They're great. No trouble."

"And Ward?"

"He seems perpetually tired." Molly sipped her drink. "It made me happy I could do something to smooth his way."

Gwen snorted. "You and a half dozen other women at the church."

"Really?"

"It's been almost two years since Brenda passed away. The single ladies are lining up."

Molly could see how older women would be attracted to the Sean Connery vibe he had going. Serious and aloof. But over the weekend, she'd seen a different side to him. His laugh might be rare, but it was contagious. He'd listened to her with intensity, as if whatever she was saying really mattered. And she loved the way he treated his kids, especially how his face lit up when Naomi ran to him and giggled as he swung her high. That was how men should greet their daughters.

Growing up, her father had tried. Although he'd never used the words *I love you* with Molly, anytime he gave her a kiss on the top of her head, she knew he did. Still, it left her envious of three children whose father offered affection so openly.

"Do you think Reverend Palmer knows they're interested?"

Gwen nodded. "He does, and he's extraordinarily courteous about it. Are you, Molly?"

What a strange question. "*No*. I'm not interested." Or at least, she hadn't been before Gwen introduced the idea. "Why do you ask?"

"Just curious. It's unusual for you to be so chatty about a man."

"It's admiration. Nothing more." And that's the way it would stay. Until she had a real job and a salary and a life, Molly was doing fine on her own.

CHAPTER
TWENTY-SEVEN

April 1973

For the last time, Molly climbed the steps to the Palmers' bungalow.

She'd been babysitting the children steadily over the past ten months. Afternoons, weekends, nights. Whatever they needed, whenever she could fit it in. She adored them.

She adored their father, too, and that had become a problem. She had to say goodbye. Tonight.

She'd practiced her farewell speech. With graduation next month, she would be turning her attention to finding a full-time job and an apartment of her own. She'd loved being their babysitter, but it was time to move on. In her head, it was a great speech. As long as she didn't cry.

On the porch, she reached to press the doorbell, then pulled her hand away. Reverend Palmer was playing something soft and melancholy on the piano. Reflecting the way she felt.

They had developed a habit of talking at the kitchen table while she packed up the books and papers for her class assignments. They'd both been raised in farming communities, him in eastern Virginia, her in the North Carolina Piedmont. He'd always wanted to be a minister. She'd never considered computers until she'd discovered the information systems degree while mopping floors. And their tastes in music? Well, they had agreed to disagree there.

She'd loved those quiet conversations. She would miss them. She would miss *him*.

It was hard to say when she'd realized what an oversize and completely inappropriate crush she had on Ward Palmer. She blamed Gwen for initially lighting the ember and, more recently, fanning the flame. But Molly had noticed that Reverend Palmer had grown "extraordinarily courteous" with her. He *knew* how she felt and was being kind.

The front door whistled open, and the piano stopped.

"Molly, why you just standing there?" David asked.

"Making sure I don't drop my books," she improvised, stepping inside. "I have homework."

"Do you have to do it right now? I thought we could play."

"We can. I'll do my homework later."

Reverend Palmer was pulling a dark suit jacket off a coatrack. "Thanks for coming over."

She nodded without meeting his eyes.

"Molly? Is everything okay?"

"Yes, sir. I'm fine." She forced herself to smile at him.

He looked skeptical as he shrugged into the jacket. "I'll be at the hospital. It shouldn't take long."

She didn't believe it, but he believed himself. "No problem." She held out her hand to David. "What do you want to do?"

"Come see."

In the library, LEGOs, picture books, and an Etch A Sketch had been lined up on the coffee table. Her evening had been planned.

"Okay," she said, kneeling on the rug, "what's first?"

The kids had been quiet for hours, and Molly had been doing her "homework" since. She had her books and materials spread around her on the kitchen table. She hadn't completed nearly enough research for her project, and time was running out.

"Molly?"

Startled, she looked up. Reverend Palmer was resting a hip against the kitchen counter. How had he gotten there without her noticing?

"Oh, sorry." She reached for the radio and turned off American Top 40, then glanced up at the clock. After eleven. "I didn't hear you come in."

"You were deep in thought." He came closer and looked at her textbook. "Statistics?"

"Yes. For my final programming project, I have to solve a question on a real-life issue I'm genuinely curious about. It's been harder than I expected."

He slipped off his suit jacket, pulled out a chair, and sat. Just as he'd done dozens of times before. "What issue did you choose?"

Dread made her restless. She ought to tell him goodbye, not have a conversation, but she wouldn't deny herself the pleasure of one last chat. Of having him focused on her. "I chose the Equal Rights Amendment. Only thirty states have ratified, and some opponents are saying it isn't needed because enough laws already exist. I thought I'd try to find out how true that was."

"I take it you support the ERA."

She bristled. Had she finally found something about him to dislike? "You don't?"

"I didn't say that. I'm on your side."

"Which side is that?"

"The one that gives my daughter the best chance at the life she deserves."

His perfect answer defused her anger—and possibly explained why this assignment was giving her such fits. She wasn't objective enough about the problem. She ought to take a step back and think analytically.

"Why has this project been hard?" he asked.

"States don't make it easy to collect the data."

"What kind of data are you looking for?"

She rested a hand on a well-thumbed set of photocopied articles. "All states have laws that discriminate against women, some worse than others. Many won't let women have a credit card without a husband's signature. Some states let employers fire women for getting pregnant. But state governments don't exactly publicize how to find their discriminatory laws. The only thing I'm certain about for all fifty states is that it's legal for a man—" She halted. The next part was ugly. His nod encouraged her.

"It's legal in all fifty states for a man to rape his wife." She became busy gathering the loose documents, newspaper clippings, and notes scattered about the tabletop and shoved them into her bag.

"When is your project due?"

"Next week."

"Have you found anything you can report on?"

"Not much." She sighed. "I have a plan B, though. I ran some analysis on which states have ratified and which have not. Like, among the original colonies, all have ratified the ERA except the four in the South."

"That's an interesting insight." His mouth relaxed into a faint smile. "What else?"

She would have to keep looking. She had a five-thousand-word paper to write on what the experience had taught her. Half of the project grade. "So far, it's the only thing I've learned."

"Except the importance of good data."

She looked over at him. Wow. There was the missing piece. A hard lesson she would take with her into the future. She could work with that. "Perfect. Thank you."

His smile widened. It was dazzling.

As she smiled back, it hit her. The moment had come to tell him she was done. She stood abruptly, clutching her bag to her chest.

He stood too. "What's wrong, Molly?"

How would she get through her speech without breaking down? "You know I'm graduating in June. I've been looking for a full-time job, and tonight . . ." She paused, her heart pounding. "Tonight is my final babysitting job for you."

He shook his head, as if stunned. "Of course. I should've thought of that."

"So, thanks. Goodbye." She hurried out the front door.

"Molly?" He was right behind her, so close she could smell the soap on his skin.

She stopped, her hand gripping the porch railing, but didn't turn. "Yes?"

"Here," he said and handed her some cash. "Did you tell the kids?"

"No." She was a coward.

"Okay. I will." There was a heavy silence. "Will you stay in touch?"

I can't. "I'll try." Could he tell it was a fib? She continued down the steps.

"Molly."

This time, when she looked at him, his face was in the shadows. What was he thinking? Was he sorry to see the faithful babysitter go? Pitying her because he knew how she felt? "Yes, Reverend Palmer?"

He stepped out into the light and studied her, unsmiling. "We will miss you."

"Thanks." She practically ran to the car, dumped her things on the passenger seat, and drove away. No second thoughts. No looking back.

Over the next month, Molly applied to every programming position she could find. Only one had invited her for an interview, and they never called back.

Her friend Jerry was having much better luck.

The two of them had had a friendly competition going in their programming classes, constantly challenging each other to write cleaner, leaner code. They'd continued their bargain too. Despite several surgeries, his left hand would never recover full dexterity, so she typed in his programs, and he chauffeured her around.

Jerry had companies seeking him out. He'd already accepted an offer with the Department of Defense and would be moving to northern Virginia in June. He'd urged her to apply there as well, but Molly wasn't giving up on Richmond.

She kept trying for another week, but the silence was wearing her down. Every job she'd gotten since moving to Richmond had come through someone else, and she'd hoped she could find this job on her own. But she was ready to swallow her pride and ask her faculty adviser for help.

"Welcome, Molly," he said when she walked in. "What brings you to my office hours?"

"Jobs, Dr. Little. I can't find one. I thought there would be plenty of companies looking for programmers, but no one seems interested."

He picked up a fountain pen and twirled it between his fingers. "They were, until recently. The economy has begun to cool, and the supply of programmers has surpassed demand."

"Oh. I worried it might be me."

"Because you're a woman? That could make a difference. But you also have a two-year degree, and some will look down on it." He jotted a note on a pad. "Let me make some calls. I'll get back with you."

He phoned later that evening and passed along three names. She arranged interviews with all three for later that week.

After the first two, she got the feeling she would hear nothing more.

The third interview was scheduled for this afternoon. She walked from the bus stop to an old brick building. Its lobby had marble floors and gilt-framed landscapes hanging on the walls.

A middle-aged woman sat at a circular desk, tapping furiously on a typewriter. Her hands stilled as she stared over the top of her round glasses. "Yes?"

"I'm here to see Mr. Bryant."

She fluttered her lashes, punched a button on a business phone, murmured quietly, then returned the handset to its cradle.

"He'll be right out." She waved Molly to a seat and returned to typing.

Five minutes passed before a door slammed somewhere in the bowels of the building. Footsteps approached, slow and deliberate. A man appeared around a corner. Tall with dark crewcut hair, he wore navy slacks, a crisp white shirt, and a striped tie but no suit jacket. His gaze met hers expectantly. She took a nervous breath and stood.

"Miss Mitchell, I'm Harvey Bryant."

"Hello."

"Thank you for coming in. If you'll just follow me." He walked back down the hallway.

She had to hurry to catch up. They made two turns, and then he ushered her through a noisy room filled with desks. As conversations slowly died, Molly felt six pairs of eyes staring. She was relieved to see that one pair belonged to a woman.

She trailed Mr. Bryant like a duckling, across the room and into the corner office.

He closed the door behind them. "Have a seat."

She lowered herself onto the chair. Fidgeted with her purse. Crossed her legs, then uncrossed them again when the hem of the minidress she'd borrowed from Gwen slid high on her thighs.

Mr. Bryant had taken his seat behind a massive wooden desk. Behind him was a credenza with a single black-framed photo of his family. Five kids. Black-framed documents hung on the wall: his bachelor's degree, some kind of data-processing certification, and an award for employee of the year.

The top of his desk was surprisingly messy. In its center rested a pad of coding sheets with a pencil and eraser on top. Several stacks of computer printouts were scattered about. One sat precariously on the edge, some of its pages spilling onto the floor in accordion pleats. She itched to clean it up.

He reached into his inbox, extracted a manila folder, and flipped it open. Her résumé. A torn piece of stenographer paper was clipped to it. He looked up suddenly. "May I call you Molly?"

"Yes, sir."

"You've completed your degree. Only two years, but VCU has a good program. And you have some experience from a part-time job at the computing center." He leaned back in his chair. Steepled his fingers. Stared at her silently for a long minute. "Vernon Little recommends you highly. Why do you think he's so impressed?"

She'd often heard Dr. Little say that she was talented, resourceful, and smart—with an *aptitude for programming*. But those words felt too braggy. She would use something precise. "I make good grades."

"I interviewed four other candidates for this job. They all had good grades. Why are you different?"

She was irritated with herself. Humble wasn't working. If she wanted a job, she had to tell him why he needed her. "My father was the principal at our county high school. I made good grades there because I had no choice." Her hands trembled, so she clenched them together on her lap. "From my first programming class at VCU, I loved writing code. Solving problems. Finding bugs and getting rid of them. I've made excellent grades in college because I love programming."

There was a glimmer in his eyes. Of approval? She relaxed the tiniest bit.

"What other qualities do you bring me, Molly? Besides an aptitude for programming?"

She relaxed to hear Dr. Little's favorite phrase about her. "I've worked a lot of jobs, Mr. Bryant, with all types of people. Sometimes I was treated well. Sometimes not. I've learned how to get along with everybody."

He stared for a long, agonizing moment, then rose. "If you'll follow me."

After escorting her back to the lobby, he asked, "How are you getting home, Molly?"

"The bus." She glanced at her watch. It would be another thirty minutes before the next one came by.

He stopped at the receptionist's desk. "Call Miss Mitchell a taxi, please."

The woman's eyes went from him to Molly. "Sure thing."

He smiled his thanks and then held the external door for her. She stepped into the sunshine, afraid to hope.

"Do you have any questions for me?" he asked, studying the traffic flowing past.

Did she have anything to lose by being honest? Probably not, and she had something she would like to know. "Does your team work well together?"

He barked a laugh. "Well enough. That's why I appreciate it when new staff have the ability to get along with everybody."

"Oh." Her words coming from his mouth sounded kind of pompous, but he didn't seem to mind. It gave her an opening to plead her case. "Mr. Bryant, when I worked at the campus computer center, I helped other students figure out where they'd gone wrong with their programs. I'm good at fixing what's broken. If you could use that skill, please consider me."

He turned to her and smiled. "Molly, I rarely make a hire decision so quickly after an interview, but in your case, I will. If you want the job, it's yours."

Oh, wow. Happy little fireworks went off inside her. Of course she would take it. Besides being the only full-time job she'd been offered, she would like working for this man. But the income was important too. "What salary are you offering?"

"Seven thousand."

She nodded as if mulling the number over. It was more than she'd expected. "I accept."

"Excellent. I'll have Personnel call you about the paperwork. When can you start?"

College commencement was this weekend. Her parents were coming with Aunt Trudy and Walter. So no earlier than Monday. But Molly would like to have a few days off to do nothing. To just *be*. "Anytime after next Wednesday."

He smiled. "I'll suggest the day after Memorial Day."

"Thank you. That sounds perfect."

A taxi stopped and honked.

"See you soon."

After the taxi dropped her off, she rushed into the apartment, eager to tell someone her news. At four in the afternoon, Gwen wouldn't be home from the bank. Molly wouldn't call her parents. Long distance was too expensive, even for this. There was someone else she'd like to speak with in her moment of triumph, but that was silly. She hadn't seen him in weeks.

As if on cue, the phone rang. "Hello?"

"Molly, it's Ward."

Oh, how she'd missed the sound of his voice! "I was just thinking of you," she blurted. And instantly wished she could take the words back.

"Really?" He sounded pleased. "Why?"

"I got a job."

"Congratulations. Will you like it?"

She dragged the phone over to the couch and sank down, elated by her good fortune, grateful that he understood the difference in taking a job because she had to and because she wanted to. "I think I will."

"Then I'm glad for you. When do you start?"

"In two weeks." Hmm. Longer than she'd noticed. She was presently unemployed. She hadn't been without any kind of job in four years.

"Good. So, I've called with an invitation."

She refocused. "Yes?"

"The kids want to throw you a party."

A party? "What kind?"

"David's class celebrated the end of kindergarten today with cupcakes. He's decided you should celebrate the end of school too. We'd like to invite you over for dinner."

Say no. It would hurt too much to say goodbye again. "Thank you. That would be cool."

"How is Saturday?"

"I can't this weekend. My family will be here for commencement. How about the Saturday after?"

"The kids will be at my brother's farm for two weeks. Maybe we should wait until they get back. I'll call later to arrange something."

"That's fine."

The apartment door opened and closed. High heels clicked in the foyer, and her friend came in. Dressed up, painted nails, new hairdo.

"Okay. Well, Molly, it was nice to hear your voice. See you soon."

As she hung up the phone, the cushion beside her shifted. She whistled at Gwen. "Do you have a date?"

"I do. Who was that?"

Not information she wanted to share. "You first. Who with?"

Gwen blushed. "Clive."

Finally. Molly was surprised it had taken him this long to ask her out. Or maybe it had taken her friend this long to say yes. "I think he's in love with you."

"So he says."

"What?" Molly felt a bit miffed that she'd had to ask. "He's told you he loves you, and you look sad?"

Gwen flung herself against the back of the couch. "He's not thinking right. He deserves the best."

"He's found it. You *are* the best."

She made a rude sound with her lips. "And you're stalling. Who was on the phone?"

Molly would try to divert one more time. "I got a job today. Mr. Bryant hired me on the spot." Repeating that would never get old. "I start after Memorial Day."

"Congratulations! So that's what the call was about?"

"No." Might as well tell. "The Palmers invited me over to celebrate my graduation."

"Oh?" Gwen shimmied.

"Stop."

"I'll bet he asks you out."

Ward Palmer could never date someone like her. "I doubt he's interested in me that way."

"I think he might be." Gwen sighed. Sobered. "Although asking you out would be brave."

"Because I used to be the babysitter?"

"Partly, but you're also nine years younger than he is. There will be some at church who don't approve, and they might raise a stink about it."

The possibility was purely hypothetical, but Molly was still curious. "What could happen to him?"

"If they approach the senior minister, nothing. Bob will set them straight in his uniquely kind way. But there are others who might try to escalate things. I'm not saying it's likely. Just be aware."

"What if our secret got out?"

"The few people who know won't say anything. If anyone did out you, they'd be outing me, and then they'd have Frank to deal with. But I won't lie. It would be worse for you, and by association, Ward."

The doorbell rang, and Gwen jumped to her feet. "Clive's here."

"And he loves you."

"Right." She grabbed her purse and hurried to the door. She spoke with him softly, intimately. And then the door closed.

Molly went to the window, watched as Clive opened her friend's car door and helped her in as if she were the most precious woman in the world. They would be wonderful together, if Gwen would allow it.

But Molly understood her friend's concern. Molly would never risk harming Reverend Palmer. Should she cancel the party?

No, the kids likely knew she'd accepted. She wouldn't hurt them by backing out. They deserved the chance to say goodbye to her. She would go, and that would be the end.

CHAPTER
TWENTY-EIGHT

Bree returned from Galen's house, wired from coffee and curiosity, on fire to learn more. She stayed up far too late, poring over the remaining documents in Granna's suitcase.

First up, a bank statement from May 1969. It had a yellowed envelope paper clipped to it, with *Everett* written in Granna's elegant handwriting. Bree opened the envelope gingerly and found two canceled checks. Both were made out to the Eastern Carolina Home for Mothers and Babies. Both had been signed by Marvin Harper. The first had been written for $200 on December 6, 1968. The second was dated April 7, 1969, for $1,000.

Twelve hundred dollars to the maternity home? In today's dollars, the total was more than ten thousand. Had her grandparents *bought* Dad?

Surely they'd known he was a twin.

Bree found the answer moments later in a letter from the director of the maternity home, dated April 1, 1969. The day after the twins were born. With shaking hands, Bree drew out a single sheet of paper. The first three paragraphs were smug fluff. The final two paragraphs read:

> As you're aware, adoptive parents are expected to cover
> the hospital costs for their babies. We anticipate that

the girl will require more hospital care than the boy, fees which we will, naturally, pass along.

Let us know how you wish to proceed.

Sincerely,

Pearl Lloyd

Her grandparents had knowingly participated in separating the twins. They'd chosen the boy and left the girl behind for someone else. How could her grandparents have thought there was anything remotely acceptable about what they had done?

The knowledge made her ill. She collapsed against the pillows of her bed and cried, hot tears sliding down her cheeks. Her beloved grandmother—a woman respected by the whole community, who became a stand-in mom when Bree's own mother moved away—had made a terrible choice.

It was an ugly story, full of pain and injustice. For all she hated the lifelong lie, she was glad she hadn't known until now.

Bree arrived at the shop early Friday but couldn't stay focused on work. She was consumed with wanting to understand what Molly had experienced fifty-five years ago as an unwed mother. How she was treated. What the adoption laws had been like.

An online search had an overwhelming number of hits. She would get back to them another time. A research library in Raleigh had caught her attention. They had items that could only be viewed in person. She emailed the library with questions and crossed her fingers that she would be able to access materials as a walk-in.

As soon as Lola showed up, Bree pounced. "Would you mind watching the shop for a few hours?"

"I would love to. Take the whole day. I'll call if I need anything." Lola's expression clearly promised, *which I won't*.

When Bree reached the research library, the librarian had resources pulled for her. She flipped open a folder filled with loose clippings. On top was a newspaper column from the eighties, featuring a birth mother who'd regretted her decision to surrender almost immediately but after the deadline to revoke. The woman had spent years trying to find her child, even hiring a private investigator. The hunt had paid off. Her story had a happy ending.

Bree got sucked in by other documents, absorbing as much as she could about the context of the time Galen and Molly had lived in. A world where the pressure on unwed mothers to surrender their babies had been at its peak.

Had Molly believed she had no choice? That giving up her children had been a foregone conclusion?

Another clipping caught her eye. In February 1970, a maternity home had been investigated for "improprieties" in the adoption practices used with their clients. "The director could not be reached for comment."

Four months later, a second clipping claimed that more evidence had surfaced of "unethical adoption procedures by the maternity home and their attorney." Rules weren't being followed. Adoptive parents were paying high fees, akin to purchasing babies. The home would no longer operate in North Carolina. And the home's name? Eastern Carolina Home for Mothers and Babies.

Her father's adoption had been managed by an entity that was dissolved a year later.

Bree left Raleigh with more questions raised than answered.

Take the whole day.

Yes, she would. She would be worthless until she knew more. Bree diverted to her apartment, surrounded herself with junk food, and continued her research.

The fees associated with Molly's maternity home hadn't been outliers. In the 1960s, babies had been commodities, with white females, especially blue-eyed blondes, in highest demand.

Did that explain what happened to Heather? The maternity home had expected a premium, and Bree's grandparents had been unable to pay?

There were many references to adoption registries, a way for adoptees and birth families to reunite. Bree couldn't get into the state-run registry, but some of the others were wide open. She typed in Dad's birth date and birth state and got a hit on the second registry.

Birth name: Baby boy Mitchell

Birthplace: Collier, NC

Date of birth: March 31, 1969

Date of relinquishment: April 2, 1969

Date of entry: March 31, 1987

And the birth mother's name? *Molly Mitchell Palmer.* Molly had been waiting thirty-seven years to hear from a son who hadn't known to look.

Did Heather have a record too? Bree did another search. A second record popped up.

Birth name: Baby girl Mitchell

Birthplace: Collier, NC

Date of birth: March 31, 1969

Date of relinquishment: April 27, 1969

Date of entry: March 31, 1987

What exactly was a *date of relinquishment*? When the birth mother consented to the adoption? Or when the child was handed over? Whatever it meant, Heather had been relinquished three weeks after Dad.

What a tragic word—*relinquished*.

Bree closed the lid of the laptop. So many complications. Missed chances. Her heart ached.

She had to find something else to do, something that wasn't sad. Small, discrete tasks that she could cross off a list, like unpacking cartons. Checking inventory. Writing newsletter content. Anything would be better than wallowing in the emotional upheaval surrounding her family.

She walked to the shop. A brown delivery truck was parked by the alley door. Kai came through it and headed for the driver's seat.

"Hi," she called.

"Hi." He leaned out of his truck. "Taking a day off when the shop is open?"

"Hard to believe, I know."

"Has that ever happened before?"

She didn't even have to think. "No."

"Hope it was fun." With a wave and a smile, he drove off.

Was she really such an obvious workaholic that acquaintances noticed?

She tapped in the key code and yanked the door open. Several cartons were stacked inside. Yay. The ideal distraction.

She had immersed herself so completely in the tedium of running a store that, when her shop clerk appeared, she jerked in surprise.

"Bree, do you need my help getting ready for tonight's class?"

A class *tonight*? She glanced at the wall calendar, and, sure enough, there was a class scheduled. She'd forgotten. Smoothing the panic from her face, she turned to Lola. "That would be great. Thanks."

"How many?"

"Attendees? Probably eight. I'm sure it sold out." Bree couldn't remember which one it was. She logged in to the event calendar on her laptop, scrambling to find the details.

She'd never been quite sure whether the success of her classes was a joy or a curse.

Last fall, as the grand opening of her shop had approached, she'd been hanging out with Allison one night, brainstorming ideas for drawing customers in. When Bree mused aloud about teaching a series of writing classes, Allison had been inspired to add an event calendar to Write Style's website. Initially, Bree had been delighted, until she learned the calendar had been preloaded with *all* the brainstormed classes. Before she could take it down, people had signed up.

Those writing classes had become some of the most low-overhead, high-profit elements of her business. They also created a monster of expectations and became the primary source of her workaholism.

Tonight's event was Extra-Special Occasion Cards, a concept suggested by previous attendees. *Congratulations on Your Divorce. You're Invited to My Fur-Baby Shower. It's a Party Just Because.* There was always plenty of laughter and creativity at the Extra-Special classes, and she loved them usually. But not tonight. Her mind wasn't sharp.

"Lola, we have seven coming." One had canceled, and it was too late to contact anyone from the wait list. "If you can set up the conversation area, I'll bring out the folding tables."

"Shall I grab the supply box?"

At least that was ready. Bree had organized the supplies last week. *Before* the revelation. "Yes."

Lola patted her shoulder. "Don't worry. We'll get this done."

The class ended by eight thirty. A triumph despite the frantic prep time. As Bree put away the tables, Lola shelved the leftover supplies.

"You saved me, Lola. Thank you."

"I enjoyed it." She leaned against the doorframe. "Bree, would you consider allowing me to expand my role in the shop? I'm confident I could add value."

A week ago, Bree would have bristled with reluctance. Today, she wanted to hear more. "What did you have in mind?"

"For starters, let me help with the classes. Turn the setup details over to me, so you can focus on teaching."

That sounded amazing, but . . . "I can't afford a full-time person."

"I don't need benefits. I just need something to look forward to." Lola's eyes lit up. "I love this job. I'd like to have more of it to look forward to."

Bree had a prickly, breathless feeling, like something unknown lay just around the bend. But instead of being worried, she was excited. "You said for starters. Any other ideas?"

"Plenty." Lola moved her fingers, as if unconsciously ticking off a checklist. "What are your least favorite tasks? Let me do them so you can focus on the things you love. Take more time off. Pick a day or a morning each week and let me handle it. You arrive when you want. Or not at all." She glowed with the enthusiasm of the MBA graduate who was ready to resume her career after raising her children. "I recommend that you charge more for rush orders. Too many people choose it, and it takes a lot out of you. Make 'em pay."

Everything Lola had said sounded tempting. Would Bree really be able to take more time off? She wasn't sure if she'd be able to relax and not worry about everything falling apart without her active participation.

Slow. Down. She wasn't committing to anything yet. "Do you have a formal proposal?"

"I could."

"Please submit it."

Lola beamed. "Thank you."

But after Lola left, Bree had a moment of anxiety. Yes, it was awful to juggle so many tasks that she couldn't recover from mistakes, and she'd loved having an unplanned day off. But labor costs would go up, with no guarantee that revenue would too. She'd also secretly harbored a goal to repay her investors early. Increasing Lola's hours meant she'd have to push out the *pay back fast* goal. But making changes was doable. All she had to do was step off the hamster wheel and yield some control.

Why did she feel like she had something to prove?

Allison had always been the capable one, gliding through life, sleek and calm, doing everything so darn correctly. And Bree had been the goof-up, distracted by shiny things and leaving messes in her wake.

Write Style was going well, and she wanted the victory to be completely hers. When had that become so important?

CHAPTER
TWENTY-NINE

Allison checked her messages as she left the office building Friday and halted in her tracks. Perry had texted her with an urgent request for help. He had a date, and the babysitter backed out at the last minute. Could she fill in?

Why, yes, she could.

On my way. Be there in 20

She hummed, literally, with anticipation as she drove to Raleigh. She loved having Liam stay over. It didn't happen often enough. She was mentally cataloging what she had available for snacks. They should meet with a kindergartner's approval.

When she parked on the street before their town house, her brother and nephew were waiting on the stoop.

Liam bounced to his feet. "Hi, Aunt Alli. Dad says I get to have a sleepover at the cabin."

"You do." She added an "oof" when her brother gave her a bear hug.

Liam was already running to her car, dragging his backpack.

As she and Perry followed, he said, "Thanks, Alli."

"I love having him." She gestured at his crisp blue shirt and white pants. "You're dressed up. Is this a promising date?"

"Very."

A good sign. The breakup of his marriage had left him messed up long enough.

Liam was in his car seat when they reached her Camry. "Can we have pancakes for breakfast, Aunt Alli?"

"You're going to Nana and Papa's in the morning. You'll have to ask them."

"Yay." Liam knew it was a done deal.

"If you're on your best behavior," Perry added.

"I always am." They fist-bumped, and Perry shut the door.

Next stop, the cabin, where spoiling her nephew commenced. The schedule for Friday night included two Disney+ movies and popcorn. Otis handled most of the heavy lifting with entertaining the five-year-old during intermissions.

After dropping Liam off at her parents' in the morning, Allison headed to the pool for her Water Tots class. Teaching babies had been something she'd stumbled into by a lucky accident. After giving her nephew a private swim lesson last summer, a staff member at the aquatic center had approached her, curious to know if she would be interested in teaching kids. She'd agreed, pursued certification, and discovered that she liked teaching infants most. They were so brave and eager and happy, reminding her of how much she loved the simple joy of gliding fearlessly through the water.

After she returned home from the pool, even though she'd promised herself not to get online, she was sucked in by yet another virtual etiquette lesson.

Communication is more than saying the right words. The right tone and attitude are essential.

It was an uncomfortable concept for her. Words had always been her focus. How to present them? She'd never thought much about the delivery of a message. But as she continued through the lesson, one of the exercises drew on something she'd observed while teaching her swim classes. Even before babies understood spoken language, they could respond to tone and attitude.

Embrace what resonates.

There it was. The light-bulb moment. The lesson that made all the others click into place.

What she would have to do to embrace this change hovered at the periphery of her understanding. Too big to handle. She could feel herself shutting down.

Okay, done for today.

Maybe she should try something physical instead. Like weeding. The vegetable garden or flower beds?

The latter. The front flower beds were in the shade.

After an hour of yanking out weeds and raking mulch around, she was showered, changed, and drinking something cold when she heard gravel popping. She looked out the front window and saw her mother's Honda creeping up the driveway.

It was unusual for Mom to come over unannounced. Also welcome. Allison went out through the carport. "Hi, Mom. Where's Liam?"

"Perry picked him up after lunch. Which was way too early."

She'd get no argument from Allison.

Inside, her mother went into the living room while Allison stopped in the kitchen. "Would you like something to drink? I have coffee, tea, and water."

"Water would be nice." Her mother sat in an armchair and promptly had a lapful of cat.

Allison set a glass of ice water near her mother and dropped sideways onto the couch.

Mom was staring determinedly out the window as she petted Otis. "I'm torn about what to do. I've worked so hard to avoid thinking about the woman who gave me up, and I won't be able to anymore." She wrinkled her nose. "It's odd that I never considered the man. I knew he had to exist, obviously, but there was no guarantee he was aware he'd fathered a child. I find myself needing to understand the full story. Whatever it is, it will hurt."

Allison remained silent. Mom would fill the silence if she wanted to. A minute passed before she spoke again. "That woman has always been more of an amorphous shape than an actual person to me. It's how I've had to handle it. No features. No personality. If she was a horrible person, I didn't want to know. If she was an amazing woman, I didn't want to know. I preferred for her to be nothing other than someone to blame for . . ." Mom bit her lip. "Blame for what? I had two wonderful parents. A healthy, happy home. Why should I find fault with the person who made that possible?

"On my eighteenth birthday, I remember waking up, wondering about the mother who had carried me for nine months and let me go. Teen-me had so many questions. How old was she when I was born? Fifteen? Twenty-five? What kind of life did she have that pushed her into that decision? If she even *was* pushed.

"I spent my whole birthday stewing over it. What would Teen-Heather do if she discovered she was pregnant? The answer was easy. I knew I would want to keep my baby. I was also grateful it was a decision I wouldn't have to make at eighteen."

Allison didn't want to stop her mother's flow of thoughts, but she felt the need to defend Molly. Provide some context, if only a little. "Mom, when you were born, eighty percent of unwed mothers like Molly relinquished their babies. By the time you were eighteen, the surrender rate for unwed mothers had dropped to two percent."

"Eighty percent," Mom echoed. "I didn't realize it was that high." She frowned out the window at the sunshine. When Otis batted her motionless hand, reminding her of her responsibilities, she resumed petting him. "Why did Everett and I have different types of adoptions?"

"I don't know. We'll have to ask Molly." It was time to feel out Mom about making the first connection. "She's open to contact."

Mom's expression soured. "So I hear, and I'm not."

Well, okay. Allison would tell Everett. Which raised another thought. "Would you like to meet with your brother?"

Mom nodded slowly.

"Do you want me to set it up?"

"Yes, but not today. I need time to prepare."

Of course. Baby steps. "Tomorrow?"

"That should work." Mom pushed out of the chair, laid Otis gently on the couch, and left.

Allison wouldn't give her mother time to change her mind. She texted Bree.

Mom wants to meet with Everett

I'll ask him. When?

Tomorrow?

Okay. Somewhere public?

Yes

Thirty minutes passed before there was a response.

Sunday at 3, town park

Should be fine. I'll let you know if it isn't

Bree was typing.

Should we go?

If it's okay with them. For the intro

Good plan

When Allison drove into the town park Sunday afternoon, she didn't see her mother's Honda, but Bree and Everett were there, waiting under a picnic shelter. Everett was half sitting on a table, head bowed, arms crossed, listening to whatever Bree was saying.

Allison got out of her car and walked over. She exchanged a smile with Bree, discouraged by the lack of a greeting. At least they were in the same physical location with no discernible negative emotion.

Everett had straightened. "Heather's not here yet," he said, stating the obvious.

"My mother tends to embrace the late side of punctual."

"Fair enough." His grin faded. "Bree discovered that I'm listed on an adoption registry. The entry was made on my eighteenth birthday."

"What?" Allison gaped at her friend.

"Sorry." Bree looked guilty. "I was planning to tell you. Heather's on there too."

How could that have happened? Allison had been checking registries for years and never found anything. Which Bree knew. "Wow."

Everett looked pained. "The birth mother has been waiting a long time for something I didn't know to do. Any updates on her?"

Allison didn't want to imagine how sad it must be to wait and hope for contact, assuming the worst, not understanding the real reason for the silence. Or how Molly would feel if she knew they still referred to her as *the birth mother* instead of by her name. "I've exchanged messages with her contact person on Ancestry. Gwen says that Molly will only respond to you or Mom." She sent him a hopeful smile. "And it won't be Mom."

"I'll do it."

"Really, Dad?" Bree stared wide eyed at him.

"Yeah. Not sure when, but I will."

Good. Allison was ready to make progress. "I'll send Gwen's contact info to you."

Her mother's Honda pulled into the lot and raced toward their corner. She parked, shut off the engine, and then nothing.

"I'll be right back," Allison said before jogging over to her mother's car.

Mom got out and pocketed her keys. "Hi." She licked her lips. "I'm not sure I'm ready for this."

"We can reschedule."

She squared her shoulders. "No, I've known Everett Harper for twenty-five years. It's not him I'm worried about." She touched her daughter's arm lightly. "Okay, let's do it."

Allison held her breath as Mom and Everett looked at each other, standing a few feet apart. How had she never seen the similarities? Same golden-brown hair and those pretty golden-brown eyes. Everett was taller. Her mother was curvier. But they definitely looked like siblings.

Her mouth went dry. The twins, so alike and yet so distant, weren't moving. Just staring. Was this meeting too soon? Should she step in?

Brother and sister spoke in unison.

"Hi, Everett."

"Hi, Heather."

They laughed nervously. Smiled. Laughed again more naturally.

"You first," he said.

"No, you. It seems like you have an idea about what to do next, and I certainly don't."

"A walk on the nature trail?"

"I'd like that."

They strolled to the trailhead, staying even with each other but with as much space between them as the path allowed.

"I never noticed," Bree said in a hushed voice. "Their resemblance."

"Me neither. We weren't looking for it."

They returned to their cars.

"You found entries in a registry." Allison's delivery had too much accusation in her tone. She had to take it down a notch.

"Yes, Friday night. *Three* registries. I'm sorry I forgot to tell you." Bree scrolled on her phone. Tapped it. "There. I've sent you a screenshot."

Allison skimmed the entry. Molly's married name was Palmer. And . . . whoa. "Your dad's birthday is March thirty-first?"

"Yes. Isn't that your mom's?"

Allison shook her head. "Mom's birth certificate has it recorded as April sixth."

"They couldn't have been born a week apart."

"They weren't. It just means the doctor who handled Mom's adoption didn't know her actual birth date, so he made an educated guess."

"A whole week off?"

"Twins are often born early. They could've been preemies."

"They were." Bree's smile was apologetic. "Galen told me that."

"Sounds like we ought to compare notes." Another day, though. Allison's mind was hung up on something Everett had said. "If Molly sent data to the registry on their eighteenth birthday, she's been looking for her children for nearly forty years. That's . . ."

"Tragic."

"Yeah." How awful the wait must have been. She blinked against the moisture in her eyes.

"Allison, I didn't keep this from you intentionally. I just got so excited about their meeting."

"It's okay." Not really, but she needed this conversation to end. She didn't have enough energy to manage recriminations in either direction. "Bye."

When she got home, she checked her slow cooker. The roast chicken was almost done. She poured a glass of tea and opened her laptop to hunt information on *Molly Palmer*. It was a popular name. She narrowed the parameters.

An alert from Ancestry distracted her. A new cousin had responded to her message.

> You and I are a shared match through my great-aunt Molly.
> Would you like a call?

She responded yes and included her phone number.

The phone rang minutes later. "Hello, Arnie here. My grandfather was Aunt Molly's brother."

"I'm Molly's granddaughter."

"Huh. No one ever said anything. She's always been a bit of a black sheep. When I was a kid, she lived in Richmond, but the distance seemed like more than miles. Molly acted like she'd escaped. And didn't know quite what to do with the rest of us."

Richmond fit with what Allison knew about Gwen Reeves. It still didn't explain why Molly was there, although Arnie had used *escaped*. But escaped from what? "Is that where she lives now?"

"No, she and her husband moved to Durham in the eighties."

Durham? That bit of information gave Allison chills. "Is her husband still alive?"

"As far as I know. Ward Palmer. He's a retired minister."

"A minister?"

"Yes. Celebrated their fiftieth anniversary last November. My uncle Walt, her favorite nephew, went to the party."

Relatives everywhere. "Do you have a family tree you can share?"

"I do, but without her permission, I won't make it public."

Reasonable. She thanked him, ended the call, and returned to search for her grandmother, armed with new data that would make it easier. And there she was. Molly Mitchell Palmer. Currently living in Durham, North Carolina. She'd been no more than twenty miles away for over thirty years.

Her husband was the Rev. Dr. Ward Palmer, a retired professor from the divinity school at Duke *and* a retired Presbyterian minister. His bio mentioned two sons, a daughter, and numerous grandchildren.

Molly had children.

There were hundreds of links, the top being Molly's website. It was Spartan. Easy to use. White text against a dark background. The bio page had nothing about her origins, although it did say she'd graduated from VCU in 1973.

Allison stared at her grandmother's photo in surprise. She recognized this Molly Palmer. Was familiar with her reputation as a software engineer.

Her grandmother had been a popular speaker, an author, and an early advocate of computer accessibility. Allison had attended a conference in Chicago once and heard Molly speak.

Someone Allison had admired from a distance was her grandmother. She closed her eyes, relaxing into memories of that trip. Molly's presentation had been useful and inspiring. Her enthusiasm for accessibility had been infectious. Allison had bought one of her books, although she hadn't waited in line to have it signed.

She'd almost met her grandmother.

Allison checked more links. Molly's Wikipedia page. Her author bio at her publishing house. A review of her latest book. Allison mentally spliced together what she'd learned from Galen with what was available online. What a complex person Molly was. A woman who'd planned to be a teacher and ended up a female pioneer in the software industry. A "wayward girl" from the sixties who had married a minister. How had *that* happened?

CHAPTER THIRTY

July 1973

After a month at her new job, Molly had reached several conclusions.

She loved the paycheck. It was nice to have money to spend without considering every penny. She was feeling secure enough to look for her own place to live.

Writing code for real customers with real problems was a blast. Much more satisfying than homework assignments.

College had spoiled her for working around women. Nearly 40 percent of information systems majors at VCU had been female. Molly could walk into a classroom and not feel like she was sticking out. Here, only two women were on the team of eight. She felt the difference keenly. The office environment was odd. Her male coworkers weren't hostile, exactly. More dismissive. When projects got tough, they welcomed her. When everything was smooth sailing or it was time to claim credit, they shooed her back into her corner.

Fortunately, she didn't worry about what her boss knew. She met with Harvey weekly for guidance, and it was clear he was aware of who was doing what. Still, it rankled that "the girls" were ignored until there were messes to clean up.

Arlene, the other female programmer, was the bright spot. At the end of Molly's first week, Arlene had invited her out for an early lunch. While they waited for their orders, the older woman filled her in.

"Don't let the way they treat us get to you. They aren't too bad. Harvey keeps 'em in line." She sipped a Sugar Free Dr Pepper. "We're lucky here. I had to quit my old job. Got tired of having my ass grabbed and pouring coffee for jerks who couldn't program their way out of a paper bag."

Aren't too bad wasn't exactly a compliment. "They have us sitting in the back of the room."

"Yeah, they do, but the joke's on them. We're by the windows. We get to see trees. They only get to see each other. Who's the winner there?" Arlene had grinned.

Arlene hadn't shied away from sharing personal details either. She was in her thirties and wanted children, but despite years of trying, it hadn't happened. She was also a policeman's wife and spent many nights alone and afraid.

Molly revealed the details of her past more slowly—with one secret she would never tell—but it wasn't long before she and Arlene became good friends.

Another man appeared in Molly's life the following Monday, a most unwelcome addition. He swaggered into the office and set an expensive leather briefcase on an empty desk in the row in front of the ladies' corner. He winked at them over his shoulder, tipped an imaginary hat, and sauntered into Harvey's office.

"Oh, Lordy," Arlene muttered. "That one's going to be trouble."

"Who is he?"

"The new programmer."

"I didn't know we had any openings."

"We didn't." Arlene knocked a pencil off her desk and leaned over to pick it up, her face hidden so no one could see or hear her. "His father plays golf with the general manager," she whispered. "He created a position for the son."

"How do you know that?" Molly whispered back.

"I have spies in the personnel office." Arlene straightened and scowled at her pencil in mock surprise. "Bummer. I broke the lead." She pushed up from her desk and crossed to the electric pencil sharpener.

Molly hid a smile as she bent her head over her statistics textbook. A customer had requested a new statistic, and it had fallen to her to program the calculation.

"Hey, babe."

She froze. A pair of manicured hands gripped the edge of her desk. Musky cologne descended on her in a cloud. She tried not to inhale.

"Hey," he repeated.

She looked up. "What?"

His gaze traveled from her left hand to her breasts to her face. "I'm Rudolph. My friends call me Rudy."

She returned her attention to the textbook.

"That's your cue to tell me your name, babe."

"No, that's my cue to leave." She rose, her chair screeching against the floor, and left.

Arlene, who'd been watching from the pencil sharpener, joined her as they headed for the women's bathroom on the third floor. Once inside, Arlene threw the lock and leaned against the wall, doubling over with laughter.

Molly went to the sink. With shaking hands, she splashed water on her face.

Her friend's reflection appeared beside hers in the mirror. She bobby-pinned a stray lock of bottle-blond hair. "You were fantastic in there."

"It still worries me."

"Yeah, it should." Arlene sounded grave. "Let's stick together. It might be the only way to beat him."

◆ ◆ ◆

Molly avoided direct interaction with Rudy for the next two days, but her luck ran out Thursday.

A pad of coding sheets slammed onto the corner of her desk. "Could you punch these for me?"

She didn't bother to look up. "No."

He waited a moment before saying, "Why not?"

She peered at him through her bangs, then down again. "Sorry, that isn't my job."

"What is your job?"

Ignoring him, she circled another bad number on a report with her red pencil.

"You punch cards for Chester."

He wasn't leaving until she was clear. She held his gaze. "Chester has his wrist in a cast. Is anything of yours broken?"

The room erupted in laughter.

Rudy's eyes narrowed to slits. "Do you know who I am?"

"No, and I don't care."

He groped behind himself for a chair. Sat. Spun around.

She released a breath. She didn't like being on his bad side. She didn't like being on any side of him.

Arlene's pen hit the floor. "He's trying to get your attention," she whispered.

"Oh, he has, but not in a good way."

"So true." Arlene waggled her eyebrows, then sobered fast. "Seriously, though, you'd better watch it with that one. You've become enemies. Someday, he's gonna make you pay."

The day of her graduation party at the Palmers' finally arrived, and she was looking forward to seeing the children. Naomi, so full of joy and trust. David, a handful and a half but oh so charming about it. Nathan, the backup parent and protector of his brother and sister.

And their father? Molly missed so much about him. His devotion to his children. How well he paid attention. The way he could walk into a room and suddenly everything was okay. No, her crush hadn't budged.

As soon as she stepped onto the porch, the door swung open.

"You're here," David said matter-of-factly and waved her in.

"Hi," she said.

He flung his arms around her hips. "It's been too long."

She stifled a laugh and rubbed his back. "I've missed you too."

"Mo," Naomi shouted as she raced down the hall.

Molly gave the girl a hug and took her hand. "Let's go eat."

In the kitchen, everything looked ready. Reverend Palmer stood at the stove, taking hot dogs out of a pot with tongs. Nathan stood soldier straight beside the table. It was nicely set, complete with a vase of red roses in full bloom.

"Wow, this looks great."

He came over to her and silently offered an index card.

Menu
1. Hot dogs
2. Macaroni and cheese
3. Strawberry Jell-O
4. Green beans

"The menu sounds fab," she said. "And what nice handwriting you have, Nathan."

"Would you like to sit? Everything is ready." He pulled out a chair.

"Thank you."

They held hands during the blessing, then pandemonium reigned as they filled their plates. Nathan watched her with big eyes as she served herself Jell-O. Had he helped to make it?

She took a bite. "This is yummy."

Nathan nodded and reached for his hot dog.

David tugged on her sleeve. "Will you still babysit us?"

"Not anymore," she said, proud of her breezy tone. "I have an adult job."

David's lower lip trembled. "Will we ever see you again?"

She glanced at Reverend Palmer, felt his interest in her answer. She smiled at David. "Of course you will. I'll always be your friend." Before she thought the next part through, she said, "Why don't I leave my phone number on the fridge? You can call me for emergencies."

"Good idea." He picked up his hot dog.

After the meal ended, Molly went with Naomi to her room and got her into her pajamas. Molly read as many books as it took for the little girl to droop. David had crept in to listen. She was pretty sure he'd fallen asleep first. After dropping a sheet over Naomi and sliding a pillow under David's head, she left.

Nathan was sitting in the living room, a lamp on beside him. She crossed to him. "Thanks for helping with dinner."

He lowered his book. "You're welcome."

"Okay. Well, bye, Nathan."

"Molly, do you promise you'll be back?"

"Promise. Friends, remember?"

Nodding, he raised his book, but his eyes stayed on her.

She had to go. Hurrying into the kitchen, she grabbed her purse. "Thank you, Reverend Palmer. It was lovely."

He stood in her path. "Excuse me," she said and went around him into the mudroom.

"Molly, wait." He'd followed her.

She froze.

He pulled the kitchen door shut with a click. "Don't leave us. Please."

She turned and there he was, so close, alone with her in this small room. "Why?"

"We miss you." His voice deepened. "*I* miss you. I'm not ready for us to be over."

She met his gaze. Didn't ever want to look away. Hoped she understood him right. "What are you asking?"

"Would you . . . ?" He crossed his arms. Scowled at his feet. "This is not the way I intended for this conversation to happen."

"About what?"

He looked back up. "Would you go on a date with me?" he asked in a rush.

Tears pricked her eyes. She was happier in that moment than she could have ever imagined being. Not after believing for so long that the terrible mistakes in her past disqualified her from joy. "I can't."

He flinched. "I'm sorry. I must've misread—"

"No, you didn't misread. It's just . . . you don't know me."

The corners of his lips curved up. "I sincerely hope not. I look forward to learning."

She shook her head firmly. She hadn't intended to give him hope, but they couldn't have a future together. "We're not right for each other."

"Why? Is it because I'm too old for you?"

"You're not too old, Ward. You're perfect."

He shuddered with relief. "Then what's wrong?"

"*I* am wrong. I have a secret." More than anything, this man was what she wanted and what she should never have, but she owed him the truth. "Four years ago, when Gwen told you about her stay in North Carolina, she mentioned her roommate, Eve."

He nodded, eyes narrowing.

"I'm Eve." She braced for rejection. Disgust. *Something.* But his expression remained calm. "Do you understand who I mean?"

"Yes."

"You're not surprised?"

"No."

What? She could hardly take it in. He'd known? All this time? "Gwen told you?"

"She didn't have to. I suspected. It didn't take long to realize that the two roommates she spoke of with such admiration had to be the same person."

Molly swayed with anguish. What had he been thinking? "You let me take care of your children."

"Of course I did. They adore you."

"You could have been in terrible trouble." And it would have been because of her. "I'm not worth it."

"Oh, Molly. You're worth so much more."

He closed the gap between them. Gently rested his hands on her shoulders. She leaned into him and, just for a moment, allowed herself to dream about being part of his life. Sighed as his hands slipped from her shoulders to her waist, pulling her close. She loved this man.

Love isn't enough.

He deserved someone whose secrets wouldn't poison his career. "What if someone finds out?"

"I'll remind them the Lord doesn't need our help judging others. *Molly.*" When she looked up, he was smiling, his eyes hopeful. "Please. Let me decide what's right for me."

He'd found the perfect words. She'd hated when others had made decisions for her. That she'd gone along with them would be her lifelong regret. She wouldn't do the same to Ward. "Yes."

"Yes."

When his arms tightened around her, she yielded to the safety of his embrace. And maybe it was wishful thinking, but she thought she heard him murmur, "Don't ever leave me again."

On the Saturday after Thanksgiving, Molly waited in the narthex at the back of the church, wearing the prettiest dress she'd ever owned. Across the room, David and Naomi were dancing around in their wedding finery, while Nathan tried to maintain order.

Mama was fussing with Molly's dress, tugging at the seams, brushing the shoulders. "I wish you would wear a veil."

She smiled and said nothing. They'd been over this. Mama and Daddy had been faintly scandalized by her nontraditional choices. Wearing an ice-blue cocktail dress rather than a formal wedding gown. The only flowers were matching circlets for her and Naomi to wear on their hair. And Molly would be escorted down the aisle by her children. It might have seemed odd to her parents, but she'd eventually persuaded them that this wedding was the right one for the Palmers.

She and Ward weren't simply marrying each other. They were creating a family.

Once the pipe organ played the processional, the first three couples to walk in were Brenda's parents, then Ward's, then Molly's. Nathan went next. The best man, he claimed. Too old to be the ring bearer. And finally, Molly holding hands with Naomi and David.

Only family and close friends had been invited. Arlene and Charlie. The newly engaged Gwen and Clive with the Abernathys. Aunt Trudy and Walt. Ward's brothers and their families. His childhood best friend. Every person who had come to share this moment with them mattered.

And then all else was forgotten when Molly saw her groom. Knowing Ward awaited her at the altar gave her such peace and hope. His smile, the intensity in his eyes were hers for a lifetime.

Vaguely, she heard the senior minister lead them through their vows. She gave Ward a plain gold wedding band and accepted one in return.

"You may kiss the bride."

Molly gathered her three children close and smiled with delight as they each kissed their new mom. And then she was in the arms of the man she loved, sharing their first kiss as husband and wife.

CHAPTER THIRTY-ONE

With a flourish, Bree pressed "Submit" for two major updates to her website. The care-package product data was going live, and her July newsletter was scheduled to publish after Independence Day. She celebrated with a Double Stuf Oreo.

The staff-only door opened. "Bree?" her afternoon clerk called.

She brushed cookie crumbs into her hand. "Yes?"

"There's a customer who would like to speak with you."

"Be right there." She closed the lid of her laptop and went out to the showroom. Hovering over the colored-pencil display was a woman holding a toddler on her hip. Two older children waited near the door.

"Hi, I'm Bree Harper. How may I help you?"

"Are you the one who teaches writing classes?"

"Yes."

"I have a request." She looked over her shoulder at the two older kids. "I'm in the local homeschooling group. Our leader says you taught a class for them on how to write thank-you notes."

"I did, and it was a pleasure." The kids had been great, and she'd been able to schedule during the day.

"We were wondering if you would consider teaching a class on reading cursive."

"*Reading* cursive?"

The woman nodded. "It's no longer being taught in public schools. Homeschools still teach writing in cursive, but we're finding it harder to get kids engaged in reading it. We were hoping that you might have ideas for piquing their curiosity. Making it appear to be a desirable skill rather than a pain."

Bree received lots of suggestions for classes, most of which she ignored. Either they didn't appeal or she couldn't bear the thought of adding another class to the schedule. But this idea intrigued her. "What age are the students?"

"Middle and high school."

With all the work she'd been doing with Granna's letters and other documents, she couldn't imagine being unable to read them and thereby missing out on the information they held. She felt a buzz of interest. Helping teens access that type of content? Definitely worth considering. She'd have to think about techniques she used to decipher handwriting that was less legible. Turn the lessons into a treasure hunt of sorts. A worthy challenge. "I'll consider it. Did you have a time frame in mind?"

"Our kids are on summer break, but most of us will start school in August."

This was how her work should feel. Intrigued by an idea so much that she couldn't wait to develop the course. "If you'll give me your email address, I'll contact you when I have a proposal."

"Thank you."

She had two new ideas to implement: care packages and a new class. This kind of excitement was what she had to get back to.

Since the afternoon shop clerk had to leave early, Bree handled the final hour before closing. She took her laptop into the showroom and focused on easily interrupted tasks.

When the door chime sounded, she saved her work, looked up, and tried to smother her surprise. "Hi, Heather."

"Hi." As always, Allison's mother looked beautiful and coordinated. Cute pink shorts with a pink-and-yellow tie-dye top. Chin-length bob of hair. No makeup because she didn't need any.

"This place looks just like you, Bree. Cheerful and efficient."

"Efficient?"

"Yes, in the best sense of the word. Charming and useful."

"Thank you." An unusual but nice compliment. Since Heather Garrett approved of efficiency, no need to waste their time on small talk. "I don't have to guess your reason for coming over."

"The revelation."

Bree couldn't help but grin at the term. They all seemed to be using it. "It's okay if we talk, but I should stay out here," she said and gestured toward the conversation area.

After they were seated, Heather said, "Allison is thrilled and bewildered that I'm not."

"Same for me."

"I'm not really sure what to think yet. The information has come in too fast for me to process it. But there has been something positive about the news. I've gained a niece."

Bree liked it, too, but was that the only positive thing? "What about gaining a brother?" Bree frowned, upset on his behalf. "You seemed fine at the park."

"*Fine* is all I can claim for now. I'm outraged that we could have been there for each other if we'd only known, and it's shrouded my positive feelings in a fog of grief. I can't be fair to Everett yet. I've been an only child my whole life. I don't know how to be a sister, but I'll enjoy learning." Her smile warmed. "I've had years of practice being an aunt to Rod's nieces and nephews, and I'm looking forward to being yours. I've always been proud of what you've achieved. This store. What a wonderful friend you've been to Allison. Now I get to call you *my* niece."

"Thank you." It was the kind of thing Bree would've known if she'd thought about it. Still lovely to hear. "Aunt Heather."

She gave a little laugh. "Don't worry. I'll get there with Everett."

"And Galen?"

"Not ready for him. Or her." Heather rose. "Sorry to bother you. Don't want to keep you from your customers."

"No bother. Come by anytime."

"Thank you." She gave Bree a hug. "See you soon."

It felt like a promise.

Heather's visit was a reminder of how important the Garretts had been throughout Bree's life. Her second family. A place to crash when Dad was distracted and Bree didn't want to be alone. It didn't make sense to distance herself from them or Allison. They'd been her found family, and now they were her real family. Why couldn't she be at peace with that?

Her phone rang minutes after Heather left. "Hi, Dad."

"Want to join me for dinner? I'm making country fried steak."

"Sure. I'm not off till six, but I can come straight there."

"Sounds good."

She hadn't had a single customer in the past hour, so she wrote in her own personal journal, pouring out her feelings about the past few days. Not only with text. She doodled flowers and rainbows. Drew cubes with lines so thick that she tore through the paper, which, weirdly, might've helped her feel better than all the rest.

A summer storm blew up out of nowhere and crashed over downtown. Rain pounded so hard it bounced on the sidewalk. She opened the door and filled her lungs with the scent. The only customers downtown were now under awnings, browsing the menus in restaurants.

Work could wait until tomorrow. Flipping the sign to Closed, she locked the front door, went to the back, completed her closing routine, and left.

Dad had two place settings waiting on the island, complete with place mats and cloth napkins and bowls of salad.

She climbed onto a barstool. "You seem very domesticated."

"I like my summers." He brought over a platter with steak and roasted potatoes. "It takes half the time to recover from the previous school year, and the other half to brace for the next one."

Grinning, she attacked her salad first. Fresh and amazing. With his own garlicky homemade croutons. She hadn't inherited his culinary gene. "This is delicious, Dad."

"Thanks. You sound tired."

"Just busy."

"Anything wrong with the shop?"

"No, not wrong exactly. More like fine, but with issues."

"Explain."

She should have kept her mouth shut. "The shop is making a profit, but it takes all my free time."

"Get more help."

"Which would rob me of the profitability."

"I have nothing to add, then."

They continued to eat in silence. When they were done, he collected their plates and put them in the sink. They carried their glasses of iced tea to the veranda and each took a seat. Her in a swivel rocker, him on the swing.

"What's the hardest part of your business?" he asked.

"The classes. They take so much mental energy."

"Then stop."

"Can't. Not when they're so profitable. And I love teaching them, although I guess I would love teaching fewer."

She could feel his eyes on her. "Why haven't you asked me?"

"About what?"

"To teach one of your classes."

She glanced at him in surprise. "You would do that for me?"

"Sure. I can't imagine something I'd like more than being paid to spend an evening with people who want to learn to write better."

Did her father really want to participate in her business? It was the best kind of praise. "I'll have to give that some thought. I've always taught them myself." She eyed him, curious about what the home-schooling mother had said. "Do kids learn how to write in cursive anymore?"

"Nah. We don't have the time for it."

"We did when I was in school."

"Since then, we've added another twenty years of history and technology. There's already too much to shoehorn into a school year to devote time to a skill kids will rarely use."

"What about reading cursive documents?"

"Doesn't happen much." He waved away the comment. "Why do *you* lead all the classes? You would have no problem finding other instructors. Like me. And you just deflected my offer."

"What would you teach?"

"What are the parameters?"

"It has to be about writing, communicating, or being creative with words. And personal. I've held classes on journaling your thoughts. Calligraphy. Homemade special-occasion cards. Anything, really, along the spectrum from wielding a pen to producing content."

"Writing a sonnet?"

She stopped rocking and swiveled to face him. "That's a great idea, Dad. Would you really be willing to teach it?"

"I'd love to." His eyes narrowed as he thought it through. "How long should it last?"

"Sixty to ninety minutes."

"Ninety minutes would work."

Dad's class would be amazing. "I might have to rent space somewhere else. The turnout will be huge."

He looked down at his hands, eyes half-closed. He had thick eyelashes, like his sister. "I doubt there would be that many."

Bree wouldn't argue with her father's modesty. He had long been a favorite teacher at the local middle school with parents and students alike. People would come.

This was the third new idea in the past week that had her smiling. Fourth, if she included Lola's set of suggestions. Bree would need to pull money from her emergency account to get them going. But if they took off, the account would be swiftly replenished.

And if a sonnets class fell flat?

No, it wasn't going to fall flat. She had to get over these arbitrary goals she'd set for herself, like repaying Dad and Allison early. They would be pissed if they thought they had become a barrier.

No, my attitude is the barrier. And that was something she could fix.

Time to rework her plans for the second half of the year. *Pay back fast* could become a stretch goal. Not *the* goal.

She pulled up the shop's calendar on her phone. "When would you like me to schedule it?"

"Give me at least three weeks to prepare, but before school starts. End of July?"

"Okay." She made a note, then held out her hand to shake on it. "Deal."

The universe was trying to encourage her to take risks and made it easier by dropping four great ideas into her lap.

They're still risks. But really? Were they?

Financial, maybe. But the imbalance in her life was its own risk. Time to get her priorities in order.

CHAPTER
THIRTY-TWO

February 1976

Molly's latest programming project had required her to spend too many late nights and Saturday mornings at the office. The long hours had permeated all aspects of her life. On weeknights, she raced home at dinnertime, threw together a meal, then curbed her frustration while she helped the kids with homework. On the evenings Ward came home late, she would point at his dinner, warming in the toaster oven, and give him a quick kiss before rushing out the door.

Thursday nights were the worst. She'd committed to keeping the nursery during choir practice and wouldn't go back on her word. But it meant she couldn't return to the office until the last child had been picked up.

She hated that her job made her sacrifice a clean house, fun with the kids, and time alone with her husband. But she couldn't afford a reputation for being the weak link on the project team. So she replaced her *good-night*s to her family with *This will end soon.*

And today, it finally had. The project was delivered when promised and on budget. Harvey had been pleased. He'd called the team into a conference room for an impromptu meeting after lunch.

"It's been stressful around here, guys, but we did it. So let's relax. For the rest of the month, no overtime. That's an order. Work eight to five, and go home to your families. Now, get out of here."

They'd applauded and headed to their cars.

After a lazy afternoon with the house all to herself, Molly was enjoying an even lazier night. The kids were in bed. With *M*A*S*H* just ended, she would read until Ward got home from his church meeting.

The kitchen door opened after nine. Her husband came to the library and smiled wearily. "What are you reading?"

"*Curtain.* It's the latest Agatha Christie. I thought I'd give it a try." Setting the book aside, she rose and slid her hands around his neck.

"Mmm." He drew her closer and kissed her. "It's nice that you're not rushing away the minute you see me."

"Tonight, I'm all yours." She relished the thought of time alone with him. "How was your evening?"

"Fine. Not too much infighting."

"Why don't you go and change, and I'll get you something to drink."

"Be right back."

She'd just finished pouring two glasses of wine when the phone rang. In a minister's home, late-night calls weren't unusual, but they were rarely good news. She picked up before it could ring twice. "Hello?"

"Molly, it's Arlene."

Her friend sounded distraught. Had something happened to Charlie? "What's wrong?"

"Harvey had a heart attack."

"Oh, no." Molly redirected her concern to her boss. How awful. Had the project been harder on him than they'd realized? He'd made it seem so effortless. She sank onto a chair. "Is he in the hospital?"

"Uh-uh. He was alone at the office, after everyone left. The janitor found him." Arlene coughed. "He's gone, Molly."

"Gone? Wow. I don't . . ." She looked at Ward, eyes swimming with tears. He took the phone from her nerveless fingers and spoke briefly with her friend.

Molly sat in stunned silence, grieving the man who, nearly three years ago, had given her a chance, taught her to be a good programmer, mentored her to be a good employee, and never once made her feel as if she were less than. She didn't know much about Harvey beyond the professional. He hadn't played office politics. Hadn't socialized much with his staff or spoken often about his children or grandchildren. Harvey's family life had rested behind a wall of privacy.

Molly had followed his lead. Ward's job could never have a clear boundary between home and office, so hers did. Other than Arlene, she had no contact with the other staff after-hours. The distance made her better at her job, and Harvey's example had given her permission.

"I'm sorry," Ward said and pulled her into his arms. She welcomed the comfort and cried.

The heavens had opened during Harvey's funeral service, with pattering rain echoing through the sanctuary and the occasional flash of lightning exposing the glory of stained glass.

Arlene and Molly decided to forgo the reception afterward, so they waited under the porte cochere for their respective husbands to bring the cars around.

Three of their colleagues hurried past, eyeing them curiously before braving the rain.

"What's up with them?" Molly asked.

"Sorry, hon." Arlene lowered her voice. "I have a bad rumor and good news. Which do you want to hear first?"

"The bad rumor."

"The general manager has named Rudy our interim manager."

"That can't be right. He's the worst possible—"

"Shh."

They went silent as another coworker walked past, struggling to raise his umbrella.

"Rudy has a business degree," Arlene said. "That seems to impress them."

"And his dad plays golf with the right people."

"That too."

Molly saw the headlights of her station wagon inching closer. "What's the good news?"

Arlene beamed with joy. "I'm expecting."

Molly let the words sink in before hugging her friend. "Congratulations. That's wonderful. Charlie must be so happy."

"Over the moon."

"Here's Ward; I have to go. We'll talk later. Are you going back to the office?"

"Yes, but Charlie's taking me out to eat first."

"See you soon." Molly ran to the passenger side and got in.

Once they were on the road, she reached for her husband's hand. "Do you have to go directly back to work?"

"No. Why?"

"We rarely have lunch at home alone. Can we? Just the two of us?"

He covered her hand with his and made a sharp turn at the next intersection.

In the kitchen, they went about their unspoken division of labor. He set the table while she stuck her head in the fridge to scrounge for a quick meal. She went with ham sandwiches and chips.

Five minutes later, she carried the plates to the table. "I have exciting news. Arlene and Charlie are having a baby."

"That's great. When?"

She couldn't believe she was about to say this. "I forgot to ask."

He took a bite of his sandwich and frowned at the plate, his face clouding over. Was something wrong? She watched him a moment, then reached for a chip. Whatever it was, he would tell her if she needed to know.

"Molly," Ward said quietly. He sounded on edge.

She swallowed her final bite of sandwich. "Yes?"

"Do you envy Arlene?"

"About the baby? No." But when his tension remained, she asked. "What are you really asking?"

"Would you like another child?"

She straightened in surprise. "I love the children I have." She studied his carefully neutral expression. Did he want more? They'd discussed the question in a vague sort of way during their engagement, but he hadn't mentioned it since. "Our kids are enough for me. They're perfect."

He pushed back in his chair, his brow creased in thought.

Maybe it was time to answer the question in a specific way. She crossed to him, sat on his lap, and waited until she had his full attention.

His arms tightened automatically around her. "Hmm?"

"What do *you* want, Ward?"

He searched her face. Whatever he saw must have comforted him, for he said, "The family we have is perfect."

She laid her head against his shoulder and sighed as they held each other.

The phone rang. Molly scooped up their lunch dishes and carried them to the sink while Ward answered.

"Hello? Yes?" He frowned. "I'm sorry, but we've been at a funeral." He looked at Molly. "One of us will be there in ten minutes. Thank you." He hung up. "The school's been trying to call both of us for an hour. David slipped on the front steps and injured his arm. The school nurse thinks it's broken. He needs to go to the emergency room."

One *of us will be there*? They both knew who had to go. Ward had a marriage-counseling session with an engaged couple this afternoon. Not to mention that when David was hurt, he wanted his mom. She left the dishes on the counter and grabbed her purse. "I'll go. Please call my office and let them know I won't be returning today."

Once Molly was seated at her desk the next morning, Arlene reached into her purse and drew out an envelope. *To Whom It May Concern.*

"What's this?"

"My resignation letter. I don't want to stay, and they would make me quit anyway when they hear about the baby." She put the envelope back in her purse. "Will you?"

Molly hadn't even considered it. "I can't. My family needs the money."

"We do, too, but this might be the push I need to start my own company."

"Programming consultants?" Her friend had read a magazine article about a woman who'd launched a business with female-only programmers. Arlene hadn't stopped talking about it in the three years they'd worked together.

"That's my plan."

A company of programmers run by a female? Nobody would hire them. Not in Richmond. "Are you sure?"

Arlene didn't pretend to misunderstand. "Charlie will be the managing director on paper. The face of the company. I'll do everything else."

"Hey, girls?" Rudy called, coming out of Harvey's office.

Molly pressed her lips together to suppress a snarl.

"Don't be gossiping on the company's dime."

She blanked her face and watched him reenter the room that still displayed Harvey's framed pictures on the wall. When his back was turned, she whispered, "Good luck."

Arlene rolled her eyes. "You'll need it more."

◆ ◆ ◆

After dinner, she told Ward about the conversation with Arlene, their concerns over Rudy's behavior once his power became permanent, and what Molly would endure as the only female in the group. "I'll get the grunt work."

"Can you refuse?"

"No. I won't hand him an excuse to fire me. It's okay. I'll be fine."

Ward drew a chair closer to her and took her hands. "No, you won't. You're good at what you do. You can find another job. If you want to, quit."

What a lovely thought. She ached to, but it was a risk she couldn't take. "We can't afford to lose my paycheck."

"We can't afford to have you miserable."

Ward didn't manage the family budget or notice the bottom line at the end of each month. His salary might cover their basic needs, and they did live in the manse rent-free. But her income allowed them the extras. Piano lessons for David. Little League for Nathan. A nice family vacation each summer. And unbeknownst to her husband, she'd been building up their savings account so that someday they could make a down payment on their own house. With *two* bathrooms. "I'm not ready to quit."

"Is money your main argument against it?"

"Mostly."

"If it gets bad, give your two-week notice. Then take the time to find the right job. Or stay at home." He pressed his lips to her forehead. "I'm going to bed."

"I'm right behind you."

She flicked out the lights in the kitchen, mulling over what Ward had said. Outside of Rudy, she loved her job. And she wasn't willing for her family to do without. So she wasn't going to quit. Yet.

It was, however, good to know she had her husband's support if she did.

With Arlene gone, Molly was the only female on the programming team—and, oh, did she stick out now. So she often left the building during her lunch break. Today, she had an appointment at the hair salon, then stopped by a travel agency on the way to the office, asking for their help with planning a summer vacation. Well, vacations, plural. A week for the family. And whatever weekend she could work out for her and Ward.

Since it was the bicentennial year, the family trip would be a mix of history and fun. Williamsburg was an obvious choice, especially with the new theme park nearby. But Busch Gardens was close enough that they could go there anytime.

Boston was her personal favorite. Rich with history, and Nathan was a huge Red Sox fan. He would love going to a Major League game in Fenway Park, and she would love taking him. However, six hundred miles each way in a car with Naomi was not for the fainthearted.

After cramming a stack of brochures in her handbag, she thanked the travel agent and walked outside. Somewhere, a church bell tolled the hour.

Darn it all. She'd let time get away from her. Rudy would be watching for her like a hawk. Well, he was the one who ought to be careful. Her emotions were on a hair trigger today. It was the twins' seventh birthday. If Rudy came after her, the results would not be pretty.

When she returned to the office ten minutes late, the room went silent. No keyboards. No conversation. Nothing but the sound of necks popping as her coworkers tracked her progress down the length of the room and to her desk in the back row. She was its sole occupant now, since Rudy had replaced Arlene with a man.

Sound resumed slowly. A nervous laugh. Pens tapping. Someone typing on a keyboard. She sat primly, set her handbag in a desk drawer, smoothed her new wedge haircut into place, and picked up a red pencil.

Rudy had her desk-checking the new programmer's code. *Again.* And she knew that a second pair of eyes was needed. The guy might play a great round of golf, but he wrote deplorable code. If it wasn't for Molly's "suggestions," his programs would have some truly disastrous failures. She didn't like her assignment, but if measured by its impact, it was huge.

Even if she hadn't heard his office door opening, she would have known her "acting supervisor" was on his way. His liberal splash of aftershave preceded him, and the room had gone silent again.

His footsteps stopped at her desk.

She merrily continued to mark the rather bad code she was correcting. Red circles and rectangles everywhere.

"Molly," he intoned.

She chuckled under her breath. His attempt at *ominous* was utterly ridiculous.

"I'm waiting."

She looked up. He had on his *I'm going to humiliate you* expression. It filled her with a weird sense of calm. She could not, *would* not let him push her around. Seven years ago, she'd allowed herself to be badgered into doing something she hadn't wanted to do. She wouldn't be pushed today. "Yes?" She gave him a cheery smile.

"You're late."

"What about it?"

His nostrils flared. He was unused to being challenged. "You can make up the time at the end of the day."

"I can, but I won't." She bowed her head over the coding sheet. Circled another error in vivid red.

"Do you know who you're talking to?"

"Yes, Rudy, I do. Clearly, the reverse is not true." And that was it. She was done.

He was in for a big surprise. He thought the tasks he gave her were busywork. A form of punishment. In reality, her efforts were critical to the company's success, and the rest of the team knew it. Even counted on her finding their sloppy mistakes. Rudy didn't get it, but he was about to.

Her only regret? She wouldn't be here to watch.

Ward had been right. *We can't afford to have you miserable.* She was confident in her decision. It made her feel blissfully free. Ripping a blank sheet off a pad, she wrote in red pencil:

I quit.

Molly Palmer

March 31, 1976

"Here's my two-week notice." She folded over the slip of paper and pushed it across the desk.

He shrank from it like it held poison. "I want you gone *now*. Clear out your things."

Could he see the contempt in her smile? "Gladly."

CHAPTER
THIRTY-THREE

Molly drove home in a giddy haze. Quitting had been so satisfying. She parked behind the house, picked up her meager carton of belongings, and walked inside. For a moment, she stood in the kitchen and soaked up the quiet.

But as she set the carton on the table, her euphoria faded, and relief turned to worry. She had to talk to her husband before anyone else did. The church grapevine was a true marvel of nature. She dialed the church's switchboard and asked for Ward.

"He's unavailable, Mrs. Palmer."

"Please ask him to call me."

A sniff. "Certainly." The lady hung up.

She didn't know how to be idle. What next? All major chores had been completed over the weekend. With a quart of spaghetti sauce thawing in the fridge, dinner was on track. Laundry had been caught up yesterday. So she took a shower, changed into jeans and a lightweight sweater, and wandered through the house.

Still no call from Ward. She tried Gwen next but had to leave a message.

Molly spread the travel brochures out on the table and got out a pad of paper. She could make plans for the trip.

Or maybe not. Had she put their vacation in jeopardy? Would she have to cut back?

She had to tell someone. She dialed Arlene's home. "Hi, it's Molly."

"What's happened?"

"I quit."

"Yes!" A laugh. "I wish I'd been there."

"It felt good at the time." She should have given herself time to think, at least overnight. Talked with Ward again and made some calculations. "Was I childish?" She groaned. She'd put her family in jeopardy. "That was childish."

"And wonderful."

And wonderful. And impulsive. On a whim, one-third of their household income was gone.

Why hadn't she thought about the consequences? Both large and small? Like the college student who walked the kids home from school and helped them with their homework. Molly could handle it now, but the young woman was relying on the money. They should let her continue through the end of the semester. "What have I done, Arlene?"

"The right thing. Now you can work for me."

"Doing what?"

"Writing code. I have two other programmers signed up. Both mothers with young children. Part time only."

"What kind of projects?"

There was silence. A sigh. "None yet, but I'm optimistic. We're close to signing a contract."

Would her friend be successful? A female-owned company with part-time, female-only coders. Molly reined in her skepticism. "I can't do anything until I talk to Ward."

"Offer stands."

"Thanks." She heard the mudroom door open, then Ward's even tread. Why had he come home? "He's here. I'd better go."

She hung up as he appeared in the doorway.

"You're home early."

"So are you." His tone was carefully mild. "Mrs. Priddy said you left a message. That you have something to tell me."

"I quit my job." She frowned at him, puzzled. "Why didn't you just return my call?"

He exhaled slowly with relief. "I heard you were fired and thought you might need me."

"No, I definitely quit." The church grapevine had tendrils everywhere, so it could be fast. This time, though, it was fast and wrong. "And I always need you." She stepped closer and rested her hands against his chest, sighing when his arms closed around her.

He kissed her forehead, her lips, then eased away. After slipping off his jacket, he hung it over the back of a chair and sat heavily. He seemed agitated.

She leaned against the kitchen counter and met his gaze. "Is there something I should know?"

"Yes. I had a meeting with my boss before coming home."

Ward's tone chilled her. "Was the meeting about me?"

"Now that you're unemployed, Bob anticipates an uptick in comments from the congregation on why it might be best for my wife to become more involved."

Being the associate minister's wife came with a lot of expectations, mostly unspoken. She knew she wasn't meeting them. Throughout their marriage, it had been a balancing act to work full-time, give her kids the attention they needed and she wanted, and be visible at church. But it must not be a problem for her husband. If Ward had had any complaints, he would have told her. "Best for whom?"

"I know. Bob knows." Ward's grin flashed and faded. "He's received suggestions."

Today? Or over time? She wouldn't ask. She didn't want to know. "Whether I work or not is between us."

"I said the same thing. They also think you should be more involved—" He clamped his lips shut.

"Where?" But she had a sick feeling that she knew.

His expression begged her to leave it alone.

"Ward. Our phone number is public knowledge. Don't let me hear it first from someone spiteful. Where should I be more involved?"

"At home. With the children."

She pushed away from the counter, crossed to the window overlooking the backyard, and pressed a fist to her mouth. For her, nothing was more important than her family. She would never knowingly cause them harm, and she didn't believe for a second that her job had either. But the attitudes of others could. "I love my children. I would never do anything to hurt them."

"I know that. The kids know that."

"What a rotten day to say such things." A sob slipped out.

Ward's chair screeched as he stood. "Molly, I'm so sorry. I forgot it's the twins' birthday." He held her close, murmured consoling words, and let her cry.

The front door banged open. The kids were home with the babysitter.

"Mom! Dad!" David shouted, his footsteps growing closer.

Molly stepped away from Ward and went to the sink, wetting her hands, splashing her face.

"Hi, Rev. Palmer. Mrs. Palmer." The babysitter walked in holding Naomi's hand. "Should I make a snack?"

"Go ahead." Molly tried to smile.

David and Naomi ran to the library. The TV went on, tuned to the educational station.

Nathan stood at the far end of the table, staring at the travel brochures. He drew out one about Boston and looked up at her, his eyes pleading. "Molly," he said, "is this for the summer?"

"Yes, it is." She exchanged a glance with her husband. Saw his nod of understanding. She would have to make the Boston trip happen, and quitting today just made it tougher.

◆ ◆ ◆

Later that night, when the house was quiet and the kids were supposed to be asleep, she and Ward were in their bed, too, lights out. But his breathing wasn't relaxed. He was awake.

"It would be easier on you if I stayed home," she said. "Do you want me to?"

He rolled to his side. "If it were only about the church, I would. We can be comfortable on my income."

Not really, although she wouldn't say so.

"But it's nice that we don't have to. It relieves pressure on me. And the satisfaction you get from work is good for all of us."

"I might find satisfaction in volunteering at the school. Or joining a church committee."

"Joining? Uh-uh. *Heading* a church committee." He raised on an elbow and grinned down at her. "Do you really think you would enjoy that?"

"I wouldn't hate it."

His eyebrow arched skeptically.

"I wouldn't *hate* it." She laughed.

He dropped his head back on the pillow.

There was a lot they'd left unsaid, and while they couldn't solve anything tonight, she was curious. She reached for his hand in the dark. "If I did find another job, how much of a problem would it be for you?"

"It won't put my job in jeopardy, but it might lessen their loyalty."

"How do you feel about that?"

He took a long time to respond. "Overall? Ambivalent. An ultimatum might force me to do something I've been considering."

She was glad he'd finally brought this up. "You'd like to work on your doctorate."

"Yes." He sounded pleased. Surprised.

"Why don't you?"

"I'm not done yet with what I'm doing."

That relieved her. It would allow her time to prepare. "Could you get started at Union?" Union Theological Seminary was practically walking distance from the manse.

"No, there's nowhere I would go nearby. We would have to leave Richmond. So it's not imminent. I just wanted you to know that being a minister at this church is not the end of my ambitions." He paused, gathering his thoughts. "Are you open to moving somewhere? After the kids have graduated?"

"That *is* planning in advance." Another ten years or more.

"You're complaining about planning?"

"No. Did you have a *somewhere* in mind?"

"Duke." He watched for her reaction.

Not only return to North Carolina but move near Marlowe? She'd never thought about the possibility. "My parents would love to have us closer."

"But would you be comfortable with moving to Durham?"

She smiled to assure him. "If it's right for you, it's right for me."

After a month of being home during the day, Molly noticed several changes. The house stayed in a state of perpetual cleanliness. Meals were less stressful, and she enjoyed cooking them. The Palmer Family Bicentennial Trip to Boston had been thoroughly planned, and the kids were getting excited. All in all, a nice four weeks.

She hadn't been quite as successful at pretending to herself that she didn't long to go back to work.

She'd made pancakes and bacon for breakfast today. Feet thundered down the stairs, until Ward's quiet "Hey" led to more sedate walking to the table. Then cheers.

Ward barely sat in his chair long enough to slurp down coffee and eat a pancake. When he headed out the back door, she followed as far as the steps. "Ward?"

He stopped. "Is everything okay?"

"Just needed a moment alone with you."

He returned and wrapped his arms loosely around her. "Hey," he said softly and kissed her.

She smiled. "Maple lips."

"Your fault."

"Not complaining."

He kissed her again. "Have you talked with Arlene? About the job?"

She shook her head.

"Why not?"

"I'm not sure."

"The Palmer family will adjust, no matter what you decide." He dropped his arms and continued to the car.

When she reentered the house, the children were waiting in the living room with their book bags and lunches. "All right," she said. "Let's go."

She escorted the kids to school now. It had been Ward's job to drop them off before. She liked this part of the morning.

They'd come up with an idea of sorts. Each day, one of the kids got her full attention on the walk. Their special time to say whatever they wanted. David had run ahead. Naomi held her hand quietly. Today was Nathan's turn. And, oh, did he talk, words gushing from his mouth. Projects. Teachers. Classmates. Knowing he had her complete attention had loosened his reticence.

He stopped within sight of the school. "Can you come to Field Day? It's a week from Thursday."

"Yes, I can." And she would.

"Can we bring a case of Gatorade?"

"Yes."

"Thanks, Molly." He smiled, one of his rare, charming smiles. Crooked teeth had him self-conscious. They would have to see about braces.

He gestured to his sister. "Come on, Naomi. Time to go inside." And off he took, his sister skipping to keep up.

Braces. Gatorade. Vacation. Why was she so torn about going back to work? They could use the extra money.

Easy answer. Because she wanted to be the kind of minister's wife Ward needed and the kind of mom who automatically came to Field Day without being asked.

Arlene's company might allow her to be all of the above. She claimed to hire only young mothers and allow her staff to set their own schedules.

If that was true, Molly would love to know more. She drove to her friend's house.

When Arlene opened the door, she stepped aside. "Come in. I hope you're here about a job." She moaned and rubbed the side of her belly. "The baby is active today."

"Only a few more weeks."

"Yeah, but I'll miss the little kicks."

"I know—" Molly stopped. She'd never told Arlene that she'd been pregnant and remembered how much a woman could miss little kicks. "How's your company doing?"

Arlene was leading the way to the den. "I hope this means what I want it to mean, and the answer is *great*. Our first project is going well. We've only had it two weeks, but we're on track to make the due date." She eased into a chair and patted her belly. "Unless Little Bit shows up early."

Molly took a seat on the couch, her nose twitching at the lingering smell of cigarette smoke. "What's the project?"

"Generating reports for the city government."

"How did you get them to hire you?"

Arlene sighed. "Charlie's name is on the paperwork. They trust him."

"Does that bother you?"

"Of course it bothers me, but it's reality. Charlie believes in me. I believe in me. And one day, I'll have customers who believe in me so strongly that they won't care the company's actually run by a woman." Arlene clapped her hands. "I can tell you're interested. Please join us. I promise you, we have the best of all worlds. Three of us are doing a one-person project. You work whatever hours you want as long as I can count on you to meet your commitment."

"Sounds too good to be true."

"Best of all worlds. We're mothers who want to stay relevant in our career and accommodate our kids' schedules. I've only negotiated the one project so far, but we're making it work. And the pay is not bad." Arlene's smile brightened. "Please give us a chance."

"It is tempting."

Her eyes gleamed with triumph. "How many hours per week could you work?"

Now Molly would see if her friend really did support part time. "Fifteen."

Arlene didn't bat an eyelash. "If you start next week, you could take my place on our current project, so I can focus on scrounging up another contract. Or have a baby. Whichever comes first."

Since Ward had practically pushed her into asking about a job, she didn't need to wonder about his opinion. "It does sound fantastic, but I'll have to let you know."

"By Monday?"

"Can I have next Thursday off?"

"You get to schedule your own hours," Arlene said patiently. "What we're doing is cool and bold. Take a leap of faith."

"Okay," Molly said, happy with her decision. "It's a yes."

CHAPTER
THIRTY-FOUR

Allison had finished the virtual lessons on customer etiquette in a week. Longer than she expected. Faster than recommended. But she was glad to have it behind her, because she started her intensive workshop today. For the next four Tuesday afternoons, she would meet in person with other software professionals needing help with their people skills.

She wasn't sure how to dress. Business casual, as a kind of pseudorepresentative of the company? Or modern American remote worker?

Better aim high.

She changed into a loose white shirt over khakis. Then added a silk scarf with an abstract pattern. Reknotted it several times. She was terrible at tying scarves. She needed her mom.

Are you busy?

No

Can I drop by? I need help with a scarf

Sure

She drove over to her parents' house and walked in the front door. "Mom?" she called.

"In the kitchen."

Her mother was sitting at the table, staring at her laptop. "Hi," she said, looking up. "You're dressier than usual."

"I'm on my way to a people-skills class. I don't want to go, and I was hoping it would help my attitude to look nice."

"Does it?"

"No."

Mom laughed as she came over. She considered the scarf and shook her head. "Let me see if I can find something else that'll pull the white and khaki together. I'll be right back."

She returned carrying a scarf with soft peach and aqua swirls, tied an intricate knot, and stepped back. "Check it out."

Allison went into the half bath. Much better.

"When do you have to be in Durham?" her mother called out.

"Around one." She went back. "Thanks. The scarf's just right."

"Would you like a sandwich? Or a cookie?"

"Cookies are always welcome."

Mom set out a large container and then crossed to the coffeepot.

Allison selected an oatmeal cookie. Still slightly warm. Mmm. She mumbled around a bite, "Have you talked with Everett since Sunday?"

"Don't push."

"I'm not."

"Yes, you are." Mom reached into the cabinet for a coffee mug. "Allison, you don't get to decide how I feel about this. You haven't lived with it for your entire life."

"Okay." Where was this coming from?

"Do you know how many milestones I've gone through, believing that I wasn't wanted? That the woman who gave birth to me cared so little she dumped me on a porch?" She faced Allison, looking like she was ready to cry. "When you and Perry were babies, I couldn't imagine letting someone take you away. Sometimes, late at night, I would nurse you, so unbelievably happy and proud, and wonder how my birth mother could've handed over her precious child—*me*—to someone else."

"We don't know—"

"*Stop!* I don't care what we don't know now. It's how I felt *then*. Finding out there might be extenuating circumstances? Doesn't help at all. The pain was real. Maybe we will learn the story I was told is flawed. Won't matter, the end result was that I was rejected."

She held up the coffeepot, and Allison shook her head. She was wired enough.

Mom poured herself a cup, laced it with cream, and carried it to the table. She took a sip. Set it down again. "I logged on to the internet in the late nineties and checked a birth registry."

Allison controlled her surprise. She'd assumed Mom's refusal to learn about her birth family was lifelong.

"She wasn't looking for me."

The whole mix-up with the birth dates in the registries? It would be a lot to unpack. Probably not the time to explain.

"I had to hide the way I felt from my parents. It stayed bottled up inside. When I met your father, I discovered that his whole childhood had been so different. Rod had this big family. Everybody seemed to know everybody else. They had family trees mapped out in their brains. At Garrett family reunions, a stranger could walk up, mention their name, and boom, instant recognition of that person's place in Rod's world. With little jokes about family traits they'd inherited or the facial features they shared. And I smiled and listened and felt left out."

Was her mother done? Allison waited through a moment of silence and hoped her question wouldn't make things worse. "Can you tell how Everett feels?"

Mom's tension eased. "He was lied to, and he's grappling with that. But he acknowledges that he was still raised in his birth family. *Our* birth family. When someone says, *you look like a Harper*, he's always known it's true." She smiled faintly. "Eventually, I will enjoy having a brother, but it will take time."

"I'm sorry, Mom. Really. I didn't understand."

"Thank you." She stared into her coffee. Exhaled a slow breath. "You better go on to your people-skills class."

On the drive over to Durham, Allison pushed that conversation into a corner of her brain, too soon to review. Besides, dread for the in-person group was taking over.

Could she tell a difference in herself after the e-learning? Maybe. She tried more consciously to "read the room," virtually or otherwise. She did consider her audience before delivering a message. It wasn't clear that she was successful, but better delivery ought to be one of those skills that improved with practice.

Her first big worry about this whole process? That her hard work would mean nothing if her work team didn't believe in the change. She'd finally become aware of how often they interrupted her or cut her off even when she was the topic expert. How had she never noticed? Had she been too focused on the message to notice how it was received?

If she had noticed, she would've put it down to mansplaining. Which wasn't wrong. The developers tried to talk over Fawn often enough, but it seemed to amuse her. Of course, she was the boss. The guys could say whatever they wanted. She would still win.

Would Allison's colleagues ever accept they didn't have to intervene before her attitude turned off a customer? She liked where she worked, but now that she was less oblivious, she would need a hard reboot of the group dynamic. Did they know she'd been assigned to this program? It would be helpful if they did. Humbling too. She would have to bide her time and see.

And there came her second big worry: How much should she fear for her job? Fawn had called her work brilliant, and she used praise sparingly. Whether training had been a salvage operation or a political necessity, the unease wouldn't let go. It would be hard to be her best if she felt monitored.

She had to relax. She'd made a mistake, and management was giving her the opportunity to redeem herself. That was all.

GPS led her to a relatively new high-rise in the downtown area, within easy walking of a parking deck. When she finally found the correct meeting room, people were milling around, none she knew.

A memory from childhood washed over her. Her family moved to Marlowe when she was five. On the first day of kindergarten, she'd stood in the classroom doorway, not knowing anyone, fighting the urge to suck her thumb. She'd worn her favorite dress because it made her happy. But seeing the other kids in shorts and T-shirts, the dress made her stand out.

Then Bree had walked over, taken her hand, and said, "Let's play together." Names had been unnecessary. A bad moment turned into one of the best things that had ever happened to her.

Maybe this workshop could beat expectations too. She went in and took a seat.

The first hour was grueling. For her, anyway. During the initial "getting to know you" section, she tried not to make snap judgments about who the others were. But it felt like people were trying to assign their own labels with their introductory remarks.

The cheerleader clapped her hands and said she was "so happy to be here."

Mr. Bitter actually used the word.

Ms. Debate wanted to pass and used more words arguing with the leader than if she'd simply given in.

"Allison, why are you here?"

She blushed, caught staring at the debater, but she had a ready answer. It was something she'd asked herself often enough recently. "To examine how I come across to people."

"So you can change?"

"It's more about learning to use the skills I already have more effectively. To detect another person's boundaries better and not cross over them without a good reason."

"What do you fear about this class?"

She hated questions about feelings. She would prefer not to say too much, but wasn't that the point? If she didn't give the class her all, it wouldn't help. Besides, she wasn't likely to see these people again. "In smoothing my edges, I'll grind away parts of me that have value."

"What do you hope for?"

"The opposite of my fear. I hope I get better without getting worse."

The leader moved along, asking each person about their hopes and fears. After the first two, Allison tuned them out to consider the group in general.

There were eight participants in total. Five dressed casually in jeans or shorts. Two in business professional. And Allison. Their expressions ranged from neutral to belligerent. As much as Allison wished she was anywhere else, the whole misery-loves-company thing helped.

"Let's get a baseline of where we are," the leader was saying. "We'll do a role-play. I'll be a disgruntled customer. One of you will be the customer service rep. Any volunteers?"

The silence was complete.

"Very well. Kirstie, why don't you join me?" Without looking for agreement, the leader dragged two chairs to the middle of the circle, back to back, and sat in one of them.

Ms. Debate stood, sighed heavily, and took her seat.

Allison wasn't sure whether the leader was brave or brilliant. Kirstie did a not-terrible job of dealing with the disgruntled customer, yet still had things the leader could correct.

By the end of the first session, Allison knew that listening to the others might have the most effect, because the other participants fell along a range of attitudes: aloof, flippant, oblivious, and intense. If she could recognize problems in others, she could recognize them in herself. Learning by *not doing that*.

Allison battled rush-hour traffic on the way home. Her typical commute doubled in length.

Too tired to face cooking for herself, she swung by a Food Truck Rodeo in a shopping center outside Marlowe. As she walked up, she saw that four of her favorites were there. She also noticed Galen looking from one to the next, his forehead creased.

"Hi," she said. "You look a little overwhelmed."

He grinned. "I've never been here before, but the guy who mows my lawn suggested it. What do you recommend?"

"Lebanese."

"Is it spicy?"

"No, it's what I'm getting, and I'm not big on spicy either."

He gave a little bow. "Lead the way."

They found two empty spots at the end of a picnic table and sat across from each other. He dug in like he was starving. There was a slight shake to his hand.

She sipped her Lebanese tea and watched her grandfather, empathy swirling inside her. He'd taken a huge hit too. In its own way, bigger than the rest of them. He'd carried the burden of secrets and regrets his whole life and had no one to share the fallout with him.

"How's life, Galen?"

He finished his bite and looked up. "I'm hanging in there. How about you?"

"Okay. Glad we had the same idea to eat here."

He smiled, took a bite of his kebab, and chewed thoughtfully. "It's been a rough few weeks, to be honest. Not only renegotiating my relationship with Everett and hoping someday that'll be all right again, but it's also dredged up parts of my past I'd rather not remember."

She nodded, containing her surprise at how much he'd shared in two sentences.

"With Molly, it was *like* at first sight. She was flustered at being caught off guard, not looking her best, but then she just went with it. That's what grabbed my attention. Most girls I knew would never let guys see them any way other than perfect. I was intrigued, and it went from there."

Did he want to talk about the past? She would ask and see if he showed interest in continuing. "When did you find out that you were expecting?"

"Around Thanksgiving. She was three months along. Apparently, she'd sent me letters and tried to call, but none of it got past my mother. Mama didn't want me distracted from my senior year.

"After my parents brought Everett home and I got over myself, I went looking for Molly. Partly to find out why she'd let him come to us. Partly because I missed her. Her aunt claimed she didn't know where Molly was. That her parents didn't either. I let it drop. I was about to start my first year of college. Got swept up in that. Then ended up in the army the next summer."

Allison had never heard that mentioned before. "Your draft number came up?"

"No, I volunteered."

"Why?"

"Molly left North Carolina after what was done to her. To find a new way to be whole again, I assume. Her disappearance inspired me to escape and experience something different. So I disappeared too. I'm not sure my parents noticed. They were too busy with Everett."

Here was a birth father who hadn't simply gone on with his life as if nothing had happened. "Did you go to Vietnam?"

He shook his head. "Germany. All I did was chauffeur senior officers around in a Rambler Ambassador. No guns pointed at me. Nothing to be scared about except a general who'd awakened that morning pissed off." He wiped his hands on a napkin, crumpled it with his trash. "I returned," he said, his voice brisk, "completed a degree in business, moved back to Marlowe, and took over the store."

"How old was Everett?"

"First or second grade. That's why it became natural to think of him as my brother. Legally, he was. I'd been absent from the US for two years and lived in Raleigh while I finished my degree. My parents never wanted to tell him. They thought it would be too confusing. I didn't, but I went along with it."

He searched her face, looking for what? Contempt? Disappointment? He'd get neither from her. She'd heard it all in her genealogy work, plenty of actions that stemmed from desperation or fear. His story showed choices both sad and selfless. "The adoption hadn't turned out the way you expected."

"No, but it was for the best." He set down his kebab, frowning at the plate. "Are you learning more about Molly?"

"We are. Slowly."

"Is she alive?"

"Yes, and open to contact with the twins."

"May I ask about her?"

"Of course." Allison smiled at his eagerness, glad she'd decided to come here tonight. "I don't know much, but I'll tell you what I can."

He drank from his cup. "This tea is wonderful. A hint of mint. Thank you for the recommendation."

"You're welcome." Was he stalling? She waited.

"Do you know where she lives?"

"In North Carolina. Not far."

"Married? Children?"

"Both, although I haven't discovered more than that."

"Did she go to college?"

"She did. She's a software engineer. Well known in the industry as an innovator." Allison had downloaded another one of the books Molly had written about the software consulting firm she'd worked at for nearly fifty years. The book was part how-to and part memoir, describing a wildly successful company staffed by young mothers who only programmed part time.

"I'm not surprised." He nodded with satisfaction. "We were only together two months and kids ourselves. I only got glimpses of who she might turn out to be. How life would change her. But I would guess spectacular."

CHAPTER
THIRTY-FIVE

September 1976

Since Molly joined Riverbend Consulting, Arlene had delivered her son, their staff had tripled in size, and Molly had become the acting project coordinator. It took a lot of conversations to make sure that three part-time women could share the same project as cohesively as one full-timer.

Despite the bumps, their results had exceeded expectations, and the client signed up for more.

Molly had discovered a talent for dividing big programming projects into smaller tasks. Although it shouldn't be surprising. Getting three kids to cooperatively clean the backyard without it devolving into the third world war had already honed the skill.

The company had grown to ten programmers, all mothers with young children, ranging from infants to elementary age. Half were married. The other half? No husbands, and they didn't ask why.

Molly was alone in the office midafternoon, monitoring the phone and keeping an eye on the clock. School would be out soon, and she'd promised to walk the kids home today.

The door to the office creaked open. Arlene appeared around the corner, pushing a stroller. "I have it, Molly," Arlene said, her perpetually cheerful face now frazzled. "The big contract."

"What do you mean?"

"The one that will put us on the map. If we pull it off."

Molly didn't like the sound of that *if.* "Are you worried we might not?"

Arlene gulped. "Less confident than normal."

"How did we win?"

"I was the only bidder. No other contractor thinks it's possible to make the proposed deadline. There's a bonus if we succeed."

It sounded scary. And fun. "What do you need from me?"

"Eight more programmers willing to take three dollars an hour."

They had ten names on the waiting list, but Molly wasn't sure that would be enough. Three dollars might not be enough to entice them off. "I'll do my best. It's a low wage."

"And a bonus at the end. Don't forget that."

Arlene was a risk-taker, which was why she was in charge, and Molly was not. "For a contract you're not confident we can succeed at."

"Not *as* confident as normal."

"Just how much of a bonus are we talking?"

Her friend quoted a figure that made Molly blink. That *dream house of our own* wouldn't be a dream anymore. "I'll see who I can find."

"Emphasize that they can put this job on their résumés."

"I always do."

But the results worked out the way Molly feared. She'd gone through the ten names on the list. Three were no longer interested. Two weren't comfortable with the money. But she had five on board.

Arlene frowned at the number. "Five isn't enough. Can you find more?"

"I can try. How involved do you want to be in interviews?"

"Not at all. I trust you."

Molly bowed her head, hiding a pleased smile. It felt as if her coordination role might be broadening to management.

Molly called the new hires to ask if they knew of anyone, but no one did. She called Dr. Little, but he didn't know of any mothers looking for jobs. She was at the office, reluctantly filling out a form to place a want ad, when she heard a voice call out, "Hello?"

She peeked in the small lobby. A college-age woman stood there, her hands in the pockets of her brown polyester slacks.

"May I help you?"

The woman's expression seemed both hopeful and resigned. "I heard you were looking for programmers. I'd like to apply."

"Follow me." Soon she was sitting across the desk from the young woman. "I'm Molly Palmer."

"Norah Wilkes. They say you hire moms. Even single moms."

"We do. We're all part time, though. Do you have a résumé with you, Norah?"

She shook her head.

"Are you employed?"

"I'm a cashier at a grocery store. But I have a programming degree from junior college."

Two-year degrees were more than fine with Molly. "Any programming experience?"

"Not yet." The woman's eyes glazed over with dejection. The look of someone certain she would be kicked to the curb.

"Why?" Molly asked gently.

"No one will hire me when they see this." Norah held up her right hand. It had only two fingers. A thumb and a pinkie. "It doesn't slow me down. Really. Please give me a chance."

Her words resonated. Harvey had given Molly a chance, and she'd been worth it. But Dr. Little had recommended her. Without experience, Norah had no one to vouch for her skills.

Although . . . maybe she could vouch for herself. "May I give you a coding test? Writing a simple program in FORTRAN?"

Norah smiled confidently. "Yes."

Molly slid over a pad of coding sheets and a pencil. "Calculate an employee's weekly paycheck. Two inputs, wage and hours worked."

The young woman sat quietly in her seat for several moments, thinking. Then she picked up the pencil and wrote.

Molly left the room to give her privacy. She went to the bathroom and checked the mailbox before returning.

Norah was sitting back, waiting with anxious eyes.

It wasn't a hard problem. Norah had coded the calculations correctly, but the details were what caught Molly's attention. There were comments for any code that wasn't self-explanatory. It would've been sufficient for Norah to calculate gross pay, but she'd included taxes and Social Security. And the most impressive detail of all? Only one erasure.

Arlene was trusting her to hire new staff. It was a scary responsibility to affect people's lives the way Molly could. Despite all that, her gut told her she was about to make the right decision. "Okay, Norah. The job is yours if you want it." When the woman nodded happily, Molly held up her hand to wait. "It's barely above minimum wage and ten hours per week to start, but that could grow."

"What kind of schedule?"

"You can generally set that yourself."

Norah looked faint with relief. "Thank you."

They dealt with the paperwork and details. Then Molly walked with her to the door.

"You said you're a single mom."

"I guess you could say I'm a single guardian. I'm raising my sister. She's thirteen. Will I have to work at night?"

"Sometimes." Leasing time on the mainframe computer was always cheapest at night. "That's when it's best to get our time-share."

Norah's smile faltered. "If I have to, I'll figure it out."

"Good. Welcome to Riverbend."

Arlene called later to check in.

Molly caught her up. "I hired someone today."

"Great. The first person you've picked on your own. When can she start?"

"Immediately."

"I sense a *but*."

"She doesn't have job experience. Or the complete use of her right hand."

Arlene sighed. "Inexperienced and disabled?"

"It'll be fine." Molly wouldn't second-guess herself. It just felt right. "Norah is hungry to show us she can do the work."

"I won't argue with your decision. But if her skills can't cut it, you're the one who'll have to fire her."

After Molly washed the dinner dishes, she checked on her sons at the kitchen table with their homework and joined Ward in the library. When she sat beside him, he set aside the book he'd been reading.

"Good day?" he asked.

"It was. I hired my first employee."

"That's great. Are you nervous about the decision?"

"A little." And she told him why.

"She'll be good, Molly. You didn't get this wrong."

They paused as David charged up the attic stairs, shouting, "Goodnight," as he went.

"One thing I worry about," she said, "is whether we should cut her some slack on working nights. She's the guardian of an eighth grader."

"Mom?" Nathan spoke from the entrance to the library.

He'd called her *Mom*. She and Ward froze in shock.

"Yes, Nathan?"

"Your new person could always bring her eighth grader over here. He could do his homework or something."

"Good idea," she said, a little breathlessly. "And it's a girl."

Nathan grinned. "Even better." He disappeared down the hallway.

She buried her face in Ward's shirt. "That's the first time he's ever called me Mom."

He pulled her closer. "He's regarded you as his mom for years. It just took a while for the name to catch up."

She knew it was true, but hearing Nathan say the word meant more than he would ever know.

CHAPTER
THIRTY-SIX

March 1987

Molly's twins were celebrating their eighteenth birthday today. Were they getting ready to graduate? Go to college? Did they have good friends? Sweethearts? Dreams?

Did they ever wonder about her?

Gwen and Molly had planned a different kind of birthday celebration this year. In addition to dessert and coffee, they had a special project to complete. Signing up for adoption registries.

She touched her stack of adoption-registry applications, filled out and ready to go. She hated how hopeful she felt. Knew that she would watch the mail anxiously for months, possibly years, desperately waiting to hear something.

"I'm scared he won't call." Gwen propped her chin in one hand and scowled at her four envelopes.

"Me too."

"But you have two children. Surely one will contact you."

If neither did, that made her twice ignored. "All we can do is wait." Molly had learned in her birth-parent group that locating a child could go very wrong. Adoptees could have a spectrum of responses, anywhere from joy to indifference to anger. She was braced for however her twins reacted. At least she hoped so.

When her cordless phone rang, she picked it up. "Hello?"

"It's Clive. Is Gwen still there?"

"Sure." She handed it to Gwen. "It's your husband."

"Hey." Gwen listened. Nodded. "Be home soon." She stood and reached for the envelopes. "Gotta go. Clive picked up Jennifer from dance lessons, and they're home now." She bit her lip. "Jennifer doesn't know she has a half brother."

Molly had never told her children either. She would one day.

Gwen stuffed the envelopes into her purse. "I hope this is the right thing to do."

"If you're not sure, hold off. You can mail it next month. Next year. Anytime."

"I know. I'll give it some thought." Gwen gave her a quick hug, murmured, "I needed this today," and let herself out.

Molly went into the kitchen to peel potatoes. She almost had dinner ready when her husband came into the kitchen from the garage.

He stopped by the table and smiled when he saw the envelopes. "You did it."

She nodded nervously. "They're ready to go."

"Want me to put them in the mailbox?"

She shook her head. She didn't want the mailman to know. "I'll take them by the post office. How was the meeting with the Personnel Committee?"

"Uncomfortable."

Ah. She'd been so focused on the registries that his big announcement had slipped her mind. Resigning as their associate minister after twenty-two years. "How did they take it?"

He shrugged. "Mostly congratulations and good wishes. A little irritation that they'll have to start searching for a replacement. And some relief."

"Those people aren't worthy of your concern." She rose and crossed to him. Slid her arms around him. Relaxed when he hugged her close. "We have some interesting years ahead of us."

"I know, my love. We'll be fine."

Ward was starting his doctoral program this fall at Duke's divinity school. With Naomi about to begin her senior year, Molly would stay in Richmond with their daughter, prepare to turn over her job responsibilities to Norah, and tackle the chore of fixing up their house to sell.

The first house they'd ever owned wasn't much to look at. A ranch with a basement and a detached garage. It had been in appalling condition when they found it ten years ago. But an interesting and rather sexy fact about her husband was that he'd worked in the construction business during college, experience that had proven quite useful in the long renovation process. All she would have to do now to have it look wonderful was clean the carpets and paint the walls.

Then Molly would be moving back to North Carolina.

She and Arlene had joked about opening a field office in Durham with a workforce of one. Molly was looking forward to it. The Research Triangle Park, a major technology center anchored by three major universities, held business opportunities for the company and talent to acquire.

Arlene's diabetes had begun to damage her heart. Another reason Molly was glad she would be staying in Richmond a little longer.

She wasn't worried about Ward. Spending his first year alone would give him permission to immerse himself in his studies. When he was able, he would drive to Richmond. When he wasn't, she would go to him. She would be returning to the familiar. And it would be strange.

After fourteen years of marriage, she would be a grad student's wife, the main breadwinner, and soon-to-be empty nester, only one school year away from having three adult children. She could hardly wait.

CHAPTER THIRTY-SEVEN

Bree had been trying to think bigger since the dinner with her father. For too long, she'd put her business at the center of her life and everything else on hold. She'd taken no vacations and pursued no social life outside her family and Allison. And there hadn't been much of Allison lately, which was Bree's fault.

She was ready to make changes. She would let Lola take over coordinating the classes, and the only cost would be giving up control. But the next two ideas would cost something financially, and she needed to budget for them. Hire another part-time clerk to take up the slack for Lola's new duties. And present a class on writing sonnets, taught by her first ever guest teacher.

She knew in her gut that a bigger-than-normal crowd would want to come to a sonnets class, and Dad deserved it. She had to find a larger venue. The library? A restaurant?

But what if she was wrong? She'd be out the cost of renting a bigger space and Dad's fee. Would he be willing to work for free?

Of course he would, but that wasn't fair. If he put in the work, he should be paid. Maybe he would go for a percentage of the registrations.

It was renting the space that worried her.

"Why do you look so glum?" Lola asked.

"The rental cost for Dad's class. The library won't let me use their room if the event is for profit. The two restaurants with private rooms require catering. Too expensive."

"Have you considered the Ivy Inn?"

Bree was familiar with the place. A 1920s-era mansion four blocks from the shopping district. "The B&B?"

"It used to be, but the business model is changing to an event venue. I think the downstairs can be rented. I attended a wedding there three weeks ago. Small. Only thirty guests. It was lovely."

Thirty? That would be more than enough. "Thanks for the idea."

"They hold an afternoon tea on Thursday afternoons. One to three."

Bree glanced at the clock. Two thirty. "I should go."

"I'll watch the shop."

It was miserably hot. Normally she would've driven, but she'd walked to work this morning. Fortunately, she was in the shade most of the way.

The mansion was beautiful and well restored, with an oversize manicured yard. At either end of the veranda were cozy groupings of wicker furniture and potted plants, a pleasant place to relax when the weather was better.

A COME IN sign hung on the door. She stepped into the foyer and surveyed the space. Gleaming wood floors. High ceilings. Arches and crown molding. The living room served as the eating area, with space for twenty or so guests. Its fireplace was framed by a gorgeous carved mantel, and its walls were papered with a soothing floral pattern. The bay window let in lots of natural light. This room would be ideal for her father's class.

The afternoon tea looked amazing, but the tables weren't full. Was that because teatime was nearly over? She hoped so. This seemed like the kind of thing that mothers and daughters would want to do together.

When she took an empty table for two by the window, a server approached.

"Hello, thank you for joining us. Would you like the full afternoon tea?"

"Yes, please."

"We offer lemonade. And tea. Hot or cold."

"Hot tea." She wanted the complete experience. Which turned out better than she anticipated. The dessert caddy held a varied selection of treats, with many of her favorites. Lemon tarts. Cucumber finger sandwiches. Fudgy brownies. All delicious. The tea was delicious, too, although hot tea on a July day might not have been so smart.

When the waiter checked on her, she asked, "Is the manager here?"

"She is. Would you like to speak with her?"

"Please."

A woman came from the kitchen. Late forties. Bright smile. Familiar-ish. "Hello. How can I help you?"

"I'm a local business owner. Bree Harper."

"I've attended one of your calligraphy classes. I'm Poppy Montgomery."

"Nice to meet you again. I have questions about the Ivy Inn."

Poppy pulled out the opposite chair, sat, and groaned with relief. "Ask, and I'll do my best."

"The tea was wonderful."

"But not well attended today." Poppy sighed. "Yes, I know. We started last month, and we're still working out the kinks."

"Do you have B&B guests?"

"We're transitioning. It's an old house, with a lot of history. The owner feels like it doesn't make sense for people outside the community to use it and not the people of Marlowe."

"What kind of events?"

"Weddings and parties. We can also put in a tent in the backyard for a larger event, but we're having good results with the small, intimate kind."

Bree was about to wing it, but her instincts were telling her this was right. "Would you consider letting me rent this room for one of my classes? If you've taken one, you know I can only fit eight people in the corner of my shop. A larger space would allow me to register more attendees, enough that I can afford the rental fee."

"I can seat twenty comfortably in the dining area," Poppy said. "More if we include the library. Did you have a specific class in mind?"

"My father's a language arts teacher at the middle school. He would like to teach a class on how to write sonnets."

"Ooh, sign me up." Poppy dug around in the pocket of her jeans. "Do you have a time frame? We could give it a try and see how it goes."

"End of July?"

"I have most Tuesday or Wednesday nights open."

"Either should be fine."

Poppy slid a business card across the table. "Bree, why don't you figure out what you could reasonably afford to pay and still make a profit on your class. If you like, I could add a sampler of treats. Free advertisement for my afternoon teas. We'll negotiate a fair introductory price." Her expression turned dreamy. "Sonnets would suggest a romantic kind of event. I could emphasize that theme. Heart-shaped cookies. Chocolate-dipped strawberries. Would your father be okay if I play up the romance?"

"Absolutely. He knows which kind of sonnets most students will want to write."

"This will be fun. We'll make it work."

Bree had been working on the numbers for Dad's class all evening. She'd sent a proposal to Poppy, it had been accepted, and Dad had agreed to the date. Now all she had to do was get the word out.

A light rap on the external door startled her. Since returning from the Ivy Inn, she'd forgotten herself, skipped dinner, too excited about the possibilities to take a break. She glanced at the time, surprised to see it was nine. Then she checked the camera feed to find Kai standing there, in a drenching rain. She hurried over to open the door.

"Come in," she said. "Why are you here?"

He shook his umbrella and stepped inside. "I was driving past and noticed the light. I didn't see your car, so I thought I'd check."

"I walked today."

"Walking home won't be much fun. Want a ride?"

"Oh. That's nice."

She backed up her computer files, locked the shop, and crowded beside him under his umbrella as they went to his car. A Honda hybrid SUV.

"Your address?" he asked and typed it into the GPS as she replied.

"Thank you so much for this. I lost track of time. Too many new ideas to play with," she said. "What had you out so late?"

"I had to take my daughter over to her mother's house."

Kai had a child. Although why Bree should be surprised, she wasn't sure. She really knew nothing about him, other than he was great at his job and had a beautiful smile. Bree had questions.

He grinned at her. "It's okay to ask."

Not wasting the chance. "Do they live nearby?"

"My ex-girlfriend lives in Chapel Hill. We share custody of our daughter, so Sienna lives with me half the time."

Bree could add *involved dad* to her knowledge base on Kai. "How old is she?"

"Four. An awesome age." He parked at the curb before her apartment.

"Thanks again for the ride." She reached for the handle.

"You're welcome. Bree? Would you . . . ?" He stopped. Drummed his fingers on the steering wheel.

Had he been about to ask her out? Well, she wasn't wasting this chance either. The past week had opened her to being bolder. "Would you like to meet for a drink sometime?"

He smiled with pleasure. "Yes."

"Why did you hesitate?"

He gave a little shrug. "It can be hard to plan something with me. My hours can be unpredictable. I don't always know when I'll be done for the day."

"Do you always know when you start? Coffee is a drink. We could meet for breakfast."

Kai's smile widened. "On a workday, it would have to be early."

"Most important meal of the day. Tomorrow?"

"I'm off this weekend. Would Saturday morning work instead? Seven thirty?"

"Seven thirty sounds great," she said and slid out. "Looking forward to it."

His SUV remained at the curb until she was in her apartment. Once inside, though, she turned on no lights, preferring the dark while she thought over how unexpectedly amazing her day had been.

Write Style was still her business, but not the one she'd originally envisioned a year ago. She'd expected to be more like a shop owner, helping customers buy just the right items to feed an interest in writing. Instead, she focused on teaching, coaching, and encouraging people to express themselves. Her business had become more satisfying once she'd let it.

And now she was taking a step toward finding a social life. A step that meant she would make herself a priority again.

CHAPTER
THIRTY-EIGHT

October 1993

When Molly originally joined Riverbend Consulting, she'd been all about writing code. But since moving to Durham, her role had changed—to something she would have never anticipated. She'd become more the face of the company. She rarely programmed now, but that was okay. She was having too much fun with travel and phone meetings and research.

Which explained why she'd spent the past four days in Washington, DC, meeting with customers and presenting at a software conference. Her topic? The joys and challenges of running a firm of freelance programmers. Happily promoting the model Arlene and Charlie had started seventeen years ago.

Riverbend had done very well. Flexibility bred loyalty, and loyalty led to a good product. The staff were still mostly women caring for small children or elderly parents. All were part time, except Norah. After Arlene's diabetes had sent her health into a decline over the past decade, Norah had assumed the role of director in Richmond.

It was surprising that, after nearly twenty years, the business model was still viewed as a novelty. They could choose the projects they wanted and hire the best. Yet the concept had never really caught on.

After the conference ended Friday afternoon, Molly had boarded a train in DC, anxious to get home to Durham. The Palmers had a big weekend planned, and she had a long to-do list. They were celebrating two events: her twentieth anniversary with Ward and the Palmer family's Thanksgiving. Early for both, but this coming weekend had been the only one that all Palmers could attend.

Ward had a long weekend off from the university where he taught others how to be ministers. He'd promised to get the house clean and a pie baked. She had her fingers crossed about the pie. Naomi had agreed to supervise. Molly wasn't sure that was any better.

David was flying in from Seattle, bringing his girlfriend to meet the family. Molly suspected they were engaged and the family would be getting the news this weekend.

Nathan was driving in from Norfolk tomorrow morning. He was coming alone, after having recently broken up with his longtime girlfriend. Molly didn't know any more than that. He'd been quiet about the details.

The train passed through the DC suburbs and headed south toward Richmond. Molly took out her notes, reflecting on some of the ideas she'd been exposed to at the conference. Advances in technology to help their disabled programmers. Conversations about the new Americans with Disabilities Act, with lots of concern expressed over how that would affect software.

But the most exciting topic of all had been the World Wide Web. The concept was frightening in its possibilities. She'd picked up documentation on HTML, determined to learn about the new markup language, and accepted a free disk copy of the Mosaic "web browser" to hand over to Norah for her opinion.

As the train slowed into the Richmond station, Molly stood, preparing to get off. But not for a smoke break. Arlene and Gwen would be waiting for her. Only a twenty-minute stop, but they would make the most of it.

It had been a tough year for Gwen. Her son had found her, but at the end of that one phone conversation, he'd let her know he was only satisfying his curiosity and wanted no further contact. Her daughter had been so upset over the secret that she'd headed off to college and hadn't communicated with her parents since.

Although both friends waited in the shadows of an overhang, Molly's focus locked on Arlene. Her friend's skin was sallow, and her body was gaunt. Molly blinked back tears as she hugged Arlene gently. "It would seem that our phone conversations have left out some key facts."

"Don't start," she said, a spirited edge to her tone. "My heart is fine. I'll manage."

Gwen was shaking her head.

Arlene glared at Gwen over her shoulder. "What are you doing back there? Get over here and greet Molly. They'll be calling her back on the train soon. I need to hear everything she learned in DC before she goes."

They found a bench, made Arlene comfortable, and Molly passed along what she'd heard about the WWW. There might not be much she could do for her friend's health, but she could satisfy Arlene's hunger to know.

After the Palmers had finished their Thanksgiving-in-October meal, they crowded into the living room.

David's girlfriend seemed charming. Shier than David, but who wouldn't be? Jill had warmed up enough to share the story of how they'd met.

"David came into the ER complaining about his ankle. The whole time we were checking it out, he flirted with me. When we discharged him, he asked me out. I told him I didn't date patients. He left, then returned five minutes later, told me he wasn't a patient any longer, and handed me his phone number." She smiled at him. "I called."

"She made me wait a week," he said sulkily.

They all laughed.

Jill linked her fingers through his and murmured something too soft to hear. He turned to his family. "We have an announcement. Jill and I are getting married."

Naomi clapped her hands.

Nathan grinned. "Beating me to the punch, little brother?"

"You always were slow."

Molly waited until the siblings had gotten their versions of *congratulations* out of their systems before asking the key questions. "When? And where?"

"December fifth in Seattle."

There was a moment of stunned silence.

Nathan shook his head. "That's not much warning."

"Tell us the rest, Dave," Ward said.

David flushed. "What makes you think there's more?"

"Statements like that."

Jill nudged her fiancé with her elbow. Gave him a look.

"Okay." His neck turned red. "We're expecting."

Molly beamed. "Oh, how lovely."

He gaped. "You're not upset?"

"That we're about to gain a daughter-in-law and a grandchild? No," Ward said. "When's the newest Palmer due?"

"In May." David shook his head. "I can't get over how well you're taking this. Jill's parents freaked out."

Molly half listened to the conversations whirling around her as she marveled at how the world had changed. Only a little but moving in the right direction. Jill had options, and the one she was choosing was David.

Ward reached for her hand, letting her know that whatever came next was fine with him.

She tightened her fingers around his. It was time. "Everyone, I have a story to tell."

◆　◆　◆

It was nearly midnight before the house grew quiet again. Naomi had returned to her apartment in Chapel Hill. Jill and David were at a hotel. Nathan was crashing in the guest room.

Molly came out of the bathroom and slipped into bed beside her husband. "I'm happy for them, Ward. Really."

"I know you are." He pulled her into his arms.

"I'm glad it's not so hopeless now."

"I agree."

"Then why am I sad?"

"Your future would've been different if you hadn't been hopeless. It's hard not to think about the might-have-beens."

But she also had to remember where she'd ended up. "I stumbled into a good life."

"No, my love. You marched into it deliberately."

CHAPTER
THIRTY-NINE

Bree had picked the outfit for her date with Kai the night before. Flirty and bright. But Saturday morning, she changed her mind. It looked like she was trying too hard. With time running out, she went with what she would have worn anyway. Basic business comfortable: coral-pink capris and a white top that felt cool and silky against her skin. She could remind Kai she worked on Saturdays, so he wouldn't be bothered if he hadn't dressed up.

She walked downtown and berated herself for that decision halfway there. It was already warm.

Kai was waiting outside the diner. In shorts and a well-fitting T-shirt, he looked great. His smile when he saw her? Even greater.

He held the door for her and followed her to her favorite booth. The waiter, who clearly knew them both, brought over the coffeepot.

"The usual?" he asked as he poured two mugs.

Bree nodded.

"Game day," Kai said.

The waiter left.

"Game day?"

"Baseball. I play in a league. So a modified breakfast today."

They smiled. Became engrossed in getting their coffee just right, which wasn't much effort on his part since he apparently took it black.

She was surprised by how anxious she was. It was really important that he found her appealing. Yet she knew he must, or they wouldn't be here.

"Are you nervous?" he asked.

She met his gaze and nodded.

"No need to be. Really."

"You don't either."

They shared smiles, and then it was all right. They were acquaintances who could become friends and maybe more. She hadn't dated since she broke off her engagement two years ago, and she was out of practice. There was a formula for first dates. To break the ice. Ask about jobs and hobbies. Movies and music. But she wasn't content to merely break the ice with Kai. She wanted to really know him. But how did she do that? Ask surreptitiously? Blurt?

He was watching her, looking as if he was on the verge of laughing. "You're thinking hard."

"Will you tell me more about your daughter?" Blurting won out.

"Oh, you're in for it now. She's just better than I deserve. My reason for being." He unlocked his phone and scrolled to an image. Slid it over to Bree. "That's Sienna."

In the photo, his little girl had big brown eyes, curly brown hair, and her father's smile. "She's adorable."

"That she is. I have her every other week. We usually hand off on Thursday nights, but next week, it'll have to be Tuesday. Sienna's mom has to go out of town for several days." He retrieved his phone. "My ex has her master's degree in crop science. She works in fields alongside farmers, helping them grow great crops. But around planting and harvest seasons, she travels a lot. Which I love 'cause it means extra time with my daughter."

"Sounds like you and her mom get along."

"Yeah. We're all about Sienna. Delivery guy wasn't on my list of what I wanted to be when I grew up. But my ex didn't discover Sienna was on the way until after we split up. We knew that one of us would have to drop out to pay the bills. I volunteered, and this is the job I found."

Attitudes were so different than they were back when unwed mothers like Molly were hidden away. Five years ago, Kai had taken on the responsibility of getting a job to support his ex and daughter. "Do you ever want to finish your degree?"

"No. My parents are disappointed, but college wasn't taking me anywhere I wanted to go. I like my job, and I'm good at it."

"Yes, you are."

Kai waited while their orders were served. A bagel for him. The full waffle-and-bacon treatment for her. Oh, well.

"Your turn to be interrogated," he said. "How are you doing? It seems like you've been riding the waves lately."

"I have been." That was a good description. Emotional ups and downs. Sometimes slapped around until she felt like she was drowning. Was she that obvious? Or was he particularly tuned in? She hoped it was the latter. "Some stuff is going on with my family. I'm also reconsidering aspects of my store, which might give me more room to breathe."

"Like what?"

After she'd explained her new options, he asked, "What's holding you back?"

"I'm not sure."

"Are any of your decisions irreversible?"

"No." She rolled her eyes. "I guess I'm just risk averse."

That drew a smile. "Cautious."

"Afraid."

"Committed to protecting your brand."

She laughed. "Protecting my brand?"

"Hey. That marketing class in college had to come in handy sometime." When his phone beeped, he pushed his plate away. "I'll have to leave soon."

"For the game?"

"Yeah. Do you like baseball?"

She shrugged. "I don't know much about it."

He shrank away in mock horror. "That will have to change."

"Will it?" Her nerves returned. This had been the best first date of her life. Fun and relaxed, mostly. She liked him, and it felt as if he liked her back. The moment had arrived to clarify what this was. What it could become.

He must have read her thoughts because he rested his hand on the table between them, palm up. "Are we going to do this?"

She linked her fingers through his. "I think we already are."

Once she'd started, Bree implemented change fast. After emailing the announcement of Dad's sonnet class to an interest list, it had sold out in two days. She had accepted Lola's proposal. And she would repeat a breakfast date with Kai Tuesday. Then nothing with him for a week. He would have Sienna back.

Her relationship with Allison had to change, too, and Bree would have to be the one to initiate an apology. She was the one who had been weird.

Are you busy?

> No

At home?

> Yes

Can I come over?

> Yes

She practiced her speech on the way, although why she bothered, it was hard to say. She would likely end up babbling while Allison listened impatiently. But Bree really *was* sorry. She'd had some wonderful things happen recently, and her best friend hadn't been part of them.

When she drove up the driveway, she saw Allison sitting on the porch steps.

As Bree approached, her friend scooted over to the side, making room.

"Hi," Bree said.

"Hi."

She would've expected arms across the chest or an injured frown. But the reaction Bree saw was more puzzled, even though this was the most sustained disconnect they'd ever had before. "I'm sorry, Allison."

"Thank you."

Her friend hadn't invited her in. Bree understood. They were barely into phase one of restoring a dented friendship into whatever it would be in the future.

Allison rested her head against the railing, staring forward. "I need you to acknowledge that you hurt me."

A legit expectation. "I know I hurt you. I hurt myself too. I don't know why I reacted the way I did, but I screwed up, and I won't make excuses."

Her friend simply nodded.

"How do we move on?"

"I am way past ready to put it behind us." Allison angled her head to meet Bree's gaze. "Do you think that once someone has decided you're abrasive that it's ever possible to get past it? Even when you're trying to improve?"

Okay, switching topics. Bree would follow. "Not impossible, but hard. It would take time and consistency."

"Yeah. That's what I think too."

"Why do you ask?"

"You know that class I mentioned about customer etiquette? It's been eye opening. Really lets me see how my *exuberance* can put people off." She smiled faintly.

Bree had to do a brain reset. The apology part of this visit was definitely over. When Allison said *put it behind us*, she meant it. "This really bugs you."

"Yeah."

"Your friends know you have good intentions."

"Yeah, but I'm not sure if my coworkers and customers do. It's been a wake-up call."

They went silent, lost in their thoughts and the gathering dusk.

Bree was used to seeing the sun set from her friend's living room, which faced west. Wild colors. Sharp images. The perspective from the east was softer. Muted. Not as pretty but interesting.

Allison straightened suddenly. "I may look for another job."

"Really?" Whatever turmoil Allison had been through, Bree had missed it completely. She felt a pang of remorse. "Why?"

"I was resistant to the training at first. It unnerved me, because it nails exactly the way I can be, valuing content over presentation. But it's beginning to make sense, and I'm wondering if it might make even more sense to get a fresh start. Find a job where my coworkers don't brace for the abrasive version of Allison every time I show up. It's just an idea. I won't act on it until my thoughts coalesce." She smiled, widely this time. "So I've caught you up on me. What's going on with you?"

"I'm marketing care packages to college students. And letting Lola take over some classes."

"You? Yielding control?"

"Yes. And get this. Dad's teaching a class on writing sonnets, and it sold out immediately."

"Glad it's full so I won't feel guilted into taking it. Anything going on with your social life?"

"Why do you ask?"

"Just curious. You seem less brittle."

Brittle? Okay, not taking the bait on that. Allison hadn't finished her etiquette lessons. And it might be true that Bree had been a bit on edge. "I went out on a date yesterday. With Kai. The delivery guy."

"I know who you mean. When you're around him, you soften."

Soften was an interesting word, and she couldn't argue with it. "It might turn into something. I hope."

They grew quiet again as darkness descended. Nothing but night noises: birds, insects, the occasional aircraft flying over. Bree should leave.

Allison stood and stretched. "I've been visiting with Galen."

"That's good." Bree was glad for them both, although it was still weird to think she and Allison had the same connection to him. "My dad is going to call Molly."

"Really? When?"

"Soon, I think."

"Once he does, let's plan a family reunion."

Bree rose and propped her butt against the railing. "Will your mom agree?"

"She'll refuse initially, but I'm pretty sure she'll show up. She's getting curious about what really happened."

"Then let's do it. How can I help?"

Allison finally turned to face her. "We should ask Molly for a reunion in person. We could go together."

"Sounds good. Have you met her?"

"Not yet. She wants contact first from one of her twins, so I'll have to wait until Everett calls her." Allison looked toward the horizon, at the moonrise. "But then I'm doing it. It's time to decide what kind of family we want to be."

CHAPTER FORTY

July 2024

Molly sat alone with her laptop on the screened porch of their home. She was participating in a software conference this week in Raleigh. Likely her last one. It was time to pass her remaining few responsibilities to Arlene's daughter and truly retire. But Molly hadn't made the *final*-final decision on that. Otherwise, she'd get too emotional.

Her iPhone chimed and VoiceOver announced a text from Gwen.

I have news

Please let it be good. A search angel had contacted Gwen three weeks ago. It had been agonizing for Molly since, wondering if she would hear something at last. She almost wished her friend had kept silent.

Ward isn't here

You'll like this

Molly put her phone aside and took a sip of cold coffee. Gwen wouldn't joke about the search for the children they'd surrendered. She had talked with her own son thirty years ago, but only the one time.

He'd been polite and pleasant and done. Gwen understood what good news was.

> Okay. Tell me

> Your son contacted me and asked for your number

Her son had reached out.

Molly felt a surge of emotion so overwhelming that she dropped her phone. Gripped the arms of her chair to keep from falling out of it. Closed her eyes and breathed slowly. This was wonderful news. So, so wonderful.

Fifty-five years had passed since she'd last seen him or held him. Was he curious? Did he want to know her? She had the shakes. Rising unsteadily, she stumbled inside, found a tea towel, and mopped her cheeks. Then grabbed a box of Kleenex and ran back to the screened porch. What had she missed?

> Did he say he would call?

> Yes, he will

> Did he say when?

> No, but soon. His name is Everett

Everett. Her son had a nice name. Okay, it was time to speak. She called.

"Hi," Gwen said, laughing. "Tired of texting?"

"I am. Did Everett say where he lives?"

"Yeah, and you need to brace yourself for the next part."

Brace herself? That felt worrisome. "Why?"

"He lives in Marlowe, Molly."

Marlowe, North Carolina? How could that be true? A couple from Boston had adopted him. "Is that a coincidence?"

"No." Gwen was distressed. "I hate to tell you this, but his full name is Everett Harper."

Harper? Somewhere, deep inside her, a wild scream of anguish threatened to bubble up. She couldn't bear the implications. "Galen's family? *That* Harper?"

"Yes, Molly. I'm sorry. Galen's parents adopted him from the Home."

Molly had been lied to all those years ago. Of course she had. She'd known that the director had been untrustworthy, but "a doctor from Boston" had seemed so specific. It had never occurred to her to question it.

Galen had been with their son his whole life. The knowledge was devastating.

"I, um, need to go. Bye, Gwen." Molly hung up, jammed the phone in her pocket, and walked into the tiny square of a yard behind their retirement home.

Had he known she'd wanted the twins back? That she'd been searching for her son for decades?

No. She might be angry with Galen, even jealous, but he wouldn't have been so cruel to keep them apart deliberately. Not the boy she'd known and loved.

Her son had been adopted by the Harpers, not a random couple. They were the people who "didn't want the girl." Or so Molly had been told. Had that been a lie too?

She had a female match who was likely a granddaughter. "Breanna H" was Breanna *Harper?*

Galen had been part of the lives of his son *and* granddaughter. Why hadn't he let her know? He could've reached her through Aunt Trudy.

No, maybe not. Her aunt would have refused.

Had Trudy known about Everett?

Molly wouldn't believe that. Her aunt couldn't have been so deceitful. Could she?

She sank onto a bench under their arbor and wept.

Ward found her there an hour later. "Gwen texted me and suggested that I check on you."

When Molly didn't react, he sat beside her, pressed a handkerchief into her hand, and put an arm around her. She slumped into him willingly.

"Tell me what happened."

"One of the twins contacted Gwen." Molly dug out her phone and handed it to him. "Read the texts."

She'd lived within a twenty-minute drive of her son for the past thirty years. She could hardly take it in. How different her life could have been if she'd only known.

Her phone rang later Sunday afternoon while she was on the porch, listening to an audiobook. She glanced at the screen. An unknown number, but her area code. She answered. "Hello?"

"Is this Molly?" a man asked.

Her heart recognized his voice. No doubt in her mind. This was her son. She swallowed hard. "Yes, this is Molly Palmer."

"I'm Everett Harper. Your friend Gwen gave me your phone number."

She closed her eyes. "Hi, Everett. How are you?" Such an inane question.

"Good. You?"

"Fine."

Not a video call. Was that a concession to her age and presumed technical skill? Or because he didn't wish to see her as they spoke?

Stop. It wasn't fair to attribute motivations to him. She knew better than to assume she understood the reasons people had for what they said or did. "Everett, please tell me about yourself."

"I'm a schoolteacher. Language arts."

Her breath caught. *A schoolteacher like your maternal grandfather.* But she wouldn't pass that along. Too soon.

"I teach at Marlowe Middle School."

"School's out now." The inanities continued. She was flustered.

"Yes, and I'm enjoying my summer off."

He told her more about his life, and she listened without comment. It was lovely to hear him speak. To let him ramble, enjoying whatever he found important enough to mention.

"So tell me about you, Molly."

"I'm a retired software engineer."

"Where do you live?"

"In Durham. With my husband."

"Oh." The other end of the line went silent.

Should she ask about Galen? She pushed aside the thought. It wasn't time for that either. She ought to establish some type of relationship with her son before widening it to include others.

She wanted to suggest a meeting, the words burning on her lips, but she wouldn't. Being rejected would be more painful than the joy of a yes. Further contact had to come from him. So she'd wait and hope. Again.

"Well, I guess I'd better go. Molly?" A sigh. "This is a complex situation. I'm not sure how to proceed."

He was in the driver's seat. Should she state that? "I understand."

"You have my phone number now."

"Yes, I do." The stress of the moment had emptied her head.

"I'll call again."

Was that a promise? Or a *don't call me* warning? "Okay. Thank you, Everett. It's been lovely speaking with you."

"You too. Bye."

Ward came out to the porch with a pitcher of sangria. When he held it up in offer, she nodded. He sat in the chair beside her and poured two glasses.

"How was it?"

"Wonderful, for me at least. He said he'd call again." Hope flickered like an ember.

"Don't worry. He meant it."

When Gwen called later that week, Molly's heart pounded. Good news again? "Hi. What's up?"

"I met someone in my travel club. We're going out tonight."

Not the good news Molly had been hoping for, but lovely just the same. Not long after Arlene died from a heart attack in the mid-'90s, Clive had passed away in an automobile accident. Gwen had found someone else on the rebound, a marriage which thankfully hadn't lasted long. It had been over twenty years since her divorce, and, although she'd dated off and on, Molly hadn't heard such happy excitement in Gwen's voice in a while. "Tell me all about him."

The next ten minutes were filled with Gwen's hopes and fears about the new man. But eventually, Gwen talked herself out and changed topics. "I haven't heard from Heather. Do you want me to contact Allison again?"

"No." Allison was the search angel who had started it all. Once Molly had learned her granddaughter's full name, she'd looked her up online and was delighted to learn the young woman was also a software engineer—a genetic predisposition—and lived nearby, in the same county as Marlowe. Another coincidence?

Molly had stopped searching for information on her granddaughter. If she'd continued, she would have discovered more, and she didn't want to. She would rather Heather's story remain blank than risk being filled with holes that distorted understanding. "We ought to hold off contacting Allison. Anything further must be my daughter's choice."

"You should consider relenting on that."

"I might. Not yet."

"Okay. Do you have anything interesting planned today?"

"I'm heading out soon for a conference in Raleigh."

"I didn't know you did that anymore . . ."

They talked for a few minutes longer before saying goodbye.

Molly looked back at her slides. They were done. Had been emailed to the conference coordinator. Nothing to change, so this review was about mentally practicing her remarks.

She rarely agreed to speak now. Although she called herself semi-retired, it was more retired than semi. Same with Ward. He'd retired from teaching ten years ago, and while he didn't actively pursue pastoral work, he could be convinced to step in at a church occasionally.

But she'd been talked into appearing at this local software-quality conference because it would be (a) a panel discussion, so she wouldn't be carrying the session on her own, and (b) purely about accessibility. She loved the idea of focusing solely on it.

She would be sharing the stage with three other panelists and a moderator. She'd only have to give a five-minute presentation, then wait for Q&A at the end.

Her phone chimed. The limo was here. She picked up her bag and went outside for the hour-long ride over to a hotel convention center in Raleigh.

Molly sat in the greenroom, waiting to be escorted onstage.

Before she left the house, Ward had mumbled something about joining her for dinner. Downtown Raleigh had great restaurants. But he hadn't texted to confirm, so he was either napping or cooking.

She was nervous. She didn't exactly hide her vision loss, but she hadn't been openly forthcoming either. Today, that would change.

Her father had lost his vision slowly. He'd stopped driving by age sixty. She hadn't noticed it was always her mother at the wheel when they drove up to Richmond to see Molly's children.

Riverbend Consulting had been active advocates for accessible hardware and software. If the people they hired required assistance to use computers, the company found or made whatever assistive technology their staff needed to be successful. It had always been the right thing to do.

Then her vision changed in her left eye, and she learned she'd inherited macular degeneration. Molly had gone from advocating for accessibility to requiring it herself.

"Ms. Palmer, are you ready?"

She stood. "Yes, thank you." She crossed to the assistant, accepted his offer of an elbow for guidance, and walked onto the stage. At her designated chair, she surveyed the room, delighted by the applause, stunned by the size of the crowd. The auditorium appeared to be standing room only.

Once the panelists were seated and mics checked, it was showtime.

CHAPTER
FORTY-ONE

Allison had debated about attending the software conference in Raleigh this year. She'd been several times in the past. Once she'd seen her grandmother's name on the list of speakers, though, it had become a given.

She sat through two morning sessions and then headed to the auditorium where Molly would be presenting. Afterward, Allison would slip away.

Her grandmother was participating in a panel session on software accessibility, sharing ideas that would benefit computer users of all abilities. The panelists would represent firsthand perspectives on visual, hearing, mobility, and cognitive accessibility.

Allison was aware that her grandmother was a longtime advocate for accessibility, but she hadn't known Molly had a personal interest in the topic. During her introduction, Molly disclosed that she was there to provide her experiences with low vision. The panel also included a man with hearing loss, another with arthritis, someone with ADHD, and the panel's moderator, a CFO from a local tech startup who was knowledgeable and passionate about the topic without addressing why she'd been invited.

After the session, a line formed in front of Molly, many holding copies of her latest book. On a whim, Allison had brought her own copy, but she hung back. Should she risk it?

Yeah, she would. She couldn't be so near and leave, but she wouldn't engage. She'd get the book signed and walk away. When they met again later, Molly might not remember.

When the line had dwindled to three, Allison joined it and took the opportunity to study her grandmother up close. Molly was below average height, with graying brown hair and blue eyes the same color as Bree's. Molly's smile seemed genuinely approachable. As she signed books, she listened, answered whatever question was posed, then sent them on their way with a firm "nice meeting you."

At last, it was Allison's turn, and that smile was directed at her.

Molly tilted her head, her smile dimming. "Allison Garrett?"

"Yes," she said, pleased at being recognized, although it shouldn't be a surprise. Her image was available on her Ancestry profile.

"I'm Molly Palmer. Obviously." She gave a slight shake of the head. "I have spoken with my son. Did you know?"

"He told me." Allison had to blink against sudden tears. She was talking with her grandmother.

"Does your mother know you're here?"

"No, I hadn't planned this. I thought . . ."

"You could speak to me, and I wouldn't recognize you."

"Something like that." They both knew she was *guilty*.

Molly looked over her shoulder, met someone's gaze out of Allison's view, and nodded. "I have a meeting in a half hour, but I'm going to the lobby coffee shop on the way. Join me."

They got in line and placed their orders. When they both had their mugs, Allison followed Molly to a pair of armchairs in a corner.

Starting with small talk might be right for someone she'd just met, but this was her grandmother, and they had only a few minutes. What Allison really wanted to know was about the reason for Molly's need for accessibility. "Molly, if this question is too personal, please tell me to mind my own business."

"It's all right. I suspect you want to know my diagnosis, and that *is* your business. Part of our family medical history." She sipped her coffee. Hummed with approval. "I have macular degeneration. So did my father. Mine's only in one eye. The centers of images are blurred. The periphery is fine."

Our family. This conversation was surreal. Allison had wondered about this woman for years. Her grandfather, too, but she'd known Galen so long that learning who he was hadn't solved as much of a mystery. Her grandmother was mostly unknown. She could learn about Molly online, but that wasn't the type of knowing Allison needed. "Thank you for telling me."

Indecision flickered on Molly's face. She wanted to ask something but wrestled with it. "I would like for whatever relationship you and I create to be open."

A wise request. No matter how much Allison wanted to know her grandmother, she wouldn't hurt Mom. "My mother is aware of my interest."

"We have to do this the right way."

"I respect that, and I think we're good, but I'll check again with her. As long as it's okay, might we meet soon? I could bring Bree. Everett's daughter."

"I would like that." Molly blew on her coffee, took a sip, and set the cup down. "What brings you here? Other than me."

"Mostly you. Although I've learned some things I'm taking back with me. Do you write code anymore?"

"I manage my own website. Experiment some with programming in Python. But my real focus shifted from technology to people thirty or more years ago."

Technology to people. What Allison had been forced to do. A change in focus. Or rather, the stretching of her skills to accommodate more.

Someone stopped at the table. "Molly?"

They looked up. It was the moderator from the panel. She glanced at Allison before smiling at Molly. "I'm heading over to the meeting."

"I'll walk with you." She rose. "Allison, this is Tamsin Carroll. Tamsin, my granddaughter, Allison Garrett. She's a software architect at . . . ?"

"Justis Software Systems," the woman completed the sentence. "I know Fawn. She's mentioned you."

Really? Allison was dying to know what Fawn had said. Or why they'd been talking about her.

Tamsin said to Molly, "Ready?"

"Yes. Thank you, Allison, for joining me."

The two women walked out together, talking as they went.

Allison stayed in the coffee shop for a few minutes after her grandmother left, not wanting to see or talk to anyone she knew until she'd processed how she felt. It had pleased her when Molly identified her so naturally as "my granddaughter." But the reminder about Mom? That was cause for concern. There must be a way to work things out.

The conference didn't end for the day until four, but Allison was ready to go home.

Over the weekend, Allison texted Molly with an invitation—to meet with both granddaughters for coffee and a proposal. They agreed on Monday at a coffee shop in Durham.

Even though Allison and Bree arrived fifteen minutes early, Molly was there ahead of them, her husband at her side. It was the first time Allison had seen him in person. He murmured to his wife and slid from his seat. As he edged by, he smiled but didn't speak.

"So how do we do this?" Bree asked.

"Why don't I take you over and introduce you to her? Then I'll place our orders."

Molly remained seated, head tilted to see them better, her whole attention on soaking up the first sight of this new granddaughter. "Hello," she said. "Thank you for coming, Bree."

"I'm glad to be here, Molly."

By the time Allison returned, her friend was chatting while their grandmother listened avidly. It wasn't much of a hurdle to clear. Bree had been more than ready.

When they broached the idea of a reunion, Molly was initially reluctant to commit without a firm acceptance from Mom.

"Are you sure it's all right?"

"I think my mother will come, and I don't think she expects the rest of us to wait."

"Okay then."

Allison sighed with relief. In her opinion, her grandmother was being overly cautious, but they would work with whatever Molly thought best. "Bree and I can plan it. Do you have preferences?"

"Outside would be nice, if you can find neutral territory."

"On a Saturday? At ten thirty?"

"A well-chosen time," Molly said, "so we can meet and talk and leave for lunch."

"Yes. To be clear, is it a requirement for my mother to come?"

There was a pause. "No, I want to meet whomever wants to meet me. Where should we hold it?"

"The Ivy Inn?" Bree suggested.

"That's not neutral territory. My grandmother, your great-great-grandmother, was Ivy Mitchell. It was her home. Now it's mine."

Bree gasped. "Is Galen aware of that?"

"It's where we met, so he knows it was my Grammy's. He might not know I inherited it. Actually, I should say that, while I own the property, it's entirely Poppy Montgomery's business." When her phone vibrated, Molly lifted it and spoke softly. "I'm ready."

They all stood.

"Ladies, it was lovely to visit with you. I'm sure whatever location you choose for the reunion will be fine. Just let me know. And please, go on. No need to worry about me. Ward is on his way."

They said their goodbyes and headed out. Her husband was entering and held the door for them.

"Dr. Palmer? I'm Bree, and this is Allison."

"Please, call me Ward." His smile was warm. "Thank you for this. It means a lot to my wife." He continued inside.

They were silent until they were in Allison's car and driving away from downtown Durham.

"She's nice," Bree said. "And scared."

"Scared of what? Rejection?"

"Possibly, but the greater worry is to be dismissed. Judged unworthy of inclusion. What she's opening herself to is brave."

"Same for us."

"True, but braver for her. We're in control." A minute passed before Bree said, "Don't be disappointed, Allison, but my reaction to her is mild. I feel admiration and curiosity, but I can't say whether it'll ever be more."

"Why would I be disappointed?"

"You're hoping for a fairy-tale ending. A reunion that leads to something big and happy."

"I'm hoping for a *positive* ending, whatever that is, and it doesn't have to be the same for each of us. I just don't want there to be resentment in any direction."

"We all know you're the most engaged."

That was true, as much as she could be while staying loyal to her mother. Allison accelerated onto the highway, merged in, and glanced at her friend. "A search angel encounters many kinds of outcomes. They can be painful and messy, even heartbreaking. Our story is edging toward the nicer kind. All we have left is to figure out the details."

"What if she wants more than we can give?"

"She already has more than she ever hoped for. Anything beyond that will be a bonus."

Bree squirmed in her seat. Checked something on her phone. "Eno River State Park."

The location for the reunion? "Perfect."

"How about a week from Saturday? Just family."

"Agreed." Allison could feel her friend's gaze on her profile. "What?"

"Did you know about Molly's connection to the Ivy Inn?"

"I did. Galen told me, but I'd forgotten."

"I think we each have discoveries that the other hasn't heard."

"Like the birth registries." Yeah, Allison really ought to let go of that one.

"Exactly." Bree wiggled for comfort in her seat and stared ahead. "Okay, let's compare what we've learned. Starting from the beginning."

Once Molly agreed to the reunion plans, Allison pondered how much time to give her mother to react. Eventually she punted the decision to Dad.

He called her back after broaching the subject with Mom. "Your mother is noncommittal for now, but that's better than refusing. So don't blunder in."

Blunder? Did he really think that of her? *Let it go.* "Okay, I get it. I'll be careful."

"Which isn't saying much."

"Thanks, Dad."

They hung up laughing.

When Mom invited her over for lunch the next day, Allison saw it as a good sign. She was itching to say something, but the back-off look from Dad kept her lips sealed about Molly.

Throughout the meal, they steered clear of the sensitive subject until her mother suddenly asked, "Will Galen be there?"

There, as in the reunion? She glanced at her father, who was trying to hide his smile. "Yes, he will."

"I'm not ready for both of them."

"When will you be?"

"I don't know. I still have questions."

"Which you can get answered if you come," Allison said, ignoring her father's scowl.

Mom sighed as she laid her utensils on her plate. "I'm not sure I want an audience when I ask them."

The curious comments and tone were permission to continue. Weren't they? "Would a one-on-one be better?"

"No." Mom shuddered. "How well do you know her?"

"I've met with Molly a couple of times."

"And?"

"She seems nice." Allison should try a suggestion she'd read in etiquette training. *Drop a tiny seed, and get out of its way.* "We owe it to ourselves to hear her story, not assume what you were told is the whole truth."

Mom shrugged, picked up her glass of tea, and headed out to the deck.

Dad gave a thumbs-up. Progress.

Allison drove to Durham for her fourth and final workshop session. Afterward, they were having an end-of-course celebration. Allison felt as if she had something big to celebrate. Navigating around her mother's boundaries without an explosion.

The workshop leader announced a final role-play, and the prompt was relevant. "Your boss has made a promise to a client in a meeting that there is no possibility her team can provide. How can you correct expectations without embarrassing your boss?"

Allison could have used this practice two weeks ago. Jax had promised something ridiculous to a group of customers on his trip to Glasgow. She had been listening in over Zoom, and embarrassing him had been unavoidable. Allison had cleared up the error with the customer, but her handling of Jax had been less than stellar. A do-over, under the insightful eye of the workshop leader, would be great.

At last, the program was over. Four brutal sessions with an unknown number of bad habits on their way to extinction. The participants didn't bother to say their goodbyes. The farewell reception at a nearby pub would be enough.

Before heading over, she made the mistake of checking her emails and got caught up in a thread, which had her showing up later than planned at the pub's private room. The good appetizers had been consumed. The guest speaker had finished speaking, and the workshop leader was giving her closing remarks.

Allison ordered a glass of club soda with lime and stood in the back, observing the seven other people who'd been in the same circumstance as she, struggling to be better, putting their vulnerabilities on display, bleeding over their failures. She'd participated while doubting that she would absorb any lasting benefits. But it had been worth the time.

She felt a presence beside her. It was the person Molly had introduced at the conference, the panel moderator. "Hi, Tamsin."

"Hello." She studied Allison curiously. "Were you in this workshop?"

"Yes. Why are you here?"

"I was the guest speaker for the celebration. I went through the program two years ago and told them I was willing to speak if they ever needed me."

Allison couldn't hide her surprise. Tamsin was at the top of her organization. "Who made you take it?"

"Me." She grinned. "Who made you?"

"Fawn."

"Do you think it helped?"

Allison wished she knew. The thing about change was that it wasn't always for the better. She was more thoughtful in her presentation of information, considering both the audience and the words. She also felt muzzled. Constantly second-guessing herself.

Maybe that would get better when her new soft skills became part of muscle memory, but it might come at a price. She was valued for how imaginative her ideas could be. In the time it took to apply the correct filters, some of the brightness could dim. The workshop hadn't taught her how to tell if she'd gone too far the wrong way. "I'm a work in progress, but I'm hopeful."

"Good response. Do you mind me asking why Fawn sent you?"

The question ought to have been too personal, but Tamsin sounded genuinely interested. "I can be rude in meetings with customers."

"Rude or impatient?"

"I guess it depends on your perspective."

"You'll figure out how to relax into what you've learned." Tamsin pursed her lips, as if mulling something over, before facing Allison squarely. "I talked to a mutual client. He says you're blunt and worth having around."

Blunt? Allison considered the word. Honesty without sharp edges. She could work with that.

"You may be where I was five years ago. Trying to speak plainly and having it interpreted all wrong. I've learned that blunt can be channeled. It's more than simply improving my delivery. It's also knowing that being direct is a tool. You use it exactly when it's needed." Tamsin rattled the ice in her glass. Took a sip.

Allison took this as encouragement to ask what she wanted to know. "Why are you doing this?"

"I'm giving you the abridged version of my speech." Tamsin's smile widened. "It was a good one."

Allison laughed. "Sounds like it. Anything else I missed?"

"Yes, but I think you're already putting them into practice. You pay attention. Adjust to what I say. React with concern when you've slipped up. I can see that you actually care about improving. The workshop was about more than checking a box. Will you ask for a coach?"

"HR said I could, but I don't know. It would have to be someone I really trust."

Tamsin gestured across the room at the workshop leader. "She coaches. If you trust her."

"Thank you."

"My pleasure. It helps to know you're not alone." Tamsin held out a business card. "I'm not a trained coach, but if you ever want a sounding board, call."

Allison accepted the card, surprised again. "Why? I can be rude."

"You took the class. You have tools now." Tamsin nodded and walked away.

Weirdly, that was one of the most comforting statements she'd heard in the past month. Allison slid the card into her pocket. Their exchange might have done her as much good as the workshop.

CHAPTER
FORTY-TWO

With her salesclerk leaving early, Bree spent the last hour before closing in the showroom. It was so hot outside, there wasn't much street traffic. The hoped-for summer storm had never appeared. She lounged in the conversation corner, laptop open, reviewing inventory data. When the shop door chimed, she looked up. "Hi, Galen. Welcome."

He approached, his smile tentative. "You're not busy."

"No, it's almost time to close."

He held up two tall to-go cups. "Orangeade?"

"Thank you. It's been a while since I had one of these." As she accepted a cup, she felt a whisper of nostalgia. Twenty years ago, while Mom and Dad had been going through their rancorous divorce, Bree had often stayed with Galen and Nell. Heading to the diner for fresh-squeezed orangeade with her uncle had been their thing. It had made her feel so special during a time when she'd needed to be noticed by someone.

She patted the empty spot beside her. "Join me."

They sipped their drinks and watched passersby. They didn't speak, but Galen was radiating tension. He must have come here to say something. Was he unsure how to start?

She would make it easy on him. "Have you come to clear the air?"

He exhaled with relief. "Yes."

"Okay, let's do it. I'll go first." She faced him. "It makes me sad that I could have had you as a grandfather my whole life. I missed out."

"I regret that deeply, not being able to act like your grandfather openly."

"Do you have similar regrets about Dad?"

He licked his lips and took another sip, his hand shaking ever so slightly. "I'm sorry he didn't know that Callum was his brother or Nell was his stepmother. He would've been closer to them, I think."

"What about not being Dad's father?"

"I regret that, too, but not quite as much. I would've been horrible at it. Between college and the military, I was almost entirely absent from the first seven years of Everett's life. My father loved being his dad, and I did a decent job as his brother, when our age difference allowed." He pursed his lips, sucked them in, as he battled through a strong emotion. Grief or remorse. Or both. "I've come to terms with the choices I had to make long ago and ultimately concluded that being a good brother was an improvement over terrible father."

Was that regret talking? As far as she could remember, he'd been a good father to the three boys he'd raised with Nell. "Why didn't you ever say anything?"

He set his cup down and stared off into space. "My parents told me that if Everett had been adopted by someone else, I would have never heard from him again. By rescuing him, I was forever in their debt, and the price was my silence."

Bree was torn between grief at what they'd suffered and outrage at the appalling things her great-grandparents had said to Galen. "That's *extortion.*"

"Whatever it's called, it worked."

"But even after they were gone, you went along with the lie."

He shrugged uncomfortably. "That's hard to explain, even to myself. It was a form of penance, I suppose. I didn't consider how the rest of you would pay."

"But DNA testing has become so popular."

"It didn't seem like the kind of thing people in our family would try. We're too careful about our privacy." He pulled a handkerchief from his pocket and patted his mouth. "I was wrong, and I'm glad of it."

She would tuck what he'd said away and think it over later. She couldn't condone what Galen had done. Not knowing the truth had cost her and Dad the chance to meet Molly years ago. But the way Granna and Grampa had treated Galen had been disgusting. Bree felt like she was waking up from a dream. People she thought she'd understood so well, she hadn't known at all. "How did their demands affect your relationship with them?"

"Kept it edgy, but I couldn't stay angry. It was clear they thought Everett hung the moon. They were better parents to him than they were to me."

"Did you resent that?"

"Not at all. I'm glad he was able to have the life he wanted." His gaze went unfocused, as if he were lost in the past. "My parents despised Molly on principle. I reminded them once that the woman they called such filthy names gave birth to their beautiful boy. They had a fit, and it got ugly. I enlisted in the army not long after that. I had to get away from them."

"How did your parents react when you enlisted?"

"Horrified at first, especially my mother, but they were eventually relieved. I'd become a surly beast of a son."

It was unreal, this portrait he was painting of Granna and Grampa. She had loved her grandparents. They had been good to her. But she had to accommodate this new information somehow. She would have to push her feelings about what she'd learned to the background, to be handled later. "Will you tell me about Molly? What attracted you to her?"

His face softened. "She was fiercely smart and very good at hiding it. She loved science, back in the days when girls weren't supposed to. Her father was a high school principal, and it put stress on her."

"I get that." Her father was the most popular language arts teacher at the middle school. It had been weird to be there and to be in his class.

"I was so proud of you and your dad for finding careers that centered around books and writing."

"Why didn't you do what you wanted?"

"The family business had been around for four generations. I couldn't be the person who let it fall apart."

"But you didn't encourage Dad to take over."

"Teaching was right for him." He toyed with his handkerchief. Refolded it. "Molly and I would sit on the veranda sometimes, late at night, talking about books. Then the conversation would drift. She would listen while I whined about my future, then cut through my self-pity and crap and push me to think bigger. It helped but only so far. She and I lived in a world where kids didn't buck their parents. Family over individual. We had no one else to turn to, so we turned to each other. She became my refuge, and I became hers."

Bree wasn't sure how to respond. The memories he shared were private and tender and achingly sad. "Why did she need you?"

"She was isolated. Boys didn't ask her out, too afraid of her father. She had to make good grades but not too good. She had to have impeccable behavior or not get caught."

"She did get caught."

"Yeah, and it was so bad." His voice had thickened.

"Did you get caught too?"

Galen shook his head. Sank lower in his seat. "No, it barely affected me. At least, outwardly. You were expected to wait until marriage back then. But if guys didn't, it was chuckled over. Something to taunt you about later. Life went on, with a bit of admiration that you'd persuaded a girl to put out. For girls? Getting caught was their ruination. Endless shame. Molly's life would've been pure hell if she'd stayed."

The conversation had affected him. Raised regrets that he'd buried to survive. Bree would leave it alone. "Thank you for the orangeade."

"You're welcome, and thank you for letting me ramble on. Bree, I hope we can . . . well, not start over. That's too much to ask. But maybe we can regroup. Discover our own path to being grands. When you're ready."

She could sentence Galen to a lifetime of apologizing. Letting this go wasn't about approving his choices. It was about not wasting their future. She leaned over and kissed his cheek. "How about today?"

His eyes glimmered. "Yeah?"

"Yeah." For so long, she and Dad had been a complete family unit. People had overlapped with them, forming other units. Mom and Bree's two half brothers. Uncle Galen's family. Cousins sprinkled about. But when she thought of *my family*, her first thought went to *Dad and me*.

Now it seemed like family was everywhere, and that was a very good thing. She would welcome it with open arms.

CHAPTER
FORTY-THREE

Reunion Day had arrived. Today, Molly would meet her twins, and they would meet her.

She got up before dawn, drank too much coffee, fretted for hours about what to wear, and paced a mile around their backyard. Nervous to the point of jittery. They'd scheduled the reunion for a Saturday morning to beat the heat. It would be held at a picnic shelter in Eno River State Park. Ward had driven her out there yesterday to make sure they could find it.

Even though she'd dreamed about reuniting with her twins for years, she hadn't accounted for her conflicting emotions. There was delight at being able to know them for the lovely people they must certainly be. But also fear that there would be nothing more than polite conversation, self-conscious smiles, and dismissal.

No. She shouldn't allow herself to believe the worst. They were at the start of something. To assume anything else would be premature.

She'd been a public speaker for over thirty years. It had been intimidating at first, but the passion for her topic, for influencing her audience, had carried her through. Yet she'd never been this anxious before. Professional speeches had been for the benefit of others, to teach or inspire. This meeting was about her. And Galen. And the twins.

"Hey," Ward said, placing himself in her path.

She stopped abruptly and looked up. She'd been circling the kitchen island. It was a wonder she hadn't made a rut in the hardwood floor. "Hey."

"You're beautiful." He slid his arms around her waist. "It'll be okay."

"Maybe."

"Just let it be."

She rested against him and breathed in his clean scent. "I worry about Heather."

"She's worrying about you too."

Molly flashed him a smile. "Probably."

"Undoubtedly." He kissed her. "If you're ready, let's go."

They were the first to arrive, just as she'd planned. Ward carried a cooler to a picnic table under the shelter. She had dithered about what to bring. They'd set the event for ten thirty. Halfway between breakfast and lunch. But she hadn't wanted people to go hungry. So water and fruit.

An SUV pulled in slowly and parked. Bree got out of the back seat and strolled to the shelter. She was smiling. "Are you ready for this, Molly?"

"I think so." She quivered with anxiety, but the show of concern helped.

Galen got out next, closed the door with a soft click, and walked slowly over. It was only her second glimpse of him in fifty-six years, but she would have recognized him anywhere. He was still tall and thin, his hair now silvery gray. He remained an attractive man.

He stopped a few paces away and took off his sunglasses. "Hello, Molly."

She wasn't prepared for how it would feel to see him. But why should that be a surprise? She should have allowed herself to anticipate what being in his presence again would do to her. The betrayal and pain she'd buried from their last meeting nearly choked her, that agonizing last meeting where he'd stood to the side, grim and silent, while both sets of parents planned their futures without consulting them. He'd let her go to her fate and never contacted her again.

Ward placed a comforting hand on the small of her back. Steadying her.

"Galen." She kept her hands pressed to her waist. She didn't want to touch him. Not sure why. She wouldn't shatter or fall apart. "You got to spend a lifetime with Everett." Why had she said that? Why had the first complete sentence from her mouth been reproachful?

"He's a fine man," Galen said, "despite me." He looked over his shoulder. The engine for the SUV finally shut off. Its door opened. Gravel crunched as the driver stepped out. Galen looked back at her. "I wasn't told the truth, Molly."

She kept her eyes on Galen, not wanting to share the moment she first saw her son with anyone but Everett. "What were you told?"

"You signed his adoption papers and walked away."

She shouldn't be surprised, but it still hurt to hear. There had been so much deception, from all the adults in their lives. "Did you believe them?"

His sigh held regret. "I wasn't sure. I should have questioned it."

She couldn't fault him. They'd been so young and a couple for only two months. It would have been hard to know what to believe.

Behind her, a man laughed. Everett. The time had arrived. She took a deep breath, turned, and drank in the sight of her son.

Everett had joined his daughter, hands in pockets. He was an attractive man, too, with laugh lines bracketing his golden-brown eyes and a captivating smile. "Hi, Molly."

She nodded, unable to speak, simply gawking, aching to hold him again. He kept a short distance between them, which disappointed her, but she understood. Maybe one day.

Beside her, Ward stirred, reminding her of the proprieties. "Everett, Galen," she said, "this is my husband, Ward Palmer."

Everett and Ward shook hands. For Galen and Ward, a single pump of their hands. Possibly the only contact that would happen today between the two sides.

Was that what they were? Sides?

Not what she hoped. She preferred to believe they would be more like misplaced puzzle pieces. Too faded and frayed to be perfect, but perhaps they could fit together again.

Would her daughter come? Allison seemed to think so, but Heather was ten minutes late.

"Molly? May I speak to you alone?" Galen's question was quiet but clear. He'd shocked Bree and Everett, because they stared, mouths gaping.

She hadn't anticipated this possibility, but it felt right. Nodding, she accompanied Galen onto the path. They turned toward the river and stopped on the bluff, far from the edge. She could hear the water rushing past.

"I'm sorry," he said.

No excuses. No dissembling. Just a heartfelt apology. Her hurt eased. Only a little, but it was enough. They had been seventeen, living in a different world. She would let this go. "Thank you."

"What I did—"

"No, please. Stop." She sent him a serene smile. "You've apologized. I've accepted. Let's not repeat it."

"You're . . ."

"Taking this well? I'm a minister's wife. Maneuvering through emotional minefields is a skill I had to develop early." They had to start anew with the tone they would follow for the future. "We have some catching up to do. Eventually. For today, we could begin with something positive. Did you become a teacher?"

"No, I managed my parents' store until they died, then I sold it. But I didn't give up on books." His smile was humble. "I'm a self-published author. The books sell modestly, and I've built a nice fan base."

"Sci-fi?"

He laughed. "Historical mysteries."

This was the Galen she'd remembered. Before the troubles came. "Tell me about your family."

"My wife, Nell, passed away last fall. I have a son with her and two stepsons. All three are fine men."

"So many boys."

"Yeah, but Nell was tough." He grinned. "Do you have children?"

Galen was either very disciplined or not technologically advanced. Once he'd learned her married name, he could've discovered nearly anything about her life that he wanted to know. "Ward and I also have three. Two sons and a daughter. Plus six grands and five and a half greats."

"Allison says you're a software pioneer."

"Retired. I got into the field by accident and stayed for a career."

"Sounds like you've had a good life."

"I have. You too."

They grew quiet. Facing out. Listening to the river, hikers tramping past, the faint murmur of conversation from the picnic shelter. How strange it was that here she stood, next to the man who'd been the boy with her when her life had taken such a dramatic, irreversible detour. The hurt was still there. Questions lingered. But it was time to put their history behind them.

"Is that all?" She held out her hands. Did he understand?

He clasped them gently. "It is. We move forward from here."

CHAPTER
FORTY-FOUR

Allison scanned the group under the shelter. Everett and Ward were swapping baseball trivia. Bree was trying to participate somewhat ineptly since she was hardly a baseball fan.

Molly and Galen had gone off together, standing on the bluff above the river, talking. As she watched, they came back down the path, the mood between them light.

Allison was glad the small talk was going smoothly. It allowed her to keep an eye on the lane without interruption. Her parents weren't here yet, but she wasn't worried. Dad would have texted her if they weren't coming.

The whine of an engine drew closer. Dad's truck traveled slowly around the circle and parked at its apex. Her parents got out and walked along the trail toward them, hand in hand.

As Molly and Galen rejoined the group, Molly tilted her head, trying to see better.

Mom's gaze scanned the group, locking briefly on her birth mother. Everyone else froze, holding their collective breath.

Molly's smile was tentative. Hopeful.

Mom stayed firmly on the pleasant side of neutral. It must be how she was holding herself together. When she and Dad entered the shelter,

Allison stepped forward. As one of the organizers behind the reunion, she would take responsibility for keeping it on track.

"Hi, everyone. We can get started."

All eyes turned to her.

"Something I've discovered when helping people on Ancestry is that the stories handed down can be exaggerated. We all have questions about this story, and I hope that Molly will be able to help us find the truth."

Molly fumbled for her husband's hand. "Okay." The word came out like a croak.

Allison looked at her uncle, hoping he would take over.

Everett accepted the handoff. "What were you told about my adoption?"

"The director at the Home said they placed you with a couple from Boston."

"Boston?" His eyes widened. "You didn't know they were my grandparents?"

"Not until three weeks ago. Although I shouldn't be surprised. The Home had to lie."

"Why?"

"If I'd known where you really were, I would've tried to find you. The staff had to tell me something to prevent me from looking."

"It didn't stop you from trying, though," Ward said. "Did it?"

She flinched and looked up at him.

Ward's smile took in the others. "We took a family vacation to Boston in 1976 and went to a Red Sox game. She scrutinized every seven-year-old boy who passed by. Wondering."

"You knew that?"

"All along."

Her smile was relieved. Grateful.

Everett asked another question. "Why weren't Heather and I adopted together?"

"I was told that your parents . . ." Molly stopped, flushed, clearly uncomfortable. She looked over at her daughter and back to her son. "I was told the adoptive parents didn't want two children."

"No." Galen shook his head firmly. It was the first time he'd spoken since the side-chat with Molly. "That can't be true. They couldn't have known."

Everett was staring hard at Bree, his eyebrow raised in question. She noticed and shook her head, confirming that Galen was wrong. She had proof that the older Harpers had deliberately chosen only one. Everett clenched his fists and looked away.

"What happened to me?" Heather asked, her voice tight.

Molly angled her head, trying to focus. "After I discovered the director had separated you, I made it clear that the twins should be adopted together. When she refused, I knew I had to do something. There was nothing I could do about Everett; he was already gone. But I wouldn't trust her with your future. So I stole you from the Home."

"Stole me?"

"Yes. I bundled you up one morning and disappeared through the woods."

"Then why did you abandon me on a porch?"

"Abandon you on a porch?" Molly staggered, falling into her husband. Her face reflected sheer horror. "That is *not* what happened."

CHAPTER
FORTY-FIVE

April 1969

Molly's first week with her baby daughter had been delightful. Just the two of them. Sequestered from the world. Unseen and unnoticed.

Diana hadn't cried or wailed. She mewled, like a kitten, sweet sounds weaving invisible threads into Molly's heart. Why would anyone want her to relinquish this precious little girl?

But the second week? Diana had colic. She flailed and screeched, not loudly but impossible to ignore. Molly had been helpless to understand how to make things better and had no one she could ask. Not her mother. Or the neighbors. Not even the local doctor. Especially him. He would want to give Diana a thorough examination. Ensure she had all of her inoculations. Molly knew her daughter needed them, but she couldn't risk being found out.

She could make no plans. Do no chores. The days became an endless round of tending to Diana's needs, doing everything possible to make her comfortable and get her to *hush*.

Mrs. Kinsley's words began to invade Molly's thoughts.

Why are you being so selfish?

Why? Why was it selfish to want to raise her own child?

You aren't the best.

But she would be. Someday.

That was the problem, though. How long would it be before she could afford to be the best? The best meant college. Becoming a teacher. How could she make that happen while raising a child? Where would they live? How would they eat?

One day, her child would go to school. What would the other kids call her? Would they let her play? Would the teachers treat her daughter differently? She and Diana might have to move to leave the taunts and judgments behind.

Would Diana understand that Molly was doing the best she could?

No, it wasn't an acceptable way to live. She couldn't allow her child to be less than.

◆　◆　◆

"Molly?"

She startled out of a sound sleep. It was dim in the room with the curtains closed, but she could tell it was midafternoon. Beside her on the bed, Diana lay peacefully. The little one had kept her up half the night. Restless and cranky. Completely awful. But she looked like an angel now.

Aunt Trudy was standing in the doorway, silhouetted by the sunlight in the hall. She came in and gazed down at her great-niece. "She is such a pretty baby."

"She is." Molly swallowed a sob as she lifted her daughter.

"Have you made a final decision about what to do?"

She had. She'd known in her heart that only one choice made sense. Only one choice put Diana first. Molly had to allow another family to give her child everything that she could not.

"I'll let her go." There. She'd said it out loud. All that was left were the details. She wouldn't think about a future without her babies. She had to stay focused on the next steps. "But I'm not taking her back to the Home."

"I agree. They had their chance, and they blew it." Aunt Trudy smoothed her hand over Diana's head. "Dr. Thompson will help."

Molly had met him once. He'd been Grammy's doctor. Really old. Really kind. Trusted by the entire town. "What can he do?"

"He knows people who are looking to adopt. And who'll be good parents."

"Have you talked with him?"

"Twice. I haven't told him who you are."

Molly nodded as she cuddled her daughter. Watched her lips suck.

"Let him help you, honey. We can trust him to find a loving family. A couple who'll take good care of her."

She had run out of good reasons to resist. It was time to acknowledge that her twins would be better off without her—the Molly who'd been abandoned herself. She might have made it with help, but the girl she was right now wasn't enough. She had to accept it and not be selfish. Not begrudge her children the advantages they would get elsewhere.

The forever of this decision hurt so badly. "I love them."

"I know you do. That's why this decision is so hard." Her aunt added gently, "Do you want me to call Dr. Thompson and see if he'll take her tonight?"

Nodding, Molly slung her legs over the side of the bed and rose, cradling her daughter.

"Okay. Go and pack. We'll leave after dinner."

"I don't have much to pack."

"There's a suitcase under the bed in the guest room. Take whatever you need. Clothes. Cash. Books. Anything."

She put her daughter in a basket and carried her from room to room, filling the suitcase. She started with the items Gwen smuggled out. From her grandmother's room, Molly added clothes that could be belted or altered, a pair of leather gloves, and a wool jacket. At the last minute, she threw in pieces of Grammy's costume jewelry.

It was good to be busy. Molly didn't have to think about how this day would end. She only had to go through with it.

When the suitcase was full, she went downstairs to the living room, pushed the recliner back as far as it would go, and settled Diana on her chest for a nap.

Too soon, she heard her aunt say, "Molly, it's time to leave."

She groaned and pushed up. Her limbs felt leaden.

On the ride to the doctor's house, she made her one demand. "Tell him it can't be anyone who lives in Marlowe."

"Because Galen is here?"

"Yes." She gazed down at her daughter. "She looks like him, doesn't she?"

"She does," Trudy agreed quietly. "I'm sure Dr. Thompson can find a couple away from Marlowe. He'll be careful. So, will you go home?"

"No, I can't face them."

"Oh, honey. Don't hide out of shame."

Molly frowned at her aunt's profile. "I'm not ashamed of me. I'm ashamed of *them*."

"They didn't have a choice."

"They most certainly did, and now I'm making mine."

Trudy parked under a tree across the street from the doctor's house. "It's best if you stay in the car. The doctor can claim he doesn't know who you are."

"Don't worry. I can't go up there with you." She wouldn't be the one to hand over her baby.

She snuggled Diana against her chest. Breathed in her sweet baby scent. *I love you, and you'll never know.* Trudy had come around to the passenger side of the car and reached in.

"Here," Molly said and kissed her daughter for the last time.

Trudy took Diana silently. Molly watched as her aunt rang the doorbell. A man opened the door and stepped aside. Trudy walked in.

Molly looked straight ahead, feeling as if she'd lost a part of her soul. The sun had disappeared behind the tree line. Houses in the neighborhood had their lights on, shadows moving back and forth across the shades.

Trudy returned ten minutes later and slid behind the wheel. "Everything will be fine. He has a wonderful couple in mind. They live in a different city." She cranked the car and pulled away. She didn't speak again until they were outside town limits. "Where would you like me to take you?"

"To the Raleigh train station."

"I doubt any trains will come through tonight."

Molly shrugged. It didn't matter. She would sleep on a bench all night if necessary. Because in the morning, she would be headed north to Richmond. And a new life.

CHAPTER
FORTY-SIX

Bree listened to Molly recount her story, crisply factual and completely awful. A scared, vulnerable teen had been forced into making a desperate choice while every adult in her life let her down.

Her heart broke for that teenage girl.

Galen might not think his parents had a hand in separating the twins, but Bree was convinced they had. Maybe they hadn't been able to afford two children. Maybe they hadn't believed they could do a good job with twins at their age. Bree sincerely hoped that it wasn't because they hadn't wanted a girl. Whatever the reason, it was consigned to history.

She owed it to her family to share what she knew. She would, eventually. But right now, this conversation could sustain only so much pain before something or someone irrevocably broke.

"We'd been living for two weeks in my Grammy's house," Molly said, her voice dull, "before I agreed my baby needed more than I could give her." When she sagged, Ward slid a supportive arm around her waist.

"My aunt called the town doctor to tell him we were coming. He was waiting at the door." She met Heather's gaze. "He said he would find you a good home somewhere besides Marlowe."

Heather's face was an unreadable mask. "The doctor told my parents you left me in a basket on the porch, tucked under a blanket—no note, no information. Then you got on a train and disappeared."

Molly shook her head slowly. "The train part was true, although how the doctor could have known that if I'd abandoned my baby is hard to imagine. So yes, I did disappear, but the rest is a fabrication. Aunt Trudy knew everything about you. The doctor could've learned whatever he wanted by asking. Perhaps he thought it best not to. My aunt later told me that your parents lived in Raleigh. Your father was an engineer and your mother, a secretary who planned to quit and be a stay-at-home mom. I was afraid to hear more than that."

Allison spoke into the silence. "That's accurate. Mom did live in Raleigh for the first half of her life. My grandparents were originally from Marlowe and moved back when they retired. We didn't move there until I was five."

Heather asked, "Why didn't you want me to end up in Marlowe?"

Molly looked primed to burst into tears. "I would've haunted the town if I'd known my twins were there."

Heather winced at *my twins* and frowned at the ground.

Dad leaned forward, engaged in the story. "Why didn't you keep us?"

"At the time, it seemed impossible. You can't know how badly an unwed mother was treated back then. I would have been reviled, and my children with me. I couldn't have gotten government assistance. No one in my family would help. I was told Galen wanted nothing to do with me."

"Not true," he said.

She exchanged a glance with him that was unspeakably sad before looking back at the twins. "The best I could've hoped for was a minimum-wage job and the lifestyle that brings. I couldn't have done that to you."

Galen nodded his agreement. The rest of them took in the words, unable to understand what that world must've been like.

"So what now?" Dad asked.

"I'm not sure . . ." Molly faltered to a stop.

Her husband wrapped his hand around hers. "Ask for what you want," he murmured softly.

She stared into his face fearfully. His nod encouraged. And some of the tension left her body. She returned her gaze to the rest of them. "I hope that we can find our way to a cordial relationship."

At the yearning in those words, Bree felt something bloom inside her. Not peace or resolution. There were still too many regrets and doubts. But she had hope for a direction out of this tangle of lies and secrets, a path to follow.

Just as strongly, Heather remained unconvinced. Bree couldn't fault that. The doctor must have thought he was doing her parents a favor. Maybe they had, too, telling her what they genuinely believed had happened. Instead, that story had been a disservice to Heather. What she'd heard brought a lifetime of pain and rejection. It wouldn't be easy to reverse.

Rod Garrett nodded, reserved and receptive.

Allison wanted a relationship, but the look she sent her mother said it all. She would bide her time until Heather was ready.

Dad wanted this reunion to lead to a good outcome. Everything about his attentiveness, his half smile, his posture, spoke of being open to knowing Molly. To someday making a place for her in his life. He moved, then hesitated, as if he knew he wanted to go to Molly but didn't know how to get there.

No one was willing to take a stand. So Molly's statement hung there, poignant and unanswered.

Ask for what you want, Ward had said to his wife. It was good advice.

Bree stepped forward and held out a hand to her grandmother. "We've missed enough of you. I'm in."

EPILOGUE

November 2024

When Molly and Ward had offered to host a potluck family luncheon at the Ivy Inn over Thanksgiving weekend, she'd crossed her fingers about the attendance. Would people come from all branches of the family? Or was it too soon? But she shouldn't have worried. There had to be nearly thirty Palmers, Garretts, and Harpers here, with a few friends thrown in.

They had gathered in the inn's annex, formerly a garage and workshop that had been converted to a dining space. It was now full of people. Chatting. Smiling. Eating. All related by blood or marriage or choice. The turmoil of the past half year had faded, not entirely gone, but the hardest part was behind them.

Molly didn't have much appetite. Between nerves and the lingering effects of a bout with the flu, she nibbled a sandwich and listened to her three grandchildren, who'd flown in from the West Coast, loving the sound of them talk about things she didn't understand.

She scanned the room for her children. Everett was helping Poppy run the show. David and Nathan and their wives sat with Ward. Naomi and Heather were talking, heads close together, a necessity for hearing with this volume of noise.

Hardly any time passed before the room began to empty again.

Molly carried a stack of plates to the kitchen. "Can I help?" she asked.

Poppy shook her head. "Everett and I have it under control. We'll have hot cocoa and cider ready soon and desserts out by two."

Her youngest son took the dishes from her with a smile. "We're good. Go mingle."

Molly went outside and looked around. The swarm of kids delighted her. They were playing some kind of game that involved a lot of movement, laughter, and falling down. Not that she could see clearly enough to tell what was going on.

When her husband joined her, she smiled at him. "Having fun?"

"Very much." Ward dropped a heavy shawl over her shoulders, then pointed to a glider positioned perfectly to provide a view of the whole back lawn. "That's yours, whenever you need a break from standing."

"Thank you. Soon, maybe."

When Ward peeled off to supervise Kai and a Palmer grandson organizing an activity for the little kids, Molly walked over to where Bree was standing.

"Hello," Molly said.

Bree gave a start, then reached for a quick hug. "I didn't hear you coming."

"You were focused on your charming young man. You've chosen well."

"Thank you. I think so too."

"Being a good father can be a very attractive trait in a man."

"That's becoming true for me. Molly, may I ask your advice?"

"Certainly."

"How can I show my interest in being part of Sienna's life without coming across as trying too hard?"

It was a good question. A tricky thing to get right. "Each child and each family we join will have its own issues to navigate. So I'd say to just be you. You're a bonus adult for Sienna. Make it clear you understand that."

"Was it hard for you?"

Molly smiled. "There were a few bumps, but no. It went well. We talked openly about Ward's first wife, and I got along with Brenda's parents. Since Naomi and David were too young to remember Brenda, I was Mom to them from the beginning. It was tougher with Nathan. Ward and I were married for three years before Nathan called me *Mom*. Quite the moment." She focused on Bree. "This will be my last piece of advice. Be mindful of what the child needs you to be for her. And do *that* well." Molly squeezed Bree's arm and headed for the glider.

She sat in it quietly, watching the crowd. There were a half dozen small clusters of people talking. Many adults were cheering on the incomprehensible kids' game. But no one was alone. Except her.

"Molly?"

She turned her head toward the sound of the voice.

Allison held out a travel mug. "Everett sends you spiced apple cider."

"Thank him. It's one of my favorites." Molly sipped. Delicious. The warmth was nice, too, with the day cooling. She patted the empty space beside her. "Join me."

As Allison sat, the glider swayed gently. "This event was a good idea, Molly. It's working out so well."

"I agree." When her phone vibrated, she raised it to her ear and listened as VoiceOver read a text from Gwen.

Got held up. Dalton drives fast so we should be there by 3

Molly sighed. "Gwen will be late. Which is in character. She'll miss a lot of people."

"There will still be some of us here. Is the grandson coming?"

"Yes." Even though the son Gwen had relinquished had no interest in being part of her life, his children did. "Dalton is the driver, so I suspect he'll make up for the late start. Will you be able to show him around?"

"Yes. Bree and Kai are joining us." Allison turned to Molly. "Are you trying to fix me up?"

"No, I promise. Doesn't seem like the kind of technique that would work with you." Molly hadn't met the young man yet, so she couldn't be sure he was as wonderful as Gwen claimed. And there was the long-distance factor. Dalton lived in Virginia Beach. "So, tell me about your new job." Her granddaughter had quit her previous position in September, convinced that the specter of the Rude Allison persona was too entrenched to overcome. She'd taken a month off, traveled to Scotland, and returned to a job offer from Tamsin.

"Still getting used to it, but I'm enjoying the work. I like having a fresh start." Allison shifted forward to the edge of the glider. "Will you be all right here? I need to check with my brother."

"Go ahead. I'm fine."

But Molly wasn't alone long. She could feel her husband approaching. "Back so soon?" she asked.

He lowered himself beside her. "How could you tell it was me?"

"After fifty-one years together, I know you with all my senses."

Ward laughed and offered her a cookie. "I stole this for you when Poppy wasn't looking."

Oatmeal walnut. From Grammy's recipe. "Thank you." Mmm, still warm.

"Are you playing matchmaker with Everett and Poppy?"

Now *that* couple was a fix-up she would have tried to arrange, if she'd thought of it first. "I didn't have to. The universe handled it for me."

He wiggled for comfort in the glider and gave a push with his foot. "Have you heard from Gwen?"

Nodding, Molly rested her head against his shoulder. "She won't make it until most people are gone, but it'll be nice to have her to myself for a while. She'll help us clean up, and we can visit better without so much going on. You can entertain the new husband." Gwen's third.

She'd remarried last month. Molly had met him and decided he was exactly right for her friend.

They grew silent as they surveyed their guests.

When Bree and Kai wandered off for a walk, Nathan's son took over managing the little kids. Galen was standing beside Perry, watching Liam kick a soccer ball. What an adorable little boy. It was Liam who had pulled Galen into the mainstream of the family more than anyone else. The two of them had just clicked. It was charming to see. Perry seemed more relaxed and open, too, now that he'd won the court case to keep his son in North Carolina.

Heather and Rod stood with them, laughing and talking. Suddenly, Heather stepped away from the group as she dug into a pocket for her phone. While she listened to whoever was on the other end of the line, she exchanged a glance with her husband.

Molly watched her daughter, unable to suppress her longing. Heather had still not warmed up to her, although she was polite and never shrank away from being in the same room. But Heather had a distinct boundary—just with Molly. She honored it. Didn't push.

Oddly enough, it was a connection Heather had made with Naomi that might, one day, make the difference. They had hit it off. Both were nurses and had several mutual acquaintances in the local medical community. Molly had sensed a slight thawing in her daughter's attitude recently. Naomi claimed that she and Heather referred to each other as sisters now. Molly had been afraid to ask if they ever talked about her.

"My daughter is still reluctant," Molly murmured.

Ward linked their fingers together. "She's relaxing."

Something urgent must have happened with the phone call, because Heather was hugging Liam and Perry. Rod was shaking hands with Galen. The Garretts turned and started to hurry down the driveway. At the last minute, Heather detoured to the glider.

"Molly, Ward, we're leaving. I'm on call this weekend and have to get to the hospital."

"Thank you for coming," Molly said and inwardly cringed. Why couldn't she think of anything clever and insightful to say when she was in her daughter's presence? Molly wished she knew the magic words to help them move on to the next stage. A friendship of sorts. But if this was the best she ever got, it was enough.

"I enjoyed this get-together. We have a nice family." Heather wasn't making her usual attempt to bolt away. "We should do this every year. I think I like it better than the actual Thanksgiving Day. Fewer hassles. Less expectations to get everything right."

"We can do that." Molly felt a thrill of excitement at the suggestion, but she kept her expression mild. With Heather, the evolution from anger to tolerance to acceptance had taken months. Had they turned the corner? "I'll tell Poppy to block off Thanksgiving weekends just for us."

"Good. Well, I really have to go. See you later." Heather gave Ward's shoulder a pat, then a touch-and-go hug to Molly before crossing the lawn to her husband.

Molly waited until they were out of sight before turning to Ward. "She said *we* have a nice family."

"I heard."

And Heather had hugged her. The first time she'd touched Molly intentionally. "What a glorious day. I could never have imagined this."

"Uh-uh. You've imagined something like this often."

Okay, true. "But not this good."

Everett had come to the door of the annex and called out, "Dessert time."

The kids' game stopped. As parents retrieved children, Perry collected Liam and Sienna. Guests were slowly moving toward the annex.

Ward squeezed her hand gently. "Look what you've done."

"Me?" She smiled over at him. She'd waited most of her life for this day. "I'm happy."

"You should be. You've earned it, my love. It's okay to believe."

"I do." She kissed the hand holding hers and savored the sight of her family.

AUTHOR'S NOTE

Readers often ask authors where we find our story ideas, and most of us would answer everywhere. With *Once You Were Mine*, I found my ideas at home.

My husband is a search angel. For years, he's volunteered to assist people with finding their relatives. He's often approached by adoptees seeking to locate members of their birth family. His efforts inspired the character Allison Garrett. She, too, is a search angel who helps others—but also herself, when she locates her birth grandmother, Molly. I had found the central story for the modern timeline of the book.

But for the historical timeline, I had to uncover what Molly would have experienced as an unmarried, pregnant teen in the 1960s. Research quickly led me to two powerful nonfiction works by Ann Fessler: the book *The Girls Who Went Away* and its companion documentary *Girls Like Us*. These works exposed a tragic and little-known part of American history, a period from the mid-1940s until the early 1970s in which these women were coerced into relinquishing their children for adoption.

While the maternity home where Molly went was fictional, her treatment was not. The young women interviewed by Fessler provided shocking accounts of the casual cruelty they faced. The mental, emotional, and physical abuse was delivered not only by maternity home staff but also by social workers and health care professionals. When these young women returned to their communities afterward, they were expected to endure their grief and regrets in silence. Many reported lifelong issues with mental health and sustaining relationships.

I wanted Molly to follow a different path, and that meant she had to find somewhere to live besides her hometown. I looked around for a new place to relocate, a city far enough away from family to feel independent, but close enough to feel familiar. My dear friend Lisa encouraged me to consider the city of her youth, Richmond, Virginia. I decided to visit.

Like Molly, I took the train from Raleigh to Richmond and discovered a city with a walkable downtown, charming architecture, amazing museums, and fabulous restaurants. Even better, its urban university, Virginia Commonwealth University, was appealing and easy to navigate. I loved the energy of the city and knew it was the right place for Molly to get her new start. However, she needed a strong draw to leave North Carolina, which is why Molly moves to Richmond to reconnect with her roommate from the maternity home, Gwen. In reality, continued relationships would have been uncommon.

Molly's professional career was informed by both research and my life. Like her, my family seems to have a "genetic predisposition" to be software engineers. Because we also share a strong focus on ensuring software is usable by people of all abilities, Molly became an early pioneer in software engineering and accessibility. The fictional consulting firm where she worked was suggested by two real companies founded independently in the 1950s and 1960s by Elsie Shutt and Stephanie "Steve" Shirley.

For more information about female software pioneers and adoption in the mid-twentieth century, I recommend: *The Baby Scoop Era: Unwed Mothers, Infant Adoption, and Forced Surrender* by Karen Wilson-Buterbaugh, *You'll Forget This Ever Happened: Secrets, Shame, and*

Adoption in the 1960s by Laura L. Engel, *American Baby: A Mother, A Child, and the Shadow History of Adoption* by Gabrielle Glaser, *The Way We* Never *Were: American Families and the Nostalgia Trap* by Stephanie Coontz, and *Recoding Gender: Women's Changing Participation in Computing* by Janet Abbate.

ACKNOWLEDGMENTS

One of the true joys of being an author is knowing that I don't have to write alone. It's a pleasure to thank the people who help.

My heartfelt gratitude goes to everyone who patiently and generously contributed their knowledge: my husband, for his expertise in genetic genealogy and ancient computing; my father, for inspiring so many women to pursue careers in IT; Larry Langston and Tom Brodie, for describing army life in the Vietnam era; Lisa Wilbourne, for her memories of the life and culture of Richmond; the research librarians at Olivia Raney Local History Library and Cabell Library at Virginia Commonwealth University; Lynda Whitcher, for brainstorming science majors and capstone projects; Jaime, for baseball, the military, or any other random trivia he might know; Elizabeth, on experiences with nursing; accessibility experts Julie and Sean; Breely C. and Benny SR, for their skill with swimming; Medora Hix, for her insights on Presbyterianism; the birth mothers, adoptees, and adoptive parents who shared their stories—Betty, Glenda, Hannah, Patti, Tom, and most especially, to Elenore Atkins, for her utterly honest perspective as both a birth mother and adoptee.

Thank you to the wonderful team at Lake Union: Melissa and Carissa for shepherding the book on its path to publication; to the entire production team for helping me create the best book possible. To Tegan, I'm so grateful to have collaborated on this story with you.

Finally, to friends and family who've been with me throughout my writing journey, I couldn't do this without you: Laura Ownbey, editor and muse; Marcia, Rebecca, and Merle, stellar beta readers and advisers; Kevan Lyon, my amazing agent; Julianna, my champion and go-to thirty-something; Amy, the best research companion, sounding board, and copyeditor; and most of all, to my husband, Rick, for your love, wisdom, and support.

BOOK CLUB QUESTIONS

1. After Molly tells her parents she's pregnant, they send her away to a maternity home, knowing she'll be coerced into surrendering her baby for adoption. Their choice was so prevalent in the mid-twentieth century that it's now called "The Baby Scoop Era." Why did society view unwed motherhood so shamefully? What societal changes in the baby boom period influenced our beliefs about marriage, sex, and family life? What might parents have been thinking and feeling that drove them to send their daughters "in trouble" away?

2. When Molly decides to work—like two-thirds of all married mothers in the 1970s—she receives unsolicited feedback from Ward's congregation to return to a more traditional role. Yet the family structure we often think of as "traditional" was short-lived, only really existing in the 1950s. Why does the myth of the traditional family linger? How has its image evolved? What does an ideal family look like for you?

3. Baby boomers like Molly could work a minimum-wage summer job and earn enough to cover four semesters of college tuition. But a similar job for millennials like Bree can't cover one semester. Yet, though half of college graduates find themselves underemployed for years

after graduation, the college dream remains strong. Has society oversold the value of college? Have our attitudes about higher education kept up with the realities of the cost? With the job market?

4. Once Galen learns of Molly's pregnancy, he chooses to walk away, leaving her to endure the consequences alone. But his decision haunts him throughout his life. By not pursuing his dream job, might Galen have been atoning for that choice? Why do you think Galen remained silent about Everett's adoption? Would you have forgiven him as easily as Molly?

5. Allison perceives her mother's mixed signals about the DNA results as a sign that Heather wants to know the truth but resists out of fear. Does Allison push her mother too hard? How might she have handled sharing the information better? Should Heather and Allison have anticipated finding a family connection that must be shared?

6. By discovering they are cousins, Bree and Allison rip the veil off long-held family secrets. How might their lives— and the lives of their parents—have been different if those secrets had been known? Did Molly and Galen have the right to withhold the truth? Do Everett and Heather have the right to be angry? Do Allison and Bree? Where do we draw the line between "I have the right to keep my secrets" and "I deserve to know the truth of my past"?

ABOUT THE AUTHOR

Photo © 2016 Wesley Smith

Elizabeth Langston is the author of *The Measure of Silence*, as well as award-winning YA fiction. Elizabeth spent a career as a software engineer before discovering she loved writing stories more. When she's not researching her next book, she enjoys traveling the world with her family, streaming mysteries, or curling up in her North Carolina home with a cup of coffee and a good book. For more information, visit www.elizabethlangston.net.